D0396755

FASHION SHOW

or,
The Adventures of
Bingo Marsh

ALSO BY JAMES BRADY

Superchic
Paris One
Nielsen's Children
The Press Lord
Holy Wars
Designs
The Coldest War

FASHION SHOW

or,
The Adventures of
Bingo Marsh

A Novel

JAMES BRADY

LITTLE, BROWN AND COMPANY

Boston   London   Toronto

Copyright © 1992 by James Brady

All rights reserved. No part of this book may be reproduced in any form or by any electronic or mechanical means, including information storage and retrieval systems, without permission in writing from the publisher, except by a reviewer who may quote brief passages in a review.

First Edition

This is a work of fiction. Names, characters, places, and incidents are either the product of the author's imagination or, if real, are used fictitiously.

Library of Congress Cataloging-in-Publication Data

Brady, James, 1928–
    Fashion show, or, The adventures of Bingo Marsh: a novel / James
Brady. — 1st ed.
        p.   cm.
    ISBN 0-316-10591-0
        I. Title.   II. Title: Fashion show.   III. Title: Adventures of
    Bingo Marsh.
    PS3552.R243F37   1992
    813'.54 — dc20   91-34338

10 9 8 7 6 5 4 3 2 1

RRD-VA

Published simultaneously in Canada by Little, Brown & Company (Canada) Limited

Printed in the United States of America

This work of fiction is dedicated to John Fairchild of *Women's Wear Daily*, who, more than anyone else, even the great Bingo Marsh, has over the past three decades illuminated and defined fashion journalism.

And it is for my daughters, Fiona and Susan.

FASHION SHOW

or,
The Adventures of
Bingo Marsh

1 ▣ A matter of some delicacy.

WHEN George Bush was elected President and the cabinet lists came out without his name, Bingham Marsh III was crushed. He thought being a Yale man still counted for something in this country. As one Bourbon after another was nominated to posts in the new Administration, Marsh wondered if he should have sent the Bush campaign a more generous check, then agonized over the propriety of having sent a check at all.

"Perhaps I committed a gaffe," Marsh told his wife. "Bush was known at Yale to maintain certain standards."

Although Bush and Bingo Marsh had been a generation apart at New Haven, both men had been tapped for Skull and Bones, a senior society so secret that, ever after, if its name is even uttered, a Bonesman must leave the room. Marsh took such matters seriously, and I doubt very much that to this day he has ever discussed Skull and Bones with Mrs. Marsh.

There was an innocence about Bingo much like that of people who have a touching belief in chiropractic.

I can say that, despite my resentment of how Marsh turned against me, and it explains why, until now, I've never written about him, not even for Tina Brown at *Vanity Fair*, who wanted me to do the definitive piece on Marsh and his magazine. You know how in baptism we solemnly renounce Satan and all his works and pomps? That was what I'd done with Bingo. Like him, I once had dreams, and when they didn't turn out quite as I expected, I cast about for someone to blame besides my father and what happened back in Ohio, the scandal and all, and settled on Bingo Marsh.

It's always more convenient to lay guilt on someone other than yourself, and Bingo would do nicely.

Then some months ago, a friend sent this clipping from the *Paris Herald Tribune* about Marsh, a man we both knew well, and in my Manhattan apartment on a bleak night, I read it over a darkly swirling glass:

3

Fashion buyers from New York and the international fashion press were mystified during last week's Milan collections when longtime fashion magazine editor Bingham (Bingo) Marsh abruptly changed hotels. Without explanation, Marsh departed a favorite haunt, the Gallia, in the middle of the night to check into the Principe et Savoie, inspiring animated speculation in a fashion community ever avid for gossip.

Asked why he'd abandoned the Gallia in what was described as a huff, Marsh declined to respond, saying it was "a matter of some delicacy."

Several sources, including a leading Italian designer with whom Marsh dined, quoted the editor as complaining, "I arrived on the late plane and was going to have a nice bath when I found a pubic hair in my tub. I phoned down instantly for my bill and left. You really shouldn't have to have pubic hairs in your bath, should you?"

A spokesman for the hotel, one of Italy's finest, remarked, "And how can Signor Marsh be certain it was not an eyelash, perhaps his own?"

There were reports the hotel might sue Marsh for slander and that he was considering countersuit for "deprivation of services."

Harsh words had apparently been exchanged as Marsh exited the hotel and one eyewitness suggested a blow may have been struck.

I scoffed at the idea of blows. Bingo was both Episcopalian and anal, which may be the same thing and certainly explains a tantrum over the condition of his tub. In recent years he'd turned down millions in advertising in his magazine simply because he refused to accept fragrance inserts. I can hear him still, his protest a refrain:

"I won't have my magazine smelling like a house of easy virtue!"

Everyone in fashion had such stories about Marsh, dining out on them. I had my own accounts of his tics and oddities, collecting them over the years for my private pleasure, a practice which drove Babe Flanagan, before she left me, to protest:

"He's absurd. And you're obsessed by him."

"I'm not obsessed. We just work in the same place."

But violence? Blows exchanged? Not the Bingo Marsh I knew, no matter the provocation, regardless of what some "wop" hotelier (as Bingo surely would have phrased it) might have said. That Bingo fled confrontation much as others of us fled commitment.

When your parents die young, you grow up wary, unwilling to share yourself fully with anyone else, lest you lose them, too. I'd forgotten that, had let down my guard and shed caution with Bingo and got hurt. Which was why now I balled up the *Herald Trib* clipping and tossed it into the basket, pouring myself a fresh drink, rid of Marsh forever, long past caring anything for him, his works and pomps.

How pleased Babe would have been to see me so crisply slam the door on memory.

In the morning, sober and recalling happier days and foolish, never-to-be-forgotten moments, I retrieved the item from the wicker and smoothed it carefully before pressing it between the pages of a favorite book, the way forsaken lovers save old flowers from the dance.

2 ▣ *She suspected Chanel was trying to get her into bed.*

BINGO MARSH and I met perhaps ten years ago. I was working in Paris for *The New York Times* and had to be in New York on some dreary business or other.

I'd been in Paris since 1970, at first living with a fashion manne-quin in a drafty old apartment on the rue de Boulainvilliers and hanging about with Coco Chanel, about whom I would write a little book that against the odds sold very well. It wasn't really important just how I got to Paris, but I did. Reporting from Vietnam for the UPI and winning some journalism awards played a part. So did my late mother, a Canadian from whom I had a slim French. The girl, Gillian, worked as a mannequin chez Chanel and asked me to accompany her one night to dinner, as she suspected Chanel was trying to get her into bed. Gillian was eighteen years old and very beautiful, and there may have been something to her concern because a lot of people kept trying to get her into bed. Anyway, I went along that first night and Coco and I hit it off and I would write the book about her that had the enormous good fortune to be published the week she died in January of '71, a coincidence of event which got it on the best-seller list and me on the "Tonight Show" exchanging pleasantries with Johnny Carson.

It was that book which drew Bingo's notice and which he remembered when finally we met.

3 ◉ *I noticed his curious gait.*

THERE were cocktails at River House, my book publisher's flat, the usual slavering of the literary crowd over an Englishman who'd just perpetrated an "important" book. The book was about T. E. Lawrence and the occasion promised novelty, or at least the opportunity to meet a New York girl. The Englishman was plump and wore a "siren suit," a one-piece coverall of the style Winston Churchill donned in the war whenever Karsh of Ottawa was going to photograph him for *Life* magazine.

The Englishman was quite drunk. When we were introduced he said, "Let me see the palm of your hand."

When I turned it up he said smugly, "Obviously homosexual."

I didn't know what to say to that, but he'd already reeled away and was scrutinizing someone else's palm. Other men, as drunk as he, shouted protest or told him, "Fuck off!" offering to take him outside. My publisher beamed, sensing an item in tomorrow's tabloids. There were women at the party, and they giggled, taking pleasure from the familiar spectacle of men being ridiculous.

I didn't know Manhattan well, but I'd seen parties deteriorate in other towns and when the author began checking hands a second time, I found my coat and left. Marsh shared the elevator with me.

"Hullo, how are you?" I murmured out of politeness, not caring one way or the other.

"Splendid," he responded. "I sleep well and enjoy a regular bowel movement. You?"

"Just fine," I said, choosing not to go into equivalent detail.

It seemed an awkwardly long time for the elevator to bring us to the ground floor. I stared fixedly at the car door, discouraging conversation, and when it slid open permitted him to exit first, marginally the older man. There being no cabs we walked west a silent block.

I knew who he was; if you were in journalism you knew about Bingo Marsh and his magazine. I was already composing in my head an anecdote about having met him and of his extraordinary response to the most banal of casual greetings.

Now, as we walked together through late Manhattan, he began to chatter amiably, a man about as tall as I and quite plump. I could see him only vaguely now in profile, but I recalled from photographs that his face had no planes or angles but only dimples and a doughy softness strengthened on occasion by a curled lip. His hair was blond and straight and parted on the left in proper prep-school tradition, occasionally falling into gentle bangs that gave Marsh something of the look of a youthful and vastly oversized Truman Capote. As we proceeded west in search of cabs, I noticed his curious gait, three or four normal steps and then a little skip. I had to hurry to keep up, recognizing I really should just let him go, skipping into the night. But Bingo was telling me he'd known Coco Chanel and how well I'd captured her in words.

I was flattered he even remembered the book. And no writer turns callously from a good review.

"You must come to lunch," he said, "the Racquet Club."

"Sure," I said, having early learned that in New York people were forever threatening lunch and rarely committing it.

A taxi slowed, but as I stepped into the street to hail it, I realized there was already a passenger, a lone woman barely discernible, with a vague but pleasing profile silhouetted briefly against the window.

"She's playing with herself," Marsh remarked in a satisfied tone.

"How can you *possibly* know that?" I demanded.

"Well, wouldn't you, if you had a nice cab all to yourself?"

Just then two empties came along, and we each waved one down.

"I'll phone," Bingo cried, skipping into the gutter. "I want to hear all about you and Coco . . ."

4 ◘ Oh, a worm!

MARSH meant what he said about lunch and got me through the switchboard at the *Times.*

"Let's make it La Grenouille instead," he said. I assumed he'd had second thoughts as to whether I was Racquet Club material. La Grenouille, on East Fifty-second Street, was obviously a favorite of Bingo's, and we were greeted at the door and bowed obsequiously to a fine corner under enormous vases of fresh flowers. A headwaiter approached.

"They have the best boiled potatoes in the world here, don't you, Marcel?"

Marcel, the headwaiter, a man the size and heft of a good middle-weight and with the ritual broken nose, nodded enthusiastically.

"They are very good, Monsieur Marsh."

Bingo beamed, delighted to have judgment confirmed.

"They have a special way of cooking them," he said.

Marcel confirmed this.

"Yes," he said, "we boil them."

Out of self-defense, I ordered a drink, and Marcel, his boiled potato badinage exhausted, went off to fetch it. Bingo wagged his head in admiration.

"I think Marcel is marvelous. And Ames."

"Ames?"

"My wife," Bingo said. "I forgot you don't know her. She admires Marcel as well."

"I see." I was making a genuine effort but not at all sure it was working.

The appetizer was artichoke vinaigrette. Halfway through his, Bingo carefully put aside one of the leaves on which a small white worm was undulating.

"Oh, a worm," I said, startled into stating the obvious.

"Of course," Marsh said blandly, "it's how you know they're fresh." He resumed eating with considerable relish, blandly insensitive either

8

to worms or misplaced modifiers, smiling and content, providing a bit of family lore:

"Ames is British. I met her in Paris when I was doing graduate work. Her maiden name is Hillary, a distant relative of the Hillary who climbed Everest. Sir Edmund. You know, the one who said, 'Because it's there . . . ' "

"I thought that was Mallory."

"No," Bingo said primly, "Sir Edmund said it. Ames's cousin, as I said, third degree of kindred, I believe. She's only an 'honourable,' because of her father. Her brother got the title."

I ignored *Burke's Peerage* to return to Everest. "And I was so sure it was George Leigh Mallory who . . ."

Marsh made a throwaway gesture, shooting a cuff and indicating none of this was significant.

"They argue endlessly over just who said what. Alpinists are apparently difficult, argumentative people, envious and litigious. Has to do with altitude and oxygen starvation. But it most certainly was Hillary got up Everest first. Sir Edmund and some coolie."

"A Sherpa guide, I believe."

"Whatever," Marsh said, waving to a woman three tables away who was smiling at him.

"That's Princess Radziwill, Jackie's younger sister. Younger, with nicer legs as well. All that horseback riding around New Jersey every Sunday with the local hunt, well, someone ought to give Jackie some friendly counsel. Anyway, Onassis had an enormous letch for Lee, such a pleasant relief from tantrums by la Callas. But once he met Jackie, it was all over. Daddy O. bought originals and not numbered prints. Someone once suggested, surely in jest, that Onassis might dump Jackie for Diana Ross and the Supremes because by then *they* were the most famous women in the world."

Bingo's voice had a way of carrying, and I glanced toward Lee Radziwill, wondering if she were catching any of this. Marsh went on, impervious.

"Her title's bogus, of course. There hasn't been a King of Poland since the third partition. She and Jackie get on, I'm told, but barely."

They cleared away the artichoke (the worm still wriggling) as Marsh identified other people in the front room.

"That's Mica Ertegun, the woman with the shiny hair. Her husband's a Turk and owns the biggest record company, so people like the Rolling Stones and Jerry Brown's girlfriend and those charming little colored children, the Johnson Five . . ."

"Jackson?"

". . . work for him. Her best friend is Chessy Rayner, who has a husband at Condé Nast, and they're in the catering business or something together, Mica and Chessy, but we always put it in the magazine, 'Messy and Chica.' If she comes over here let me do the talking. She can be arch."

"But doesn't that confuse your readers, using the wrong names?"

"Oh, but that's the fun of it. We mentioned La Grenouille so much in print people said I was getting free meals, so then we called this place The Frog Pond and then everyone started using that so now we call it 'Restaurant X.' Readers like puzzles, the way some people enjoy S and M and things."

"I suppose so," I said, starting to lose him.

"We also publish a list of who's In and who's Out. It's an old staple of the magazine business, like the best-dressed list and the ten worst movies. I stole the idea from one of the Mitford girls, who wrote a book about just who was U- and non-U, U- being upper-class . . ."

"Nancy Mitford. I know the book."

"I'm sure you're right, though I thought it might be Jessica. I knew it wasn't the other one, Verity . . ."

"Unity."

". . . because she was Hitler's girlfriend. And John Fairchild, as well."

Astonished, I said, "She was John Fairchild's . . . ?"

"No, I mean Fairchild stole the idea, too, and uses it at *Women's Wear*, who's In or Out. I like to shift people from list to list every year just to confuse things."

I was thinking of the thick book of editorial rules at the *Times* and how slavishly we subscribed to its . . .

"Oh, good, here's Marcel," Bingo said, rubbing his hands. "Marcel," he said, his voice falling conspiratorially, "today's boiled potatoes, are they really good?"

Marcel looked about cautiously before answering.

"Monsieur Marsh, my word as a Breton."

Marsh beamed again. When we'd ordered he turned to me and in a voice suddenly amplified, demanded:

"Tell me about your Pulitzer, tell me of the horrors of Vietnam."

I provided a brief, bowdlerized version, not knowing him well enough for candor and uneasy with his penchant for shouts. I wasn't halfway through the story of Da Xiang when he said:

"It's amazing, how each of us has had to struggle, you versus the Communists, me against Nunc."

"Nunc?"

5 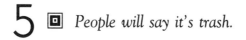 *People will say it's trash.*

IT was 1960 and Jack Kennedy had just, and narrowly, been elected President, and Bingo was in Paris, a Yale man loafing through lectures at the Sorbonne for exams he had no intention of taking, when he fell among expatriates short of money.

"They thought they discerned in me an easy mark," he was admitting now over our Manhattan lunch.

The expatriates had been running, and doing poorly at it, an obscure little trade magazine in which Bingo saw possibilities. The magazine bore an unwieldy title, *Bruit de la Mode,* freely translated into the "noise" or "gossip" of fashion. Before closing the deal, as a matter not only of finance but of courtesy, Marsh flew to New York to present the purchase to his Uncle Elmer, known as "Nunc," and chairman of the Marsh clan's profitable if undistinguished chain of provincial newspapers. When Nunc objected, Bingo threw up his hands.

"You object to everything new, Nunc. You're personally affronted every December thirtieth when the year changes."

"It changes the thirty-first," Nunc growled.

"Whatever."

Elmer Marsh possessed a long red nose, keenly pointed and generously dotted with small seeds like a raspberry, part genetic, part

alcoholic, at which he pawed and groped when distracted. He was pawing and groping now at his nose.

"What's it called again?"

"*Bruit de la Mode.*"

" 'Brouilly of the mud?' " Nunc demanded. "I thought you said it
was about fashion, not some cheap wine."

Bingo explained the name. "We'll rename it, of course, call it *Fashion.* Or *Gossip.*"

"You can't publish something called *Gossip,*" Nunc declared. "People
will say it's trash. *I'll* say it's trash."

"People will *buy* it, Nunc," Bingo said triumphantly, with the confidence of young men with trust funds. "People love gossip; women are
mad for fashion. They'll storm the kiosks to buy it."

Nunc groped again at his great nose. "I won't have the family's name
sullied."

"Fine," Bingo said airily, "keep the family out of it. With Jackie
Kennedy taking over the White House in January, fashion will be the
national rage. I'll buy the magazine with my own money."

"Oh?" said Nunc, expecting he was about to be mulcted and giving
his nose an enormous going over.

"Yes, and it'll make tons of money."

"Well, then," said Elmer Marsh, suddenly very much the crusading
journalist, "Marsh Publishing ought to give it a try, don't you think?"

"Yes, Nunc," Bingo said piously. "What a splendid idea."

He returned to Paris to wrap up the deal for a derisory price, remained
long enough to absorb what he could about running a small magazine
and, incidentally, about fashion, using his connections to get invited to
the collections and to meet a few of the more influential designers and
hiring a disaffected former employee of *Women's Wear Daily,* an aging
fashion expert named Regina Stealth, to put him through a crash course
in women's clothes.

"It all begins with the cloth, Bingo, you must never, never forget
that. Within the fabric, erratically spinning, is the nucleus of every dress
ever made."

A chum from *Paris Match* filled in with gossip from the bistros and
the discotheques, a lover of Cocteau offered news of the arts, and a
broker with a seat on the Bourse provided confidential information on
the finances of Jean Patou, Lanvin, Dior, Rodier, and the other major

houses. Marsh, who for all his faults was never lazy, took assiduous notes. Then, almost in his spare time but in an inspired moment, he married a pretty young Englishwoman he'd met over dinner at the American ambassador's residence.

Halfway through 1961 Mr. and Mrs. Marsh were back in Manhattan, and Bingo's little magazine, now titled simply *Fashion* and translated into an English-language weekly for the delectation of monied America, had been installed in unused space of the Marsh Publishing building on lower Fifth Avenue. Staff was hired, and Bingo set out to sell magazines and intimidate people, ever preaching the one gospel:

"People are more interesting than things."

He was not yet twenty-five, and already he understood vulnerability, knew that while other people were difficult, even dangerous, he could frighten the designers, the driving force of fashion. And from the very first he set out to do precisely that, alternately the wealthy, naive, charming boy and, through the pages of his magazine and using its leverage, the powerful, menacing bully.

I was a newspaperman; I knew how a call from the *Times* made people nervous. But these were wealthy, successful people of international rep-utation, these fashion designers. How could they possibly have been intimidated by what Marsh admitted was at first a small, obscure weekly?

I asked Bingo.

"The designers are the fashion locomotives, a few dozen men and a few women in Europe mostly, a few here. Get them scared, get their attention, get them reading the magazine every Monday morning and you've won the battle. And all you have to remember is, no matter how sophisticated and rich and tough they seem to be, they all started out as little boys playing with and dressing dolls."

I laughed, unsure he was being serious, and said:

"Jan de Hartog wrote a novel, called *The Ship*, I think, about an old tramp steamer captain who on long voyages kept an inflated, life-sized rubber doll in his stateroom and . . ."

"John, I'm not suggesting the designers are slipping Barbie or Rag-gedy Ann between the Porthault sheets and having affairs. I mean, they dress the dolls and sew up little costumes . . ."

"Oh . . ." I let my face go stern and attentive.

"Yes," he said, pleased I was back on his wavelength, "and the odd thing was, years before, it was worth a lady's reputation to go

13

unchaperoned to a fashion fitting. The designers then were all rakes, with scores of their wealthy clients and fashion mannequins tumbling in and out of bed night and day. Jacques Heim told me when he was a boy and his mother still alive and designing, the first pederast was hired by a Paris couture house as an assistant and everyone laughed and made rude sport of the poor boy. Within a generation they were all that way, or almost all. And the dashing dressmaker roué of French farce was banished, virtually forgotten."

Marsh sighed, as if mourning a better time. Then, brightly:

"So the designers are easily intimidated and tell us almost anything we want to know, just to stay in our good graces. And Fairchild."

"Fairchild?"

"The *Women's Wear Daily* man. The designers are afraid of him, too."

Remembering Chanel, I was still skeptical, a furrowed forehead showing it.

"But don't we all have our secrets, our little guilts?" Bingo asked. "Your background or mine or Calvin Klein's, don't we all have something we'd prefer never to see in print? Isn't everybody vulnerable?"

My stomach tensed. I thought of my father, the look on his face that day when I was nine as the local paper screamed its headlines and my mother wept.

"Well, sure, I guess so . . ."

Marcel returned now with the next course, inspiring Marsh to such ecstasies it was a simple matter to change the subject, and I did so, reasonably sure Bingo had seen nothing in my face.

6 ▣ *As soon as I was suckled, she was off.*

I admired people who went out on their own and did original things, and I said so now.

"I'd have just gone to work on the family newspapers," I said, "and not taken the risk."

"You don't know my family, especially Nunc."

Not knowing Nunc and having no family myself, I was ignorant of such matters. Nor was I quite ready for Bingo's account of his mother's death, an account that seemed to flow seamlessly from his impatience with Nunc.

"She was what in those days was called an aviatrix," he said, shoveling up the potatoes, "a female pilot, like Amelia Earhart. Or Beryl Markham. Mother was said to be jealous of Earhart, always talking about the sheer bad taste of that histrionic 'last flight.' A publicity stunt, that's how my mother saw it, faked for the Hearst Sunday supplements. Anyway, she married my father because he was rich. He could buy airplanes for my mother to crack up. She had little interest in him or home and almost none in me. I was an accident of passion. When I was born the war was nearly upon us, and as soon as I was suckled — they tell me I was nearly four — she was off."

I dove into the wine, unaccustomed to having total strangers tell me about being nursed. Marsh, abstemious, sipped a Perrier and went on.

"Mother joined an Air Corps auxiliary, ferrying planes across the Atlantic to England, courageous, embattled England. In 1944 she disappeared on a flight from Newfoundland to Croydon, and it was said in the newspapers that she died a heroine's death, shot down by the Nazis, the only American woman pilot shot down in the entire war."

"Well," I said, casting about for the proper blend of horror and condolence.

"My father," Marsh said equably, "never believed that, about the Nazis. 'She was always a careless person,' he said when I was old enough to understand, 'and probably forgot to check a fuel gauge or something. She simply ran out of gas and fell into the sea. Nothing heroic about it. She was always running out of gas in cars.' "

I shook my head in sympathy, trying to communicate a sense of loss such as Amelia Earhart might have inspired, even if her death was concocted by Hearst.

"President Roosevelt sent a medal of some sort," Marsh said. "I have it still, I think. Father didn't want the horrid thing. He was a Republican, very staunch about it, too."

He talked then a bit about himself.

"We live simply, my wife being English. They so hate display. There's nothing I'd rather have for lunch than a thick slice of homemade bread slathered in preserves put up from our own fraises and framboises."

Bingo had just finished, along with his boiled potatoes, a goujonette of sole, and had tasted the extraordinary Graves (Château Laville-Haut-Brion) I was drinking and he had selected.

They had several homes, also simple, he insisted, especially now that the children were away at school. There was an apartment at 834 Fifth ("not even a duplex"), the cottage in Barbados, a weekend place on the Vineyard ("wrong end of the island, I assure you, totally unfashionable"), and a place out west where they skied.

"I dream one day of operating a ski lodge, perhaps an entire resort," Marsh said.

Bill Blass, whom even I recognized from photographs, interrupted Marsh's reverie as he took a table nearby, shouting a cheerful and apparently quite sincere "Hallo!"

"I had the impression designers hated you."

"Oh, that's just Bill," said Marsh. "He'd love to be an Englishman. He's from one of those square states in the middle, and he affects this little accent and holds a cigarette as Noël Coward might and we always put in the magazine, 'Bill Blass of London comma Indiana.' Drives him mad."

"He seemed genuinely friendly."

"They're terrified of us, Blass and all of them. Deep down they're resentful, we poke such fun. Bill and I were walking across town one day and we passed a firehouse and he remarked, 'You know, Bingo, most firemen are gay,' and I said I certainly didn't know that. And Blass said I was naive, that it was so obvious, the boots, the rubber clothes, the male bonding, the phallic symbolism of the hose and that pole they slide up . . ."

" . . . down?" I murmured.

"Well, I thought Bill was talking rubbish, but I put it in the magazine, quoting him by name, and he was furious."

Marsh paused. "And you know, despite myself, I've never passed a firehouse since without wondering just what *was* going on inside . . ."

Chic women, slim and suntanned out of season, stopped at our table. So did a bald, flabby little man. Bingo introduced me to each with exquisite courtesy.

"Mr. Sharkey won the Pulitzer, you know," he said, mispronouncing "Pulitzer," as most people did. I was dismissed. These people cared about Marsh and his magazine and not about faceless strangers. They paid him gushing tribute and were off, waving to others and blowing still more kisses.

"That was the Social Larva," Bingo hissed, the small, flabby man barely out of hearing, "not quite a moth and certainly never a butterfly."

He went on like this over the coffee, charting the restaurant with his eyes, occasionally jotting a note on his shirt cuff, trashing people in the room, cattily, entertainingly.

"That's Mollie Parnis over there. She's dressed every President's wife from Mamie Eisenhower on, except Jackie, who has taste."

He pointed out Marvin Traub, the chief executive of Bloomingdale's.

"Marvin's turned the store into a phenomenon. It used to live on bargain basement business. Now it's the trendiest place in town. Marvin puts on a big international promotion every year. It doesn't seem to matter to him if the United States and the foreign country involved are at war or at peace. Marvin says Bloomie's has a foreign policy of its own. And the house furnishings floor, I'm assured, is where all the Saturday afternoon pickups take place. The store pullulates with sex, hetero and otherwise."

Bingo looked extremely pleased, as he tended to do when discussing sex.

He also enjoyed recounting stories of impending bankruptcy, marital discord, incipient madness, lawsuits, and terminal illness among people sitting within twenty yards of us. I found myself, to my marginal shame, listening avidly and even laughing along.

Then, again unsettling me with an unexpected question on another subject about which I would be less than frank:

"You and Coco," he said, "did you have sex?"

Bingo's high-pitched voice carried, and I glanced about, wondering if this were the sort of thing about which fashionable people spoke aloud in famous Manhattan restaurants. Marsh continued.

"There are those who say it was your ardor as much as anything that killed her. That at her age the passion of young men was not to be borne."

I said nothing, too stunned to respond. He must have taken an uneasy silence for confirmation.

"I was just curious," he said, not at all apologetic, "because when I knew Coco, I often experienced erection in her presence." He paused, thoughtful. "But she was younger then, not yet eighty."

17

As we finished coffee and he called for the check, Bingo offered me a job writing for his magazine.

I'd grown wary, as I say, suspecting God, or the World, had it in for me, and as a result, I questioned motives, sniffed out conspiracies, and withheld judgments. So I told Bingo, not entirely honest about it, that I was quite happy at the *Times* but flattered to be asked, and we must really keep in touch. What I actually felt at this moment following the fine lunch was quite different. I knew Bingo was married and had children. Yet I was uneasy, suspecting without the slightest evidence beyond a skip and a giggle, that he might be homosexual, that this was not so much a job offer as an elaborate pass.

When he'd signed and Marcel came to pull out the table, Marsh said, "Right back," and disappeared toward what I assumed was the men's room. When he reappeared he said brightly, "I had to floss. Do you floss after every meal?"

I confessed I didn't, and then we were on the sidewalk and he was climbing into a chauffeured car.

I waved him off and walked toward Madison, realizing uncomfortably he'd been more than generous, exceedingly generous, especially since I was not all that happy with the *Times* nor they with me. That weekend I flew home to Paris, suspecting that despite Marsh's oddities, I was the one acting very much like that English asshole in the siren suit reading palms.

7 ▣ *When they shot Dr. King and then Bobby Kennedy . . . I decided to get out.*

IN some ways, I missed the seventies, Watergate and the hostages and baby boomers and all that. But if you had to misplace a decade, Paris was a pretty good town in which to do it. I mentioned I had French. In all honesty it wasn't great French, even discounting its Canadian origins. An Englishwoman I met my first year in Paris put her finger on it.

"I love your French, Jack," she said, not being at all snide, "so easy to understand, the way you don't bother with accents and things."

Nor did I bother with much else, being young and careless and in love with Paris and drinking more than I should. In a sort of entente cordiale, the British correspondents got drunk at the bar of the Hotel Crillon, while the Americans favored the small bar of the Ritz Hotel on the Cambon side, where Bertin the barman once handicapped horses for Hemingway and arranged outings to the big rugby matches.

Being an amiable sort, I drank in both places, plus others, and was therefore popular with all my colleagues.

Later, however, in the old curiosity shop of the magazine Bingo Marsh published and the rest of us sooner or later would inhabit, I was considered something of a crank, notorious for my complaints about synthetic people.

No one ever seemed to me quite genuine or unposed, no one unrehearsed or taken by surprise, either at the magazine itself or in the elegant milieu on which it weekly reports. There were so many domino masques, so many psychological facelifts, so many disguises. Yet when seized by a rare candor, I must admit that to an extent, I am someone else's creation.

Bingo Marsh's, of course.

But as I insist, only to an extent. Before Bingo and I ever met, and at an implausibly early age, I had already been briefly famous.

Twice.

The first time was when I won the Pulitzer reporting for the UPI in Vietnam. That fame endured only until they handed round next year's prizes, but it put money in my bank account and got me hired by *The New York Times*, which sent me to Paris, where I wrote that book about Chanel which became a best-seller.

I was by then twenty-three. And had begun complacently to feel, like the early Scott Fitzgerald, that life was something you dominated if you were any good. It would not take "life" long to knock that misconception out of me.

In Paris the *Times* bureau assigned me to work with an older man who was being retired and whose grab bag of assignments I would be inheriting. He was a decent old gent named Tuthill who drank a little and who, as I would come to do, loved France and the French. Tuthill had become incontinent and something of an embarrassment to the bureau, occasionally wetting his chair, so no one wanted to sit near him. They laughed at Tuthill behind his back, saying you always knew when he was in the office from the trail he left behind in the corridors. I'd seen worse, and smelled worse, in Vietnam, so I took the desk next to Mr. Tuthill and we got along fine. I even told him over a glass one night how all that happened, Vietnam and the Prize.

"When they shot Dr. King and then Bobby Kennedy and when everyone went nuts at the '68 convention, I decided to get out. Not running to Canada to dodge the draft, because I had a shortstop's knee and was deferred, but just wanting to get the hell away. My parents were both dead, and I was twenty years old and going into my senior year at Ohio State where I ran the student newspaper and worked summers at the *Plain Dealer* up in Cleveland as a city room gofer, and one of the editors made a phone call that got me a job at UPI, which was always looking for promising young people to underpay."

Mr. Tuthill laughed. "Nothing changes, does it," he said, listening and not patronizing.

By Christmas of that year I was in Saigon, where they'd done a crash buildup of the bureau. I made coffee and answered phones and ran errands. The war was boiling over, and even kids like me and burned-out old drunks in the Saigon news bureaus found ourselves being sent upcountry on assignment, there being too much war to be covered by the real pros. I was dispatched to a provincial town checking out a nothing story on syphilis rates among American troops. Lousy town, lousy story. "Ma boys don't do that shit, son," a career colonel assured me. "Ma boys don't screw slopes."

Lepers were more popular up there than I was, and I didn't get a damned thing from anyone, but that night Charley came in over the wire and I was pinned down there for nine days, sending out my stories by radio dictation. It began small and became the Siege of Da Xiang, the biggest battle since Tet, and all I did was write the play-by-play. By the third day my stuff was on every front page in America that took the UPI. Some people later insisted I'd been a hero, but I knew better; I was scared shitless.

I admitted as much to Mr. Tuthill.

"Shows good sense," he said.

So I told him about the fourth or fifth night of the siege, when I got the old gunnery sergeant in trouble with the Geneva Convention, something I never put in any of the stories and for good reason.

"We were living underground by then, in bunkers. No one could live in the open with the shelling. I bunked in with this old gunny who ran the mortars, but of course there was a young officer over him who had the rank, but the gunny had the brains and said yessir and then went right ahead and did what was right. The gunny knew how important ammunition was, and he fussed over it and kept maybe a hundred rounds of mortar shells with us there in the bunker to be sure it was clean and dry. We slept right next to the shells, and when incoming hit, sand filtered down on top of us through the logs and sandbags and the bunker shook and I wondered what it would feel like to be blown up. Then, during a bad night, the worst shelling we'd had, a trooper dove into the bunker, moving fast.

" 'Gunny! Ammo's runnin' short! Corporal sent me!'

"So the gunny scrambled out after him and I was afraid to stay behind and I went too and the night was like noon from the explosion of the shells, theirs and ours both, and the gunny sergeant yelled to start passing up the shells from our bunker, a sort of bucket brigade, and they got that started and I was crouched there watching when a man went down, holding his stomach and rolling around screaming, and I jumped into that line and started passing the ammo, too. I had to be doing something or I would have gone nuts from fear, and I realize like everyone else I'm yelling and shouting and flipping those shells as if they were nothing and I look up and there's our lieutenant.

"He glares at me and then he says to the gunny, 'Sergeant, this man is a correspondent, a civilian. He can't handle ammunition. It's against the Geneva Convention.' "

Mr. Tuthill gave a little laugh and shook his head, and I poured us both some wine and went on.

"Well, the old gunny looks up but he just keeps right on passing the shells and ducking, as we all did, whenever one hit near, and the lieutenant is really mad now, shouting about how I'm not in the army and we're contravening the Geneva Convention, and finally the gunny says, 'Lieutenant, them Vietcongs get through the wire they're gonna shoot us all up the ass, including this here civilian, so I think we ought to just feed the guns and to hell with the Geneever Conventions.' "

I got a real laugh out of Mr. Tuthill on that, and it wasn't just wine laughter, either, and I told him other stories and he told some and then had to go to the bathroom, but when he came back he bought us a *fin* and lifted his glass in a gracious little toast to my Pulitzer Prize.

He'd been in the newspaper business forty-three years, he said, and never won a damned thing.

8 ▣ *Cheering and applauding, weeping and carrying on.*

FOR the first time I had a few dollars and a decent salary coming in and this big, drafty apartment on a hilly, winding street above the Seine in Passy, two blocks from the Metro Muette and down the street from the shoemakers where you could buy firewood. It was damp and cold that first winter and you needed a fire. Or other alternatives to central heating.

Her name was Gillian, and I won her by offering to buy lunch.

"If I can have a steak," she said. Gillian had a keen sense of the priorities.

"Sure," I said, thinking how cold it was in my bedroom.

She was English, a mannequin working in the Paris couture, planning either to be discovered by Hollywood and become a cinema star or go home to England to get into university. I told her she was the first English girl I'd met and I liked her accent.

"You just want me to go to bed with you," she said.

"Come on, let's get that steak."

She was eighteen years old and that season was the top model at the fashion establishment of Gabrielle Chanel.

"They're so cheap there," she complained, "and Mademoiselle is always going on about my appetite."

From the way she demolished the steak, I could believe it. Then I called the office and told them something had come up, and we went back to my place and went to bed for the afternoon.

"That was really an excellent steak," Gillian said.

The following week she moved in with me, which certainly made things cozier on chill nights, and it was convenient for her as well.

"I can save on the rent," she said, "they're so cheap, the French . . ."

Gillian was astonishingly shallow and obsessed by herself, clothes, and men, in that order, and had absolutely no interest in my work, my writing, or my war stories, but in bed she was sweetly tolerant of my innocence and performed prodigies of which I had no conception. I paid the rent and she bought the food and the cheap wine and for a time it was a splendid arrangement.

Then Mr. Tuthill died, which I think was a relief to people in the bureau, and I took on his beat, loosely branded "culture." That meant it consisted of unimportant things no one else wanted to cover, opening nights and art galleries and film crews shooting in Paris on location and stuff like that.

And the fashion business.

I wasn't actually expected to know anything about clothes; they sent a woman named Morris twice a year from New York for that. I was supposed to know just sufficient about the fashion designers in case they went bankrupt and to be able to update their obituaries.

Although the bureau discouraged it, I did attend one fashion show, curious to see how they did it. Most startling, after my brief season at the *Plain Dealer* and then UPI and now at the *Times*, was how the fashion editors rooted for the designer. Or for the clothes. A sportswriter in a press box manifesting such partisanship would have been escorted out, his credentials confiscated. At the Paris showings the fashion editors kept leaping up from their little gold chairs cheering and applauding and carrying on. It almost seemed to be expected that you whoop and fan yourself and rend your garments and suffer nosebleeds and faint with emotion. Weeping also seemed to be encouraged, especially at the end. John Fairchild, who owned *Women's Wear Daily*, appeared to lead the cheers, and occasionally the weeping, poking people on either side of him to stimulate their enthusiasm, or their grief, stamping his feet whenever mere hand-clapping was insufficient.

The second fashion collection I ever saw was that of Gabrielle Chanel, known as Coco, and I went to that because she invited me.

9 ▣ *"Mon petit Indien,"* murmured Chanel.

CHANEL lived in a small suite above the inner garden of the Ritz, but atop her fashion establishment just opposite on the rue Cambon, she had a large apartment, and it was there Gillian and I dined. Downstairs, at street level, the shop was officially closed but still brightly lit, and we were let in by a shop girl, chic in a little black dress, kept after hours just to welcome us and to alert Coco by phone as we mounted the stairs. Chanel met us at the opened doors of the apartment, a slender woman with alert eyes under a flat straw hat and a fringe of brown bangs, with a wide mouth capable of a broad, tightlipped smile. Gillian received a kiss that barely brushed her cheek, hardly the passionate embrace I'd anticipated from a woman scheming to get her into bed.

"May I present Monsieur John Sharkey, Mademoiselle. He is the editor of the *Times* of New York and insisted on meeting you."

I muttered something about just being a reporter and was ignored.

Chanel was a very old lady, but she gave me that flat smile and a brisk handshake and then, her arms around both our waists, walked us into the most elaborate room I'd ever seen, full-sized ceramic deer, coromandel screens everywhere, piles of leather-bound books stacked about, a suede sofa that might have been eight or nine feet long on the edge of which she balanced while pouring me a neat whisky over ice. I am dark and lean with a ruddy complexion and my nose was once broken playing ball and knit badly, and Chanel somehow got the idea I was an American Indian.

Gillian sat near her on the sofa, and I perched on a footstool, and we sat there in her incredible apartment over the fashion salon and talked, or rather Coco talked and we listened. It was rapid-fire and fascinating, much of it slanderous, and I was glad I had French. Gillian knew how to get her started, something about the miniskirt.

"Ah, that," Chanel said, *"dégoûtant.* Tasteless. *Une exhibition de viande* . . . a show of meat."

The actress Romy Schneider had long been a client, and now, in a new film, was being dressed by a rival, Pierre Cardin.

24

"But what is she, after all?" Coco demanded. "A little Swiss milk-maid."

I'd recently interviewed Brigitte Bardot and asked if she'd ever done her clothes.

"Yes, yes, I tried to do something with her. Here it is very nice, *très jolie*," she said, stroking her buttocks, "but up here?" cupping her own minimal breasts, "it is too much."

Over drinks Gillian just sat there looking beautiful and being bored, crossing and uncrossing her legs and admiring them. She'd heard all the Chanel stories before, during fittings. At eight o'clock we went into the dining room to be served by a fat waiter wearing white gloves and livery. The food was astonishing, glutinous Scottish smoked salmon served with chilled ponies of Polish vodka, blue trout with the heads still on, one eye regarding us, tiny quail, three to each plate, skin as crisped as Peking duck, asparagus and haricots steamed rather than boiled, a cheese platter and mille feuilles that challenged description, three wines, two white, the red a private Rothschild label.

"Marie-Hélène sends it over," said Coco. I assumed this was the Baronne Rothschild.

Despite her great age, Chanel seemed to eat and drink everything, occasionally pulling out a cigarette. By now I was *"mon petit Indien,"* ignoring the fact I was nearly a foot taller and not an Indian.

Feeling the wine I made the mistake of mentioning another designer I'd interviewed, a Spaniard named Castillo who stuttered in four or five languages and claimed he'd once as a young man been Chanel's principal assistant.

"Ah, that one," Coco said disdainfully, "he may have held the pins."

Having dismissed Castillo's significance, she recounted a salacious story to the effect he retained an assistant who hired Gypsy boys to come to the cellar of his castle in Spain to be whipped. I didn't know just what to say to that, but Gillian brightened.

"I never heard that before," she said, always alert to any story with sexual overtones.

"Voilà, la télévision," Chanel announced at ten o'clock as the waiter switched on a big set hung at the far end of the dining room.

There was a taped interview Coco had done with a French version of Phil Donahue, and we sat there and watched while the waiter fetched cognac. Questions were asked and she answered, rambling on but getting off some good lines. A couple of times, looking up at herself on the screen, Chanel nodded and said, "*Tu sais, elle a raison . . .* You know, she's right."

It was as if she were watching a stranger and agreeing with what the woman on television was saying.

Then the talk-show host asked if Chanel had a favorite client.

"The one who pays her bills," she snapped. "Keep your princesses and comtesses and pretenders to the throne. Such women are so impressed by their own nobility, to send a check is beneath them. Give me the chic, second wife of a rich businessman who cheats a little on his government contracts. Such a woman is too insecure to posture; such a woman pays her dressmaker."

Going home in the cab Gillian was sulky.

"Did you notice how she gestured to Antoine to give you another quail, and I was neither offered nor given one?"

"Well, she kept saying I was skinny, and calling me her 'poor Indian.' Maybe she thought I was starving."

"We're the ones who starve. The girls of the cabine. They're so cheap, the French."

"Yes," I said noncommittally.

"Well, what did you think of the old girl?" Gillian asked.

I said what I thought, that Chanel was incredible.

"I know," Gillian agreed, "just imagine, nearly ninety years old and still fucking." Gillian's mind ran along such lines.

10 ▣ *Eating asparagus with their fingers and the butter running down their chins.*

IN Paris they stage the big fashion shows in January and July. The fall fashion collections were shown the last week of July, but except for what I'd learned listening to Chanel and a rooting interest in it for Gillian's sake, it didn't excite me at all. Gillian, of course, was highly stimulated; it was the work she did. Coco's show would draw the American buyers and the fashion editors and the paparazzi and the rich women who could afford the clothes and the network television crews who would shoot both the clothes and the rich women.

And the fashion mannequins.

"Why shouldn't I be discovered?" Gillian demanded. "Lots of model girls have become cinema stars. Lauren Hutton, Betty Bacall, Twiggy, Suzy Parker, why not me? I've got legs as good as any of them and boobs as well."

She was Chanel's current star and would wear the classic suits, the slinkiest evening gowns, and with that face and legs and her coltish grace, you weren't likely to miss her. Gillian kept after me to write a story about her. She didn't understand *The New York Times* frowned on stories about one's friends. I must say it was pleasant how Gillian kept trying to convince me.

Then she got the notion a PR man might help, getting her name around, generating a little publicity. So she got me to take her to lunch with Percy Savage, an Australian pal of mine who did publicity for the fashion house of Nina Ricci. Gillian kept promoting herself, but Percy kept talking about a new account he had with the cotton trade.

"It's a real challenge, you know," Percy enthused.

"Do tell us about it," Gillian said finally, in some exasperation.

"Well, it's to convince everyone cotton is superior to synthetics. You know, getting nuns to use cotton tampons instead of polyester."

That same week I saw my second fashion show. It was important to Gillian that I see her performance, and Coco had invited me. We'd had dinner with her again, and then Coco asked me for lunch a couple of times. Without Gillian.

I've called Coco "fascinating." That's just an adjective. She was eighty-six years old and still the single most influential force in world fashion. She knew everyone and had an opinion on everything. She was crotchety and prejudiced and tactless and stubborn and very, very wise. Best of all, for a newsman, she was quotable. Even my bureau chief at the *Times*, who considered me an infant, was impressed I knew her.

"Ten years in Paris and I've never met the woman. Saw her once lunching with the Duchess of Windsor at the Espadon in the Ritz. Never forgot it, the two of them eating asparagus with their fingers and the butter running down their chins." Then he paused. "During the war she had a Nazi boyfriend, didn't she?"

Coco scheduled her fashion show for three in the afternoon, precisely the time of the Cardin show on the other side of town, so editors and buyers would have to choose between the bitter rivals. I got there about two-thirty to find a queue of people, most of them women, jostling slowly through the ground-floor shop toward the stairs and the salon, waving their invitations and being ignored by the staff. I'd been told what to do and just went up without asking, starting to take a chair toward the back in the third row when a directrice grabbed my arm.

"No, monsieur, up there," she said, pointing toward the second floor.

I wasn't to sit in the audience with the rest of them, but with Coco, up at the top of those famous mirrored, winding stairs where habitually she perched on the top step to watch the show, as she made catty remarks about people and even about her own work, chain-smoking nervously and elbowing me to pay attention and never shutting up.

"Regard that woman in gray on the left. Have you ever seen such ankles? And they speak of the Swiss disdainfully as cows. Now, this next suit, in navy, the proportions are important. Can you believe that photo of Mees Fonda [this was Jane, I assumed] in the current *Match?* Why don't such women act their age? Now, this little dress, charming, I have to say, don't you think? I've caught fashion editors fast asleep during a show, you know. They drink themselves into insensibility during lunch, and there is a monumental struggle to remain awake. One is dozing off even as we speak, there in the second row. I'll show that one the door next season. Now, there is your girlfriend, Gillian, in the evening suit. I once had such legs, a century ago. Give me another cigarette, *mon petit Indien,* I know they're bad for me, but what is one to do?"

By the time it was over, my head was a kaleidoscope of color and shape and form, all of it set to the rat-a-tat of Chanel's comments. Gillian crossed the rue Cambon to meet me afterward in the small bar of the Ritz.

"You were terrific," I said, meaning it, "the way you move, how you carry those clothes."

"Shaun, the bitch, had one more *passage* than I did. Did you notice?"

"I only noticed you, how lovely you looked."

"Oh?"

"Even Coco talked about you, admiring your legs."

"And you?"

"I admired them, too."

We went on to dinner and home early and Gillian demonstrated her gratitude several times during the night and in quite extraordinary ways.

It was shortly after that Chanel told me there really ought to be a good book about her, an honest book, "and not that filth and piggishness they always write. Or the rubbish Mees Rosalind Russell talked after I rejected her for Broadway in *Coco*."

She asked me to do such a book, but I was uneasy about it. I'd been trying to write a novel about Vietnam and couldn't get it going, the words and images all conveniently in memory; I just couldn't seem to get them down on paper, not so it seemed like Vietnam, and so I said I didn't seem to be very good at full-length books.

"It's easy," she said. "Proust told me he just listened to what people said in the Ritz and wrote it down. We'll do it like Proust; I'll talk and you write it down."

I didn't have an agent or a publisher but you didn't say no to Chanel, and I was trying to become a writer, not just a reporter, and I had a primitive sense of just how unique an opportunity this might be, spending hour after hour with this extraordinary old woman who must be nearing the end of her life and had so many memories, so many scores to settle, had lived the kind of life few of us even dreamt of living.

So I said yes, and we went to work on it that same day.

Coco stroked my face and ran arthritic fingers through my hair and murmured, "Mon Indien, mon petit Indien," and chain-smoked cigarettes while I puffed a Punch cigar she clipped with a gold cutter, and she poured whisky over the ice from a decanter that must have been Waterford and said, her voice husking and rasping as she leaned close, "Ask me anything, anything you want, *mon petit Indien*."

She talked and I took it down, and afternoon after afternoon we grew tipsy as the shadows lengthened in the rue Cambon.

It was that little book which years later would draw the sensitive antennae of Bingo Marsh.

11 ▣ *Suppose someone came after him with a horsewhip?*

I didn't kid myself, then or later, that I knew much about fashion.

Bingo, in contrast, seemed instinctively to understand and really cared about it.

Before he was twenty-five and by no means yet an expert, Bingo already had a precisely delineated vision of a different breed of fashion magazine, harder edged, stripped of puffery and pretension, of the sort of bullshit where they run on the inside pages an editorial credit for a perfume the model is supposedly wearing on the cover, simply to please the advertiser with a mention.

"The clothes," he informed his first employees years before I met him, "are incidental. The people who design the clothes are the story, the people who sell them, who wear the clothes, who pay for them. Creative designers, beautiful women, and the rich men who finance both. That's who and what *Fashion* will be about."

What began under his direction as a small, obscure, elitist, and rather cleverly snotty little slick, virtually a newsletter to the chic, a modest counterculture response to the authoritative, powerful *Women's Wear Daily,* would become a publishing phenomenon.

I was a newspaper reporter, trained by a wire service and the *Times* to ask questions. After I got to know him, I pressed Marsh.

"But how did you know this stuff? You were only a child."

"I guess at the very beginning it was 'the little monks,' " he said, pleased and complacent. "They told me what was going on, passed me the secrets. All the best scoops at first came from them."

"And just who are 'the little monks' when not at prayer?"

"The boys who work for the designers in the studio. Every designer has a half dozen assistants. Balenciaga was the king of fashion when I bought the magazine, and he was like the Pope, this austere old Spaniard, so everyone called his assistants 'the little monks.' They wore these darling little smocks. Anyway, the designers know everything, they know all the gossip. Their models gossip through their chewing gum as they're being pinned and basted, rich women come in to be fitted and they talk, the designers themselves talk, and the little monks never stop talking."

"A reporter's dream," I murmured, remembering how Coco rarely drew breath.

"Exactly," said Bingo enthusiastically. "In the fashion business no one is discreet, no secret ever kept, circumspection is considered the . . . how many deadly sins do Catholics have?"

"Seven."

". . . well, the eighth deadly sin. The designers and the little monks and the models and the clients together hour after hour, hermetically sealed into a fashion studio, the women half-naked all the time, in and out of their underwear, wine may be handed around, perhaps a little pot is smoked, and all of them talk, all of them listen. The rich bitches jabber on about their husbands' businesses, about their lovers; they slander their enemies, they pass on state secrets, and all the while the little monks listen, so pleased to be part of this lush, ornate, monied world; ragamuffins welcomed to the ball. And at night all the little monks spend what few francs they have to go dancing. By day, slavishly faithful retainers to Dior, to Givenchy, to Saint Laurent, to Valentino. By night they revert to silly young boys who giggle and tell tales and drink too much. On the dance floors or in bed, they talk, they tell everything."

"But you didn't spend your evenings out dancing with these kids."

"Of course not," Marsh said, prim as Cotton Mather. "I was home with Ames. But I learned which of the little monks had talent, which might soon launch himself into a career and open his own studio. Those little monks I invited to lunch. Those I flattered with curiosity about their work, and they responded by telling me the shape and spirit of the new clothes which no one else would see for weeks. And, as I say, they gossiped."

"And you took notes."

"And encouraged the careers of those who told me what I wanted to know."

On that, Bingo was totally candid, cold-bloodedly so.

"But this was Paris," I said. "In New York . . ."

"There are little monks in New York, as well. Blass has his assistants, Beene, Halston, Trigere . . . only the smocks are different."

Marsh worked them all, he cheerfully admitted, gleaned their secrets, picked their brains, and betrayed confidences every Monday.

31

He had other sources. Designers who fed him advance sketches or permitted him to attend a circumspect dress rehearsal of the season's new clothes found themselves lavishly featured in the magazine, their work praised beyond its inherent virtues. Those who refused to cooperate were ignored, maligned, slandered.

"And there are others who talk. Photographers, fashion artists, the fabric salesmen, the jewelry designers, milliners, the purveyors of expensive shoes, the hairdressers."

All these worked inside fashion's silken curtain. But, despite his willingness to exploit them and use their knowledge, Marsh drew the line at socializing with hairdressers, maintaining toward them, at least, a decidedly stiff line:

"Society collapsed when the first hairdresser was invited to dinner at a decent table."

When he became vague, fobbing me off with aphorisms, I persisted, demanding just how a young man came to develop such keen instincts so early. Bingo turned playful:

"They teach you at Yale."

Maybe they really did, I thought, product of the Big Ten and square Ohio.

His vision of a different genre of fashion magazine established, Marsh had thrown family money into the new weekly, hiring the best young writers and photographers and editors (he turned out to have a feel for talent) to cover and report on not only fashion but also the fashionable. And on movies and restaurants and books and ski resorts and architecture and scuba diving and the new cars and low-cholesterol diets and the America's Cup (it was a *Fashion* reporter who coined the term for Newport's luxurious spectator yachts, "floating gin palaces") and on network television and Sotheby's auctions and dinner parties and country weekends. On wealthy women and their lovers. The weekly frequency of *Fashion,* on sale every Monday morning, gave it an edge in timeliness over established monthlies such as *Vogue* and *Harper's Bazaar;* Marsh's editorial knack gave the magazine an instant identity with the surgically precise nickname, the "hot, new" personality, the latest trendy look, the scandal filling with pus but not quite yet erupting. Circulation soared from a few thousand to more than a million copies a week, with a pass-along readership claimed to be five times that. In a single week when Jackie Kennedy, then between widowings, posed prettily on its cover in a miniskirt (only to be scolded in the headline as "bandy-legged"), some twenty thousand subscriptions were sold. Nor was it cheap. When tabloids at the same supermarket checkout sold for twenty-five cents, *Fashion* cost a dollar. *Fashion* was nasty, it was smart, it was In. Bingham Marsh III had arrived, outdoing three generations of publishing Marshes. His idiosyncratic genius provided the uniquely tangy (some insisted "gamy") flavor its readers, most but not all monied and leisured women, lapped up as Wimbledon devours strawberries and cream. Some readers, who were also his victims, actually seemed to enjoy being humiliated in print, as a Good Friday penitent might welcome the lash.

Time magazine, in a cover story on Marsh, called his career "one long-running essay in elegant bitchery."

Bingo, delighted, pounced on "elegant bitchery" and used it in ads.

Men who'd been with him at Yale wondered how a well-bred young Protestant developed such an effectively vulgar instinct for attracting attention.

"The biggest gossips in town," he declared in an editorial manifesto, "are Irish priests, desk clerks, and fashion designers. *Fashion* will concentrate on the latter and will report every week what they say, what they whisper, what they may only suspect."

This cheeky declaration, typical of Bingo in full flight, scandalized the Archdiocese and annoyed hoteliers. But it got his little magazine talked about. Readership and circulation soared, the advertising poured in. In a way, the reaction frightened Marsh. For the first time he realized the passion a single editorial could arouse. And despite the bravado, he shrank from personal confrontation. As someone once wrote of Sartre, another timid man, "he could be violent on the page." In person, it was something else again, and after that first, inflammatory editorial, Bingo rarely signed a piece of copy.

"Terrible things are done in my name," he protested, claiming innocence while, in private, urging his editors and writers on to further outrage.

Lawsuits and irate letters were no problems. Attorneys and editors could handle those. But as his little magazine grew in influence and wealth, as he himself lashed the staff to new excess, "Vex them! Vex them anew!" Bingo's insecurities deepened.

He could cope with arm's-length hostility; it was the face-to-face meeting, the ugly scene, the slim potential for actual physical attack, that terrified him. Suppose they sent a lynch mob? Or, as wronged parties did in Victorian novels, came after him with a horsewhip?

Marsh had read somewhere about Joseph Pulitzer, years before, having shot at a man in the city room (he missed), and considered applying for a pistol license, only to be talked out of it by his wife, a sensible woman.

"Bingo," she predicted, "you'll just shoot yourself. Or worse, an advertiser."

So when celebrated victims complained, he lied, claiming the item slipped past him or the reporter was to blame or that he was out of town or lay ill. While behind the barricades of the magazine, sheltered by guards and anonymous staffers, he continued to demand more and more from his editors and writers, a man torn by the conflicting emotions of crusading zeal and rank cowardice.

Of course I knew scant little of this when I first met Bingo.

12 ▣ *Have you noticed her liver spots?*

THREE thousand miles and eight or ten years apart, I, too, was learning my trade. Though I still didn't understand about clothes, not even Coco's, I got to know the designers, and not only Chanel. As part of my *Times* beat, I learned the difference between Pierre Cardin and Pierre Balmain, and I met Emanuel Ungaro, who raised the five thousand dollars for his first couture house taking out a loan on his girlfriend's Porsche and who rarely touched the brakes when I drove with him, the car radio blaring operas I didn't recognize and chamber music Emanuel assured me was Beethoven; and Givenchy, who had a title and manners and who was said to be the handsomest man in Paris, though he lacked small talk and did needlework in his lap during dinner parties; and Gérard Pipart, who was always broke but could never pass the front door of Hermès without going in to buy a few silk squares on tick.

And I met André Courreges, lean, balding, intense, a young man from Pau who'd worked as a tailor under the genius Balenciaga and who was taken with the messianic conviction he'd invented modern dress.

André had a girlfriend named Coqueline who had a crewcut, and she and André wore identical white pants and tops and shoes. It was Courreges who got me playing rugby in the Bois Sundays with a club team and going out with him and Coqueline and sometimes Gillian to the Stade Colombes where they played the big rugger internationals and the French sang, "Allez la France!" and the English cried, "England and Sin George!" and after the match twenty or thirty thousand Frenchmen lined up outside to piss against the stadium walls, there being no urinals, while Gillian and Coqueline urged us to hurry to a café with a rest room so their turn might come.

So I had a job and money and a girl and an apartment for which I bought a secondhand grand piano which neither of us could play and I smoked two or three packs of Gitanes a day until the cancer stories began and I became a famous consumer of foot-long, near-black cigars I liked even better. I also drank a lot and learned about bed from Gillian and was having a pretty good time being young and in love, not with her or with anyone, really, but with Paris.

And maybe, in a crazy way, with Coco Chanel.

I said I was uneasy with Marsh. But there was more to it than naïf concerns about my precious virtue and the remote possibility he lusted after me. While I hadn't admitted a thing, had barely responded, it was unsettling, uncanny how Bingo was able to winkle out guilt. For, during those weeks I'd worked together with Coco on her book, I, too, had found myself, as Marsh so delicately put it, "experiencing erection."

Each day at noon she crossed over the rue Cambon from her suite in the Ritz to her apartment over the shop, and unless I had an assignment, I would be there by one, climbing the stairs to her drawing room with its chinoiserie and coromandel screens, where she greeted me reclining on the long, suede couch. I fetched a footstool close to her knee and she poured us both neat Scotch or Polish vodka and I asked questions and recorded answers of a sort. And got drunk.

Over drinks, during lunch, through the long afternoons she talked, telling me of love affairs and betrayals, of ecstasies and crushing loss, of intrigues and riches and wartime flights, all the while calling me her little Indian, reaching out to touch my hair, my shoulder, occasionally to trail arthritic fingers lightly across my face and lips, fixing me with those dark eyes, dancing old eyes, and continuing to talk, talk, talk.

Gillian, encountering me on the stair or crossing the salon as I came and went, snarled with the fury of a discarded lover, and I wondered just what I would do if one day Coco took my hand and led me drunkenly deeper into the mysterious apartment to a lover's bed.

Maybe it was the whisky, maybe the long hours together, perhaps it was just Paris or the stories of her lovers, or simply I was still an impressionable boy, and yet as we talked over a meal or a glass into the dusk, Paris darkening beyond the tall windows of her apartment, I thought what it might be like to be Coco's lover, this extraordinary woman whose triumphs and romances, whose life had become legend.

With the instinct women possess from birth, Gillian sensed it.

"It's ridiculous," she cried, "infatuation! You're my age, and she's ninety if she's a day. And bald as an egg under that silly wig. I doubt she's a real tooth in her head. Those arthritic hands. Have you noticed her liver spots? Do you imagine what her breasts would be like . . . ?"

"Gillian," I lied, "there's absolutely nothing like that. She . . ."

"It's her money, her fame, her bloody celebrated charm. It's despicable. You're using her and she's using you." She paused.

"Star fucker!"

Pompously, I defended myself. "I'm writing her goddamned book, is all."

We both knew it was more than that.

13 ▣ *At this rate you'll never bury the poor chap.*

IT wasn't always tense, rarely Sturm und Drang. And there were distractions. Gillian, when in the mood. And Coco herself, who could be damned funny, unintentionally.

She'd fired a new directrice, a chic, dignified woman who was to have brought order to the establishment. "That bit of filth," Coco raged, "I had to show her the door. Now she drives 'round and 'round the block every afternoon, knowing I have the windows open to the breeze, shouting up obscenities at me. I'll have the police on her."

Also dismissed, her longtime manager, a sleek and corpulent man, self-important, with a Légion d'Honneur in his buttonhole Chanel claimed to have petitioned for him despite her contempt for de Gaulle and his regime. "The *salot* repaid me with larceny!" she said, the manager having punched a hole through her wall into a vacant building next door where seamstresses sewed up "false" Chanels, counterfeit suits and coats fabricated from cloth and braid and buttons stolen from her ateliers.

"The man's entire career: *zéro à gauche!*"

"Zero to the left," of course, meaning nothing.

Sometimes she spoke of her youth, of the Auvergne, where she was born. "The Auvergnats are so close with their money that during the Revolution they sold drinking water. If travelers and refugees couldn't pay, they died right there of thirst."

She sounded rather proud of that, pleased with her fellow Auvergnats.

But she held in contempt the Swiss who owned her company, especially the latest Swiss, a man in his fifties, whom she dismissed as a child. "He belongs in *l'école maternelle* . . . the nursery school. They don't permit him to order pencils for the company."

Yves Saint Laurent had just shown a collection critics said was inspired by Chanel. "I respect Monsieur Saint Laurent," she said sweetly in response, "and the more he copies me, the greater my respect."

Cardin, that season's especial rival, had, she insisted, floated the rumor Chanel died over a weekend and the Ritz had stored her body in the freezer of the Espadon Grill until the morticians reopened Monday.

But she spoke also of herself with a candor I'd not expected. Looking back now, perhaps she knew death was near, and there was little profit in discretion.

She talked of Westminster, her ducal lover, the wealthiest man in England, who took her cruising on a destroyer purchased after World War I and painted white, with a crew of a hundred and eighty. "Churchill dined with us on board one evening. He kept teasing, asking when I would visit him in England. Nonsense, of course. Westminster had a wife and I couldn't set foot in her country. It would not have been *comme il faut.* He loved to tease, *pauvre* Winston; you couldn't take him seriously."

I thrilled to hear one who'd actually known him refer to "poor Winston" and poke fun.

I was too naive, I lacked the sophistication to do a proper job of biography, to punch holes in her narrative and demand dates, witnesses, corroboration. I simply took down what she said, which may be what made the book readable, and a seller.

She was paranoid and a mass of contradictions, blaming the Jews for a rainy summer and last year's poor vintage in Bordeaux and then rattling on about her great pal who was coming to lunch, Marie-Hélène de Rothschild. In one breath she talked of having to move her seat in a movie theater on the Champs Elysées because a black man came to sit nearby. "He smelled so, the way they do." Then, without pause, rhapsodizing about another black, an American boxer she'd known in the twenties. "Ah, that man, how we danced." Conversationally, she leapt about, rabbits on an April lawn, but that was what gave the book its pace, its bounce.

Among her fulminations, a cheerful readiness to agree that, if not truly a fascist, she was sympathetic.

"Despite Napoleon, who was a Corsican and therefore never understood, the French and the Russians should have been allies. We're much alike, two nations possessing underclasses in need of the whip and the knout, both with their aristocracies preening and bullying."

"But the famous French middle class, Coco . . ."

"Ah, don't speak to me of the bourgeoisie. One is either peasant or prince."

Mussolini she had found a cordial fellow, except for his unfortunate style of dress ("Can you imagine white spats with a black shirt?"). "A bit windy, fond of the elaborate gesture, the strutting posture, but at bottom just what the Italians need." Hitler, she dismissed. "The usual Teutonic efficiency, of course, one expected that. But no family or background whatsoever. And have you ever looked closely at those watercolors, his architectural renderings? Childlike."

During the war, she said, Pétain threatened her with arrest because she wore trousers on holiday in the South. "In Occupied France, I was curtly informed, 'women are to wear skirts, churn butter, and behave!' Although she had her differences with Pétain and the other Nazi collaborators, she despised de Gaulle. Part of that stemmed from her post-war difficulties when she was accused of collaboration by the de Gaulle regime, when it was really de Gaulle, in her view, who had broken the law. "A gangster, a criminal," she protested. "It was France that called for an armistice. To do that and then go out and shoot Germans and derail locomotives was simple banditry. Had the Germans caught de Gaulle it would have been only justice to hang him!"

But there was more to her distaste for de Gaulle than narrow legalisms.

"Some men age well," she informed me, "as you surely will, *mon petit Indien.* But not General de Gaulle. Regard his chest, how it sinks below his belt. *Dégoûtant!* Disgusting! A woman's breasts inevitably sag with age unless one keeps them small, discreet. Blame gravity. But for a man of de Gaulle's great height and a man in the public eye to reshape himself into a ripe pear, plump end down, ah, one really must protest!"

An invitation to dinner at the Elysée Palace had been turned down so she could dine one evening with Gillian and me.

"But Coco, to be invited by the President?"

"I will attend his funeral," she cooed.

She also shared her comments on Neiman Marcus, the Catholic Church, Jackie Kennedy ("a silly woman but at least she has a rather fluent French"), Robespierre, and Jean Cocteau.

"It was during the First War, and Cocteau was staying with military friends in a château near the front, a place where generals and colonels went to rest, when a German zeppelin flew over dropping bombs. There was a great commotion, with officers routed from their beds tumbling downstairs to shelter in the wine cellar, and among them, in a very pretty little pink peignoir, came Cocteau!"

Some evenings her banker dined with us, a prudent man who confided to me, "Mademoiselle knows the value of a safe nine percent"; sometimes Herve Mille, fat and clever, the man who directed *Match* for Jean Prouvost and addressed her always as *"chère Coco,"* deftly drawing her out.

"Tell Monsieur Sharkey about Mees Rosalind Russell, *chère Coco.*"

"Ah, that one. Her husband, Monsieur Brisson, quite nice. And naturally as the producer, he wished to have his wife play the leading role. I agreed to meet with her. The woman came up and I was hospitable. After all, I'd seen her films, and Brisson spoke highly of her as any husband would. But after one hour, surely after two, I knew the role of Coco on Broadway was not for her. Talk, talk, talk, endlessly, and with no more content than a gourd. What a treat when Mees Katharine Hepburn was presented to me a few months later. A delightful woman who knew how to listen."

She talked of lovers, of the young aristo who set her up in a milliner's shop in 1914 before going off to die on the Marne. Of other men, vaguely identified. And always of Westminster.

"We were cruising when Diaghilev died in Venice, and Westminster agreed to put in so I could attend the funeral. It was already in progress; White Russians, dancers, musicians, choreographers, all emotional, all of them crazy, mad with grief, swearing to follow the body on their knees all the way to the grave. 'A tribute, Coco!' they cried out. 'We suffer as the master did!'

"After a few hundred meters they were groaning and weeping, not for Diaghilev but for their torn knees. 'Get up!' I shouted, 'at this rate you'll never bury the poor chap.' "

She gave me a flat, wonderful smile. "They got up, of course, thanking me profusely for absolving them with honor."

Only about her wartime lover, the German noble with whom she shared her bed at the Ritz, was she mute.

When the book was sold to a good New York publisher for fifty thousand, for the hardcover and paperback both, I told Coco, very excited.

She didn't ask for a cut of the money or even to read the manuscript, but only fretted that I'd gone too cheap, always the fiscally shrewd Auvergnat.

"*Mon petit Indien*, I trust you," she murmured, running old fingers through my hair.

When the book came out she was dead, and for thirty weeks it was on the *Times* best-seller list and a television producer bought it for a miniseries that was never made, but I got money out of that, too. And a good thing. My bosses at the *Times* were not happy. There was some sort of unwritten rule I didn't know about that you offered your book first to Times Books, and I hadn't done that. While I was in New York on leave doing the talk shows and answering dumb questions about Coco, I dropped by Forty-third Street a few times, getting the very distinct impression my future at the paper wasn't nearly as promising as it had been when I won the Pulitzer and was first hired.

Not that Mr. Rosenthal or Mr. Gelb ever said anything. There was just an . . . atmosphere.

"Trouble with you, Sharkey," a city-room friend informed me, "is that you're cavalier. They don't like that here, you know. They like people to worry. And sweat. You don't seem to give a shit."

We were drinking at Bleeck's, and I thought he was drunk and laying it on a bit thick, but I was just twenty-three and quite pleased I'd been able to mask vulnerability, to conceal my demons. Why should it be anyone's business at the *Times* what happened to my dad?

At my age and with what I'd accomplished, I could afford a little swagger.

14 ▣ *The mandolin lady was very old and had whiskers.*

GILLIAN was gone when I got back from New York. She left a long letter, affectionate, ill-spelled, and erotic, reminding me of acrobatic interludes. But she realized she would one day be twenty. Hollywood beckoned, she said, and if that didn't work out, there was always university. Over the next few months I received girlishly scrawled postcards, a few from London, from Rome, several from the Beverly Hills Hotel, with a view of the Polo Lounge. In each she spoke briefly of influential men she'd met, and hoped I was well. There were no longer dirty passages, and the cards were signed "Fondly."

I knew love had fled.

I kept the apartment, despite its being too big and where, for purposes of tax evasion, the gas and electric and the phone were all listed in the names of other people, presumed long dead. The rent was paid in cash to the elderly countess who lived upstairs. We would meet once a month across the street in the zinc bar where she drank and flirted and sent out the boy to buy cigarettes she stained crimson with her uneven lipstick and tossed away after a few puffs to light another.

My Vietnam novel finished, I sent it off to New York, and on the momentum of the Chanel best-seller it was published but went nowhere. I was now seeing a Goucher girl who worked for *Vogue* in the Place de Palais Bourbon who read *everything*. I mean that, she read Dreiser! But she couldn't finish my novel.

"I tried, darling. I really did. It must be me."

She was sweet, but she lied. Even in Paris where anyone should be able to write, I was punk. In a thousand words I could pin a character to the corkboard; at three hundred pages I was unreadable.

It was the era of the discotheque, and I hung out at the best of them, one run by Regine, a red-haired Polish woman, the other by Jean Castel, an old rugby player going to fat. There was the new music and always plenty of pretty girls, models and actresses and whores who worked for Madame Claude, and one got to know the barmen and you could always get a table, even at three in the morning when the crush was on and the music was the best. Downstairs at Regine's at six in the morning people lay on the dance floor and staged pasta fights, throwing cold pasta at each other; at Castel's you saw Jean-Paul Belmondo with Ursula Andress and Mick Flick and Sasha Distel and Kim d'Estainville and the other "locomotives" of Paris, the best-looking girls and the men who held their drinks best, and you watched the most beautiful young women dance or you danced with them and tried to seduce them. At the entrance to Castel's, the mandolin lady, who was very old and had whiskers, played the mandolin while men shoved hundred-franc notes at her to keep from being kissed. Girls who worked on the fashion pages of *Elle* took their lovers to Les Nuages to drink brandy and argue politics, and when we ate we sat late over steaks and pommes frites at La Coupole, downstairs from where the Gestapo used to interrogate the unfortunate.

That was how it was being a journalist then, especially if you were unmarried.

The most interesting of us were French and worked for *Paris Match*. Jean Prouvost, who ran woolen mills and owned *Match*, a sporting weekly he'd turned into a Gallic *Life*, bought himself off from collaboration charges after the war, much as people said Coco did, and rebuilt his staff. Not a journalist himself, Prouvost recruited tough boys from the Maquis, the French Resistance, ex-paras, racing car drivers, ski instructors, bouncers, tennis players.

"He went into the nightclubs," said one of them, "and picked out the guys who had the best-looking girls. He hired us, and his editors gave us a crash course in the questions to ask and how to get the stories back. Fast."

One night Sinatra showed up at Castel's with his gorillas and someone said something drunkenly and the gorillas started after a boy who looked easy, but he worked for *Match* and before it was over two gorillas were in the American Hospital in Neuilly and Mr. Sinatra was in his hotel making plane reservations out. I drank and partied with the *Match* boys, too much, and went home to the Goucher girl who read Dreiser or to a wealthy divorcée with a profile who stuck her finger down her throat after every meal. Sometimes it was to a model, any number of fashion models.

And of course I worked for a living. People died and retired and were transferred home from the bureau, and by now I was on general assignment, no longer the new boy and permitted by the grown-ups to stay up late and everything, covering summit conferences and writing profiles and doing features. The *Times* even let me go to another war.

"Sharkey, wake up. Are you sober?"

It was the bureau chief. It was four in the morning.

"Yes."

"Colonel Khadafy is wigging out again. His army's invaded Chad."

"Chad?"

"Yes, it's in Africa somewhere. The Quai d'Orsay's sending a regiment of paras down there. They okayed a gentleman from the *Times* to go along. Your plane leaves at eight."

Chad was in Africa all right, south of Libya, west of Mali, east of the Sudan, and north of someplace else. Chad was also empty, a hundred miles between towns, between oases. The Libyan army wasn't much, the Chadian army was even less. Libya, at least, had a few old tanks. Chad had recoilless rifles mounted on trucks. The paras were pretty good, and after a few days the Foreign Legion came in and things got sporting. There were other reporters in the country by now, from the wires and one of the networks and a couple of papers. Chad didn't sell the way more picturesque Third World countries might, but I'd been there first, I spoke French, the Légionnaires and the paras and I had spent a few nights over the vin rouge.

Mr. Gelb sent me a gracious note from New York congratulating me on my coverage.

But you know the best part? For the first time since Da Xiang I'd been in a firefight and I was able to function. Scared, as sensible men always were under fire, I could still work, take notes, registering the scene, getting it down and writing it up. I can't tell you how good that makes you feel. Even better than notes from the *Times,* even from Mr. Gelb himself.

I did other grown-up stories as well, in Paris and around France and elsewhere, hard news and features and personality sketches and literal question-and-answer interviews. They got their money's worth out of me and always did. Where I failed the *Times* was on attitude. As my friend remarked that time at Bleeck's, I didn't seem to give a shit. But it only seemed that way. I wasn't very good at bureau politics or writing memos or getting my expense account right and I *had* gone to a rival publisher with the Chanel book, and the bosses were uncomfortable with that, recognizing I would never become one of the bright young men on the newspaper's promotion track, knowing I was no Max Frankel or Joe Lelyveld or Warren Hoge.

But they knew something else, that I worked the correspondent's trade, and as Thurber said once long before he applied for a job in Paris, I could get it, I could write it, I could put a head on it.

So went the seventies.

Toward the end of the decade, I had to be in New York on business and first met Bingo Marsh.

I was always honest with myself and as I entered my thirties, I knew how lucky I'd been young, winning the Pulitzer and then having a bestseller. Such things sort of made up for my dad. Now, in a journalistic limbo, a competent journeyman or maybe a little better, luck was leveling out. Well, the hell with it.

It was in that restive, queasy mood that I met Marsh. And then, back in Paris the *attaché du presse* of the Chambre Syndicale, the fashion trade association, took me to lunch at the Ritz, pumping me about New York. I mentioned having met Bingo.

"Mind you," she said brightly, "I don't believe a word of it. But when Bingo was living here and buying *Fashion* and first getting it launched, there was a lot of talk."

"Talk?"

She leaned closer. "They said he had affairs with animals."

15 ▣ *You know what they call him on Fire Island?*

DESPITE the animals, it was comforting to know that if things really deteriorated at the *Times*, I had Bingo's offer of a job.

In July he was in Paris for the collections and laid siege to me over drinks downstairs at the Georges V. For all his curious obsessions, he was certainly brisk and businesslike when it came to getting what he wanted.

"Working on another book?" he asked right away, sniffing out vulnerability like a ferret.

"Oh, you know," I said, wary of giving too much.

"Book publishers are awful little people. Not our sort at all."

"Well," I said, not knowing precisely what "sort" I was.

Then, shifting gears, Bingo announced, "Abe Rosenthal resents you."

I had to laugh.

"Abe is barely aware of me," I said honestly. The editor of the *Times* was famous for distancing himself from mere reporters.

"Nonsense. You have a Pulitzer, you wrote a best-seller. It's common knowledge the man is writhing with jealousy. It's all New York is talking about. You've got to get out of there."

Since Rosenthal had his own Pulitzer, had written his own books, I mumbled something, and then Marsh swiveled again, without warning, master of the non sequitur.

"See that fellow there, the sleek Rudolph Valentino spic with the greased hair?"

A rather good-looking young man waved to Marsh from one of the more desirable booths.

"Yes," I said, unsure if I were to say more.

"He's a fashion designer from New York. Here to buy fabric and sniff the air, which is how designers always describe stealing someone's idea."

"Oh?"

"Yes. He spent last summer on Fire Island, recruiting lovers and attempting to arrange financial backing for his Seventh Avenue house."

"Mmm," I said, attempting to be blasé.

Marsh leaned closer to me at the bar, dropping his voice. Obviously, this was to be some variety of confidential remark.

"My informants tell me he's exceedingly modest when it comes to sexual organs."

"Oh?" I gripped my old-fashioned glass more tightly.

"Yes, a penis about so long . . ."

Bingo held up two fingers, not very far apart. I glanced about nervously, wondering who else might be listening.

"And you know what they call him on Fire Island?"

"I have no idea."

Marsh smiled in triumph. Then, in a much louder voice: "Princess Tiny Meat!"

He left me soon after to visit what he called, also aloud, "the little boys' room." I ordered another drink, quick.

When Marsh returned, he again abruptly changed subjects.

"I'm absolutely sure . . . now don't deny it . . . that Coco seduced you."

I pushed back from the table a bit. "How can you be sure about something like that?"

"There's passion in every line of your book about her. I wouldn't say so if we weren't such good friends, but you wrote a very randy book, John, very randy." I wasn't sure whether he was chiding or becoming aroused.

"She was extraordinary," I said, choosing prudence.

"I flew over for her funeral," Bingo said. "It was all *comme il faut*, everything but a Nazi honor guard standing attention at the Ritz."

I'd been in the States for the book's publication and had missed the old girl's funeral and felt bad about it, and Bingo sensed that.

"People living off her for years couldn't bestir themselves," he said. "The Seventh Avenue manufacturers, the fashion editors, most of the retail buyers, Rosalind Russell and Freddie Brisson, who made a fortune off the musical. I called Freddie in Cleveland or some vulgar place and screamed at him. He kept saying, 'Dear boy, dear boy,' so I hung up on him. He and Miss Russell sent a floral arrangement. The sort of thing you might send to the requiem of a distant aunt." He brightened. "But an entire clan of Rothschilds came, even knowing how Coco felt about the Jews. Givenchy was there, but not Balenciaga. He never forgave her for saying he was too old, and she a decade older."

I was aware of who these people were, just, but knew little of their feuds and alliances. Bingo sensed that as well.

"There are dozens of reporters who know such things, any number of them at *Fashion*. And scores of fashion experts, who realize, for example, that men should have short necks."

"They what?"

"Short necks. Look at Cary Grant sometime. Or photos of Jack Kennedy. Fredric March. Nice, short necks, so the suit jacket sits more elegantly. A long neck on a woman is swanlike. Consider Babe Paley. But on a man . . ."

"I see," I said, though not really. Bingo was in full flight, quite excited.

"Through the years all the really well-dressed men, the great old actors, men like, well, Herbert Marshall . . ."

"Who?"

"Excellent actor. Did some movies with Bette Davis. An Englishman who had, I believe, a wooden leg. From the war. In fact, I'm quite sure about that, the wooden leg, but a nice, short neck . . ."

I was blunt.

"No, Bingo, I don't know about short necks."

". . . and Bette Davis herself, you might not be aware, had a very low bosom."

"Well, she's hardly in the first blush of . . ."

"No, even when she was young. Quite low. The brassiere industry keeps very careful track of such matters, statistics and such, when they involve the bosoms of famous people. Women, I mean."

Despite all those hours with Coco, I was a fashion illiterate. I admitted as much now. Bingo accepted my confession as enthusiastically as they welcomed back the prodigal son.

"But you're a writer. You got Chanel down on paper. Memorably so." He understood flattery.

47

"Well . . ."

"That's why you've got to join the magazine, why you simply must work for *Fashion*."

He dealt in imperatives.

16 ▣ *Tell Sharkey about the Blue Train, Olivier.*

HE was also persistent. A month later he called me from New York. An airplane ticket was en route. Open dates, round trip, first class. All he asked was a good, serious talk about my leaving the *Times* to come to work for him.

That fall I flew over, taking a week's vacation.

Lunch was in that season's fashionable restaurant, La Côte Basque, where we were greeted with enormous enthusiasm by an ugly woman and shown to a banquette in the front, more desirable, room.

"That's Madame Henriette," Bingo hissed. "She hates me."

That he and Madame Henriette had exchanged delighted kisses went unremarked.

"We're lunching with Olivier," I was informed. "You'll love him."

I thought we were having lunch to discuss my career, but I said that was fine and just who might Olivier be?

"Olivier of Hollywood."

"A director?"

"No, he makes dresses."

"Oh."

"Yes," Bingo went on, "he was a great hero during the war, in the French Resistance. Well, actually he wasn't a hero; he was the *boyfriend* of the hero, a truly sainted man."

"Oh," I said again, queasily aware of how Bingo's voice rose on such disclosures.

"The Nazis were closing in, so the hero confided to Olivier where the money was hidden, gold the British and Americans dropped by parachute to finance the Maquis and disconcert the Germans. Anyway, here was the Gestapo at the door and the Resistance hero gave Olivier a final, surely passionate, kiss, and shoved him through the window into a convenient alleyway, patting his little bottom as he went."

"And what happened?" Bingo had a way of leaving a story in mid-crisis.

"Oh," he said offhandedly, "the Gestapo pulled out the hero's fingernails and did beastly things and then shot him or something and within a few months the Allies were in Paris. Olivier surfaced, pried up the floorboards, and retrieved the gold. Anyone else who knew about the fortune was dead, and the Americans had plenty, so Olivier made an instant moral judgment and kept it. 'As a small tribute to a man I loved' was the way he later put it.

"Olivier moved in with an American colonel from Des Moines with a penchant for young boys, got the colonel to arrange for a visa, and by '46 or '47 Olivier was in New York, a rather wealthy young man."

Marsh paused, calculating.

"He must have been just eighteen."

I cleared my throat, wondering how much of this the waiter was getting.

"So you see," Marsh said, "that, after all, the fairies really did play a major role in the war effort."

Olivier of Hollywood came in a few moments later, a tough-looking, slim, dark-haired man.

"This is Mr. Sharkey, Olivier, of *The New York Times*."

"You a fashion editor?"

"No, Olivier, John knows nothing of fashion. He may just be joining us at the magazine to write about people."

"No shit?" said Olivier. I don't know where he learned his English, but from its Brooklyn accents, it could have been Huntz Hall. Or Leo Gorcey.

Wanting to be cordial, I said, "And you like Los Angeles?"

"Huh?"

"I mean, Hollywood, where you live."

"Hollywood is shit," he said.

"But you live there . . ."

"Nah. It just sounds good, you know, 'of Hollywood.' Gives dames a thrill."

"It does have a ring," I agreed.

"Sure," said Olivier, "but L.A. is bullshit. I don't never go there. I got Mexican wetbacks sews up the goods. In this business you need a name. You think dames buy sexy dresses from 'Olivier of Thirty-eighth Street'?"

It was Bingo's lunch, but Olivier had already called for the wine card.

"The Pétrus '61," he said.

I had a vague idea what that cost.

Marsh, simpering with satisfaction and ignoring the price, said, "John was Chanel's last and closest friend."

"You fucked her?" Olivier inquired, looking at me with a new respect.

"They were *friends*, Olivier," Bingo said sternly. "John wrote a book about her."

"Oh." He sounded disappointed.

"It's possible for people to have a relationship without its involving sex." Bingo was starting to sound almost schoolmarmish.

The wine arrived and Olivier tasted it. "Fucking great," he enthused.

"Tell Mr. Sharkey about the Blue Train, Olivier," Marsh urged.

"You know," the Frenchman told me, ignoring Bingo, "I like your name. It's sexy."

"The Blue Train," Marsh insisted sternly.

It turned out that while traveling on the famous Blue Train between Nice and Paris, Olivier of Hollywood had actually seduced a young American bridegroom while the man was on his honeymoon, luring him from the nuptial compartment to Olivier's narrow berth as the train sped north. He told the story with considerable spirit and in great detail. Bingo smiled smugly, satisfied that Olivier had performed as advertised.

"Gee," I said, unsure if that covered the situation.

Olivier apparently thought it sufficient. "Maybe you write in the *Times* about me?"

"Sure," I said, carelessly and insincerely. I could imagine Mr. Gelb and Mr. Rosenthal seeing a feature on Olivier of Hollywood and the Blue Train cross their desks.

"I got a new boyfriend now," Olivier went on, "a New York cop. I wear his uniform around the apartment, and he lets me blow his whistle."

Bingo giggled.

I lifted a wineglass, smothering confusion with the Pétrus. It was an extraordinary wine. I liked Olivier better already.

Madame Henriette, the ugly woman who'd greeted Bingo with such zeal, hovered as we ordered.

"She's Henri Soulé's old mistress," he confided. "She was the hatcheck girl at Le Pavillon, and in a moment of weakness he took her to bed. Great chefs are so vulnerable, slaving over hot stoves all day, tasting things, stirring the *bonne soupe*. I'm sure she took advantage of him while he was enervated by spices. Can you imagine waking up next to a face like hers?"

I wondered if she could hear him, if people at other tables were, as Bingo often did, taking notes of overheard conversations. I wondered about the laws on slander in New York State. When we'd lunched and were on the way out, Bingo introduced us, again embracing Madame Henriette with enormous affection, turning to me while still in her arms:

"Madame Henriette is so nice, John. And Ames . . ."

17 ▣ *Stepping down to enter Dracula's castle.*

AS Olivier of Hollywood left us on the sidewalk, Marsh peered at his wristwatch.

"Come on," he said, skipping east on Fifty-fifth Street, "it's after two and I hate to miss the start."

"Of what?"

"There's this new movie I'm dying to see. Don't you love going to movies in the afternoon?"

"Well, I guess so . . ."

"This one's about lesbians. Come on, I want to see how they do it."

Evenings were for Bingo's wife and his children and their home; afternoons, when he could sneak away like this, delighting in the joy of truancy, were for movies. He liked having company, and I was drafted. I'd always felt furtive about afternoon movies, coming out while it was still daylight.

Less than two hours later we were back on the street. The film turned out to be exceedingly dull and not about lesbians at all; he'd gotten that wrong, and I was a bit huffy about it.

"Well, I certainly *thought* it was going to be about lesbians," Bingo said lamely, "the ad in the paper looked that way."

I admitted then I was uneasy about movies in the afternoon.

"Yes," he said, "it all has to do with being a Catholic. Guilt and all that. You are a Catholic, of course. The eight deadly sins . . ."

"Seven."

He was again regarding his watch, tempted to try to catch a four o'clock show somewhere. Then, resignedly, he shrugged. "I guess we'd better go back. I promised to show you around the office."

In the cab downtown he talked about film, saying that while he despised most American culture, he thought Hollywood made the best movies.

"Including my own personal all-time favorite."

"Which is . . . ?"

"*Laura.*"

Not, he told me confidentially, because it was a whodunit or because of the romance between Gene Tierney and Dana Andrews.

"At Yale they were always pushing British films at us, art movies like *Les Amants*. Or *Hiroshima, Mon Amour*."

"Thought they were French," I said.

"Or the Laurence Olivier movies about Shakespeare," he went on, unperturbed. "*Hamlet*. Or *Henry the Fourth*."

"*Fifth.*"

"Whatever."

He also liked *Citizen Kane* and *Pandora and the Flying Dutchman* and *Singin' in the Rain*. And . . . *Laura*.

"It's the Clifford Webb character . . ."

"Isn't it 'Clifton'?"

". . . yes, the evil columnist besotten with love for Laura. Who certainly wasn't really worthy of him, not up to his standards at all, but isn't that how men are, always pining away for . . ." He searched for the word.

"The 'unattainable,' " I offered.

"Just so," Bingo said. Then, more thoughtfully, "You know, had they made *Laura* a few years later, after I got the magazine started and began to be talked about, it would have been actionable."

"What would?" I asked, thoroughly lost now.

Bingo regarded me with something less than tolerance.

"The Waldo Lydecker character. Clearly inspired by me." He paused. "I mean, if at the time they knew who I was."

He'd lost me again, in the details, but I was beginning to grasp his thought.

"I really liked how Waldo typed his column, on a sort of little platform erected over the bathtub. I thought of doing that myself, you know, but Ames talked me out of it."

"Why?" I asked, genuinely curious.

"Well, Lydecker used an old-fashioned typewriter. I use an electric. And Ames said if it slipped off and fell into the tub, I'd be electrocuted." He paused again, "Just as surely as they electrocuted Hoffman, who kidnapped the Lindbergh baby."

"Hauptmann."

"Yes, that fellow."

I really didn't know what to say at times like this, when Bingo thoroughly befuddled me with vagaries of grammar and the mythic nature of his thought processes.

"Don't you think I would have had a case? I mean, you've seen the film, how Lydecker is modeled on me."

Well, I said, there certainly *was* a similarity . . .

". . . as if they knew there'd be someone like me, before the movie was ever made . . ."

Only Marsh, I thought, a man who could consider a libel action over a work made years before he could possibly have been its putative subject. . . . I was still mulling this when he was saying it was his nightmare to be caught coming out of the movies some afternoon by one of his many enemies.

"If Nunc came along, for example, and saw me. I mean, I'd never hear the end of it. Or the Social Larva . . ."

It was, he concluded, part of the fun of afternoon movies, the thrill of risking exposure. "You know, how sex maniacs really want to be captured and write their names on mirrors with the victim's lipstick."

He was rhapsodizing now about Japanese monster films, the ones starring B actors like Raymond Burr and always starting off with some idyllic picnic or boating scene when suddenly, set free by postwar nuclear underseas testing, an enormous prehistoric monster emerges to . . .

"We're here!" Bingo cried, rapping at the plastic window between ourselves and the driver and pushing bills into the cash tray. I looked out to see what looked to be a turn-of-the-century mansion, mullioned windows, turrets and all, looming above us, everything but cast-iron Negro jockeys flanking the enormous front doors.

"This is it!" said Bingo enthusiastically. "The Marsh building!"

For some obscure reason I thought of the young solicitor, new to Transylvania, stepping down from the carriage to enter Dracula's castle.

18 ◙ *Pinsky does not do donkeys.*

"THIS is Mr. Sharkey," Bingo said over and over as we entered and began to climb through the old building, floor by floor. "He won the Pulitzer Prize," as childishly proud of me as of a new puppy.

The magazine's offices rabbit-warrened through gallery, floor, and wing of the handsome period mansion on lower Fifth, where the city's publishing business once clustered and flourished, the anachronism conscious and charming. There were pretty, leggy girls at every turning; bent old men in vests; dashing postgraduates who affected suspenders; chattering typewriters, ringing phones, cigarette smoke hanging blue, brimming, reeking ashtrays, mugs of black coffee gone cold and sour. In all, a marvelous facsimile of real journalism.

No one seemed aware of the imposture.

Several floors up was the advertising department. The ad director, sullen and a drinker, was nodded to and ignored. We moved on swiftly.

"And *this* is Mr. Pinsky," Bingo said, voice cracking with emotion. "He sells absolutely *all* the advertising."

Pinsky, tall and craggy with thick, graying hair and a cordovan suntan no salaried worker ever comes by honestly, smiled his tolerance.

"I bring in a few dollars," he admitted.

Marsh beamed on him. I had a Pulitzer; Pinsky brought in the dollars.

We were both important, one actually, the other potentially. Perhaps it wasn't all that different from the dusty, accustomed precincts of the *Times*. Pinsky, I would learn, was an office legend, living splendidly with a baroque style all his own. Arriving at a grand hotel, a resort in the islands, or the shingle at Portofino, Pinsky instantly summoned whoever was in charge — concierge, mayor, chief barman — to issue a terse announcement:

"I am Mr. Pinsky," he would say, pulling out an impressive wallet and holding it above his head, pointing to it with the free hand, "and this is Mr. Pinsky's wallet. You take care of Mr. Pinsky and Mr. Pinsky's wallet takes care of you."

Pinsky, it was said, invariably received excellent service.

It was not simply his largesse that impressed the natives on his travels. During a trip through the Greek isles Pinsky was offered the ritual tour of a down-at-the-heels Orthodox monastery of enormous sanctity set atop a towering peak accessible only on the back of a small, sure-footed Aegean donkey. Pinsky would have none of it. To the local Pope he declared:

"Pinsky does not do donkeys. Four natives carrying a basket, maybe. But Pinsky does not do donkeys."

The monastery remained unvisited.

As we departed Pinsky's realm into the stairwell, Marsh hissed, apologetic and pleased both, "Great salesmen *ought* to be vulgar. He's terribly good, but not our sort, not our sort at all."

I was again unsure just what sort that was. Bingo went on:

"We employ Jews, of course," he said murkily.

As we ascended through the building, cheerful (or intimidated) smiles greeting us, we encountered an extraordinary sight, a slender young black man, dizzyingly tall, smoking, or rather posturing with, an ivory cigarette holder and wearing a soft gray flannel vested suit that murmured Savile Row. I suddenly felt rumpled.

"This is Elegant Hopkins," Marsh said brightly, "one of our most truly talented young people."

Hopkins extended a languid hand as I was introduced, preferring not to expend energy on the unimportant and not yet having measured my role.

"Charmed," he said, in a studied Oxbridge drawl.

As he passed on, Bingo giggled.

"Isn't he marvelous? Shoes by Lobb, shirts handmade at Charvet. And not even Gielgud sounds as grand."

"Is that really his name, 'Elegant'?"

"I asked the same question myself. Looked it up on his withholding forms. I questioned him about it, and he said his mother was a prodigious reader of romantic novels. He has sisters called Utopia and Bountiful and a brother named Zealous. Or maybe that's a sister as well."

Then Marsh thought of something. "But he hadn't been here a week when the girls christened him. He's always carrying on about becoming a fashion designer, that this is temporary, a kind of summer internship. Very superior he is. So the girls gave him a pet name."

"Yes?"

Marsh swiveled his head to see if we could be overheard.

"The African Queen," he said. "Delicious, isn't it?"

"But they don't call him that, not to his face?"

Bingo looked pained. "Of course not. Colored people are very sensitive. I'm most particular about such things. And Ames."

Now he skipped ahead of me through another department where "the girls" worked, where even now they might be concocting nicknames for newcomers like me. One looked up from a typewriter and briefly held my eyes. This might not be a bad place to work after all.

Bingo's office was lushly carpeted, book lined, with pictures I assumed to be originals, more a comfortable study than a place of work. Marsh fell into a deep leather armchair and motioned me to another, before embarking on an impressive *tour d'horizon* of fashion journalism, from *Vogue* to *Women's Wear Daily*.

"*Vogue* is the biggest and richest," he began. "Si Newhouse and his brother own it, and the publisher is a salesman who keeps getting married again. But the man who really runs it is named Alex Liberman. He's an artist. He cuts up iron girders and things with a blowtorch and puts them out on lawns to rust, and Hilton Kramer at the *Times* and Tom Hoving at the Met go crazy."

"I think I've seen some of his . . ."

"He's an aristocrat as well, you know, just getting out of St. Petersburg before they shot the czar or something, and he's very bright. He has the art directors all terrified of his sheer good taste. They retired the editor of *Vogue* a few years ago, Madame Vreeland, a woman with lacquered hair who resembles the last Empress of China."

"Coco used to speak of her," I said, "called her 'the most pretentious woman ever . . .' "

Marsh loved to hear people he knew being trashed, and he got up and skipped about a bit.

"Did she? That's splendid. I remember Walter Hoving saying when he was running Lord and Taylor, he had Vreeland come in and look over the store and tell him honestly what she thought, this was when she was still at *Harper's Bazaar,* and so Diana went through all the floors and then she got to Mr. Hoving's office and she said, 'You know, Mr. Hoving, your store would be ever so much nicer if there weren't so many customers.' "

Back in his chair, Bingo resumed his appraisal of the magazines.

"*Bazaar* is a disaster area. Hearst keeps changing editors, firing publishers. Winston Churchill's mother used to write for the *Bazaar* a hundred years ago. Did you know that?"

"No, I . . ."

"It's true. She was broke and having affairs and Winston and his brother were still in school or in the army or something and Lady Churchill wrote free-lance pieces and now they publish features on corrective footwear. I wish she were still alive; I'd love to have Churchill's mother on *Fashion,* wouldn't you?"

"Sure. She'd certainly sell some maga . . ."

"*Glamour* and *Mademoiselle* are both owned by Condé Nast. Newhouse, again. Both make money. *Glamour* is very smart in its marketing, lots of pretty girls fresh out of Sarah Lawrence and Bryn Mawr running around showing their legs and charming the retailers. But they have zero influence with the designers . . ."

"The Sarah Lawrence girls?"

"No, *Mademoiselle* and *Glamour.* The designers are key to the entire business. They're all crazy except for Sarmi and he has no talent. *Town and Country* has a very good editor named Frank Zachary, and they read it in San Diego, all the admirals' widows. Fleur Cowles used to have a magazine, too, but she got divorced. *Women's Wear Daily* has the most influence, even more than ours. The daily frequency gives it a tremendous edge, and Fairchild is a clever man, smarmy but shrewd. He went to Princeton . . ."

I had visions of a feud that began at a half-forgotten Yale-Princeton game a generation ago.

". . . and frequency is why I made *Fashion* a weekly. Not as good as a daily, obviously, but so much more timely and fresh than a monthly. That's why *Elle* magazine is the most interesting fashion magazine in France. A woman named Helen Gordon Lazareff runs it. Quite mad, totally gaga."

"I met her at Coco's. She had both of us for lunch and . . ."

"Well, then, you know. Certifiable but cunning. She's the reason every little French shop girl has at least a suspicion of chic."

He went on like this, ending up with *Fashion*, never apologizing for it, always talking it up, real passion in his voice. He wanted it to be *more* than a fashion magazine, the *Vanity Fair* of its time perhaps, saying something and saying it memorably, good writing, great art direction, cutting criticism, acutely honed commentary. That was where I came in, the commentary.

"Not about clothes. You don't know enough to write fashion. We have people to do that. I want you to write about the designers, these mad, glamorous, tortured people, the way you wrote about Colonel Khadafy for the *Times* when he invaded Mali . . ."

"Chad."

". . . their wealth, the scandals, their incredible lifestyles, the jealousies. That ripe stuff you pried out of Coco for your book. All about the designers and the rich bitches who support them and the richer men who support the rich bitches and the whole phony society that leeches off all of them." He paused for an instant. "Is it true Khadafy's a transvestite, or was that just propaganda the CIA put out about him?"

"Well, there was a story that . . ."

Bingo waved a hand. Then, as if realizing he was confusing me, he concluded, "Well, you know what I mean."

I didn't, not really, but I didn't say that. He offered to start me at fifty thousand a year.

A week later I returned to Paris, sending Bingo a note thanking him for his graciousness and the handsome offer, suggesting that if at any point I left the *Times* but remained in Paris, perhaps I could write the odd free-lance piece for him. Journalists talk endlessly of money, but most of us are snobs and I wasn't yet sure I really wanted to trade in *The New York Times* for something called *Fashion* that employed people named "Elegant Hopkins."

19 ▣ *The creator of the New Look ate himself to death.*

IN the 1920s the American poet Hart Crane scrawled on a postcard this description of Paris:

"Dinners, soirees, poets, erratic millionaires, painters, translations, lobsters, absinthe, music, promenades, oysters, sherry, aspirin, pictures, Sapphic heiresses, editors, books, sailors. And How!"

I hadn't tried sailors. But fifty years after Crane I recognized the town.

The New York Times doesn't sack young men with Pulitzers but they give you hints, and after another year I resigned, writing Marsh to tell him I was staying in Paris but would be open to writing assignments. In January, he replied, he would be over for the fashion shows, staying at the Lancaster, and suggesting lunch.

I was airy about the *Times*. You don't confess failure to people you're hoping will hand out plummy jobs.

"I knew you weren't their sort," Bingo said with considerable satisfaction, "Abe Rosenthal and Artie Gelb."

Actually they'd both been more than generous with me, so instead of responding, I talked about Paris.

"Don't tell me about Paris," Marsh said impatiently. "Don't forget, it was here I bought *Fashion* and gulled Nunc into financing it, where I met Ames, where I learned French and lost innocence."

I sat back, swirling my wine, dark and wonderful, recognizing I was about to be treated to Bingo in full flight.

"Dior was king then. I was at the Sorbonne in '59 when he died on a voyage his astrologer warned him against taking. People who liked Dior said it was a cardiac. Or stress. It was none of those things. It was gluttony. We had mutual friends through family and I'd been taken up by him and I can testify what killed him. This patron saint of couture, the creator of the New Look, ate himself to death. Oh, you could see it coming. The pâté, the pot-au-feu, the sausage, the rack of lamb, the faisan à l'orange, the lunches of choucroute at Lipp, the crevettes at Méditerranée, the dinners Chez Allard. And desserts! The fraises de bois, the framboises, the peaches swimming in kirsch, everything smothered in crème fraîche, the tortes, the profiteroles, the cheese platter and petits pains thick with slabs of butter!"

Bingo enjoyed himself a good meal and ate all through this account, his slight tummy pressing against his vest and the beltline of his gently pleated trousers, but there was no mistaking his righteous indignation.

"Dior," said Marsh, "was a pig."

After Dior as king came Balenciaga.

"He and his little monks," Bingo said with some asperity, "all in their surgically pristine neat little white smocks. Those juicy boys and this ascetic old Spaniard, a man of such taste and artistry, of discrimination and genius. And what was he doing? Getting down on his hands and knees for the little monks to mount and bugger him. Really, you had to be there."

"Were you?" I asked, unable to resist.

"Of course not. But by then I had my sources. Gérard used to tell me everything. Discreetly, of course."

Who Gérard was, was not explained. There had been a falling out between Balenciaga and *Fashion* magazine and Bingo was now banned from the house.

"I wrote that he and Givenchy strolled hand in hand. The most innocent of similes, meant stylistically of course, but Balenciaga took it to have a sexual connotation. So we're banned from seeing the collections. I send pretty girls to work the sidewalks outside, swinging the bag like streetwalkers, and peeking in through the windows during rehearsals. Once I dressed up a young editor as a florist's assistant, cheap plastic smock and carpet slippers, and sent her in with a vulgarly enormous bouquet for Monsieur Balenciaga, to be delivered personally into his hands and with a card I forged with the name of the man who owns Bergdorf's. Balenciaga can't resist flattery. So he took the flowers and signed for them, all the while letting the girl get a look 'round at the work going on and taking mental notes of the drawings. But as she left he suddenly called her back. Had she been discovered?"

Bingo halted dramatically.

"No, he wanted to give her a franc tip." Another pause. "The skin-flint."

Balenciaga was so obsessed by secrecy and so distrustful of the press, Marsh said, he entered and left his own *maison de couture* in one of its black-lacquered little delivery vans, getting in and out in the interior courtyard and riding in back with the racked dresses, "lying on the floor so no one could see him through the windows."

Balenciaga and his acolyte Givenchy were *not* favorites of *Fashion*.

I decided to put in an anecdote of my own, about Castillo, the Spaniard Chanel despised.

"Coco told me he once tried to set her on fire. There was a garden party one evening off the Etoile, lighted by tapers, and she was wearing something flowing . . ."

"Chiffon, I would think," Bingo put in expertly.

". . . and he surprised her by asking her to dance. Until she realized he kept steering her and the flowing stuff . . ."

". . . chiffon, surely."

". . . toward the flaming candles."

"They've always had difficulty with chiffon and the flammability standards," Marsh said pedantically, hating to have an anecdote topped. I decided against telling him about the Gypsy boys in the castle basement. It was just as well.

Bingo related a preposterous tale about a famous American political figure's second wife and a German shepherd.

I must have goggled. "You know this?"

Bingo looked at me tolerantly. "Everyone knows it, just everyone."

For all his journalistic lineage, a family in the business, Marsh was astonishingly vague about libel law, marvelous at winnowing out shameful secrets but erratic when it came to the reportorial conventions.

"But just how do you prove such a story?"

He fixed me with an incredulous eye. "Don't be naive. It's common knowledge."

You didn't win arguments like that with Marsh, and before lunch was ended we'd agreed on a dozen pieces a year from Paris for *Fashion* magazine at two thousand apiece. It wasn't a lot of money to him, but it would keep me going until I figured out just what I was going to do with the rest of my life.

And it didn't pin me down to full-time work for a man and a magazine I didn't yet quite understand. And a man who didn't know as much about me as he thought he did.

20 ▣ *I didn't want to be laughed at.*

IT bothered me, going to work for a man as relentlessly curious as Marsh and keeping things from him.

"We all have our secrets," he'd said. "Everyone has something to hide."

He was only blathering, going on as he did about the fashion designers and their little scandals. He didn't know a thing about my people, and I hoped he never would. No one wants sandpaper rubbed across scabs.

I was nine years old and came home from school to learn about it. I'd left that morning a reasonably well-adjusted third-grader who lived in a nice clapboard house on one of the better streets on the right side of the tracks in a prosperous Ohio town where my mother, who had social ambitions, and my father, the county attorney, cut a certain figure. Then came the afternoon paper with its headlines:

"County Attorney Sharkey Accused!"

And the subhead: "State Alleges He Faced Evidence to Insure Convictions."

"Mom?"

She sat at the kitchen table, sobbing. It was unlike her, both the tears and the kitchen table. We had a maid, and my mother, who never wept, preferred the sitting room.

"Here, read it for yourself. You'll hear enough about it."

I picked up the paper, an old-fashioned broadsheet not yet owned by Gannett or Knight or anybody, an ornery, independent small-town daily. There was my dad on the front page, a three-year-old photo from the last election. The paper said he had been indicted, that he would shortly be arraigned, that he was suspended from his job as county attorney. I knew those terms; lawyers' sons hear them around the house, over the dinner table.

When my father came home he went into the den alone for a while. Then he called for me.

"Son, you saw the paper."

"Yessir."

"You understand I'm in difficulty. Legal problems. And that in school tomorrow your friends may talk about them, about what the newspaper said. They may tease you a bit."

I nodded, not really knowing.

"If they do, don't get into fights, don't argue. Just say you know about it, or say nothing, or go your way."

"Yessir."

"And, Johnny, are you listening?"

"Yes."

"Don't say you're sorry, don't apologize, remember that? Nothing they say I did calls for any apology from you or your mom or anyone but me."

"Yessir."

"All right, you go now and play."

When I went out of the den I looked through the open door into the kitchen where my mother stood, red-eyed, over the afternoon paper.

A week later my father killed himself, using the old shotgun he kept in the cellar for shooting crows. My mother went sort of funny after that, drinking a bit. She died when I was thirteen, able to take disaster but not embarrassment.

Uncle Ab and Aunt Micki brought me up until I went away to school at Ohio State and applied right away for the staff of the newspaper as a freshman. I figured if a small-town afternoon paper could change people's lives, being on a newspaper was the thing to do. Not even lawyers, or county attorneys, were as important as newspapers. And their headlines.

So when Bingo Marsh talked about newspapering and coming from a newspaper background and about the journalist's code and ethic, I knew as much as he did. In a way, I wanted to tell him about my dad and the trouble so he'd understand why being a good newspaperman was important to me.

But Bingo had that way of snickering and making sport of things, and I didn't want to be laughed at. Or gossiped about. Or felt sorry for. Anyway, it was none of his business. His life, his wife and home, whatever Marsh was beyond the office and the magazine, were kept guarded and private. Why not my life?

So I held old secrets close.

21 □ *He's a hundred years old and he has a girlfriend.*

THERE was a final dinner with Bingo. "You've got to meet Bergé before I leave. The smartest man in Paris."

By now I recognized the patterns in Marsh's speech. One "must" do this and "never" do that. People were "the smartest . . . the most dreadful . . . my best friend." He dealt in absolutes, chiaroscuro, no grays or pastels on Bingo's palette.

I'd seen Pierre Bergé around town, of course, once at a cocktail at Saint Laurent's flat on the Left Bank, the one decorated with narwhal horns. I was standing there with a glass when a New York coat-and-suit buyer cornered Bergé, Saint Laurent's partner, and was asking impertinently if he spoke English.

"I . . . can . . . *count,*" Bergé responded with malicious glee. My admiration for him derived from that moment.

"I don't know if they, you know, sleep together . . ."

"Who?"

"Yves and Pierre. They've been, well, together for years. Pierre is from La Rochelle and came up to Paris to paint, but he lacked the talent. Even he'll tell you that, so I'm not being bitchy. While still a teenager he was arrested at the Palais de Chaillot demonstrating on behalf of Garry Davis. You remember him? The 'citizen of the world' who burned his passport."

"I think so."

"A poseur, that's my opinion, but it was American MPs who arrested young Pierre, so he hates us. Not you or me or Ames, for goodness' sake, but us in general. He's a bolshie, red flag and all, and a millionaire. Drives a Bentley and blathers on about the redistribution of wealth. Didn't that fellow John Reed go to Princeton, the one who wrote about the Russian Revolution and was so chummy with Lenin?"

"Harvard, I believe." I wondered what any of this had to do with Saint Laurent's partner.

"You may be right. Harvard's always been rife with bolshies. Free love, Timothy Leary, vegetarianism, all that sort of nonsense. Anyway, Bergé's first fortune was made with Bernard Buffet, managing his career, marketing his pictures. I've been through Bergé's apartment, end to end, it's chockablock with Buffets, even the bathroom. There must be a hundred of them, and they've got to be worth forty thousand apiece, that is, if you like the linear style."

"Well, I often . . ."

"Since 1960 or so Pierre's been with Saint Laurent. He'd been clever about discerning talent, and he's been a tremendous help to Yves, who tends to faint, and things."

"Literally?"

"Oh yes. When they drafted him into the army to fight the Algerians, Yves had a nervous breakdown. All those lusty young French boys, and here was poor Yves among them in the barracks, weeping and sobbing, and having to go pipi in front of everyone. They used to make him iron their underwear for inspection."

"Man's inhumanity to man . . ."

"And Pierre saved him from all that after the army threw him out. A very clever man, Bergé. Not that Yves doesn't still have his little problems, such as the time when . . ."

The cab chose this promising moment to pull up at last, having missed the restaurant several times and going back.

"This is the most obscure street in Paris," Bingo said proudly.

Bergé was there ahead of us, reorganizing the table according to his own seating plan.

"Hallo, you rat fink," he greeted Marsh.

"No, you're the rat fink," Bingo responded.

"No, you are."

"The smartest man in Paris" and Marsh embraced. I was introduced.

"This is John Sharkey, Pierre."

"Ah yes," Bergé said, hissing his esses, *"le requin."*

"What's that? What's that mean?" Bingo said hastily, suspicious he was missing something, his French rusty.

"The . . . shark!" Bergé said, smacking his lips, then calling imperiously for a waiter.

Marsh had called him a Communist; what he was, theoretically, was a socialist. In actuality, he was in style a monarchist, of the strict construction.

They fetched salad reeking with garlic, and we dove in, Bingo and Pierre swapping stories about people in the fashion business, most of them scatological, all of them libelous.

"Cela ne fait rien," Bergé would say, "that's nothing," and he would tell another story.

They even told stories about themselves, Marsh recounting the tale of a celebrated man who once broke into his stateroom on the *Queen Mary* and offered to perform base acts.

"You invent these things," I said incredulously.

Bingo looked at me. "Everyone knows about him," he said.

"But . . ."

Bergé snapped his fingers for more wine.

"Don't ever be provincial, John," Marsh said seriously. "More is expected of you."

Bergé told a story about Pierre Cardin's being gulled again in yet another confidence scheme, while Marsh countered with an anecdote about the Baron Nicky de Gunzberg of *Vogue*.

"The *salot!*" Bergé exploded, "the way he turned his vest."

The baron, who did fashion things for *Vogue*, had apparently been overheard being complimentary about the current Dior collection. When Bergé went to the men's room, Bingo leaned his head close to mine. "You never, *never* praise one designer where another might hear of it."

Women's Wear Daily had recently launched a new biweekly spinoff, a handsome broadsheet called *W,* and it was making something of a success in America.

"They're so cheap," Bingo said in irritation. "It's all recycled material from *Women's Wear* . . . words, pictures, everything. They haven't hired a single reporter, just some ad salesmen."

Bergé, who understandably wanted to stay on the right side of

Women's Wear Daily, said he did not agree, that the new paper was quite good. Now it was Bingo's turn to sulk. The old man who owned the bistro, Monsieur Mangin, came out briskly to greet us and to praise the gigot d'agneau.

"He's a hundred years old," Bingo whispered when Mangin returned to the kitchen, "and he has a girlfriend."

"He can't."

"But he has. Everyone knows it. And Ames."

The lamb was wonderful, and after we went to Regine's to dance with two lesbians, both of them handsome women. I was getting rather drunk and Bergé kept pushing the Black Label on me, enjoying watching me play the fool. Then one of our lesbians spied a very pretty girl dancing with a good-looking boy.

"I'll wager I can get her away from him," she said. Stakes were arranged and money put up. Bingo said he never gambled. But just this once . . .

Bergé made a book.

When I left, alone, about four A.M., the woman, Betty, was dancing with the pretty girl and the good-looking boy was sitting morosely at the bar.

22 ▣ *Howling, cursing, singing, often in Gregorian chant.*

FOR a year I did pieces on the European designers. Not only Paris. Mary Quant in London and this new man Armani in Milano, the odd Japanese setting up shop on the Faubourg Saint-Honoré. At first I was shy about imposing myself on them, exotic creatures of rare plumage. It was one thing to play rugger with Courreges or hang out with Ungaro or get tipsy with Chanel; then I had the *Times* behind me. A simple reference to the paper opened doors. Now I was a freelance, representing something called . . . *Fashion*.

What I failed to realize was that in this milieu, *Fashion* was as potent as the *Times*. Maybe more so.

Bergé arranged an interview, and I asked Saint Laurent about fashion, whether it was an art. He responded more eloquently than any of them, which was odd, for Yves was faun-shy, self-conscious, nearly tongue-tied with strangers.

"Fashion isn't art," he said, "that's too important a word. It's a trade, a *métier. Un métier poetique.*"

"A poetic trade." I used his phrase to open a profile of Yves, and Marsh cabled his delight. I was not always as fortunate. Touted on his talent by several dubious sources I wrote what could only be termed a "puff piece" about another, "promising," young designer. His collection was an enormous flop.

Bingo called from New York. "What did you expect? The man's happily married."

Marsh had the knack of fashion, not only the clothes but the men and women who conjured up the magic. I didn't. Not that I didn't learn something. Certainly I got to know them, the designers. Theirs was a narrow, special gift, the proper draping of cloth, the comprehension, without desire, of a woman's body, and more than the body, knowing how a woman felt and what she wanted. A sense of proportion, an eye for color, an understanding of time and place so that the clothes would work now, and not a year ahead, a year ago, or on some wench in another country.

Not an art, yet I haunted fashion's ateliers. "The designers, the designers, the designers," Bingo carped at me by phone and cable, "they're the engines of fashion."

And when you got to know the designers, sitting late with them over dinners on the Ile or lunches Chez Allard, you were inevitably invited to the new fashion show.

"It is my work, it is what I do, it is my life. If you care anything for me you must come and bear witness to my genius."

So ran the appeal. And so I became a regular at the fashion shows of Paris, and surprised myself by enjoying them. The clothes held interest mostly because I knew who had designed them. I was intrigued by the beautiful young women who wore them on the runway and by the less beautiful and somewhat more mature women who could afford the clothes. I'd begun learning about fashion shows from Coco and from Gillian. Now I was tutored by Bingo, from whom I would learn the fashion show had a dynamic, a flow, even an ethic all its own.

"You simply must sit in the front row and on the first day," Bingo lectured me. "If there are two shows the first day, attend the earlier. The models get sloppy and the energy goes, and at the second show there are Germans."

By "Germans" Bingo subsequently made clear he meant any Europeans who were not French.

"If when you get there and there's no front-row seat reserved, leave instantly. The designers have utter contempt for people who accept a place in the second row. It's far better to insult a designer by walking out. He'll respect you for it. And don't fret if he bursts into tears. Designers always weep on the day of the collection. It's how they pay homage to themselves."

Gillian had had her own set of rules, agreeing with Bingo about the necessity of the front seat but enlarging on it.

"You've got to sit up front, of course, but you must also smoke cigarettes constantly, lighting one from another, and laugh a lot and when John Fairchild or the editor of *Vogue* rolls his eyes backwards, you look stern. And after the show has gone on for a certain period of time, anything over an hour, pretend to be Italian and cry 'Basta!' and perhaps throw your program. At some shows, the Cardin for example, crying 'Basta!' commences quite early."

I also learned it was permitted to faint at shows. The woman who wrote fashion for the *Herald Tribune* in Paris did this frequently in order to escape early.

I had an advantage over most newcomers writing for fashion magazines. I had the *Times;* its severe disciplines and its stylebook, to which its writers adhered with the fervor of religious conversion; and I had something else, a conviction that as lousy as I might be writing books, I was pretty good at short pieces. Maybe very good. And there was one more thing: Da Xiang and the cockiness combat gave a young man that he would never entirely lose no matter what happened.

I think the designers sensed it, opening themselves, their minds, even their homes to me so that I was able to write about them with a familiarity, a near intimacy, that brought the pieces vibrantly to life. Other fashion writers asked them about their designs, about the clothes; I asked them about themselves. It worked, and more and more often my pieces found their way to the cover of the magazine and it was by cover stories, as much as by money, that a magazine writer's worth was calculated.

Not that I had no other life. This was still Paris; there were women.

The designers sent them, they came on their own, some I sought out. The designers tried me early with the subtle bribe, the bespoke suit, the pricey meal, the case of Latour, sometimes blunt and vulgar cash. I took the meals and a discount on the clothes, and the occasional vintage bottle (an entire case I rejected righteously as immoral!), but turned down the rest. Bingo's warning echoed: "They'll try to buy you. They tried to buy me." It was apparently an honored and ancient tradition among French fashion editors to be bought; the Italians insisted on it as an inherited right. So I said no to the cash.

It was more ticklish with the women. To reject them without at least sharing an apéritif or an evening would have been unconscionably rude, since they were amiable young persons but doing their job.

One of the Paris designers not only sent no bribes but refused to receive me.

This was Paul Profonde, the "intellectual," known more familiarly as "Pipi." Profonde was said to be "too grand" at this stage of his career to receive the press. He was contemptuous of publicity; too busy thinking.

"A genius!" cried his small but growing cult of admirers. As profound as his name, Profonde was known to slave through an entire day and night over a shoulder pad, howling, cursing, singing, often in Gregorian chant (vestige of an education by Jesuits in Lille), occasionally crying out in anguish to God to witness the perfidy of silk prices and the embroiderers' union, pointing an elegantly narrow foot (he'd done time at the barre as a child in ballet class), and slavering slightly at the corners of his aristocratic mouth.

"Secretly a heterosexual," the nasty-minded whispered.

Others, knowing Pipi, thought this unlikely. And when unconfirmed reports surfaced from Tangier that Pipi on holiday had been beaten up by Arab boys in a communal bath, had in fact been severely bitten, and painfully so, in strategic places, there was in Paris considerable smirking.

So ran down the seventies. Hostages rotted in Tehran, a movie actor was running for President, Ethiopians starved, governments were overthrown, continental plates shifted, the Amazon forests were set ablaze, while in Paris at Regine's and Castel's I played with the boys of *Paris Match* and strapping Swedish blondes from the cabine of André Courreges, and wrote long pieces about fashion designers like Karl Lagerfeld, who drove a Bentley, denied his mother was a Nazi, wore a pigtail, and everywhere carried a tortoiseshell fan with which to stir the languid air.

I felt only the occasional guilt which, as a Catholic, I was able to enjoy fully.

23 ▣ Terrible for the country. And Hart Schaffner and Marx.

EVERY few months, Bingo descended. I don't know that Henry Luce flew about so, inspecting *Time's* correspondents. The difference was, Luce terrified his employees. I began to look forward to Bingo's descents. Well, most of them.

We were on a Channel ferry, the two of us, crossing from France to England on an April day, tossed and bucketed about on a Force 9 gale.

"We could have flown," I complained, "Paris to London, less than an hour . . ."

"Nobody flies who has time for the ferry," Bingo lectured me tolerantly, "just inhale that salt breeze." He then broke into a little sea chantey.

All about us tourists and day-trippers vomited on their shoes and clung grimly to railings, apparently convinced none of us would survive to see the white cliffs of Dover or anything else, blotted out by spray coming over the bows. Marsh and I were headed for London so he could buy some suits and attend a dinner given by the British menswear industry, where he would receive some sort of decorous honor. I was fetched along for company and to gather material for a column.

The dinner was being jointly sponsored by the Bespoke Tailors & Cutters Guild of the United Kingdom and by the Woolmark label.

"What's that?"

"If a manufacturer uses all wool in a suit and none of that synthetic stuff Du Pont foists on people, he gets to put a Woolmark label inside the jacket, and they buy lots of advertising for him and he gets invited to things and Prince Philip comes."

This was about as clear as Marsh ever was on anything, so I accepted it. And the award the tailors and cutters were giving him?

"I believe it's for my courageous statement on behalf of the double-breasted suit."

"You wrote something about it?"

"No, I had a couple made and I've been wearing them recently, which made the menswear people happy. The industry loves it every ten years or so when everybody switches from single- to double-breasted or vice versa. It's like women's hemlines. That way we all have to buy new suits to be in fashion, and it stimulates business. Like the miniskirt. You ought to get one while we're in London."

"A miniskirt?"

He looked bleak. "You know what I mean, a double-breasted suit. We owe it to the retailers."

Marsh was solicitous of good tailors, always was. He expounded on difficulties in the men's suit trade as we did another lap around the ferry's deck, buffeted by the wind but driven from the salons by the stench.

"Someone did a survey once, and it turned out the average American man buys one suit every eight years. And that included people like me, who might buy four or five suits a year, as well as suits for graduation and getting married and even navy blue suits to be laid out in by the undertaker. Though with cremation even that trade is said to be dying off . . ."

"Ha ha ha," I said, pleasing him.

" . . . and people live in sports jackets these days, and jeans. And that's terrible for the country. And Hart Schaffner and Marx."

Bingo's own suits, most of them, came from London.

"I used to go to Dougie Hayward on Mount Street," he said. "Very nice suits, single stitching in the lapels and four cuff buttons, the usual thing, and Dougie liked to lounge about in the afternoon during fittings chatting and pouring an excellent dry sherry, not the Tio Pepe you get everywhere in London, and passing on cinema gossip and the latest about Princess Margaret and her current boyfriend, a boy called Rodney Something, whom they all called 'sweet, impetuous Rodders,' which made him sound rather dear and vulnerable and she a monster, and Michael Caine came to Dougie for suits and people like that and then they all got drunk and went to discotheques and places. It all became just too hectic for me, so I switched my custom to Gieves and Hawkes. They're very good on Harris tweeds. You can actually smell the heather and the gorse and the eternal mists of the Islands on those tweeds, a sort of oatmeal odor."

"I've gotten a few suits from Henry Poole," I said, unwilling to let Bingo have all the Savile Row lines. "They're really quite . . ."

"I know the house. They do the Queen's riding britches and uniforms for Haile Selassie. Or used to, until he was bumped off."

". . . solicitous about fit. My man there had a client who insisted on getting down on all fours to crawl about before accepting a suit, just to be sure it didn't bind."

"I daresay," said Bingo vacantly, hating as usual to let anyone else have a good story about fashion. "Isn't that Dover just ahead?"

We stayed at the Connaught, Bingo in a suite, and went to Moss Bros. to rent white tie and tails for the Bespoke Tailors affair. While we were being fitted, Marsh skimmed the letters page of *The Times*.

"I think it's so clever that Rupert Murdoch left *The Times* the way it was, nice and dull, and didn't try to tart it up like the *New York Post*."

"Well, they're hardly the same thing . . ."

"Hello, hello!" He was peering intently at the paper now, not just skimming.

"What?"

"There must be a half dozen letters here, all on the same subject. The Bishop of Chichester apparently wrote to the editor recently, inquiring why English country inns and provincial hotels no longer offered chamber pots."

"Oh?"

"And there are all these letters telling of hotels that still have them."

"Letters to the editor of *The Times* of London, with all that's going on in the world, and they're about chamber pots?"

Marsh put down the paper.

"Isn't it one of man's most fundamental concerns, John?"

The dinner went off brilliantly. Prince Philip actually did attend, and it was reassuring to see that he walked about with his hands behind his back just as he does on television and in the papers. Marsh's award went down quite nicely, and he wasn't asked to speak, which was a relief to me, sure as I was that those letters to *The Times* about chamber pots were still very much on his mind and might conceivably work their way into his speech.

Before he left London to go back to New York, we dined with Hardy Amies, not yet a knight but one of the glories of English fashion ("Such as it is," quoth Bingo), and an officer in wartime British intelligence.

"I want John to write something juicy about "Bomber" Littlejohn while he's here, Hardy."

"He should, you know," said Amies.

I knew a little about Littlejohn, who worked for Amies's great rival, Norman Hartnell, one of several London couturiers whose principal role seemed to be making the Queen Mother and Princess Margaret, and even the Queen herself, look dowdy. "Bomber" Littlejohn, a corpulent Englishman who resembled my (and Hollywood's) idea of an aging RAF wing commander, which he may well have been with his mustachios and puffs of fur on his cheeks and ruddy complexion, was said to be happily married, with a number of children; he reputedly kept an extremely ripe young mistress; and he was believed also to be Mr. Hartnell's lover.

"I can't write that, Bingo. It's libelous on the face of it."

"We're too cautious, Hardy," Marsh grumbled. "The magazine's getting predictable and dull." Then, brightening, "Hardy, have you been following the correspondence in *The Times*, the Bishop of Chichester and the country inns . . . ?"

24 ▣ *South of Rome you always carry your billfold inside your underwear.*

USUALLY, I was more pliable than in the case of "Bomber" Littlejohn's impressively busy sex life.

In July, Marsh was back in Paris for the collections. On the day of the last show he announced, "We're going to Italy tomorrow. Oscar has a house and we've got to visit."

I had no rational excuse, and we flew to Rome. I didn't know Oscar de la Renta and he didn't know me, but we were "to visit." Once again, the absolute imperative. From Rome there was a fast train to Naples.

"Anywhere south of Rome," Bingo confided, "you always carry your billfold inside your underwear."

I resisted the temptation to go into the lavatory and shift my money to my jockey shorts, but in Naples no cut-purses attacked us and we got a courteous cab to the waterfront, where we boarded the *aliscafi*, the hydrofoil, for Ischia. It was a forty-five-minute ride, very rough, bang-bang-banging against the waves. When we got to Ischia Oscar de la Renta was at the quay. He was a tall, tan boy from the Dominican Republic who'd worked in Paris as an assistant to Castillo, the one who may have whipped Gypsies, and was now an important designer in New York. Oscar greeted us both very graciously and went off to summon his driver.

"Dominicans are all part black," Bingo hissed.

I didn't bother asking details or how he knew. Oscar was married to a very chic Frenchwoman, Françoise de Langlade, who'd been editor of French *Vogue*.

"She was Rothschild's mistress," Bingo informed me with some delight as soon as no one was listening.

The Rentas were very nice. They'd rented a large villa on a hill overlooking the sea, and the first night they had some people come over from Naples for dinner, Go Go Berenson and her husband.

"He speaks no known language, the husband, including Italian," Oscar warned us before they arrived.

"We wanted Alex and Tatiana Liberman, too," Françoise said. "They're here, taking the mud."

Ischia's volcanic mud was imbued with apparently miraculous properties, I gathered, but the Libermans were unable to join us.

Go Go was a very attractive American who was the daughter of the great designer Elsa Schiaparelli. Go Go had two daughters of her own, Berry, who was married to the actor Tony Perkins, and Marisa, the cover girl and actress.

"I never had a chance in life," Go Go complained in mock despair over dinner. "I used to be 'Scap's daughter'; now I'm 'Marisa's mother.' "

Her husband, the "barone," smiled broadly but offered nothing beyond views of his excellent teeth. It was a very pleasant dinner and we got drunk and then a motorboat came, all mahogany and gleaming brightwork, to take Go Go and the barone home. Next day we were out diving and the skipper of the motorboat, speaking rapid Italian, told Oscar, who translated for us, that Go Go and her husband had been to Ischia before.

"That first year he was *cavaliere* (gentleman); the next year *commendatore*. Now, he's *barone*." The sailor paused. "Next year, *principe!*"

Oscar was a powerfully built man in swim trunks, not the delicate designer I'd expected, and a very good swimmer. I flailed about while Bingo squeezed fresh lemons on his hair to make it blonder (it may have worked, but when it dried the pits remained there and looked silly), and Françoise sunned herself. Before the sport ended I had sea urchin spines in my foot.

"You get a young girl to bite them out with her teeth," Françoise said lazily, smiling at me through her suntan oil.

"Oh?"

"Yes," said Bingo authoritatively, "everyone knows that. And Ames."

Though the sea urchin spines were more annoying than painful, I would not have minded having a girl, even one without accurate, urchin-seeking teeth.

Several days passed like this, and I thought how blue the water was and how the rocks looked beneath it when you dove with a mask and how warm the Med was and how good the white wine tasted in the sun and how I'd owed myself a holiday like this, pampered and lush.

And paid for by Bingo Marsh.

I mentioned my uneasiness. "Catholic guilt, I guess."

"Don't be puritanic. It's part of the job," Bingo said. Then, "Is it true about nuns and priests, that they have to sleep with their feet toward Rome?"

It occurred to me this trip was but another movement in a seductive dance. But there was the sun on my back and the taste of wine on my tongue and I could hear the splash of Oscar's efficient dive from the forward deck and I didn't care, awfully.

25 ▣ *How can you find bad pizza in Italy?*

VALENTINO was now the most important of the Italian fashion designers, Bingo said, and we had to see him while we were here.

"Otherwise, he'll be slighted. You know how vulnerable they are."

A decade earlier Roberto Capucci had been the leading Italian, but when Bingo persuaded him to relocate in Paris ("It's where the buyers are, Roberto") from his native Rome, his gift disappeared.

"Some wine just doesn't travel," Marsh said piously, as if the move had been Capucci's idea.

The other important Italians were Armani, with whom *Fashion* was now feuding; Emilio Pucci, whom Bingo for some reason, perhaps because they were both snobs, couldn't stand; Princess Galitzine, who was a White Russian, a member of royalty, and a great beauty ("but without a clue when it comes to designing a dress"), and Simonetta & Fabiani, who were husband and wife.

"They're washed up," Bingo informed me. "He plays cards with his cronies and keeps a young film actress. Simonetta dabbles in Orientalism and mystic numbers."

So that left Valentino, whom we were about to visit.

The Rentas came with us to Capri, invited along by Bingo, who may or may not have bothered to inform Valentino. Ischia was but an hour's bumpy speedboat ride from Capri, about which I knew nothing, only the famous song. Bingo, as he did on many subjects, seemed to know everything, much of which would prove inaccurate. Four taxicabs were waiting, and on luxurious impulse, we each took one. I remembered the night Bingo and I met and went in search of cabs. Capri looked like a good town for walking, with bars and outdoor cafés and trattorias and shops open to the noon heat, with men in smart sports clothes strolling with pretty women in slacks and shorts and summer dresses, basking in the hot sunlight and looking seductively at each other, a sense of pleasant indolence. Valentino's villa was behind a wall, and a servant came to the gate to let us in. The house was U-shaped, built around a pool, with at its far end an awninged cabana.

77

"The only private fresh-water pool on the island," Bingo remarked. "They're short of sweet water and Valentino had to pull all nature of strings."

Servants — there seemed to be a score of them, all in livery — took our bags and led us upstairs. Oscar and Françoise had a bedroom, of course, and Bingo and I were to share.

"Uh-oh," I thought, slightly ashamed even to think it, the last vestige of disquietude.

The bedrooms were beautiful, if impractical, draped from ceiling to floor in luxurious fabrics I didn't recognize, creating a tented effect and holding close the heat. Slatted doors opened onto an outside balcony that seemed to run all the way 'round the house. It was hot at midday, and I wondered about the night under those draperies.

Valentino greeted us when we came down, a slender man desjtined to plump up, hair neatly sprayed so there wasn't a strand out of place, face deeply tanned by something that came out of bottles. His eyes were expertly made up and I wondered if he did it himself. He was very cordial, considering I was a stranger and the Rentas last-minute additions to the party. His partner, aide, chum, whatever he was, Giancarlo, was a handsome boy with a mischievous smile.

"All the really important designers have a 'Giancarlo,' " Bingo informed me, "someone to smile yet do the nasty business and fire people and keep the books and curse at the press and to talk to over dinner and," he paused, "and, in some instances, to sleep with."

We swam in Valentino's rare and famous pool and lazed in the sun while servants fetched the drinks and I smoked Havana cigars. Oscar and the Italians told stories and laughed a lot, stories about people I didn't know but whose names anyone would recognize, celebrated folk. They seemed to know all of them personally, intimately, you might think from the degree of lubricious detail their anecdotes contained. Madame de la Renta, who had a marvelous body for her age and enjoyed showing it off, sunned herself in a chaise and napped, having heard all these slanders previously.

There was something admirable, even gallant about Françoise. Not a great beauty, she'd married this much younger, more celebrated man I'd wrongly assumed to be homosexual. Bingo, who claimed to know such things, went on and on about her sensuality.

Now she was married to Oscar, a genial, eager boy who stammered. They seemed marvelously well mated. Why couldn't more of us encounter women like Françoise?

Valentino was less content with events and conditions. There was a spate of kidnappings throughout Italy.

"It's not as political as the time of the Red Brigades," Giancarlo explained, "it's simply business. They demand a fortune or they start to cut off fingers and ears."

"And I am so obvious a target," said Valentino, not at all happy at the prospect of losing an ear. Or even a finger.

He had, at that moment, the villa on Capri, another on the Via Appia with twenty-eight rooms, a chalet in Gstaad ("I am taking ski lessons. At my age, imagine"), an apartment in Manhattan overlooking the Frick, and a ninety-eight-foot yacht.

He was also, he said, learning to swim.

But because of kidnappers he had given up his chauffeured Rolls and was now getting around in a Fiat.

"He drives himself, you know," said Giancarlo. Several of us clucked our admiration.

I think Bingo felt left out of all this high drama, for suddenly he blurted out:

"There's this new magazine. Princess Tiny Meat sent me a copy. He gets it every month and it's all about spanking."

"Spanking?"

"Yes, but not for punishment. For pleasure. Though I've looked over the photos rather closely, and I really don't see what's so pleasurable about handcuffs and gags and being paddled with squash racquets and such. Do you, John?"

I shook my head: "I'd be a lousy spy. Just show me the pliers and I'd tell them anything they wanted to . . ."

"Nathan Hale was a spy," Bingo said. "A Yale man. And they hanged him. I mightn't mind, being hanged I mean, if it were absolutely essential. I just couldn't stand anything more elaborate."

Madame de la Renta revived and told a rather good story about an attractive woman she knew and her lover, something of a sadist. "He kept trying to get her to have her nipples pierced . . ."

Valentino cringed. "Ooo, I wouldn't like that."

"Who is Nathan Hale?" Giancarlo asked.

"Why, he was at Yale," Bingo said, surprised someone didn't know, "and he stole all the British plans and General Washington gave him a medal but the British caught him. It was something about Benedict Arnold."

"Who?"

"Our most famous traitor," Bingo said, getting it approximately right.

"But that friend of yours, Françoise, did she go along with it, I mean, having her nipples . . ."

"I always get mixed up," Bingo said, "do I have a low or a high threshold of pain? I mean, if I can't stand having my teeth cleaned unless the dentist gives me Novocain . . . ?"

Giancarlo asked for the name of the magazine Tiny Meat sent Marsh.

"*Spanky.* It's called *Spanky.* I'll call my secretary tomorrow and get you the address. It's really quite well done and on very nice quality stock, so the pictures reproduce very attractively."

Dinner was quite formal, the waiters in white gloves, the plate gold, the stemware excellent leaded crystal.

"Gold plate and they serve bad pizza," Marsh complained later in some exasperation. "How do you find bad pizza in Italy?"

We all got drunk, all but Bingo.

When we'd gone upstairs he decided we shouldn't undress yet. "Let's tiptoe around the balcony to Oscar and Françoise's room and look through the window and see if they do it."

Marsh had been married nearly twenty years and he still used such euphemisms.

I was drunk enough to think it an amusing idea. The balcony ran at bedroom level, and Marsh and I, still dressed but barefoot to achieve surprise, walked around to the slatted doors of the Rentas' room.

"Darn," said Bingo, trying to peer through the slats, "I can't see a thing."

"Maybe they'll put the lights on for us," I whispered, drunker and as giddy as he.

"It's so unfair," Bingo said, "so frustrating."

In the end we satisfied ourselves by pounding on their door and then sprinting away as lights suddenly blazed through the house.

Bingo remained chastely in his bed and I in mine, and we slept as innocent as schoolboys. In the morning, before going down to breakfast, I remarked on how childishly we'd behaved.

"That was pretty sophomoric last night, like a couple of kids at boarding school."

Marsh shrugged off criticism and pulled out one of his instructive anecdotes.

"At prep school we had double-decker bunks and the boy who slept above me, Windsell, used to whack off every night into a sweat sock. I remember, the bed used to shake and then, a little groan of delight, and then down would come the sock, plopping on the floor. It was disgusting."

He was grinning as if in pleasant reverie.

"Yes?" I said unsurely, wondering what might be coming next.

"Everyone called him 'Socks.' We put him in the yearbook that way, 'Socks' Windsell." Bingo looked inordinately pleased with this little story.

We toured Capri that day, mostly on foot, which was the way to see the island, and took cooling drinks in cafés and watched the strollers. All the women seemed astonishingly beautiful. Even Françoise said so. People waved and called out; Valentino and Giancarlo seemed to know everyone by name. That night there was a sort of festival and we went to that, swept along by the street crowds, and then to dinner and finally to a nightclub. We got drunk again. Everyone said "*Ciao!*" or "*Ciao, babeee!*" even to me, whom they didn't know. Marsh beamed, for once nearly as drunk as I.

I was very pleased with Capri and I thought Valentino a capital fellow and whose business was it if he painted his eyelids?

Especially was I becoming fond of Capri when a young Italian woman in the nightclub asked me to dance and came back with us to the villa and sat late with me by the pool when the others had staggered up to bed. I told her about the sea urchin spines.

"Oh," she said, "there's nothing simpler. You just bite them out."

Before I could say more she was kneeling before me on the marble, removing the appropriate shoe, and then leaning down and biting me fiercely, suddenly, at which I gave a yelp, and then more gently with an inhaling motion, all the while looking up at me, large, dark eyes solicitous and caring. I thought of Coco, murmuring "*Indien*" and gazing at me like that.

"See," the girl said, "it'll be fine now. Please, the brandy?"

I passed her a snifter and she took a mouthful, squirting it caressingly on the place where the spines had been. It stung, but only briefly.

"So you won't be infected," she said.

"I think I love Capri," I said soddenly.

"Yes, *caro.* "

In the morning Bingo and I took a cab up to Alta Capri for the noon helicopter to Naples. Valentino and Giancarlo saw us off, waving silk handkerchiefs and pretending to weep.

In Rome we dined with Fellini and a cardinal and a movie actress of incredible sensuality whose teenaged boyfriend spent the entire dinner with his hand on Bingo's knee. Or so Marsh later swore.

"He kept whispering that she drained him totally and could I arrange for him to escape to America and get his green card."

"Damned cheek," I said.

"John," Bingo said tolerantly, "Europeans aren't like us. You make exceptions."

26 ▣ *There was no one or nothing holding me in Paris.*

A month later, in Paris, I received a letter from Bingo, wanting me to come back to New York and to write full-time for *Fashion* for considerably more money.

"This time I won't take 'No,' " he wrote. "I'll give you your own column."

My most recent novel was being remaindered, my publisher had rejected the new one, there was no one and nothing holding me in Paris but the lovely, wonderful city itself. The idea of becoming a columnist sounded appealing, the money was generous, Marsh persuasive.

I lunched with my lawyer, Tom Webb, at the Travelers Club, where he'd once introduced me to John O'Hara and where Hemingway used to drink, "a man barely under control."

"How long have you been here?" Tom asked.

"Ten years almost. And I'll soon be thirty-two. Maybe it's time."

"You'll have to make up your own mind," Webb said. "After a certain number of years you either put down roots and become an expatriate as some of us do or, eventually, you go back. It's a simple question only you can answer: where will you have the more pleasant life, where will you write better, and, perhaps most important, in which country do you prefer to die?"

We were drinking martinis, a chill, windswept day with the Champs Elysées beyond the windows, while in the big fireplace a good fire burned. Tom Webb and I talked some more. He didn't push one way or the other, too good a lawyer to do that, knowing that on certain matters the client must decide. Counting Vietnam, I'd been away from the States more than ten years. Yet I wasn't really sure I could answer Tom's question about where I wanted to die.

"Tom," I said, swirling a second martini gently against its ice, and trying to sound a lot cockier than I felt, "if I knew where I was going to die, I'd move."

Tom laughed.

"O'Hara once wrote a story about a man who did just that. And Death met him in Samarra."

27 ◙ Tom and Huck, Damon and Pythias.

SO I came home, having put away toys to become a grown-up, swapping the pleasant trompe l'oeil of Paris for the reality of a salaried job, and a very good one, in the most serious city in America. I'd served my apprenticeship, honed my craft, and now a man who put out a successful magazine was giving me my very own weekly column and a lot of money and dangling fame. A magnificent scenario for adulthood.

Which wouldn't quite work out that way.

Maybe fashion was to blame for what happened between Bingo and me, the industry or the magazine that weekly chronicled its excesses. Fashion with its bitchery and petty cruelties, its instant millionaires and overnight bankrupts, its breathtaking beauty and sleazy vulgarity. Or

Fashion, the magazine he owned and for which I now worked. Perhaps it wasn't fashion at all but that we fell victim to gossip, loose mouths, and careless people.

You know those stories ignorant party-goers at West Egg told about Gatsby, that he was a gangster . . . or the Kaiser's son . . . that he killed a man. Almost from the first day I went to work at Bingo's magazine, false and slanderous tales were told about me and about us, about our friends and those we loved. People said a girl came between us, Babe Flanagan, that it was a lovers' triangle, that because of her Bingo and I fell out and I betrayed him. Until she came along, it was said, Marsh and I were Tom and Huck, Damon and Pythias, the Boy Allies in Flanders.

Little of that was true. Bingo and I were very different people with distinct private lives who happened for a time to travel the same, rather fast, professional track. For years I wasn't asked to his house, hadn't met his wife, and in ways he was a mystery. We just worked together and laughed at some of the same things.

And if it ended badly it wasn't Babe Flanagan, or certainly not Ames Marsh, who was at fault.

For a long while Marsh was smug about the gossip. "I recognize it's intolerant of me," he said loftily, "but I can never quite forgive people for not being perfect."

Which was what made our relationship so odd. Like Tristram Shandy, or the hero of one of those old, picaresque Spanish novels, I kept trying to do the right thing and it kept going wrong. I tried to do right by Mr. Rosenthal, editor of the *Times;* I tried to do right by the cover girls in Paris; I tried to do right by the novel. All these went at least partially wrong. Yet Marsh not only forgave my failures but paid me a handsome wage and promoted me shamelessly. It was said by wicked folk he was in love with me, and I suppose in a way he was, though we were both (I firmly believe) heterosexuals, and Bingo never so much as laid a caressing hand on mine.

Yet, because I was perceived as Bingo's protégé, resentful and jealous men created monstrous tales which were passed along with lip-smacking malice. Nor did Marsh's own loose tongue and careless exaggerations help.

It was said my war experiences were fabricated; that I killed Coco Chanel with my youthful passion; that fashion designers bribed me with girls; that I conspired with greedy men attempting to take over Bingo's magazine; that I introduced Balmain to his lover, the Franciscan monk; that I actually helped Castillo whip the Gypsies; that I was Elmer Marsh's illegitimate son.

None of these allegations was *entirely* true and several, such as being Nunc's bastard, palpably false.

Yet even before taking the boat train out of the Gare St. Lazare for Le Havre and the QE2, where Bingo had typically and generously arranged for me the right stateroom on the right deck and a window table in the Princess Grill, my excitement about homecoming was dampened by a certain trepidation. A New York acquaintance learned I was coming back to take full-time employment at the magazine.

"You know, of course," he wrote, "that Bingo has a history of taking people up. And then, for whatever reason, he just cuts them dead."

My friend went on to alert me about someone called Peter Quinn.

"Pete was with Marsh almost from the start. A terrific writer, very nice guy. He did some of the best early stories *Fashion* ran. He and Marsh were peas in a pod, lunches together, slipping out to go to the movies, laughing at the same corny things, coming up with great story ideas. Then Hearst hired Pete away, gave him big bucks and a magazine of his own to run. He'd always wanted to be an editor, this was his big chance, and it wasn't anything like *Fashion,* no competitive situation. Quinn rushed in to tell Bingo, he was delighted and he thought Marsh would be happy for him as well, excited over his prospects. Marsh just went icy, turned away, told him to clear out his desk that day, never spoke to him again. Even assigned a reporter to dig up negative stuff about Pete's new magazine. Never mentioned Quinn's name in print except when he was in difficulty. The magazine eventually folded and Quinn was fired and Bingo ran a prominent story about how he'd flopped, much more prominent a story than the news was worth. Inside the mag, people said that was one story Bingo actually wrote himself.

"Much of this may be bullshit," my friend concluded, "but Marsh can be a petty, malicious son of a bitch is all I'm saying. So, take care of yourself, Jack, and guard your ass."

Then, in an ominous postscript:

"Funny thing, this guy Pete Quinn that Marsh played up and then dropped sort of looked like you."

28 ▣ Fortunately, I had a revolver in my stateroom.

BINGO was swift to put me at ease.

I returned to my own, my native land, a couple of weeks after Reagan's election and a month or so before his inaugural, a clear, chill Thanksgiving week. Bingo dispatched a limo to pick me up at the pier and a man to haggle about the luggage. I sailed through customs and immigration and plopped myself temporarily in a decent hotel just off Madison in the seventies for which the company was paying until I found digs. That very first day in New York Bingo called the hotel before I was fully unpacked.

"I want to show you something this afternoon. Be downstairs about four, and I'll pick you up."

He sounded so pleased to have me there, I shrugged off concern.

The limo swung downtown on the FDR Drive and around the Battery and into the bowels of the World Trade Center. We took an elevator to the roof, to a private club. Functionaries genuflected and led Marsh and me to a private dining room overlooking the city. It was just sundown, Bingo's timing impeccable, a lovely evening with the east in dusk and New Jersey and the Hudson and the taller buildings about us clinging to last light. A man brought wine, a blanc de blanc, and Bingo had him uncork and pour it. When we each had a glass he motioned me to the window, where we both stood, silent for a moment. Then, with a stagy gesture:

"There it is. Vanity Fair. Paname. Gotham. Baghdad on the Hudson. The world's greatest city." He paused. "I unleash you on it!"

I didn't know quite what to say, so I remained silent, thinking that surely he would say more. And then he did, slightly more subdued:

"Subject only to the laws of libel. And a good newsstand sale."

The grandiose, typical of Marsh, made the midwesterner in me squirm. But I was sufficient of a journalistic predator to relish the task. It really was a dream assignment, to write about anyone or anything I wished, so long as it interested, inspired, irritated, informed, or enraged the readers of *Fashion* magazine.

And it was over our private dinner that evening high above Manhattan and the harbor, that I became "The Shark."

I may not have mentioned that I have rather prominent canine teeth. In a profile of me written at the time I won the Pulitzer, a woman writer said I was a cross between "David Steinberg-good-looking and a young shark." A David Levine caricature at the same time, otherwise flattering, exaggerated my canines. But it wasn't my teeth that held Marsh in sway. He sought and believed he'd found a shark with words:

El tiburon. Le requin. The man-eater. Dangerous in any language and on any coast. Funny how Pierre Bergé had, jokingly, suggested so years before.

A day or two later I had dinner with an old friend from the *Times* and told him of the assignment.

"They're going to pay you, too?"

Were they not. A hundred thousand a year. I thought of it as all the money in the world. An expense account, besides. And I was expected to spend: the right places, the right tables, the right tips. Bingo was good about things like that. He might refuse a twenty-dollar raise to a file clerk or cancel a subscription to the *Wall Street Journal* for the ad department. But he believed we were dealing with people who spent money, and we were expected to spend. Not that this always pleased Nunc.

When one of my earliest expense accounts reached the office of the board chairman, Elmer Marsh sent a testy note. Rather than insinuate myself into a family argument, I showed it to Marsh.

"Should I respond or what?"

Bingo waved a careless hand. "That's just Nunc making himself important. He's up there in his private shower with Miss Fuchs, anyhow. Throw it away."

"Miss Fuchs?"

"Nunc's secretary. They take showers together."

There was no evidence this ever occurred but whenever Miss Fuchs's name was mentioned, Marsh smirked and spoke airily of showers.

It must have been my cavalier attitude, making no reply to his chiding note about expenses, that impressed Elmer Marsh. A second note arrived from the old gentleman inviting me to lunch with him at what Bingo assured me was a bad club. Nunc told everyone he was a Dartmouth man, or a Cornell man, sometimes it was one and sometimes the other, the truth being he hadn't attended any college at all and consequently could belong only to a club that welcomed people like himself. Or so went Bingo's description of the place.

The club dining room was just off the bar, and when I got there and was seated, Nunc came in from the bar pulling at his nose and sat down opposite me. "Had to make a phone call," he said.

I said the right thing about how handsome the room was, and the waiter came and handed us the cards and then asked if we wanted a drink.

"I never drink at lunch," Nunc said, "but you go ahead."

I ordered something and then we ordered lunch, but before the salad had cleared Nunc got up.

"There's a phone call for me," he said.

Since no message had arrived at the table, I was rather mystified. Then, through the swinging doors that separated dining room from bar, I could see Nunc standing at the bar, downing a quick one.

"Sorry," he said when he returned, "long distance. Business matter."

Twice more during lunch Nunc was "called away." Each time I glimpsed him enjoying a furtive drink. Over the meal he said some nasty things about Bingo and Bingo's late father and talked eloquently of his own colorful history.

"You sailed back?"

"Yes, on the QE2."

"I crossed once on the *Queen Mary*," Nunc said, "when there was a mutiny. Fortunately, I had a revolver in my stateroom, and with the help of a few officers and loyal members of the crew, I was able to put it down."

I'd never heard of a mutiny aboard a Cunard liner, not in this century, but it wouldn't have been polite to say so.

"Nor do I travel often by subway anymore," Nunc was saying. "And I'd advise against it. On the Lexington Avenue line a year or two ago a band of spics began abusing passengers. I stood up, grabbed two of them, and knocked their heads together. The others fled, and when we came into the Fifty-ninth Street station, passengers rose as one man to cheer me."

I shook my head in admiration.

Nunc hadn't been in the war, he said, his one great regret.

"I wanted to go but they'd assigned me to head up civil defense for New York City."

I asked Bingo about that. He looked impatient.

"Nunc was air raid warden for the Marsh building," he said.

29 ▣ *She had Paris, of course, and all its carnal arts.*

IF Bingo saw through Nunc's boozy, rather pathetic, posing, he was less astute judging me, from the first endowing me with qualities I didn't have.

For one, he assumed sophistication; that was Paris and having known Chanel. The fact was I was the product of the smokestack Midwest and as awed by New York as the most casual provincial lately arrived on the Greyhound bus. For another, there was the Pulitzer. People sneer at prizes and insist the best-seller list speaks only to the cleverness of the book publishers, but Marsh was impressed. More important, I'd attended a war and he hadn't, and the several young women he'd seen with me were attractive and he considered me something of a rake, continuing to insist I'd been Coco Chanel's last lover. What I didn't see until later was the detail with which he embroidered the legend and how energetically he broadcast it.

"It was Sharkey's ardor, as much as age and decrepitude, that finished off the old girl," Marsh would confide over the dinner table or in the intimacy of the Racquet Club. "He was a boy and she near ninety. But she had Paris, of course, and all its carnal arts, oils and unguents, pomades and fixatives. She lured young Sharkey to her couch above the shop, to her bed at the Ritz, to the chalet above Geneva. She was insatiable, he tireless, and the combination killed her." Pause. "It's said, though without corroboration, that the concierge on the rue Cambon side of the hotel smuggled Sharkey into an anonymous cab in the night so that she could be found discreetly alone in her deathbed."

This was rubbish and Bingo knew it, especially that part about sharing her deathbed, since I'd been in America at the time, plugging my book. Not that fact ever interfered with a good story, not for Marsh. Nor always for his magazine.

For all the sophistication of his audience, he could be extraordinarily gullible.

Of course Bingo knew about Pierre Balmain and his boyfriend, the Franciscan monk. He expected such things of Catholics. As a good Protestant he was full of misinformation, and knowing I was a Catholic, even if not especially pious, he questioned me closely and confidentially about it:

Was it true that nuns and priests were routinely, though secretly, married to each other; could you buy your way into heaven with large donations; did Christ's wounds on the cross hung in Saint Patrick's Cathedral actually bleed if someone used Jesus' name in vain or was it a clever trick to gull the faithful?

I invented ludicrous replies which he swallowed whole and then passed on in conspiratorial tones as having been privately confided to him by "one of the holiest Catholics they have."

So Marsh saw in me virtues that didn't exist and vices that weren't there. He'd just taken me up to the roof of Manhattan, as Satan once did with Jesus on the mountain overlooking Jerusalem, showing me this world and the glory of it. And then assigned me the daunting task of dissecting New York, this latter-day "Vanity Fair," probing its rich and powerful.

"Vex them, vex them!" was his cry, as he urged me on, demanding that week after week I tell millions of readers things neither they nor anyone else knew of this most subtle of societies and the grandees who inhabited its more elegant precincts.

I should have cringed at his presumption, and mine, and petitioned Bingo for a return ticket, economy class, to Paris. I knew, deep inside myself, he was as mistaken about me as he was about nuns having to sleep with their feet toward Rome.

I knew I could write; I had a functioning ego. But did he expect too much?

I thought back to whisky-soaked afternoons with Coco when nothing seemed difficult and how I expected one day to write novels, dreamt of becoming . . . Somerset Maugham. A modest enough ambition, surely, for a young man. Now, more tolerant in my thirties than

I'd been at twenty, I knew as a novelist how far beyond me even Maugham was.

What I *could* be, and owed it to Bingo, was the best magazine writer he had, maybe the best there was. I owed that to Bingo, to his magazine, to myself. Even owed it to Nunc, who when not in the shower with Miss Fuchs signed the company checks.

Oh yes, there was one other thing bothered me those first weeks in New York. For all my rakishness, for the "carnal arts" in which Coco had supposedly tutored me, I had never really been in love and, in truth, knew very little about women.

30 ◨ *This is Count Vava . . . active in émigré circles.*

NOR did I know much about the internal workings of a great fashion magazine. Or its politics.

Being a fashion magazine there was, of course, a fashion department. Not that this was my concern, nor did Marsh encourage me to make it so.

"They're certifiable, fashion editors," he cautioned, "and they conspire."

Bingo had two of them, two fashion editors instead of one. This, too, I suspected, reflected a certain insecurity. Not one that he admitted.

"I play them off, one against the other," he said smugly, "you know, like Julius Caesar."

"Caesar?"

"Yes, all Gaul being divided into two parts."

I refrained from correcting the quotation.

"It's the classic balance of power," he went on, smiling, assuming I understood. Then, seeing a certain blankness in my face, he elaborated:

"Ames, who is quite a student of the matter, tells me that in its dominant period Great Britain always allied itself with the second most powerful nation on the Continent. And against the first. If France, for example, were on top, the British sucked up to the Germans. If the

Belgians seemed about to overrun Europe, getting too powerful . . ."

"Hardly the Belgians," I murmured.

". . . London hatched treaties with the Dutch," Bingo said, ignoring protest. Then, once he was sure I understood, he concluded, ". . . and that's why I insist on having two fashion editors on the magazine, maintaining the famous 'balance of power.' "

Now I was to meet them.

"This is Count Vava," Bingo said enthusiastically. "He's active in émigré circles."

"Quite active," said the Count, extending a hand.

"Delighted," I assured him.

Count Vava was six and a half feet tall, a Mittel European of enormous charm and dash, who on this occasion was wearing a long black leather trench coat. He rather resembled photos of Hitler's architect, Albert Speer. His enemies on the staff suggested Vava and the unfortunate Speer shared fascist sympathies. This rather pleased Bingo, who held no great brief for democracy.

"They sit about and plot," Marsh said, going on as if Vava weren't there. "His best friend is King Tupa, whose late father was Zog of Albania. King Tupa sells jewelry for Van Cleef's, but Vava tells me he lives quite modestly, in a furnished room, conserving funds for the counterrevolution. He keeps a machine gun under his bed, I'm told."

"He does, Bingo," said the Count, "for I have seen it there."

The other fashion editor was Regina Stealth, invariably addressed as "Madame," at one time an editor at *Women's Wear Daily.*

"This is John Sharkey, Madame," Bingo said perkily as he introduced us, "our new columnist."

Madame Stealth extended a liver-spotted hand about a foot to the right of mine.

"She's nearly blind," Bingo whispered, "you have to point her in the right direction."

It was Regina Stealth whom Marsh early on hired to teach him about fashion, and he was, in his way, grateful, so that despite fading eyesight she was kept on, not simply as an aging pensioner but in a major role, balancing Count Vava. As we made small talk I mentioned to Madame that I'd met the Count.

"Ah yes," she said, "he once was a personage of some substance, apparently. Now he wears an elastic stocking."

I was curious as to how Madame could edit a fashion magazine if she couldn't see the clothes or discern color.

"She has a Seeing Eye dog," Bingo said.

That year's "dog" was named Blanche, a Radcliffe girl with sufficient ego to have later done a year at FIT. She sat with Madame Regina at the shows and told her what she was seeing, lighting her cigarettes and holding the ashtray. Count Vava, who saw in me a potential ally, claimed they spent the entire fashion show conspiring against him.

"Regina hates me," he said, "resents my proximity to Marsh; envies my education and breeding. She would give both her unfortunately sagging breasts for a European title of any legitimacy. She is, as you know, from . . . Pittsburgh."

I wondered over lunch at La Caravelle how Vava had gotten into fashion.

"You're right to ask, of course, since I'm not a pansy. It happened this way. When I got to America there was a recession. No decent jobs. A friend, a certain Archduke Vassily (the title may be flawed, I caution you), had been taken on as a perfume salesman by Prince Matchabelli. He got me an appointment as well. The title did it, of course. We lived on commission, selling perfume to debutantes and their mothers, sleeping with the debutantes, and when unavoidable the mothers, and escorted them to nightclubs and polo matches and played tennis with them weekends. The debs picked up the checks. It was a marvelous, irresponsible life, so much better than rotting in a gulag somewhere or being shot. From there I dressed windows at Saks and drifted onto *Bazaar* and ended up here. Bingo's mad, of course, but we get along splendidly."

Vava liked it that I knew Europe.

"So few Americans really do. They don't understand what it was to survive the war. When the money began to run out, I knew Europe was finished. I purchased a one-way ticket on the *Ile de France,* confident I could make my way in America. With the thousand or so (in dollars, I assure you!) I had left, I took over a private room at Maxim's and invited my friends, people I knew, people I knew *of.* A marvelous evening. I ended, drunkenly, I am willing to admit, in bed in a hotel particulier on the Avenue Foch, with two women, a mother and daughter, each quite appealing in her own debauched way. I arrived in Manhattan with perhaps twenty dollars."

I cleared my throat.

"But surely, dear boy, you have had even more exotic experiences, a man of your background and breeding."

"Which of us doesn't, Count. But there are things, even now, too painful to . . ."

"Of course," he said solicitously, one man of the world recognizing another and saluting discretion.

He was less discreet about his own affairs.

In the weeks and years to come, I would learn more of the Count's activities, on behalf of everything but the American Indian Movement and Boris Yeltsin.

"Never," he told me. "The man's a charlatan. Several Obolenskys have warned me against his counterrevolutionary posturings . . ."

On efforts to restore the Greek monarchy he was more sanguine.

"Things are definitely afoot in Athens and Piraeus. I have my sources."

Regina Stealth, suspecting I might be Bingo's lover and could be undercutting her with him, sent the Seeing Eye dog, Blanche.

Over drinks in a booth at the King Cole Bar in the St. Regis, she said, "Mind, I don't believe any of it. Mr. Marsh, if so inclined, would surely choose juicy little boys . . ."

I remonstrated.

"You know, this is all foolishness. I barely know Vava. I have no influence on Mr. Marsh. Please assure Madame Regina . . ."

" 'Vagina,' " she said, giggling, pronouncing the noun with a long *i*.

I tried to look stern.

"Your boss, your editor, a woman of breeding!"

"Yes," the Seeing Eye dog said, cowed. I smiled, knowing I'd made my point.

The girl looked at me, with something resembling affection.

"But Madame told me to go to bed with you. She'll be furious with me if I don't . . ."

I empathized with the child. First Vava had wooed me; now Blanche had been sent to offer herself up. It would have been brutal and un-thinking of me to have sent her away.

Later, as we lay together following a somewhat less than frenzied passage at arms, the Seeing Eye dog murmured, "Is that how you did it with Chanel?"

31 ▣ Vulgar people pretending to have taste.

ACTUALLY going to work at *Fashion* magazine, as opposed to writing for it from Europe, was a decided cultural shock.

I'd been in the magazine's offices before, of course, shepherded about by Marsh, provided the grand tour, cozened and cosseted, shown the Sphinx and the Pyramids and a few of the lesser tombs. Now I was there, not for a matter of a few hours of handshaking and smiles, but day after day, sometimes the day long.

"There's this little oddity they have in the art department," Bingo advised, proceeding in a cautionary and uncharacteristically tentative manner, "to which narrow people might take offense."

"Oh?"

"Yes, but what it really is . . ." Bingo paused, seemingly embarrassed, ". . . is that some of the boy artists . . ."

"Yes?"

". . . prefer to wear dresses."

I wanted to hold Bingo close and comfort him.

"It's called cross-dressing, Bingo. One season the star mannequin in the cabine of Balenciaga was a paratrooper."

He looked relieved. "Good, then you know about it. I was afraid it might, well, intimidate you."

"No, it's okay. Chanel's secretary, a guy named Jackie Iskandere, used to . . ."

Marsh was off now, on a hobbyhorse, enthused the way he often became, rather excited.

"Ames informed me there was historical precedent," he said, "a royal governor of New York under the British, a Viscount Cornbury. He posed for his formal portrait wearing a very nice dress, the bodice just so, the usual lace trim and softly belled sleeves, rather flattering actually."

My eyes may have begun to glaze, but Marsh soldiered on:

"Various historians have referred to Cornbury as a 'notorious transvestite.' But Ames assures me the Viscount had a fixation he facially resembled Queen Anne and was in fact a distant cousin. So his turning up to preside over city council sessions wearing a dress was a rather touching little tribute, and not at all a perversion, his attempt more closely to resemble his royal cousin."

He recommended I boycott American fashion ("Seventh Avenue doesn't have a clue!"), but when Count Vava asked me to come along to Geoffrey Beene one afternoon, out of curiosity I went. The editors and clients behaved just as badly as they did in Paris, squealing in delight and weeping with emotion.

"Splendid," Vava enthused, "so many vulgar people pretending to have taste."

He scribbled in his program, cupping his hand so no rival editor could crib. We had front-row seats on one side of the salon, Regina Stealth and the Seeing Eye dog on the other, Beene being a diplomatist aware of the realities. Madame chain-smoked throughout, staring at the clothes a yard or two off target. I'd seen her arrive, lurching through the room, a spotted hand extended, feeling her way by touching the backs of chairs, the wall, women's elbows. She was laughable, she was gallant.

"She has her horoscope drawn every morning," Vava assured me, cold and unforgiving, "before she chooses her underwear."

Madame took me to lunch, attempting to maintain parity in the internecine struggle with the Count. I told her I, too, had attended Geoffrey Beene's collection.

"Such a nice boy," she said, "a Southerner, you know. His real name is Willie something. He and *Women's Wear* had a tremendous falling out when he let *Architectural Digest* photograph his country home before *W*. Years ago he did the wedding dress for one of those Lyndon and Ladybird Johnson girls, the tall, gawky one who used to be seen about with George Hamilton . . ."

"Lynda Bird, I think."

"That's the one. She married someone else. So naturally Bingo plays up Geoffrey in the magazine because *Women's Wear* won't. It's a sort of game."

"Yes?"

"And they say Beene attends leather bars on weekends. That can't be so. Plump people avoid leather and wear something slimming."

Eventually, over the poached salmon, she moved on to Count Vava.

"One evening at Mortimer's words were exchanged between Vava and the barman. Vava cuffed the man. The next day he was quoted as declaring, 'I shall never again patronize a saloon where one is not permitted to strike a barman.' "

She dove into a Gucci handbag to pull out a yellowed clipping of the incident.

"I'm only trying to save Bingo," Madame assured me. "Vava is a notorious voluptuary, out to destroy him, take advantage of his sweet innocence. There are evil men in this city, clever, ruthless men . . ."

Vava exploded when I mentioned we'd lunched.

"She'll bring the magazine down one day, the old bitch! How does one employ a blind woman to critique fashion? She'll announce burnt orange is the season's color when it's snot green. Pension her off! I say. If she had a sense of honor, she'd kill herself. It would be the noble, selfless thing to do . . ."

Elegant Hopkins was no longer there, having gone off to make his mark on Seventh Avenue as a designer, presenting a small first collection of a dozen dresses done in muslin to save money. The few who saw his work remarked it was not bad. Bingo, who thrived on litigation, wondered aloud if it was possible to sue Elegant Hopkins.

"On what grounds?"

"Well, I gave him a job. And he left. Isn't that sufficient? And Ames . . . ?"

My second or third day there an unfamiliar figure approached me.

"You must be Sharkey."

"Yes."

"I'm le Boot, the managing editor."

He was tiny, wizened, perhaps forty, and at ten in the morning smelled of barrooms.

"What can I tell you about this place?" he asked pleasantly.

"Well, Bingo's taken me around. All a bit different from the *Times*."

"The *Times*? This place makes the *Woonsocket Call* look serious."

"Oh?"

"Sure, I drink out of a primitive instinct for self-survival. Have you met the fashion editors?"

"Yes."

"Then you know. Two years ago the FBI was in here questioning Count Vava about threats he'd allegedly made to a pretender to the throne of Montenegro."

For the first time I was working on a publication where the strict rules of wire service procedure, where the stiff rituals of *The New York Times,* did not apply. At the *Times* reporters were discouraged from writing unattributed quotes, and there was no such thing as a "blind item" in which the reader was supposed to guess just who was being libeled. At *Fashion* magazine, such practices were positively encouraged. As Marsh pragmatically put it, "How can we be expected to report the dirt if we quote people by name? They'll simply keep it to themselves or tell John Fairchild."

I balanced the technique against my own ethical concerns and found it wanting. For the moment, at least, I would continue to work under older, stricter rules of play.

Through P.J. le Boot, the managing editor, I began to meet my fellow workers in Bingo's vineyard, even though he kept warning me to maintain a distance.

"They're simply not your sort."

On this, as on some other things, I disregarded Bingo's advice and occasionally went out for a drink with other people in the office. On one such outing with le Boot, he informed me over a glass that he owned a parrot.

"A parrot? A live parrot?"

"It was my wife's," he said apologetically. "I didn't like having the damned thing in the house squawking and crapping, but I wasn't home much nights and she deserved to have company."

His wife left two years before, fed up. But the parrot stayed.

"He's a savage little son of a bitch," P.J. said, and could have been speaking of himself. "He'll go right at you, and not just a nip on the finger. He goes for the eyes. I can't keep a cleaning woman."

For this reason P.J. had to go home at least once every twenty-four hours to air and water and feed the beast, the one constant in his otherwise anarchic existence. "Keeps me sober," he said. It didn't, of course, but it kept him functioning. Now, over gin, he asked if I liked Kipling.

A drinker standing next to us groaned. "Jesus, not 'Gunga Din' again."

After several stanzas, followed by a passable impersonation of Jimmy Cagney singing the title song from *Yankee Doodle Dandy,* P.J. left, urged on by a chorus of fellow patrons.

"I know some good piano bars if you're in the mood some night," he shouted to me as he went.

"Le Boot isn't your sort, John," Bingo chided, "not your sort at all."

I thought that on this, at least, Bingo was probably right.

32 ▣ *It's historic: the long-anticipated return of the peplum!*

THE magazine went to press Thursday evening for publication coast to coast Monday morning. Being accustomed to the daily deadline of the *Times,* I assumed this meant Friday would be an off-day or at least a time of muted frenzy. Not so. It was the day on which Bingo laid down parameters for the next issue of *Fashion,* the one to come out ten days from now. We met in his office, a room too small for the purpose.

"It's good for them to have to stand or sit on the floor and squeeze in together," he told me once. "It creates esprit de corps, a sort of . . ."

"Togetherness?" I offered as he groped for a word.

"That's the motto of *Redbook* magazine and is never used here!" he snapped, decidedly curt.

We pressed in shortly after ten of a Friday morning in one of those first weeks I was at the magazine. Young women, who knew their place, perched on windowsills or sat on Bingo's Aubusson carpets, tugging short skirts primly over handsome knees. The couch, the several chairs, were reserved for more senior staff, Madame Stealth and Count Vava (strategically situated at opposite ends of the room), Rambush the art director, P.J. le Boot, with people like me left to find available space. Marsh began sitting upon one buttock at a corner of his Louis Quinze desk but was swiftly up and about, skipping here and there as ideas flew about the room for the next issue. His remarks, awkwardly phrased, vague, unexpected, often unintelligible, seemed to spark more cogent suggestions and ideas from his captive audience.

But he commenced slowly, almost diffident.

"Does anyone see lapels? Over lunch Ungaro was talking lapels. Is anyone in New York into lapels at the moment?

There seemed little enthusiasm for lapels. One young woman stroked her breasts, as if wondering.

In swift succession Bingo mentioned a recent chat with Giorgio Armani (the latest feud having been adjudicated) in which Armani was "definitely thinking padded shoulders once again, very Joan Crawford," a veritable splurge of Mondrian-type geometric prints he saw coming out of the silk mills of Lyon, a telephone conversation with Yves Saint Laurent during which pleats were mentioned most prominently, and the merest hint from Pierre Cardin of a flattened, boyish bosom.

Cries and little gasps and muted groans went up from his staff at each of these dangled suggestions. No one knew which were simply stalking horses, false clues dropped by Marsh to get the rash to betray themselves into premature ejaculation.

Then, satisfied, Bingo went on, moving into more substantive fashion directions.

"Jimmy Galanos tells me the new show at the Modern will have everyone agog."

"Everyone!" came a swift, agreeing chorus. Galanos was America's fashion intellectual. And if *he* said the new show at the Modern . . .

"It's bound to have influence." That was Vava, his resonant Mittel European accent unmistakable.

"We've been betrayed before by the Modern." That was Madame Stealth, canny, anxious to distance herself from the Count.

"Tyson?" Bingo asked, seeking out the art director.

"Mr. Marsh, I'd first like to scrutinize the catalogue. Just what do they mean by 'Sources of the Twentieth Century'?"

"We ought to know that, surely," murmured Regina Stealth.

"Should the Modern really be delving back that far, into a previous century?"

"Don't be so literal," Bingo cautioned. "Send someone around to ask Bill and Geoffrey and Calvin and Ralph what they think."

"It's not Ralph's period at all . . . ," a young woman crouched near me whispered.

"And tell Paris to ask Yves and Hubert. Emanuel might possibly have a notion, having been so close to Balenciaga . . ."

Count Vava dared float a suggestion of his own.

"From what my sources tell me, Paris today is much more concerned with the 'Le Boy' look . . ."

100

"It's darling," squealed a young editor before she could get control of herself, drawing an exceedingly narrow look from Madame Stealth.

The meeting meandered on to other matters, to story ideas and interviews to be sought and collections to be covered and artwork considered and just which of a dozen possible pieces might mature into the cover story. When a fabric editor rhapsodized about a new dress fabric "inspired by grandma's sofa slipcover material," I shifted uneasily.

"Can a museum show really turn around an entire New York fashion season?" I asked him later.

"One *movie* can do it. *Bonnie and Clyde* . . . *Jules et Jim* . . . *Love Story* with Ali McGraw in those wool hats tugged down snug like an Ivy League cloche . . . *Annie Hall* with that Diane Keaton layered look . . ."

"And the Seventh Avenue designers take the look as inspiration for . . ."

"No, no," Bingo said firmly, "the Seventh Avenue designers *steal* the look. Then they congratulate themselves on their originality."

"And *Fashion* magazine says so? You accuse them of stealing?"

"Absolutely. It's why they have to read us every Monday morning. And Ames."

But for all Marsh's airy assertions of infallibility, even on matters about which he was clearly in error, his histrionics at staff meetings, his skipping and capering, the man really had a fundamental appreciation of just how fashion worked and which were the new and important directions.

"Old Stealth taught him," Count Vava conceded to me one evening over drinks. "When he started up in Paris with his new magazine he was still an amateur, but he recruited her over there somehow to provide a crash course. She'd been managing a brothel, I believe, and in return for her guidance he bribed the authorities and got her out of the country and back here. He's grateful, and so he keeps her about now, blind and gaga though she is."

But it went beyond Regina Stealth's teaching.

"He's neither a woman nor a Jew nor a fairy," Vava concluded, "yet when it comes to predicting the dominant fashions as each new season looms, Bingo is uncanny. An American Protestant has no business having such instincts. Unheard of. But he knows, Bingo *knows!*"

While convinced Marsh was at least slightly insane, there was no mistaking Vava's respect for his employer as unfeigned.

"Season after season, I've seen him come skipping into the fashion department, crying 'Sportive is out!' or, 'I see dirndls!' Or, perhaps, 'It's historic: the long-anticipated return of the peplum!' "

As the Count shook his head admiringly, I imagined I caught the glint of a tear. At *Fashion* magazine they took seriously such matters as the return of the peplum.

I asked Bingo about it, how he knew, how he was so sure.

"There's nothing new in fashion. Everything's been done before. Well, perhaps the duffel coat. Or blue jeans. And they were invented in 1849 so the miners had something to wear while they dug for gold in Alaska . . ."

". . . California? Sutter's Mill?"

". . . and the pullover. And that was invented by the navy for sailors to wear. Chanel once told me that was where she got the idea for women's sweaters, from gondoliers . . ."

When he talked about fashion, he was almost articulate, talking of the different ways in which the great designers worked, right down to the use of toiles, light canvas, or even brown paper, in the early stages of cutting and fitting and basting so that the garment could begin to take shape and mistakes be corrected in the studio, without cutting into remnants fabric that sold at ninety dollars the yard.

He knew the *métier* so intimately and his enthusiasm was so genuine, I thirsted to interview *him*.

"You saw Coco work," he said, "how she built a dress on the girl."

"Yes, many times. She liked an audience." I didn't mention what sport it was to look at the girls on whom she built the dresses.

Bingo went on, still serious.

"And did she work from sketches? She did not. Chanel never sketched in her life. Even before the arthritis got into her fingers. She worked from the original fabric, no cheap toiles for her, shaping and fitting right on the naked girl with her little tailors in their white butcher coats kneeling there, terrified of displeasing her, basting and pinning, snipping and tugging."

"Yes," I said, "that's how it went."

Bingo nodded happily, always pleased to be proved correct.

"Whereas Saint Laurent can't cut or sew at all. Never could. Yves

works with a pencil, sketching the coat on long, narrow white card-
boards. And then the tailors take over, cutting and sewing. Cardin
can do it all. I know he's impossible, I know his collections go on
too long, but the man knows. And Ungaro as well. I recall a season
when . . ."

Then he was off on his hobbyhorse.

When he explained all this to me, I said, meaning it, "But that
makes a good deal of sense."

"Yes," Bingo said, getting up from his chair to perform a brief skip
of glee. "You see, I'm not entirely mad, am I?"

33 ▣ *Call Roy Cohn. . . . Roy's organizing everything.*

MARSH wanted me to slip gradually into the weekly grind of a column
by writing a few longer pieces to acclimate myself to America. Being
Bingo, his notion of a simple little first assignment was the 1981 Reagan
inaugural in Washington. He gave no instructions as to how to cover
the festivities or the news angle on the story. Bingo was not precisely a
political scientist.

"I know Reagan's a Republican, and that's about the extent of it,"
he admitted. "The key people to see down there are Blass, Jimmy
Galanos, and Adolfo. Adolfo's a spic who has a little dog, and I believe
he's from Cuba or somewhere. Does very good Chanel copies. Between
the three of them they do all Nancy's clothes. They'll have the inside
story on what's happening, and Bush went to Yale, so if you meet him,
tell him you work for me."

"Are you and Bush friends?"

"No, but being a Yale man . . ."

I went down by train, stayed four days, attended a number of inaugural balls and some other parties, sat way back on the Capitol Hill
parking lot watching the official ceremonies, and then wrote precisely
what I'd seen and heard. Which was what got me into trouble with the
First Lady and her confidant, Zizi Orlando, and would eventually lead
to difficulty with Marsh.

Zizi didn't work. He had inherited money, and according to legend spoke every day on the phone to Nancy out in California, filling her in on the New York gossip and reading snippets to her from that morning's tabloids. Later, when she was ensconced in the White House, he continued to fulfill the same function. His fame derived both from friendship with the First Lady and his hotel ashtrays.

"It is the most famous collection of hotel ashtrays in the world," *People* magazine said in a profile, "some 11,000 different examples of which occupy an entire floor and the cellar of his double townhouse in Manhattan's posh East 60s."

Others were less impressed.

"The silly little eunuch, who gives a fuck about his ashtrays?"

Zizi was short and dumpy, with a black-dyed Zorro mustache he waxed each morning that gave him something of the look of the gentleman caller in an old-fashioned stag movie. He also had a mouth on him. People used to call him "Orlando Furioso," but then Bingo Marsh and *Fashion* magazine offered another nickname, "The Social Larva." It was the name I'd heard at La Grenouille during that first lunch with Bingo so long ago. Now I was to record his *pensées* at the inauguration.

The entire week was a circus and quite marvelous. Maybe they all were; this was my first. P.J. le Boot gave me a little paperback, *Inaugurals throughout History*, that I read on the train south. I decided my favorite was Andy Jackson's.

Jackson, the book said, invited his good ol' boys from Tennessee to help him celebrate. Three days later they were still camping out in the White House in their coonskin caps, pinching the maids, drinking whisky, setting an occasional fire, and, when things got dull, firing their long rifles out the windows. In the end Old Hickory got them to leave by rolling the whisky barrels out onto the White House lawn.

Mr. Reagan's first inaugural wasn't quite up to those standards.

The usual press credentials didn't count for much, these being Republicans and suspicious. Then someone from the *New York Post* gave me a tip. "Call Roy Cohn," she said, "Roy's organizing everything."

I knew who Cohn was, one of Joe McCarthy's bully boys and now a very successful New York shyster and influence peddler. Where he got his purchase with the Reagan crowd, Californians cool to both gays and Jews, I didn't know. I called and was immediately invited over to his hotel. Cohn loved reporters; he understood the publicity apparat and figured he could manipulate most of us. He was probably right. From the moment I entered the suite I was "Jack," he was "Roy."

"Just use my name at the door," he kept saying. "You'll be on the lists."

Cohn was as good as his word. At one of the early events I went up to him to say thanks. "Say hello to Barbara Walters," Roy said. "Barbara, Jack won the Pulitzer in Vietnam. A great reporter."

I hadn't recognized Miss Walters, and I said hello. Roy beamed. "Barbara's my dearest friend."

Bingo dealt in absolute imperatives; Roy Cohn in superlatives.

"Thank God those shitkickers are finally gone," a pretty woman told me, and I jotted it down. Washington was fed up with the Carters after four years of Jimmy and Rosalynn, with brother Billy getting stewed and little Amy up in the tree house and old Miss Lillian and her good works.

The Reagans were to change all that, restore elegance to the White House, inspire a Republican Camelot.

The leading fashion designers were there. I recognized Blass, who did some of Nancy Reagan's clothes, but not Adolfo, the Cuban émigré who made very nice copies of Chanel suits. And then there was Olivier of Hollywood, who was not impressed.

"These people, strictly from Zinzinnati," he complained. The few exceptions were women wearing "Oliviers."

Olivier passed on a few items of salacious and obviously unprintable gossip about the celebrated and powerful. I mentioned that the new President's son wanted to be a ballet dancer. Olivier brightened.

"No shit?"

"Ted Graber's the Reagans' decorator," a woman offered as she saw me jotting notes. "He does all their private homes, and he'll be doing the White House."

"I didn't know the White House needed 'doing,' " I said, drawing her.

"After four years of the Carters? Ted's been in there quietly already. He says even the dinnerware has to go. There's a private fund being pledged, a couple of million so far, so no tax money will be needed to clean up the mess Rosalynn and Jimmy left behind . . ."

I got the woman's name, had her spell Graber for me.

"The man to see in the new Administration will be Charlie Wick," a cheerful drunk informed me. "His name used to be Charles Zwick but he changed it. Now it's Charlie Wick and Z is his middle name. Get it?"

"Sure."

I saw a tall woman I suspected might be Betsy Bloomingdale but it wasn't. I asked her anyway about Nancy's clothes.

"She's a size six. Maybe a four. Some people very close to the family don't think she'll live out the first term, the way she's shrinking."

"Shrinking?"

"She's terminal. Some dreadful sort of cancer, I hear."

I was jotting furiously now, but the woman was gone, blowing kisses.

Someone pointed out an official with the Reagan party, an assistant to somebody. Notebook out, I started to ask about Nancy Reagan's "shrinking" and if by any chance . . .

"The First Lady is in the best of health. She's just petite."

"Oh."

A hearty man with a suntan took me aside. "I hear that when they got in there today they found the White House basement just filled with peanuts. Hundreds of burlap bags full of peanuts. Do you think that's possible? I mean, I thought Jimmy was an asshole, but . . ."

Some of the Republicans I met were quite nice, especially the ones who were drunk. In a way, my ignorance was a help. I had to ask questions, having so little background, and after a few drinks, people tended to give you rather interesting answers. I even got to see the President once, at a distance. I wrote it all down and put it in the story, including what Zizi Orlando told me.

"Some nominations clear through me. I know the eastern players more intimately than does the Beverly Hills bunch."

"The Beverly Hills bunch?" I asked. "Who are they?"

Zizi looked at me pityingly. "My dear young man, the California Mafia, of course. Don't you know anything?"

A few months before I'd been living in Paris and, no, I didn't know much.

But I put Zizi's quotes, tactless if anything, into the story. I wondered if Bingo would let it run untouched. Not that he was that enthusiastic about Reagan, but he and George Bush were Yale men and I knew about the old school tie.

It was one thing to tease the fashion designers; quite another to annoy a new President and First Lady and their cronies.

My account, spiced with drunken quotes and earthy asides from party guests, ran in *Fashion* the following Monday, diplomatically balanced by some swell fashion photos of Nancy and her chums, plus a few cheap shots at the Carters (written anonymously by Bingo). It was the first time Bingo's magazine had taken on the political Establishment, and by some fluke the thing came off. Marsh and I were political illiterates, but *The New York Times* quoted the magazine on its assessment of so-called "California chic," while the next week's *Time* would take note of several of my bitchy snippets, including Olivier of Hollywood's dismissal of "the new Camelot" as "strictly from Zinzinnati."

"Zizi's more furioso than ever, I'm told," Marsh enthused, rubbing his hands as we sat in his office. "Next time let's misspell his name."

Most of my newspaper experience had been at the *Times*. I couldn't quite imagine Mr. Sulzberger and Mr. Rosenthal sitting around giggling over stories and plotting to misspell names. But Bingo looked so beatifically happy it would have been churlish to protest.

A week or so later it was reported to me Zizi Orlando complained to Marsh on behalf of the First Lady and himself and that Bingo denied culpability.

"We have this new man, Sharkey, just in from Paris. He doesn't understand how things are done in this country. I'll speak very sternly to him, Zizi. You can count on it."

I laughed off the report. Editors and publishers stood by their reporters; part of the journalism ethic. Surely I could trust Marsh.

34 ▣ *I wonder if Nunc wet the bed. I must ask him.*

PINSKY, the salesman, bought me a welcoming lunch, shrugging off thanks.

"It goes on the swindle sheet. I select the name of a valued advertiser and put it down. These are the accepted conventions."

Over the meal he filled me in on some of the magazine's cast. It sounded pretty much like that of any big publication, drunks, misers, a guy who spent his lunch hours surreptitiously photographing women's backsides, an elderly reporter so cheap he suffered a cardiac moving from one Village apartment to another by using the subway.

"I met Tramlett," I said, naming another character.

"Then you know."

The first day on the job I'd gone into the men's room to encounter a silver-haired fellow standing atop a toilet seat, tossing scraps of torn newspaper, confetti-like, up toward the air vents. When I stared at him, curious, he cried out in anguish as the bits fluttered down:

"Call this a venting system? And there are men in this building who've not yet sired children!" This was Tramlett, the environmental quack.

"There are also a few sane people," Pinsky said complacently, "not necessarily including anyone named Marsh."

Not feeling it appropriate to criticize the man who'd so recently hired me for a hundred thousand a year, I said blithely, "I had lunch with the chairman."

"Ah yes," Pinsky said, "Nunc. You never knew Bingo's father, of course. Nice, decent man, very good with his people. Maybe not as creative as Bingo but you couldn't snow him, couldn't scare him."

"Bingo told me about his mother's death, first time we had lunch."

"Yes, blame it on that," said Pinsky, choosing not to elaborate.

P.J. le Boot was less circumspect. Tiny, capricious, clever, obscene, he had a hard-edged wit and too much courage, whisky and otherwise. In a dim, local bar a large black man, surly and panhandling, braced us. I tensed, anticipating a scene if no worse. Not le Boot.

"Pal," he said amiably, "if you've got an attitude, don't blame me. I'm not Achmed the slave trader . . ."

The black, befuddled, walked away.

P.J. and I got along, began having a drink together after work. Marsh pulled me aside.

"He's not your sort, John, not your sort at all."

"I hope not," I said, having seen le Boot drunk. The stab at humor seemed to elude Bingo.

When le Boot propositioned female employees or fell down drunk or erupted in tantrums or got into fistfights, most of which he lost, Marsh shrugged.

"He gets the magazine to press every Thursday night. I need him."

And when P.J. got into a punch-up with a movie producer during a black-tie premiere party at the Pierre and people from the studio came next day in delegation demanding le Boot be sacked, Marsh refused to see them and called for his car, to be taken home faint.

"I can't stand scenes. They make me physically ill."

Le Boot was the one who looked sick but he smirked, ignoring his black eye and swollen lip.

"Hollywood guys can't hit for shit," he assured people.

For days after, Bingo ducked down corridors or sheltered in his office when he saw P.J. coming, just so he wouldn't have to face chastising him.

Why was Bingo this way, why couldn't he tell off a Zizi Orlando or chew out le Boot?

Over the next few years in unwonted, unwelcome spasms of self-revelation, while we traveled in airplanes or sat late over dinner in a distant city, he would lift corners of personality, drop tantalizing hints.

"I was a bed-wetter," he said brightly. "Were you?"

He was as frank about that as he was about his preference for suppositories, a subject on which he would expand in near clinical detail.

"I'm sure a qualified psychologist would know," he told me once, "some link to aviation . . ."

"Aviation?"

"My mother. Something Freudian." Pause. "Or is Freud only about sex?"

He was contemptuous of Nunc but in an odd way envious.

"I worry too much," Bingo said. "In ways I wish I could be like Nunc. There's consolation in being so dumb you don't know it."

"Invincible ignorance," I murmured, a phrase from a long-lost lecture.

Marsh looked as if he were about to pursue the line, and then, abruptly, he returned to an earlier, more familiar, theme.

"I wonder if Nunc wet the bed. I must ask him one of these days."

There was a naiveté about Bingo his enemies never saw. But then he would slink off behind half-truths and mendacity, as when I asked him casually about Peter Quinn, the editor who abdicated Marsh's favor by going to work for Hearst, the fellow who was said to look like me.

"Quinn? I barely knew the boy. He worked here, I believe."

No reference to afternoon movies or giggles together. It was like Chanel's chill dismissal of poor Castillo, who "held the pins."

35 ▣ Hush! That's Lindbergh in his gallant silver plane!

THERE were enormous feuds among the fashion magazines and their editors. Most of them bloodless.

"They threaten each another," Vava cried. "Beaded purses at three paces."

Especially hostile, Bingo and John Fairchild of *Women's Wear Daily*, who swapped insults, slyly recruited star reporters and artists from each other's staff, and engaged in deadly earnest competition to break the new fashion sketches first. In the middle, the poor designers, both bullied and bribed. If Donna Karan gave Fairchild an advance look at the new collection before providing equal justice to Bingo, *Fashion* magazine was sure to savage her in its next review. If Gianni Versace slipped Marsh the new sketches before anyone else, *Women's Wear Daily* could be counted on to suggest his impending bankruptcy.

Especially infuriating was *WWD*'s latest hurled defiance. Fairchild had taken to featuring the designs of Elegant Hopkins in his newspaper's pages, once, particularly galling, on the front page.

"They do it to exasperate me," Bingo complained. "They know I discovered and nurtured that boy, gave him his chance to escape the ghetto and build a decent life, and then he turned on me, ratlike and cunning, abandoning this magazine. And Ames."

Vogue and *Harper's Bazaar* hated each other for more mundane reasons: advertising dollars.

"They bicker and haggle endlessly about position," Bingo explained. "The two biggest advertisers in the fashion business are Revlon and Estée Lauder. Mrs. Lauder couldn't stand Charles Revson; he despised her. Ever since, even after Charles's death, they continue to argue over who gets the first right-hand page up front in the magazine. If Revlon gets it in *Vogue,* Lauder threatens to take its advertising to *Bazaar.*"

"And do they?"

"No, they bluster and whine, but *Vogue's* so much stronger, *Bazaar* has to walk a knife's edge and try to keep everyone happy. Years ago Bill Fine was the publisher, and when he put a Lauder ad ahead of a Revlon ad, Charles Revson threatened to pull every ad not only from *Bazaar* but from the other Hearst books, *Cosmo* and *Good Housekeeping* and *House Beautiful* and so on. Poor Fine had to crawl on hands and knees to apologize."

Seventeen drew his ire. "It's run by a nun. And the readers are all twelve years old."

Why this should aggravate him eluded me. But Bingo's talk of rival publications convinced you the fashion magazines, like the Balkans, were constantly at war.

Madame Vreeland, retired by *Vogue* a decade before, remained to many of her old competitors a hissing and a byword. Carmel Snow, dead twenty years, was still the target of lip-smacking bitchery.

"When she ran *Bazaar* there was a young fashion editor assigned to Miss Snow in Paris who had but a single task," Madame Regina informed me, "to iron Miss Snow's underwear and dresses and to lay out her stockings. She set up an ironing board borrowed from the housekeeper of the Crillon. More senior editors attended the collections, while this poor girl was transported from New York twice a year to iron petticoats."

Vava also had a story about Carmel Snow.

"She was past seventy and on the train from Rome to Florence for the July collections, and, the train having no air conditioning, Carmel went to stand between the cars to catch a breeze. A young Italian pushed by, bumping her slightly, before vanishing into the next car. When Carmel got to Florence she discovered her necklace was missing. She'd been wearing it when she left Rome, and now it was gone."

It must have been the boy who bumped her, they told her.

" 'Oh,' said Miss Snow, 'and I thought he was just being amoreuse . . .' "

I thought that story reflected rather well on a seventy-year-old woman, but when I said so, Vava scowled. In fashion's feuds, you gave no quarter. Certainly Bingo gave none.

"Fashion editors," he warned bleakly, "all have dubious motives. And wear bladder control devices."

He didn't say which was worse, and then, having warned me off but being Marsh, he suggested I go uptown to see Diana Vreeland.

"She lives all alone and grinds her teeth. Very bitter. She'll tell you everything. Just like Chanel."

I knew who Vreeland was, of course. Everyone knew about her. She'd been editor of *Harper's Bazaar* and then of *Vogue* until 1971 when they retired her and put in her assistant, Grace Mirabella, whom Vreeland had regularly reduced to tears and sobbing. Grace, pale blonde, pretty, ladylike, nervous, and gracious, was now running the magazine as a superior sort of clerk supervised by the true editorial power at Condé Nast, Alexander Liberman. Mrs. Vreeland had been sufficiently colorful as an editor to inspire a Fred Astaire movie called *Funny Face* in which Kay Thompson portrayed her, mouthing lines like "Think pink!"

There was an even better Vreeland line, too subtle for Hollywood: "Pink is the navy blue of India."

So, at Marsh's urging, I went uptown to see her. Regina Stealth, who'd learned my destination, sent the Seeing Eye dog with a sprig of wolfsbane for me to wear as protection.

"She considered providing a crucifix as well," Blanche said blushingly.

Madame Vreeland, whom friends addressed as "Dee-Anne," lived in a small apartment enameled red. I'd sent a note, introducing myself, and she received me graciously but, unlike Chanel, serving no drinks. Vreeland really did resemble one's image of the last Empress of China, with black hair, surely touched up, no gray anywhere. Although she now worked for the Met, the Metropolitan Museum of Art, as curator of its costume wing, she had no money to speak of beyond a generous pension from *Vogue* and was understandably cagy about her former employer. Bingo wanted very much to get her to trash *Vogue* and Grace Mirabella and just about everyone else.

"It'll make a great piece," he said, rubbing his hands and skipping about the office.

But Madame Vreeland fenced deftly, or perhaps I simply lacked cleverness, and I got very little that was quotable. Which didn't mean it wasn't a pleasant hour or two. Like Regina Stealth, she had trouble with her eyes. And with facts. Perhaps it was her memory that was bad, but I tended to think she just made things up, quite marvelous stories.

Legs Diamond, the gangster, for example. Diana told a complicated anecdote about Legs and his "moll" — an expression Madame Vreeland enjoyed — an incredible slut of such sensuality and raw beauty that Ernest Hemingway, who didn't realize to whom she belonged, picked her up one night at the "21" Club and took her back to his hotel, where they spent two days in bed until a pal called.

"Ernie, don't you know who that dame is?" and Hemingway departed that very afternoon on the plane to Cuba.

Then there was Diana Vreeland's account of that day in 1927 when she dandled her infant son in the garden of Tuxedo Park, "waiting for the bootlegger to arrive," when Lindbergh flew over the garden on his way from Mitchell Field, Long Island, to Paris.

"The bootlegger arrived at that very instant," Vreeland told me, "but I ran across the lawn with my baby and cried, 'Hush! That's Colonel Lindbergh overhead in his gallant silver plane. We can discuss the gin order afterwards.' "

How it was that Lindbergh, heading northeast to France, was flying almost due west over Tuxedo Park that day, I was unable to fathom.

Diana Vreeland, leading me unsteadily to the door, issued no feasible explanation. "You must call me Dee-Anne," she said, looking past me at a large vase, "and return often."

36 ▣ *They'll swim naked each morning and drink a lot of wine.*

AT times it seemed as if Bingo had appointed himself adviser and counselor to people in fashion, alternately stern and consoling as a chaplain might be, a latter-day Father Flanagan ministering to the spiritual and other needs of a chaotic home for aging boys.

"Sol Blum's wife, lovely woman, is dying of cancer," he told me one morning, Blum being quite aged and a towering figure in brassiere manufacture.

"That's sad," I said.

"Yes, they went everywhere together, and he was just devoted."

I began to say something pious about there being so few good marriages when . . .

"But he has this fantastic mistress."

"Oh?"

"Yes, and Princess Tiny Meat told me recently her sexual demands are such that Mr. Blum's been totally distracted from depression."

I cleared my throat.

"So you see, John," Bingo said, smiling beatifically, "that even a silver cloud can have a lining."

"Yes."

At moments like these I was tempted to hug him and pat his cheek.

Bingo's specialty, of course, was the libido. He may not have known the term, but much of the energy he expended counseling the designers dealt with their sex lives. One of his favorite subjects was Clive Neville, a good-looking man going to fat, and for many years one of Seventh Avenue's most consistent designers.

"He never does anything original, but then neither does he offer the merest vulgarity," was how one of *Fashion*'s reviews of a Neville collection concluded. "The man simply has too much taste ever to be great."

"It's really so courageous," Bingo began as we slid into his accustomed banquette at Le Cirque for Tuesday lunch, opening his remarks as he frequently did, in media res.

"What is?"

"Well, you know Clive Neville."

I did, and for all his pretension (he'd seen too many Cary Grant movies growing up in small-town Missouri and was given to wearing Oxford bags and hacking jackets and gesturing with a cigarette holder), I found Neville a good fellow.

"Yes."

"Anyway, he and Emma are going to spend a month together in the South of France, at Cap d'Antibes in a villa of the most extraordinary lavishness, to see if they can . . . 'do it.' "

He pursed his lips and wagged his head knowingly, as if I, too, were now in on the secret.

Oddly, I did happen to know who "Emma" was, an attractive and very wealthy woman in her thirties, recently divorced from an eight-goal polo player of international renown, and perhaps Neville's best friend. They went well together, if you know what I mean, good friends with common interests. Now, according to Marsh, they'd leased a villa in France in an attempt to "do it."

As soon as we'd given Benito our order, Marsh resumed, literally rubbing his hands in excitement.

"Yes, it's an extraordinary situation. Everyone knows Clive's gay, just everyone. But he keeps pretending he's straight. I don't know how many times I've lectured him, 'Clive, be yourself. There's no shame in it.' But no, not Clive Neville. He's a sweet boy but so stubborn . . ."

"Bingo, he's fifty."

"Boyish for his age. Anyway, now that Emma divorced the golf pro . . ."

"He's a polo player."

". . . she and Clive are perfectly free to marry. And it's just a perfect match; she being made for his clothes, you know, and Clive always needing someone to go to dinner parties."

It didn't seem to Marsh there might be other criteria for a successful marriage.

"But he confessed to me in a conversation I pledged to keep entirely confidential, and I shall! that he isn't quite sure he can, you know, *do it* with a woman. So they've taken this place at Cap and Clive says they'll swim naked each morning and drink a lot of wine in the afternoon and then, at night, they'll share a bed he tells me is authentic Louis Quinze and they'll see what happens."

He paused and I said nothing. What possible comment could suit the occasion?

"I do so hope it works and they can have an orgasm," Bingo resumed. "They've spared no expense."

"Yes, well . . ."

"But I'm hardly optimistic," Bingo said, his voice stern, less lilting. "You know what they say about tigers never changing their spots . . ."

37 ◙ *Face of a monkey, mouth of a sewer.*

BEFORE being diverted by Lindbergh, Madame Vreeland had told me about China Machado, who'd been a leading cover girl.

"Oh, don't write about her," Bingo said. "Models spend their time examining their underarms."

I wrote about China anyway.

"China (which Vreeland pronounced 'Cheena') was just glorious," Dee-Anne had assured me. "You never saw such a beauty. The men were all mad for her, duels in the Bois and diamond necklaces dangled, the keys to Bentleys proffered, that sort of thing. But she never made the money she should have. Some magazines wouldn't have her on the cover. She was half-Portuguese and half-Chinese or Thai or something and had been born in Macao or someplace exotic, and so, in the crude terms one then used, she was a 'half-breed.' Some of the magazines wouldn't use her at all as a model lest it upset more sensitive readers. Those were the days, of course, when no one ever dreamt of using a black model except for hair-straightening products in *Ebony*. And in the models' cabine were girls who wouldn't dress with China or use the same mirror or makeup tables.

" 'Not with a nigger,' one girl told me, a simpering little blonde bitch quite put out to have China sharing the bathroom."

Vreeland paused, an elegant hand touching her lacquered hair, as if seeking to recall. "A lovely girl, China. A scandal there was such prejudice, such pride."

She really spoke like that.

Journalists are a lot like policemen. We pick up a clue here, a clue there, a lead from one person to the next. In the end, you may have a story, or an arrest. Since my assignment as the magazine's new columnist was vague as to its restraints, and I knew so few people in New York, Madame Vreeland's little vignette caught at my reporter's instincts. And so, despite Bingo's objections to models, I went to see Miss Machado, finding her in a vast, echoing apartment on Central Park West that had once belonged to Ring Lardner.

116

She was, as Dee-Anne insisted, very beautiful still, and had gone on from modeling to become fashion editor of *Harper's Bazaar* and later become a designer herself, something I thought might enable me to slip the story past Marsh.

"When I quit modeling," China said, "and was the most junior and humble of magazine editors, I was assigned to sit next to our Paris editor, Marie-Louise Bousquet, in the front row of all the fashion shows."

"I know who she was. Chanel despised her. 'Face of a monkey, mouth of a sewer.' " I could still hear Coco, her voice full of contempt.

"That's Marie-Louise. Anyway, I was to help her in and out of her chair, to tell her what she was watching, to get her to the ladies' room. And she chain-smoked, as all the fashion editors did, but she was so old and trembled so, everyone was terrified she'd set herself on fire. At Lanvin they kept a fire extinguisher always at the ready. Balenciaga considered banning her on grounds the insurance premiums would rise. We were at Dior, right up front along with the Duchess of Windsor and Babe Paley and the Rothschilds, with Marie-Louise puffing away, the ashes falling on her lap, coughing and hacking like a tubercular, talking endlessly throughout, slandering everyone and barely watching the dresses pass, lighting one cigarette from the other and dropping the burning butts on the pearl gray carpet. I haven't to this day seen a single dress of that collection, I was so busy watching her cigarettes and snuffing out fires.

"Blah blah blah, Marie-Louise goes on, and then suddenly right in the middle of a puff, she loses a cigarette! It's dropped down inside the bodice of her dress and I can't see it and she's mystified as to just where it might have disappeared, looking around for it on her lap and then giving up and starting to light another. Then I see smoke starting to rise up out of her dress. I jump up crying, '*Au secours! Au secours! Help! Help!*' and begin slapping at her chest with both hands to extinguish the fire. The Dior directrice, in silky tones, ignores the distraction and continues to announce the numbers, the models still coming out for their *passage*, pirouetting ever so gracefully, with everyone watching and taking notes, to polite applause, superior to it all, the way the pious might ignore a vulgar outburst in church during High Mass.

"All the while I'm beating at Marie-Louise's bony chest and she's trying to fend me off, crying 'Assassin! Madwoman!' and demanding aloud have I gone berserk or am I molesting her sexually?"

When the interview ended, I took China Machado for a drink. "Do you know Regina Stealth?"

"Oh yes," she said. "There was one season when Bingo kept trying to marry off Regina. He'd picked out the groom, middle-aged, as she was, a coat-and-suit buyer, very nice man. But homosexual, completely uninterested in marrying Madame Stealth or anyone. Bingo kept pushing, though, forever throwing the two of them together."

"He's like that," I agreed, thinking of Clive Neville and Emma.

"Oh yes," China said. "He doesn't think people know what's good for them and have to be so informed, the way one does with small children."

38 ▣ Was Moby Dick the man or the fish?

BUT why, with all his blind spots, his fears and evasions, the vast ignorance that made one question Yale, was Bingo so good at what he did?

Even he shrugged helplessly when I asked. He had no rational explanation why he and John Fairchild and Diana Vreeland and a few more were great fashion editors while others flopped.

"You just . . . *know*," he said weakly.

I realized being eccentric helped, setting him apart from the crowd. He was bitchy, and that provided among the designers a certain entrée; ruthless, and that frightened some into telling him and showing him what he wanted. But Bingo had a big talent, an absolute editorial instinct, an untaught gift for knowing what the fashion story was and what it meant, a talent few possessed.

Marsh could sit through a Pierre Cardin collection of three hundred dresses and come outside to tell you, right there on the sidewalk and with certitude, just which single coat or dress would be that season's "Ford," the copyable number after which women would lust and that Seventh Avenue would make up in the tens of thousands, the one dress or coat that, as the retailers put it, "walks out of the store."

Not that he would have flourished on another kind of magazine.

He knew nothing of sport or finance or politics, could not name half the states, and didn't know, I believe, if the Mississippi flowed north or south. Like Harold Ross of *The New Yorker,* another great editor, Bingo was capable of asking, "Was Moby Dick the man or the fish?"

Yet he winnowed out, hired and promoted, the brightest young women and homosexual men and more conventional types and seemed to understand the raw clay at his hands and how to mold it. When it came to needing precisely the right free-lance writer to tackle a subject, Marsh's mind became a swiftly spinning and fully annotated Rolodex. He knew the names, he knew their strengths, he had their unlisted phone numbers and could reach them. And he had the money to pay them and the charm, when turned on, to lure them into his employ. And it wasn't just freelances. He had his contacts among the sketchers and photographers and layout artists and assistant art directors. He always *knew.*

And, like great editors from Mencken to Luce to Felker, he could be unforgiving. In Marsh's case, he was contemptuous of most journalists who didn't work for him.

"They're shirkers, lazy or drunks or both. They pad expense accounts and hang around bars interviewing each other and acting the pundit. They'd rather talk about being reporters than be one."

As an editor he knew the worth of a great headline, of a repeatable phrase. He was forever seeking the perfect word, the totally apt sentence. He didn't know those words until he saw them; couldn't write that sentence, but he knew it when someone else wrote it. That was what he saw in me, that I could write.

"That interview you did in the *Times* about Nureyev."

"Yes?" It had been at least two years ago, in Paris, yet Bingo remembered.

"It was the first time I ever read that, about his knees, how after all those thousands of hours onstage, jumping up and down, lifting ballerinas and leaping about, his knees were as damaged as those of an aging football player . . ."

"Yes," I said, "and that after every rehearsal, after every performance, he had to ice them down in order to be able to walk the next day."

Marsh nodded. "I remembered that, about the ice. If you remember one new thing you didn't know before, then a story works."

But perhaps the true reason for *Fashion's* success was that it reflected, as *Forbes* magazine did Malcolm or *The New Yorker* first Ross and later

Shawn, or the early *Time* Mr. Luce, the personality of the man who ran it. *Fashion* was Bingo's creature; its idiosyncratic personality *his* personality, its lapses and failings *his.*

As Pinsky the adman put it, "We are not dealing here with the *Ladies' Home Journal.* Mister Marsh does not do recipes."

For all Bingo's cavalier attitudes, his disdain for so much and for so many, Bingo was one of the least secure men I'd ever met. He himself put it down to bed-wetting. Or his mother's disappearance.

Count Vava and Madame Stealth, who differed on everything, differed on this.

"He should have been breast-fed," Regina Stealth announced, inaccurately.

"He was suckled too long, until the age of eight or nine," Vava declared, also without great accuracy.

None of us really knew. But it says something for Bingo's fascination, his tap dance at center stage of our lives, that we wondered and bickered endlessly about him. The Count and Madame Stealth, convinced I held keys, that I wielded some influence over Marsh, laid campaigns, inviting me to lavish dinners, suspecting after a tepid report from the Seeing Eye dog as to my libido that a good meal might be a more effective way of wrestling for my soul.

In ways it was like being back in Paris, subject to bribes from the designers, and I thought back wistfully to those jolly days and nights, those splendid meals and those amiable round-limbed young women with their lovely, knowing eyes.

39 ▣ *So cheap he sends his socks to France to be washed.*

ALMOST from the first, Marsh took me into his confidence, summoning me to his office, closing the door with a great show of circumspection, and then telling me the most outrageous things. Perhaps he'd run out of gullible people.

"Olivier," he informed me in considerable perturbation one morning, "is going to kill himself."

I asked Bingo if he'd notified the authorities. "Maybe it's not too late to prevent tragedy."

Marsh gave me a sour look.

"We don't want scandal. Let's take him to lunch. Olivier's so cheap he'll postpone his own death for a free meal. You've got to come along. He respects you. And Ames. I can't handle emotion alone."

Olivier and I had met twice in our lives.

During a television interview, Olivier of Hollywood admitted that in the true peasant mentality, he sent his wool socks back to France for his mother to darn. This admission was made with a certain pride, but *Women's Wear Daily* got it wrong, suggesting the designer was so cheap he sent his socks to France to be washed, dispatching them "by private courier."

"What does that mean?" I said.

"Anyone he can persuade to take his dirty socks to Paris," Marsh said.

So Olivier of Hollywood was being pilloried in print not only for being cheap but for transporting soiled laundry across the Atlantic. We took him to lunch at Orsini's to save his life.

"I don't mind they write shit about my collection," Olivier complained. "But smelly socks? Maybe I get a good Jew lawyer and sue."

I was relieved Olivier was talking litigation and not suicide.

But Bingo, anxious to discomfort his chief and most hated rival, John Fairchild of *Women's Wear*, egged Olivier on.

"They've held you up to ridicule, Olivier. To opprobrium."

"What's that?" Olivier demanded, suspicious of words he didn't know.

To my surprise, Bingo provided something of a definition:

"Suggesting you're a cheap shit."

"Oh," said Olivier mildly. He knew himself and had no argument for that.

Bingo wasn't ready to give it up. "That's how Fairchild is, insensitive to the feelings of creative men."

Olivier shrugged off piety.

"All fashion editors are shit."

"Well, now," Bingo said, "I wouldn't . . ."

"Sure, your Regina . . ."

"Yes?" Bingo said, leaning close, always eager to hear some dirt, even about one of his own oldest and most faithful employees.

"Ask her," Olivier insisted, "about her dildos. Electric ones, too. All sizes."

People at the next table seemed to be listening with a certain curiosity, and I said, more loudly than I should, "Might we have some wine?"

By the second bottle of Chianti Classico (Marsh was paying), Olivier was feeling more cheerful.

"I went horseback riding last weekend," he said, "up in Connecticut (he pronounced the second *c*). But I can't do that no more."

"Why not?"

"I get too excited. Every ten minutes I got to go in the bushes and whack off. I used to think there's nothing like a clean twelve-year-old boy. Now I think horses is better."

I regarded the restaurant's ceiling. Olivier's voice carried. But Bingo, entirely unperturbed, was up to the occasion.

"That's why so many young girls learn to ride," he said. "It stimulates them. A rather innocent way of deriving sexual pleasure without losing their virginity or becoming emotionally involved."

"No shit?" Olivier said.

Conversation then moved on to a discussion of true love, just how did you define it. I said something banal, and Bingo talked about his wife. Then Olivier waved us off.

"Lemme tell you. I got this new boyfriend, you know, a kid from down South, some shit place like Georgia."

As their relationship deepened and ripened, Olivier said, he asked the young man about life at home.

"I said, look, here in New York you find horny guys like me all over the place. Down there on the farm, what the hell you do? So the boy says, 'Well, Olivier, on my farm I have a mule.'"

"That's nice, I say."

One day, infatuation having become real love, Olivier told us, "This boy looks in my eyes and he says, 'You know, Olivier, I think my mule would like you, too.' "

Olivier of Hollywood paused, triumphant.

"Now that," he said, "is true love and not what Regina Stealth does with dildos or shit about my socks."

Headed back to the office by cab (his limo was transporting Bingo's wife somewhere), Marsh said, "You know, that was interesting, Olivier and horseback riding."

"Very."

"My father wouldn't let me own a bicycle. I didn't have one until I went to Yale. I bought it out of my allowance to get around the campus, and I didn't tell him about it until sophomore year."

"Oh?"

"Yes, Father had a theory that bike riding got boys randy. You know, the vibration and the bar between your legs and all those abnormal pressures on your groin region . . ."

I glanced at the driver.

". . . and he didn't want me to be like Olivier, jumping into the bushes every few miles to whack off."

"Your father knew Olivier?"

Marsh gave me a sour look. "Well, you know what I mean. Generic whacking off, not Olivier in particular."

The driver nearly hit a crosstown bus at Thirty-fourth Street, running a red light, so I assume he'd followed our conversation.

40 ▣ *The macaw perched on his shoulder, where it subsequently enjoyed a small bowel movement.*

I found an apartment, on Second Avenue in the forties, and out of some vestigial ache for Paris, bought another piano, this a modest upright in deference to the size of the place.

"You play?" asked the man who moved it in.

"No."

He shrugged. New York was full of nuts and fashion designers.

"You've got to go," Bingo pleaded. "I can't face those two alone."

He'd been invited and in a weak moment accepted a lunch date with

Mister John, who was billed, modestly, as "Emperor of Fashion," and his roommate and partner, Peter Brandon. Mister John made hats and was apparently quite successful at it.

"I don't want to have lunch with Mister John," I said sulkily. "You keep telling me to be aloof, to stay away from Blass and Calvin and Trigere, and you keep making me go to lunch with suicides and hat designers. I won't do it."

Bingo wheedled. "I'm desperate," he said. In the end I went along. How bad could Mister John be?

John and Brandon had a wonderfully large apartment in an old building with high ceilings. Peter met us at the door on a ten-speed bike that he rode up and down the apartment's corridors and in and out of rooms.

"John will join us momentarily," he said. We were given a drink, and then Mister John entered, the Emperor of Fashion, a plump man with thick glasses and bee-sting lips. A macaw sat on his head and squawked at us.

Mister John was very nice, hospitable and gracious, only once essaying a mild complaint that Bingo's magazine should expand its coverage of the millinery market, which Mister John naturally felt was very important and was being overlooked. Bingo was evasive, blaming his editors and promising to look into the matter. The macaw remained on Mister John's head for the first course and then flew across to perch on Peter Brandon's shoulder, where it subsequently enjoyed a small bowel movement. I was hoping the damned bird wouldn't come near me, and I wondered just what Bingo would do if it flew in his direction.

I knew he was nervous about it because he talked constantly.

"I was thinking about Helena Rubenstein just the other day," he said, "and what a pig she was. She had this sublime apartment in Paris and I was asked up there once for lunch, much as we're doing today, and she received me sitting up in bed, this little old lady wearing a hat . . ."

Mister John looked pleased; milliners like stories with hats.

". . . and I sat down on a straight-backed chair near the bed. Patrick O'Higgins was there, her flunky. And when they served lunch it was cold chicken, the sort of thing you might find at a picnic, and we sat there eating chicken with our fingers, with Madame Rubenstein telling stories about how she became a designer and wiping her greasy fingers on the bedsheets and sucking them clean. Silk sheets and she wiped the chicken grease all over them."

In a way, I enjoyed lunch. This was how I thought fashion designers ought to be, awarding themselves grandiose titles and living splendidly, riding bikes about the apartment and being shit on by birds. I mentioned how I felt on our way back to the office.

"Nonsense," said Bingo, "you've got to be more aloof."

During another lunch our host passed around some grass, a single cigarette passed from mouth to mouth in the affectation of the moment. I took a puff and passed it on. When it got to Bingo, who had never in his life smoked as much as a Camel, he positioned the joint delicately between two fingers, opened his mouth slightly, placed it to his lips. And blew!

For months after that he informed anyone who'd listen, "You either dominate drugs or they dominate you."

Smug, oh, but he was smug. I suppose it was bred in him, those Roman numerals after his name, third-generation Yale, old money and all it meant: manners, the right clothes, the social connections, the effrontery to wear cracked old wing-tip shoes so long as the cracks were waxed and polished, the sense of caste and of belonging, the haughty, know-it-all tone even when he didn't, the complacent sense of superiority and class.

I felt rumpled and homespun around him, suspecting my suit needed pressing or my tie was spotted, a rustic attempting to make my way in the great city, forever in peril of using the wrong fork.

But you couldn't really resent him, this aristocratic snob, in those endearing, and frequent, moments when he proved himself as gauche and awkward as any hayseed, referring, inevitably, to Mario Cuomo as "Como," misplacing entire states and nations, unsure at all times whether the sun circled the earth or the earth the moon.

"Galileo, I think it was, found out which. But I forget," he would confess.

Fascinated as he was by masturbation, he seemed interested in all biological functions, discharges, emissions, and the various bodily orifices, telling anyone who would listen how he took all his medicine ("especially aspirin!") in suppository form.

"The only sensible way, really," he would inform a luncheon or dinner table, "so that it gets into the bloodstream quicker and doesn't upset your digestive tract. Many people can't tolerate aspirin taken orally; in some instances suffering antiperistalsis, or what's more commonly referred to as vomiting. And Ames."

Strangers, at such moments, cleared their throats and looked away, hoping desperately someone would change the subject. Those of us who knew Marsh dove into the claret or pushed vegetables around the plate.

41 ▣ *Calvin Klein, hiding in the men's room.*

UNDER terms of my deal I didn't have to spend a lot of time in the office. Bingo might be petty about some things but not that.

"I don't care where you write. So long as everyone's talking about it Monday morning."

"And if I irritate your pals, the rich and elegant?"

"Vex them! Vex them!" he cried, bold in the certain knowledge we were alone and I was the only one who could hear his cry of defiance.

He had these histrionic moments; you learned to discount them, for surely a cautionary word followed:

"But don't upset everyone. If you trash Macy's be sure to puff Bloomie's."

For those hours I spent in the Marsh mansion I was assigned a small office, a mere cubicle, really, but with a door you could shut and a window on Fifth Avenue through which you could watch pretty women heading for the New School or to the Lone Star Cafe.

"It used to be Schrafft's," Pinsky said, "where old ladies drank Manhattans in the afternoons and the drinkers who worked for Marsh could get their first of the morning, drinking it straight from the glass sitting on the bar so their hands wouldn't tremble and spill any."

Pinsky was full of local lore.

Although I wasn't there nine to five, you know how it is in an office, you get caught up in the rhythm of the place, absorbing office politics and hanging out. The art department was the place to hang out; it was where the models spent their time between shoots, cover girls lounging in their jeans and tank tops smoking grass and gossiping and watching themselves in mirrors. Even without the models, the art department had a charm of its own.

Tyson Rambush was the art director, tall, handsome, courtly, about fifty. It was Rambush who gave the magazine its distinctive look, selected its crisp, readable typeface, at ten points just slightly larger than that of most magazines, convinced Marsh early on to make *Fashion* the same size as *Time* and *Newsweek* rather than outsized, like *Vogue* and *Bazaar*, all the better to emphasize its timeliness, more like the news weeklies than the leisurely paced monthlies. Rambush was a genius at photo selection, had an unerring eye for just the right model, possessed the subtlety to manage a large art department of unconventional talents. He was also somewhat intimidated by Marsh and often reduced by him to nervous stammering and wildly rolling eyes.

Bingo recognized and admired his talent and bullyingly delighted in tormenting him. But then, the reticent, mannered Rambush was an easy target for any of us. He owned a gracious brownstone in the Village where he lived with his friend, another sedate middle-aged gentleman. One evening P.J. le Boot and a space salesman and I went drinking, starting at Bradley's on University Place, a joint for obscure reasons known as "the evil place." By two in the morning and quite stewed, we found ourselves on the street where Rambush lived. A noble elm fronted the house.

"Let's climb up and look in the window," le Boot suggested boozily. I started to tell him about the night long ago when Bingo and I attempted to look through bedroom windows on Capri, but I was too drunk to get the story out and by then, le Boot's having been a very witty notion, all three of us were climbing the tree. When you are very drunk, a thin idea gains dimension. P.J. le Boot led the way, the salesman following. I had difficulty focusing and because some tiny remnant of sanity remained, I decided after all to remain on the sidewalk below in case someone should fall. When the others were level with Rambush's windows, le Boot called out:

"Tyson's friend, can Tyson come out to play?"

We found this very amusing, and I fell about in laughter while P.J. kept up the chanting, echoed by the salesman.

Then the lights blazed on and Rambush pulled open the blind to look out. He was in pajamas but he looked very stern. In an angry, but very controlled voice, he spoke.

"I think . . . you . . . are . . . *disgusting.*"

Cowed, le Boot and the salesman made their way down, the salesman falling the last ten feet to the sidewalk, knocking me down.

Rambush had more than a house in the Village and a convenient elm — his *équipe* of artists, mostly young, all talented, underpaid, most gay. Mostly, the artists socialized together. Occasionally, they made exceptions.

"Chester's having people in for cocktails. It's rather special," I was told.

Chester was small, ugly, and bald, with a mustache, and he was mad for the work of Luis Estevez, a California designer who did not currently enjoy Bingo's favor, whose name never appeared in the magazine.

Bingo would debate "never."

"If they die or go into Chapter 11, we always write about them."

Bingo had his biases, and they were respected. Not, however, by tiny, ugly Chester, who had purchased for his own personal wardrobe an eight-hundred-dollar Estevez dress. Now, in excitement bordering on ecstasy, Chester threw a small cocktail party to show off his purchase. We stood around his loft drinking wine in plastic glasses while Chester went in to change, emerging triumphantly in the new Estevez, an off-the-shoulder number which I privately felt was in no way improved by the kinky black hair that covered Chester's shoulders and back.

Still, *ave atque vale!* We all saluted a man in Bingo's employ with the courage to wear a dress created by a designer of whom Marsh did not approve.

Many of the young artists dreamt of becoming designers themselves. It was how Calvin Klein got started, working as a copyboy at *Women's Wear Daily*, running errands and sharpening pencils, hiding in the men's room when the publisher walked through because Calvin was afraid of him. *Women's Wear Daily* discerned no talent in young Klein, and eventually he left to find greatness elsewhere.

We had a young star of our own at *Fashion*, and he too had slipped through the magazine's seine: Elegant Hopkins.

"Don't mention that fellow's name!" Marsh ordered. Rival publisher

John Fairchild had just anointed the "African Queen" one of the year's ten most promising young designers. "I'm sure there are grounds for a suit."

The office offered other divertissements. I may have mentioned how I enjoyed hanging around the art department. There was a sort of screened-off area where cover girls changed their clothes and where, if you were deft, you could watch them.

The models didn't seem to mind being ogled, and I thought, not for the first time, that exhibitionism came with their calling. I remembered Paris, and Gillian.

With a certain wistful emptiness.

42 ▣ *Please tie me to the bedposts.*

OCCASIONALLY the art department produced. Her name was Sabra and she was an Israeli. I'd known one Israeli mannequin in Paris, very beautiful and quite conservative, dieting and doing yoga and drinking only hot water, even at the small bar of the Ritz. Sabra was also very beautiful but not at all conservative. She posed for the underwear and swimsuit shots in the magazine. She also worked for other magazines and showed clothes in some of the collections. Her father was a famous tank general who was now in the Knesset, the Israeli parliament.

"Israelis," she told me, "are all crazy. That's why I like the fashion biz."

On our first date I took her to a dinner party at Calvin Klein's apartment. Sabra diplomatically wore one of his evening dresses, and Calvin was charming.

"You made quite a hit," I said in the cab.

"Oh, designers are so stupid. You wear one of their dresses, they wet their pants."

I suggested, with my usual subtlety, a nightcap at my place.

"No, I want to go home."

So much for subtlety.

But when we pulled up in front of her apartment, Sabra said, "Why don't you pay him and come up?"

"Sure," I said, feeling a bit better about things.

We had a drink in her living room and listened to some music, heavy metal I didn't like but to which Sabra moved her hips, even while seated, crooning along.

"I'm mad for dancing," she said.

"Yes," I said, noncommittal, afraid she was about to suggest we go downtown to Heartbreak or one of the other new clubs.

Instead she said, "I heard about you and Chanel. Let's go to bed."

It was a very large bed, a four-poster. Sabra kissed me and started to take off her clothes without a wasted motion. The tank general's genes were evident in her crisp efficiency. When we were both undressed, she went to a wardrobe and came up with four neckties, men's silk neckties.

"Please tie me to the bedposts," Sabra said politely.

I'd never tied a woman to bedposts before, not even in Paris, but I'd read *The Story of O*, so I knew that people did such things, and since it was our first date and not being rude, I complied.

"A little tighter, please," Sabra said. "I like to be stretched."

Sabra and I spent considerable time together that year, and then *Sports Illustrated* asked her to go to Madagascar to pose for the swimsuit issue, and while she was there she met someone else who presumably tied her up tighter and I got a postcard from Jo'burg telling me I was sweet and she would always think of me fondly and why didn't I take up jogging and get in shape and, oh yes, quit smoking cigars.

Bingo somehow heard about our affair and for months after informed anyone who'd listen, in admiring terms, "Sharkey ties up girls. And everything."

I'd have protested except that this sort of PR, erroneous as it was, did generate interest on the part of any number of attractive women. And got me invited to a party in Guccione's backyard, not the sort of thing Bingo approved, but I was curious and I went.

Bob Guccione and Kathy Keeton had a townhouse in the sixties near Fifth Avenue, a house filled with important pictures and patrolled by huge dogs, African ridgebacks, I think, bred to fight lions. The occasion was publicity, of course, to promote a new issue of Guccione's magazine in which Pia Zadora, a young woman married to a very rich older man named Riklis, was the subject of a photo essay, somewhat more adequately clothed than the run of *Penthouse* beauties.

The press was there. And the usual Manhattan cocktail party trash. A summer's evening and we filled the garden. I stood on a sort of patio, watching and taking mental notes.

"Mr. Riklis," a paparazzo shouted, "put your hand on your wife's leg." "Higher!" shouted another. Always in good taste.

The couple had been christened "The Young and the Riklis" by the tabloids. The husband, thirty years older, was asked if he worried about the disparity in age.

"No," he said, "if she dies, she dies."

Pia wore a summer dress slit high, and we all had drinks thrust upon us and were encouraged to ask questions, but I couldn't think of any. Andy Warhol was there next to me, pale and apparently incompetent, fumbling with a camera and getting in his own way.

"Lift your dress again, Pia," the paparazzi shouted.

Guccione, slung generously about with gold chains, gave me a tour of the house, the dogs padding along behind, drooling and panting. There were some marvelous pictures, and Guccione pointed them out and told me when he'd bought them and where.

Downstairs there was a small indoor pool, occupied now by young women in swimsuits, splashing about. Guccione gave them a languorous wave.

"A few of the Pets," he said.

I marveled at Kathy Keeton's tolerance.

Back in the garden the paparazzi were now urging Miss Zadora to remove her dress. I finished my drink and left. On the sidewalk I paused to consider a cab, but it was a pleasant evening, soft in the half light, and as I hesitated, Warhol came up. I introduced myself and he said, quite earnestly, "I *know*," and we walked together toward the avenue.

"She's just so greeaaaatttt," he said.

"Pia Zadora?"

"Yes, have you seen her new movie?"

"No."

"She's such a greeaaattt actress."

I assumed Warhol was having sport with me, and when a cab rolled up I let him get it and said good night. In the morning I described the scene to Bingo.

"Don't write about people like that," he said, lips pursed. "They're tacky, not our sort, and it just demeans you."

"I hadn't intended to," I lied. Actually, it would have made an amusing piece, but it was Marsh's magazine and he set its standards.

Standards of a sort.

43 ▣ *He makes these things up. I KNOW he does.*

THAT same week Bingo returned from lunch in a state of considerable excitement, summoning me to his office.

"Close the door," he said. "We can't afford to be overheard."

He could be the most careless of men, imprudent and tactless, yet at times he was seized by the paranoid certainty he was being spied upon. I flopped into one of his easy chairs while Bingo buzzed his secretary, Mrs. K.

"Get Ambrose down here, right away." He turned to me. "I love to shock Ambrose. He gets all red."

Ambrose was the in-house lawyer, a bright young man who went home nights to wife and children. He came in now, disgruntled.

"I was chairing that meeting you wanted with . . ."

"Never mind, Ambrose," Marsh snapped. "This is important." He started to pace a bit, as if unsure just how to start, and then, with a joyous little skip, he began.

"I had lunch with Norman."

Norman Delavan was perhaps the greatest of all the American designers, a lean, aging, elegant man of near ponderous dignity. I'd met him and found myself intimidated even though I knew that under that courteous, magisterial shell, he was as wacky as any of them. On the afternoon of a collection Norman worked off tension by getting down on hands and knees with a bucket of soapy water and an old-fashioned brush to scrub the floor of the entire showroom before bathing and changing into a dinner jacket to greet the fashion editors with champagne and a new line of dresses.

"Well," Bingo said, again glancing toward the door to be sure it was closed, "Norman tells me the designers have a new thing. You'll never guess."

Ambrose no longer tried. I said, "No, what?"

"It's so disgusting, you won't believe it." Bingo didn't look disgusted. He looked elated.

Ambrose perked up a bit. "Oh?"

"Yes," Marsh said, pacing faster now, tossing in the occasional skip, "they get a live goose. There's a place out on Long Island you buy geese, and they get undressed . . ."

"The geese or the designers?" Ambrose said, his lawyer's face carefully blank.

"The designers, of course. Don't be gross."

"I just like to be sure."

Marsh stopped pacing now and faced us. ". . . and they take this goose and put its head in the bureau drawer, and then they close the drawer slowly on the goose's neck so it can't get away. And then they . . ."

I confess I found myself tensing, leaning forward.

". . . *slam* the drawer suddenly on the goose so it strangles and they're mounting the goose from the rear while the poor goose is in its death throes."

My mouth was hanging open, and the lawyer sat there silent, kneading his hands.

"Isn't that awful?" Marsh said. "And all the designers are doing it."

As he and I walked through the city room from his office, Ambrose said, "He makes these things up. I *know* he does."

I stared at him. "Ambrose, how could you make up something like that?"

"Jesus," Ambrose said, shaking his head, "you're right. How could you?"

44 ▣ *He stroked a beautiful piece of cloth and wept.*

BY now my pieces had been institutionalized as a regular weekly column, entire page, facing what's called the third cover, the inside back page, a position for which advertisers pay a hefty premium. The column even had a title. Originally Marsh suggested the headline:

"Shark Attack!"

"Oh, come on, Bingo," I protested indignantly, vestiges of *The New York Times* stubbornly still with me.

"Gives people fair warning," Marsh said. In the end we settled for "Shark!" though I continued to grouse about the exclamation point as stagy and self-conscious. In vain.

Fashion and the fashionable were still the magazine's main thrust, but the coverage and material had broadened over the years to what people now called "lifestyle." *Fashion* was doing as many pages on houses and their decor as were *Architectural Digest* and *House & Garden*, nearly as many on wine and cuisine as *Gourmet*, and running book and film reviews that would have done nicely in the *Atlantic*. I continued to see the designers and record their oddities, but in any week I might as easily be writing about Billy Joel or Henry Kissinger or Meryl Streep or Norman Mailer or about Martina Navratilova's entourage, tennis and otherwise.

"Write whatever you want," Bingo told me. "A single caveat: that people be talking about it Monday morning."

Monday was when both *Fashion* and *People* magazine, its putative rival, appeared. Time Inc. was considerably larger and more powerful than Marsh Publishing, and Bingo viewed *People* as the enemy. Having himself the attention span of a gnat, and assuming our audience did as well, Marsh harped on the need for editorial impact.

"If they're not talking about the magazine by Tuesday at the latest, I know that week's issue is a flop."

And while he didn't want me writing about Warhol and Pia Zadora, he wondered aloud if I couldn't somehow get in there the story of Delavan and the goose.

"Bingo, besides being disgusting, it's clearly libelous."

"Oh, I dunno," he said. "You could say Norman told us the story, not that he actually did it."

He was now paying me more, something over a hundred thousand a year, something that did not go undetected by Elmer Marsh.

"Nunc sent me a note about you," Bingo said, "wanting to know why that lad Sharkey was making so much money."

Nunc called everyone "lad," no matter your age.

"What did you say?"

"I told Nunc if he raised the matter again, I'd pay you one fifty and how would he like that!"

He looked and sounded pleased, like the mischievous boy who'd just put one over on an unpopular master. I made no attempt to mask a grin.

"One fifty would be splendid, Bingo," I said, rubbing my hands in obvious avarice.

He blinked then. "Well, I was threatening Nunc, you know, and not really doing anything about it." To punctuate the fact it was only sport, he got up and skipped a little.

But I could not escape wondering if over at Time Inc., where they published *People*, or at Mr. Newhouse's Condé Nast, where they published *Vogue*, they had conversations like this, and concluded not. Time Inc. was run by grown-ups; Bingo and Nunc behaved like unruly little boys in a schoolyard.

One of the first "Shark!" columns was a vignette of Barbra Streisand, a megastar with the reputation for being difficult. I'd wangled my way into a rehearsal studio where she was working on dance routines for a television special, and I was fully prepared to dislike her. But after she'd run through a routine she took a break, toweling off and sitting next to me on another wooden folding chair and talking. She was small and ripe, sexy in a pouty-mouthed sort of way and with the sweat-soaked leotard glued to her body. I assumed the charm was turned on and off at will, but it was effective and with me she was cute and flirtatious but very intense about her work.

"Y'know," she said, "I met Chanel once myself."

I was flattered she knew about my book, and I asked about Chanel. It turned out a mutual friend had arranged the meeting the first time Streisand was ever in Paris, and she'd memorized a gracious little speech. In French.

"So we get up there, climbing those damned stairs with the mirrors,

and Chanel opens the door to us. 'So?' and I shake hands or curtsy or
something, I'm so nervous, and I launch into my speech in French,
memorized, of course. I've got a singer's ear, so I guess it sounds okay,
and when I'm finished, Chanel gives me this big smile and starts in, a
mile a minute. I don't understand a goddamned word she's saying and
she thinks I speak French and she's going on and on and finally I grab
this guy's arm who made the introductions and I hiss in his ear, 'Get
me the hell out of here!' "

I wrote it just that way in *Fashion,* and even if it wasn't sufficiently
bitchy for Marsh, who didn't like Streisand, people were talking about
it that next Monday, and he was mollified.

I wrote about Walter Matthau, chewing gum like a cow working the
cud, big, lumbering, slope-shouldered, flat feet pointing out, just as he
looks in movie roles, exasperated, fatigued, reluctant to give much of
himself; and about Richard Chamberlain, vain and fretting about
whether his hair was combed as the interview proceeded; about the
seventeen-year-old cover girl Paulina Porizkova, who greeted me wearing a T-shirt that said "Let's Fuck" and told me "Modeling is such shit,"
and claimed what she really wanted to do was write children's books;
and about race car drivers and television anchormen and politicians and
once about a bordello keeper. And about the designers and the rich
women who patronized them and about storekeepers like Marvin Traub,
who still limped from having been shot by the Germans while serving
with Patton, and about Gustav Zumsteg, the great Zurich silk designer,
who told me as a child that when he touched and stroked a beautiful
piece of cloth from one of his mother's dresses, "I wept."

I wrote about grotesques and I wrote obituaries.

When Jackie Iskandere died I wrote a column. Jackie ran a transvestite nightclub in Paris on the Rive Gauche, and when I went there he
invariably offered to find me the prettiest boy with whom to dance. I
settled for a scotch and yarns from Jackie about the old days when he
worked as Chanel's private secretary. And when the old girl was in the
Ritz, Jackie sat at his little desk, and, instead of typing and filing, he
sewed up little dresses by hand from filched materials, dresses he wore
at night.

"When I'd hear her coming, heard her step on the stairs, oooh! how
quickly I slipped my needlework into a little bag and shoved it out of
sight with my foot."

When Jackie Iskandere died I wrote that story for the first time.

We were in Rome for the collections the week it came out, Bingo and I sitting there in the sun looking out over the Hilton's pool as the sun fell toward the tall cedars, and he put down the magazine, freshly arrived by courier, and smiled beatifically at me.

"It's really a fine story, showing that the fairies have feelings, too, even if some people don't like them and make fun. And everyone on Seventh Avenue will talk about it. And Ames."

"Why, thanks, Bingo." I meant it.

Just then a girl in a bikini passed, sleekly wet from the Hilton's pool, casting a brief shadow in the hot sun.

Bingo was still smiling, savoring the account of Jackie Iskandere's secret needlework.

"Think of all the people we know in joyless jobs," he said, stretching almost catlike in contentment.

"Yes," I said, following the girl with my eyes, but knowing precisely what he meant. At that moment, lolling poolside in the Roman sun, I shed the last of whatever reservations to which I still clung about Bingo Marsh and his magazine.

"Yes," I said, "I wouldn't trade with anyone."

45 ▣ *Park Avenue sucking up to the Black Leopards.*

ELEGANT Hopkins looked down at me from his great height.

"Ah yes, Mister Sharkey, isn't it?"

He had put aside the proper Henry Poole suit and Turnbull & Asser shirts and the other accoutrements of Savile Row and the West to move, gradually, toward the Third World in a sort of tropical uniform, a khaki affair with matching fez that suggested President Mobutu of Zaire or some such African despot.

"Hello, Elegant."

It was late September at the U.N. in New York, start of the new session of the General Assembly, and I'd strolled over to attend one of the receptions for delegates. No matter how broke the U.N. claimed to be, they were never short of cocktail parties, and I went thinking there might be a column in it, you know, pious Muslim delegate from Mecca in Manhattan gets stewed.

Elegant tarried with me only a moment. He'd been taken up by the diplomatic set, and it was said he had a private tutor from Alliance Française laboring over his French.

"Congratulations on the new collection," I said. "It seems to be doing very well."

"Yes," he said complacently, "quite well."

His handshake was as languid as his tone, and he passed on, beckoned to by a fashionable Nordic blonde and a turbaned fellow in aviator shades.

Women's Wear Daily had recently anointed Elegant one of the top five designers in America, elevating him from top ten.

"John Fairchild hates me!" was Bingo's reaction. He saw malign motives in most things and certainly in this.

In that season there was no end to Marsh's suffering.

"Who was it turned into a pillar of salt in the Bible, Noah?"

"I think it was Lot's wife."

"Well," Bingo said, "I'm next. Either that or the plague of boils that afflicted Babylon."

"Egypt."

Fortune did a feature on Elegant Hopkins's burgeoning network of licensing deals, a favorite with the Japanese and the Germans. Liz Smith reported Elegant was negotiating the purchase of a Georgian house in the Lake Country and was learning how to ride.

"Sidesaddle, I assume," snarled Bingo, by whom no betrayal was ever forgiven.

When Elegant was profiled by Enid Nemy in the *Times* he spoke, with some eloquence, of his work, saying it derived from the primal ooze of his tribal roots, cadence and beat, origins deep in Africa.

"For God's sake!" Bingo cried in exasperation. "He was born in New Jersey. I looked it up. He'll be wearing a bone through his nose next and carrying a spear."

But on this, Bingo was wrong. Within a year Elegant Hopkins had moved his entire operation west, to Los Angeles, to take advantage of, he said, the exploding markets of the Pacific Rim.

"He means the cheap labor of Mexican wetbacks," Marsh insisted.

It was now, in the picture magazines and on "Entertainment Tonight," that Elegant entered his Los Angeles Lakers period, hanging out and exchanging high and low fives at the basketball games with Eddie Murphy and Jack Nicholson.

It frightened Bingo, this sudden and extraordinary celebrity of a former employee, especially one Bingo was convinced he had single-handedly raised from poverty and the ghetto. But then he was frightened of almost anything new or strange or which he didn't understand.

"You see," he said, waving a copy of *Sports Illustrated* under my nose, "all these phony white liberals and black people going around together. Just like Lenny Bernstein and everyone on Park Avenue sucking up to the Black Leopards."

It was symptomatic of Bingo's time warp that he mentioned the Black Panthers (or very nearly did) and felt threatened by them. All the Black Panthers of those old Radical Chic days were dead or on the faculty of the University of California. Yet Marsh sensed their menace in a photo of Elegant Hopkins at a basketball game in Los Angeles.

"Look at them, scheming and plotting, with Hopkins at the very heart of the conspiracy. I suppose Nicholson provides the bankroll."

"Oh, hell! It's just another movie star fawning over people even more famous than he."

I started to tell Bingo how much money a Magic Johnson made but stopped myself, not wishing to upset him further.

The Yale of his years had not prepared him for a society in which tall black men could become millionaires.

46 ⬚ *Do we have a picture of Lucille Ball without a gin bottle?*

"I have but one thing to ask," Bingo was forever saying, and it was always something different.

"Be yourself . . . be controversial . . . be the one columnist everyone is talking about Monday morning."

With Marsh the goad, Monday after Monday I pinned someone to the corkboard of the column as Bingo rubbed his hands, the victim groaned or raged or consulted eminent counsel, readers clucked, rivals ground their teeth, and *Fashion* walked off the newsstands.

For obscure reasons he despised Leonard Bernstein.

"He's such a phony."

"I dunno. Surely a great musician."

"John, why don't you write something nasty about him?"

It was often on my tongue at such moments to say no, to tell Marsh to do the dirty work himself. I rarely did. I was the hired gun or, as less generous folk would have it, "the hatchet man." Besides, the column would be fun.

I knew Bernstein was in many ways a preposterous man, a poseur, reeking with false modesty while consumed by vast ego. A column about him would get people talking. I found my focus in Bernstein's penchant for melodramatic tears, for jags of crying onstage at the first or last performance of just about anything. He seemed to revel in public grief. Throughout the piece I referred to him as:

"The weeping maestro."

Bernstein quite naturally took exception. I never heard whether he got to Marsh with his plaints, but less than a month later *Fashion* published an obvious puff piece about an otherwise routine charity concert of which he was both sponsor and performer. I asked Bingo about the story.

"Why not?" he said huffily. "The man's one of the few geniuses we have in this country. And Ames."

Other demeaning nicknames were invented by us and by others: "The Prince of Swine" . . . "The Wee Haberdasher" . . . "The Social Larva" . . . and, of course, "Princess Tiny Meat." Calvin Klein graciously devoted an afternoon demonstrating Nautilus machines and other body-building equipment installed at great expense in his fashion establishment, lecturing me on fitness and good health. I rewarded his zeal by doing a column on this "curious new fixation" of his, suggesting narcissism run riot.

Bingo was delighted when Klein issued instructions I wasn't to be assigned a seat at his next collection.

"Sharkey gets so upset," he informed people.

John Dodd, shrewd and hearty, an important book editor with beefy thighs and a wheezing laugh, proposed putting together a collection of my columns between hard covers. As part of the wooing process, he produced his wife, Vivian Vance, the actress who played Ethel Mertz on "I Love Lucy." They lived out on the Coast, in San Francisco, but kept an apartment in Manhattan where I was asked for drinks.

"Do you ever see Lucille Ball?" I said.

"Not often, but we stay in touch," Miss Vance said, prim and thin-lipped, nothing like the Ethel Mertz of television. "Lucy's my best friend."

"And how's she doing?"

"Oh, fine," Vivian Vance said, "if you think it's fine to sit in the house all the day long with the blinds drawn and a gin bottle on your head."

It was hardly a line you could simply drop into the column, but neither did you ever forget it, tucking it away, knowing one day there would be a way to use it. Like most reporters, I have the curse of indiscriminate memory; things stick there and never leave. And eventually you use them. I understood about memory; I also understood the reporter's trade and its primitive ethic.

What I didn't understand is how people can say such terrible things about their "best friend" to strangers.

Marsh never agonized. "Publish it," he said, "the reader delights in these little insights into famous folk."

"It's actionable, Bingo. Lucille Ball's lawyers . . ."

"She's a public figure. Besides," he said, becoming sly, "you can also say lots of nice things about her and we'll run a flattering photo so she can't claim malice and you can slip in the quote about the gin bottle."

When I continued to object, he called for Rambush, the art director.

"Tyson, do you have any really pretty pictures of Lucille Ball? Without a gin bottle?"

Rambush, who'd worked years for Marsh, just stared, eyes bulging.

There were those who found Marsh amusing, dismissing his venom as adults shrug off dirty words hurled by children in tantrums. There were those who disliked him, a few who moved beyond dislike to hate.

Some people thought I acted despicably.

"Marsh is a bastard. But at least he says what he thinks, right or wrong. Sharkey does these things because he's paid."

I heard such criticism but tried to shrug it off. When you are a professional you take the money and do the job. Nothing I'd done for Marsh or the magazine yet tripped ethical alarms. Let others complain about the work we did. I was comfortable with Bingo and the job, both.

Then something happened that wasn't the job, but personal. And that detonated the first real trouble between us.

47 ▣ *Everyone has a morgue folder somewhere.*

IT began, innocently enough, over girls, as important things often at first seem frivolous.

I'd now been in Manhattan for a couple of years where, as a single man, I was forever being invited to dinner. Eventually, I stopped accepting these invitations, which always involved being paired with a woman, usually recently divorced, widowed, or otherwise abandoned. The women were invariably intelligent, frequently quite attractive, and always and understandably resentful. Since their former husbands (or significant others) had in one form or other fled the scene, sooner or later I became the focus of their anger. I can't tell you on how many Park Avenue evenings I heard a variant on the phrase, "You men, you're all . . ."

For this reason, among others, I gravitated toward younger women, not recently entangled. It was just . . . simpler.

Marsh, among others, occasionally remarked my cultural lapses, to which I offered protest. I read a lot of books, I said, I watched PBS, and while living in Paris had been any number of times to the Louvre, shepherding visiting Americans to the three things that had to be seen. Still, I recognized some merit in these cultural rebukes and embarked on ambitious self-improvement programs, the reading of the hundred most important books, for example, actually succeeding in getting through a number of them. My latest enthusiasm was ballet.

Her name was Lise, she was a Russian émigré, and she was a promising member of the corps de ballet at the Met. With Lise, I was learning about ballet. Bingo heard about her, of course, and started right off.

"How was the ballet last night?"

"Oh, fine. Tchaikovsky. *Petrushka,* the one about the puppet that falls in love and comes to life and in the end . . ."

"Yes, yes," Bingo said briskly, getting out of his chair to skip a bit, "so much better than that dirty modern stuff they dance these days. I like all those swans and nutcrackers and things. I believe most decent people do."

"This one had snow falling at the end and the puppet is lifted up toward heaven and . . ."

"I think I've seen it. I probably wept. And Ames."

Then abruptly, he said, "Is she still with that boy?"

"Who?"

"Jessica something. The actress."

"Lange?"

"That's it. She's the one."

"Baryshnikov, the fellow who replaced Nureyev. Aren't they having a thing?"

"There was something in Liz Smith . . ."

"I warn you," Marsh said, suddenly stern, "ballet dancers never did anyone any good. Men or women."

"Well, I . . ."

"It's like Mayerling or wherever that place was they had a hunting lodge and the Austrian crown prince shot himself and then his mistress . . ."

"In that order?" With Bingo, I couldn't resist.

"Well, you know what I mean. The both of them dead, and she was a ballerina. A commoner, I believe."

"And not his sort at all."

"Precisely," Bingo said, "and I'm quite sure the czar had a ballet dancer, too, right down the street from the Winter Palace, and I believe that was really what started World War One, Mayerling and the czar and the ballet dancers being shot. So for goodness' sake, John, be careful."

My passion for ballet didn't last. Lise was demanding and worked theater hours.

"You have a nice body, but you could get yourself into better shape," she hectored me. "Feel how firm my thighs are, my buttocks."

They were admirable, I eagerly conceded, noting the rest of her was admirable as well.

"Don't credit me," she said, "it's all a tribute to the efficacy of the barre."

"I dare say."

Lise was succeeded by a twenty-five-year-old on the pro tennis tour. "I'm never going to be Evert or Navratilova," she admitted. "I'm never even going to be Pam Shriver, for God's sake. I'm too old."

I commiserated and attempted to console her.

Marsh learned of her as well.

"They're all tailored women, those tennis players."

"Tailored women?"

"Don't be naive. Princess Tiny Meat says they're all, you know . . ."

I didn't mind being teased about my girls, about what he supposed was my extraordinarily active sex life, about exaggerations dating back to Chanel. It was amusing, it entertained Bingo, and it did no real harm. Or so I thought until the day he was sufficiently encouraged by my good nature to proceed from teasing to what I angrily thought of as unconscionable prying and none of his damned business.

And it had nothing to do with Russian ballerinas or "tailored women" who played tennis. It was about my family, about my father and what happened when I was a kid, which I never talked about. Not to anyone.

"I know about your father," Bingo said, just like that.

"Oh?" I said, my insides jumping, my face flushing red.

"Yes."

We were at lunch, the Veau d'Or over near Bloomingdale's, an authentic French bistro with plenty of noise and people with napkins jammed into their collars and their vests unbuttoned, people who concentrated on their food and wine with deadly seriousness and seemed uninterested in what was being said at the next table. Maybe this was why Bingo chose the restaurant.

When I said nothing, he went on. "Yes, I knew there was something. Knew it instinctively. So I sent for the clips. Everyone has a morgue folder somewhere, everyone has his little envelope of clips."

"Do you mind telling me why you bothered?"

"Because we work together. Because I care about you."

"I work *for* you, Bingo," I said, quite cold. "You own the magazine; I write for it."

"Oh, don't be shirty. I wasn't intruding. And, besides, such things happen."

"Sure they do."

"Teapot Dome. Watergate. The South Sea Bubble . . ."

"For God's sake, my father was accused of impropriety in gathering evidence, not trying to steal or overthrow the fucking government!"

"Well," he said mildly, "I was simply pointing out historical precedents to indicate your father was hardly alone in . . ."

"Bingo . . ." The warning was implicit in the word and he sensed it.

"Well, I'm sorry. I'm just normally curious and sometimes it gets me on to a good story and sometimes it gets me into trouble. Journalists ought to be curious. For example, just who was Charles of the Ritz, and why did they name a perfume and all those creams and toilet waters and things after him? I worry about things like that. You're not the only one with doubts. And so I dig into it and find out eventually and it was like that with your father and what happened back then in . . ."

"Bingo, about my dad, about my whole damned family, just shut up. We're not a cosmetics company and we're none of your goddamned business."

He should have fired me then; I would have fired me.

Instead, he looked at me, startled, eyes huge, fearful perhaps of violence. And for once, he said nothing more on a subject. Ever.

To use *his* word, I had been "shirty," oversensitive, surely, after all these years. But it was none of his damned business and I didn't regret blowing up.

48 ▣ *I suppose we'll have to stare at her armpits all day.*

HE held grudges, Marsh did, with the designers and rival editors, but for some reason, not with me. Now, forgiving me my anger and without actually saying so, a week later he was making peace by taking me uptown to a splendid lunch during which he so studiously avoided any mention whatsoever of my family, you would have thought I'd been discovered newborn in a wicker basket on a doorstep on a snowy Christmas Eve.

After being salaamed to our table by captains and waiters, he launched right in as if I'd never told him to shut his damned mouth about my dad.

"You know, you really ought to do a piece on John Weitz. He hates *Women's Wear Daily* and married a movie star and claims to have invented American sportswear, though how can you overlook Bonnie Cashin or Claire McCardell, and the Japs spend millions on his license deals and he went to Oxford or someplace and studied this British accent he has, all very grand, but he's German and used to live in China to get away from Hitler and he's very handsome and owns a yacht and some race cars."

All this in one breath. And since his voice carried in a restaurant like La Grenouille, where they'll always squeeze in one table too many in the front room, people nearby were involuntarily included in the conversation.

"Yes, I'm told he's fascinating . . ."

"And he was a spy during the war. Did you know that?"

"No."

"Yes, in the USO. He used to jump out of planes in parachutes and land in Germany and blow up things."

"Probably the OSS, what the CIA later would . . ."

"Well, one of those patriotic organizations. You're probably right." Bingo paused. "Do you see that woman over there, with the bare arms?

"Yes."

"No woman over eighteen should ever attempt a sleeveless dress. Coco first taught me that. I suppose we'll have to stare at her armpits all day. It really shouldn't be allowed."

The woman saw him looking and waved, thinking she might know him.

"Hello, there. How *are* you?" Bingo shouted. Then, to me, but hardly in an aside, "I haven't the foggiest who she is, do you?"

Pierre Cardin was in town to open a restaurant, and that swiftly became Bingo's surpassing concern.

"He knows literally nothing about food. The only couturier in Paris who doesn't. So what does he do, naturally, he opens a chain of restaurants, all of them named Maxim's, where Toulouse-Lautrec used to go and dance the cancan."

"No, Toulouse liked to watch the cancan dancers. And it wasn't at Maxim's. It was up the hill in . . ."

"John, you know what I mean. You don't have to pull out the Michelin Guide."

"Sorry."

"Anyway, he and André think they can just put a Maxim's anywhere and so now they've found a place on Madison Avenue and I just can't quite imagine Toulouse-Lautrec and that crowd flocking to Madison Avenue of a Friday night, can you?"

"Who's André?" Because of my intimacy with Chanel, Cardin had maintained a chill distance.

"André Oliver, Cardin's assistant. Everybody knows him. During the Algerian War André was drafted and Cardin made him his uniforms. The only couture uniforms of any private in the French army, I'm told. And when the collection is shown it's never quite finished and poor André is there on his hands and knees still basting a hem on at least one of the dresses when the model walks out. It's a popular feature of any Cardin collection, André basting and sewing in front of everyone. People would feel let down if it didn't happen."

Once the menu was examined and Marcel or one of the other captains consulted, Marsh could relax. The room had been surveyed, waves and blown kisses, snippets of gossip exchanged, and he could range more expansively in conversation.

"Speaking of Paris and Toulouse-Lautrec and that crowd, did you know James Gordon Bennett, the publisher?"

"Not personally. I believe he died some . . ."

"Oh, I know he's dead. But he lived there for a long time and got the Paris *Herald Tribune* started and later Art Buchwald worked for it and Mr. Bennett was strange but that was before Kay Graham and the *Times* bought the paper."

"How so?"

"He liked to ride around Paris at midnight in a carriage stark naked."

I glanced about, wondering how much of this was being overheard.

"People do weird things. When I lived in Paris and before I met Ames, the big sensation was a place in Montmartre, the rue Lepic as I recall, where people used to do it on motorcycles."

"On motorcycles . . . ?"

"Yes, in a nightclub, this girl and this boy would get on a motorcycle onstage and take off their clothes and the motorcycle was on a stand or bolted down or something, I'm not precisely sure how all that worked, but they had floodlights on them and the front tables were always filled up with cloak-and-suiters from Seventh Avenue every night for the late show because the word got around about the motorcycle so everyone went."

That little account led him to further musings on the neighborhood. "There's a wonderful restaurant on the rue Lepic, halfway up on the left side, I forget the name, where they serve the most marvelous soufflé de turbot. I'd never had it anyplace else and it . . . ."

Just then Madame Masson, the owner, passed by.

"Madame Masson, the soufflé de turbot at rue Lepic, isn't it good?"

"Pardon, Monsieur Marsh. Is it . . . ?"

"Oh, it's incredible. I've got to tell Cardin about it, for the new Maxim's. And André, if he isn't doing any last-minute sewing and basting on his hands and knees, ha ha."

Madame Masson, a pretty, blonde woman, smiled nervously and went off in some confusion.

"John," Bingo said sternly, "you're just toying with your food. Eat up."

"Yes, Bingo," I said dutifully. There were things worth arguing about with Marsh, but food wasn't among them.

49 ▣ *That's when you called her a geisha girl?*

MARSH tried to discourage me from writing about other writers. I'd known Irwin Shaw in Paris and through him I'd met Mailer, and a girl I went out with a couple of times introduced me to Capote, whom I admired greatly for the lovely economy of his writing. I was still slightly in awe of all three, but not Bingo.

"They drink too much and get married and then they shoot themselves. You look it up, Hemingway and Thomas Wolfe and that lot, and didn't Mailer stab somebody . . . ?"

"A wife, or an ex-wife, yes."

"See! And Irwin Shaw has an artificial hip. I'm quite sure of that. It was the talk of Gstaad last year. And Capote can't drive anymore because he's always drunk and they took his license or something. I'd stay away from them if I were you, John."

"Sure, Bingo."

I didn't, though. Old English majors are allowed our heroes.

Capote and I went to lunch at a place he liked, La Petite Marmite on Forty-ninth Street, directly across from where he lived. Jeane Kirkpatrick was there with people from the U.N., and Truman was very late. He arrived drunk and wearing a broad-brimmed plantation hat, which he declined to take off. At such times, one admired him . . . less greatly.

When the captain came over, Truman said, "You grow strawberries on the roof, don't you?"

The Frenchman had been through the routine before. "Ah yes, Monsieur Capote, and peaches and arugula and pommes de terre."

"We'll have some. But first, a double bourbon."

His fly was open and there were spots all over his jacket and shirt, and when he ate he drooled and dropped food. Every so often he waved to Ambassador Kirkpatrick, who was stern and disapproving and did not wave back.

"And people say I'm difficult," Truman remarked. "Look at the bags under her eyes, look at that face. Tell me she isn't into the sherry every afternoon in the Delegates' Lounge."

We talked about his unfinished book and other things, and he drank a lot.

"I get my hair cut right down the street," he said in that whining voice. "Tino and George. George is the juicy one. They shave me every morning because my hand shakes, and they give me a shampoo. Sometimes they have to help me back to the apartment. I'm not well. I've been through sort of twenty bad periods. One was right after *In Cold Blood* and then I began another book and I'm just now getting towards finishing up and I ran into a lot of trouble with it and I stopped. I had various forms of illnesses that took on all kinds of disguises. One was drinking, one was taking too many sleeping pills, this, that, and the other, but then I pulled out of it. I've been writing pretty steadily for the past five years."

I was taking notes, and he noticed, but he didn't stop or ask me not to, so I continued. And so did he.

"My mother was a great beauty, what in the South they called a belle. And I was an embarrassment and an inconvenience to her, and once when we were on a train, she threw me off. I was raised by aunts, maiden ladies."

Since he spoke of his youth, I asked about the character Dill, in *To Kill a Mockingbird,* the little boy supposedly based on Capote.

"Oh, he definitely was. Miss Harper Lee and I grew up together in a very small rural town in Alabama and her father was a lawyer, the hero of the book, Atticus, and I was a character called Dill. I taught Miss Harper Lee to type, but I was the one who wanted to be a writer. She wanted to be a lawyer. She won the Pulitzer Prize, but she is now a lawyer and never has written another book."

I'd read in Thurber's *The Years with Ross* that Capote worked at *The New Yorker* as a copyboy.

"Well, actually," he said, "I wasn't a copyboy. I was working there in the art department and then after a few months on 'Talk of the Town.' It was a very hectic place. Mr. Ross was a very formidable man, a very rough fellow. He was extremely nice to me. He was amazed by me because I went to work there when I was seventeen years old, and when I was seventeen, I looked about eleven. Every time he'd see me in the hall he'd stop and shake his head and then walk around muttering about child labor."

"Thurber said one of your jobs was to get a drunken writer out of the Algonquin bar and back to the office."

"Namely, him," Capote said, laughing, and when he was like that you forgot about the stains on his clothes and his open fly and the drooling. So I got him talking about some of his chums who were sore at him.

"Lee Radziwill, your old pal, did a little screaming about what you said about her and her sister Jackie."

"No, no, no, that's not what Lee and I had a falling out about. She was quite pleased with the book. We had a falling out because Gore Vidal brought a libel suit against me for a million dollars because of something I said about Gore in an interview. And the source of the thing that I said was Lee Radziwill and in the thing I had to give to the court, the deposition, I named the different sources. So that's what we had the big falling out about."

"That's when you called her a geisha girl?"

"No, no, no, that was really a compliment."

"Did Jackie like that, too?" I asked. This story was beginning to write itself, and I was scribbling faster and faster.

"Yes, that was meant as a compliment."

"That they were beautiful . . ."

". . . and they're geisha girls, not prostitutes. Geisha girls are just highly accomplished girls who are sort of meant to be charming and cultivated and entertaining."

I knew he disliked Ted Kennedy and asked him if he thought we might ever have a "President Teddy."

"Some things just run their course," Truman said, "and I think his has run its course in every conceivable direction. I don't think he is very intelligent."

"Is Jackie intelligent, do you know her that well?"

"Yes, I know her very well. And, yes, she is."

After lunch he waved his hat at Jeane Kirkpatrick and was again snubbed, and he staggered out. On the sidewalk he was so shaky I walked him across the street to his building where the doorman took him from there, giving me a look as if to say, "Yes, I know, we're used to this."

I told Bingo about lunch, and he was so excited he forgot he'd told me to stay away from Capote.

"And Ambassador Kirkpatrick wouldn't wave back?"

"No."

"I never liked her. Until now."

Bingo was especially interested in Capote's decline, manifested by his appearance and the drinking, because he'd known Ann Woodward, who killed herself, it was said, over something Truman wrote.

"I was in San Sebastian for the Tir aux Pigeons," Bingo said. "All the chic people were there from Paris and Madrid and a few from London, and all anyone talks about down there is the shooting. I'm less keen on the shooting than on the ambience, and Ames, because I never hit anything. Anyway, we went down on the overnight train from Paris, this was years ago, shortly after Mrs. Woodward shot her husband and claimed she thought he was an intruder, and that first night I was in the library, waiting for Ames to change and looking for a book, and this attractive woman came in in a velvet dress. I'm always fascinated by women in velvet dresses, since they can't sit down, the fabric marks so. But in any event I said hello and she said hello, obviously American, and I said, since it's how you start every conversation at the Tir aux Pigeons, 'Do you shoot?'

" 'Not any more,' she said, giving me the sweetest smile.

"Over dinner we learned who she was. A handsome woman, tall, with good manners. And your friend Capote killed her."

"Well, she killed herself."

"Same thing," said Bingo, immensely pleased, getting up to skip across the room.

50 ▣ *Are we in favor of the ozone layer or opposed?*

"IT'S corporate blackmail," Bingo complained, "the curse of being a publisher in New York."

What had him incensed was a charity black-tie dinner at the Waldorf for some worthy cause or other, and Pinsky the adman convinced Marsh that if his magazine were to continue in business it must purchase a table for ten thousand dollars.

"Pinsky rarely panics, nor does he exaggerate, Mr. Marsh. Our biggest single advertiser is being honored and a gun has been placed at my head. The magazine buys a table so trees can be planted in Israel, cedars of Lebanon I would not be surprised, or they cut our ad pages next year."

Bingo raged and then, as he usually did, capitulated. I was drafted to attend, and several of our major advertisers were invited. Bingo surprised me by going along himself. I think he suspected the magazine was being bilked and wanted to be sure there really was a dinner.

It might be a tiresome bore to Marsh, but such evenings in Manhattan were new to me, exotic and flamboyant. Over cocktails I wandered about, drink in hand, slipping away from Marsh and his round of reluctant handshaking, to absorb the moment's flavor, noisy, glittering, vulgar, fascinating, irresistible. The recognizable faces of famous men, the jeweled and powdered old women with their evident wealth, the ripe, younger, obviously second, wives, the bearded rabbis, the lush gowns, the gross and the elegant; the scene was intoxicating. In Bingo, of course, it was sufficient to alert every latent snobbish impulse.

Over dinner in the garish ballroom, routine food and bad music, interminable tributes and fawning recognitions of great men, and then the speeches, on and on, our table attempted to divert itself. One of the women with us, married to an advertiser, tried to draw Marsh, bored and making no effort to conceal it. The woman had a small child and had turned the desultory chat to child-rearing techniques.

"A fascinating topic," Bingo intervened unexpectedly, brightening perceptibly and eager to talk. As he often did when among strangers or nervous, he would go on, compulsively, the words tumbling out almost without regard to meaning or sense.

"Why so, Mr. Marsh?" one of the men asked, surprised Bingo had interests beyond fashion and publishing.

"We've made a considerable study of it," Marsh said, warming swiftly to the theme, "and Ames."

"Ames?" someone asked, befuddled. Bingo didn't explain, just launched into his lecture, telling the table how his children were encouraged to address him, somewhat stiffly, as "Father."

"I don't feel this 'Daddy' business is healthy. Breeds a contempt for authority, bringing the father figure down to a cute diminutive."

"Oh?"

Then, rather winningly I thought, he revealed that his wife had early on bestowed on him a pet nickname.

"What is it?"

"Soames," Bingo said, "after the leading character in that television series, 'The Forsyte Affair.' "

" 'Saga,' " I said, suspecting Marsh knew nothing of Galsworthy and believed the Forsytes were characters a BBC scriptwriter had made up.

"Whatever. Charming of her, don't you think? I like the sound of it, 'Soames.' " He smiled broadly, enjoying the notion he and his wife could share such a middle-class concept as a nickname. How could anyone have the heart to tell him what an insufferably righteous prig

Soames was? But you also had to like the never-seen Ames Marsh for a sense of humor.

Marsh, totally insensitive to others at the table who were regarding each other narrowly, was already embarked on another aspect of raising children in the eighties.

"You have to be concerned about things. And ecology."

"Oh?"

"Yes, disposable diapers, for example. We're opposed to their use. Because of the ozone layer."

"Diapers? The ozone layer?"

"The earlier you begin potty training, the better," Bingo said firmly, leaving the ozone layer to its own resources. "We put them on these little potties the French make, porcelain and quite attractive, no one else does them half as well, before they're a year old."

"Terribly young," a woman clucked.

"That's the point of it," Bingo said enthusiastically. "Some of them are so ill-coordinated you have to sustain them at their activities. But once they grasp the concept . . ."

"About the ozone layer . . ."

"All the best child psychiatrists warn us against becoming anal retentive. But what of 'anal expulsive'? Such behavior, and Ames is more knowledgeable on this than I . . ."

"Ames?"

"Mrs. Marsh," I put in, impatient for Bingo to get on with the narrative, wondering where it was leading.

"Yes," Bingo said, "especially between the ages of two and four, the problem ought to be somehow worked out. If not, well, I guess we all appreciate the problem . . ."

"No," a man next to me said, "I can't say I . . ."

Bingo fixed him with a patronizing smile. "Then later in life you have all sorts of people who've experienced arrested development in terms of wanting, fruitlessly, I might add, to assert their autonomy. And, when they fail to do so . . ."

I must admit, I was myself leaning forward. Up on the dais a rabbi of extraordinary piety was describing a grove of spruce on the Golan Heights. Bingo waited that brief moment during which tension tested restraints and then said, in a rather loud voice:

". . . people then find themselves defecating in the most unusual places, in formal flower gardens, in the drawing rooms of great homes, even in the backseats of hired cars. You see, it's a sort of protest which . . ."

There was a sort of mass paralysis at our table, and, I suspected, at neighboring tables, people hearing what they heard and trying to believe they were, somehow, mistaken.

Bingo, in full flight, went on:

". . . Hitler, for example . . ."

"Hitler?" a gruff voice demanded, Hitler not being a name often invoked at UJA-Federation dinners.

"Yes," Bingo said primly, "it's not generally known, but he was a victim of a mild form of anal expulsion. Teutonic people tend to hold back, which probably explains his particular form of malaise."

"Madness?" one of the women asked.

Bingo shook his head. "You can be perfectly sane and have these little difficulties. With Hitler it was called 'dynamitism.' "

"Dynamitism?" several of us asked, I among them.

"Yes," Marsh said, lips momentarily pursed.

"Uncontrollable farting."

Several heads at our table swiveled abruptly, to see if we were overheard, and one of the two women got up and excused herself.

I'd myself always been sensitive to Bingo's needs, rarely, for example, making reference to the last flight of Amelia Earhart lest it remind him of his mother's unfortunate death. But he never failed to dismay me when he got on to the subject, in whatever form, of bowel movements. Behind me, on the dais, someone was calling for monetary pledges. The someone was, I believe, Joey Adams. But I hesitated to turn 'round, lest I be right.

"Bingo, the new fashion collections," I said desperately, "they sound fascinating."

He bathed me in smiles.

"Why, John, they are, you know. Olivier of Hollywood was telling me just last week . . ."

I was terrified one of our guests might ask just who Olivier was, and we would be favored with one of Bingo's little essays on bike riding and masturbation, or perhaps a few other selected quotes.

Fortunately, we were spared, and Bingo limited himself to a dazzling report on the season's new clothes, a subject which the women found mesmerizing.

As we made our way out, the evening over, Bingo pulled me aside.

"You know, I was pleasantly surprised. I thought an entire evening among Jews would be banal. But there was really some rather good table talk, wasn't there?"

Uncomfortable lecturing him about how patronizing he sounded, I tried sarcasm.

"It's like blacks having innate rhythm. Jews are famous for their verbal skills."

"Oh? That must be why things went so well," he said, very satisfied.

Then, as he spied his limo and waved it toward us, a man immune to sarcasm as to so much else, Bingo suffered one final moment of insecurity.

"John, what I said tonight about disposable diapers and the ozone layer . . . ?"

"Yes?"

"I sometimes become confused, John. Are we in favor of the ozone layer or opposed?"

51 ▣ Go to work for Hitler or play piano in a cabaret.

FOUR or five years passed this way, a dizzying kaleidoscope, brilliantly colored but unfocused, shapeless and chaotic.

Then, on a spring evening, while drunk, I met Babe.

By now I was one of the highest-priced journalists in the country. A few editors made more; more publishers surely did; but among pure writers maybe only Buchwald and Russell Baker and broadly syndicated feature writers like Erma Bombeck were better paid. At one point King Features offered to make me "the new Jim Bishop," and dangled riches.

I didn't agonize over the money, suffered few guilts. I recognized I was Bingo's creature, that I went along with most of his pettiness, joined in his feuds, promoted his agenda, deviled his enemies, and smarmed over his friends. There were empty nights and hangover mornings when I disliked myself for not declaring independence and going somewhere east of Eden to write more serious stuff, something better than journalistic bitchery.

And then on a television talk show or in a magazine someone would refer to me as "the most powerful" magazine writer or some such rubbish and I would cheer up and admit, well, it's not all that bad a job, is it?

Head swollen? Of course. I was still honest enough to admit that (at least to myself).

But there was something beyond money and celebrity. By now I was so inextricably entangled with Marsh there had developed between us such a genuine, if antithetic, affection, that we seemed often to be halves of the same curious brain, one starting the sentence, the other ending it. Marsh wasn't anything like my father. Nothing like! And yet . . .

Bingo even tolerated anger, which he rarely did from others, hating to be opposed. I think he put it down to petulance. Or my liver.

At Le Cirque one day Karl Lagerfeld sat across from us at lunch, his hair in a pigtail, his red-lacquered fan languidly moving the elegant air.

"He's such a phony," Bingo hissed contemptuously, "a baron or something in Germany where they haven't had royalty since the Kaiser was shot . . ."

"Didn't he abdicate?"

". . . and he's forever telling people to look him up in the *Almanach de Gotha*. It's just like Egon von Furstenberg. Or Egon von und zu Furstenberg, more properly. Can you imagine being 'John von und zu Sharkey'? Besides, the Agnelli side of the family have all the money, and they're wops. Poor Egon. He and his wife split, and she was the smart one. Now he's working for a shirt manufacturer, selling menswear. It's like Putzi Hanfstaengl in 1930, a Harvard man at that, either go to work for Hitler or play piano in a cabaret."

Marsh could manage such mental gymnastics, from Lagerfeld's "phony" title to going to work for Hitler. The appalling thing was, by now I could follow his tortured thought processes.

Then Lagerfeld saw Bingo and waved. Voice shrill with delight, Marsh called back, "We must have lunch!"

157

We argued again about cover girls. I was doing a column, and Bingo thought it was beneath the magazine even to acknowledge their existence. As I did increasingly, I told him he was wrong.

"Little girls in America used to want to grow up to be nurses or stews or Rockettes. Now they want to be President or Christie Brinkley."

A streak of puritanism ran pure in Marsh and he regarded me narrowly.

"You just want to have S-E-X with them." He spelled it out, really he did. There may have been an element of truth in that, but I did the column. Bingo wasn't happy until he saw the newsstand sale.

I'd come back from Paris the end of '80, a foreign correspondent for the *Times*, a Pulitzer laureate, a man who'd been to war, a best-selling author who knew . . . and legend had it had loved . . . Coco Chanel. And ever since I'd lived for Bingo's job and Bingo's magazine. Marsh paid me with more than money, with that weekly fix of a column with my name at the bottom and a thumbnail photo at top, just to the right of that ridiculous exclamation point at the end of "Shark!" Every fortnight or so "Good Morning America" had me on as a sort of "guest columnist," chatting with David Hartman about the rich and celebrated I'd just pinioned. And the ABC checks came without carping notes from Nunc about "that lad Sharkey" and how much I cost. With such clamor and popularity, I should have been content.

Instead, I felt the weight of vacant years, a single man halfway through his thirties, making a lot of money and owning nothing. My apartment was rented, my car was leased, there were a dozen girls and not a single important woman, pleasure but no true joy. And if love came my way, would I even recognize it?

Bingo made sport of me when I complained.

"You're having a midlife crisis. Or a change of life. Or what is it women have these days, PS something?"

"PMS."

"I knew there was a *P* in it somewhere," he said, rather pleased.

For all my vaunted knowledge of European women (courtesy of Bingo Marsh), it was in the pickup bars of Manhattan's East Side that I would discover the great erotic secret: there is nothing more exciting than a young American career woman who's just shampooed her hair.

It was Babe from whom I learned.

52 ▣ *Go to Woody Allen and turn right.*

A soft evening rather late in a bar on Second Avenue. There was this Babe Flanagan standing there talking to people I knew. I hardly noticed her, concentrating instead on an American Indian lady with whom I was necking as we sat on adjacent bar stools, I attempting to put my tongue into her mouth but ending up inaccurately somewhere around her right eye, startling her so that she toppled from her stool, dragging me with her.

The American Indian lady, embarrassed, fled into the night. And as I attempted to regain my feet, tangled in one of the bar stools, Babe Flanagan looked down at me.

"You're drunk," she said.

"Yes, I am."

So began a candid relationship.

The man with Babe introduced us, and as I rearranged my ensemble, she said, more matter-of-fact than solicitous, "Can you get home by yourself?"

"I live right over there," I said, weaving slightly but seeking precision as if it were vital she know the latitude and longitude, "right across the street. A small but tasteful apartment."

She looked past me through the window. "Over the deli?" she said. "You can't live over a deli. Think of the roaches."

"Where in Manhattan are there no roaches?" I demanded in some perturbation.

"I find Roach Motel pretty effective," she said, serious about it.

"Forget roaches. Pigeon lice are the true peril."

"Pigeon lice?"

"A man named Marsh warned me when I first came to New York: 'Examine the windowsills carefully,' he said. 'If there are pigeons roosting you get pigeon lice. And if you ever do, you'll have to move. There's no way to rid yourself of them. There's no escape.' "

"Who's peddling this?" she said, brow furrowed.

"Bingo. His vision is apocalyptic, seeing plague and disaster looming everywhere."

159

"He's nuts," she said pleasantly, "and so are . . ."

"Yes," I said firmly, "he's nuts. But in the morning I'll be sober."

"Hey, that's pretty good, falling down drunk and paraphrasing Churchill."

Sodden as I was, I knew we'd begun well. She'd read Churchill; more significant, her candor. Two people meet by chance who actually tell the truth, each of them, with just about the very first words they speak; her allegation of drunkenness; my shamed agreement that, yes, I was indeed drunk. I had theater tickets for the next night and I told her where and when and I went home to sleep it off. I wasn't at all confident she'd show up. It was George C. Scott in *Volpone*. Babe Flanagan surprised me by getting there. George C. Scott didn't.

"An indisposition," we were informed nervously from the footlights.

"Stewed," Babe announced.

Bingo would like her, I thought, like him, ascribing motivation and thinking the worst of people.

The understudy played the role, and we left halfway through and went uptown to Elaine's. I was something of a regular by now, but she'd never been there.

When they took our order, Babe said, "I like the waiter. Knowing but obsequious."

"Sure. Considers himself better than we are, but he wants the tip, too."

Her first name was Barbara, but she had always been called "Babe."

"I'm youngest of five, the baby of the family. But I was never really the 'baby' type. Too rambunctious and noisy. So it was 'Babe.' "

Her father was a city cop, now in retirement. Her mother always worked, teaching school mostly. They lived way out on Long Island, someplace I never heard of, and all five kids had gotten through college. Babe was in law school now, at Fordham, over in Lincoln Center near the opera house.

"I targeted Harvard," she said, "or at least Columbia. But I screwed up the math on my LSATs and missed out by a couple of points. Math and I co-exist uneasily."

Until now, a familiar story: lower-middle-class overachiever getting her law degree and then going down to Wall Street to join one of the big law firms and become a Yuppie, get rich. But there were things that made Babe . . . different.

She was not the most beautiful girl I'd ever seen. After all, I inhabited the realm of models. She had freckles and over her right eyebrow a small but discernible scar. And she was solid. You had the feeling that if she ever stopped exercising, with her appetite, she might weigh one fifty, one sixty. But she was startling to look at, with extraordinary eyes that bored right into you. And she was honest to the point of blunt, maybe of all the people I ever knew, men and women, the most direct.

"I don't do bullshit," she told me once, and it was true.

And she was smart. And a bit wacky. I liked that, too. But there was one other thing that set her apart, and it was that first night over dinner at Elaine's that she told me about it, the other thing that made her different.

"I didn't tell you where I went to college, did I?"

"No." I hadn't asked. People in New York were always sizing you up by your college, which I found phony.

"Well, it was West Point. I'm in the army. I'm a first lieutenant."

They brought the drinks just then, and a good thing.

"Well," I said, "I never dated a first lieutenant."

She grinned. "Is it that bad?"

"No," I said, "different but decidedly not bad."

She'd graduated a couple of years earlier and spent a year down South, at Fort Benning, where she qualified for parachute duty. Her grades at West Point had been excellent and the army needed lawyers, and now she was in New York at Fordham Law. She and another woman officer, who worked in recruiting, shared an apartment in Forest Hills, where they used to play tennis.

"It isn't Manhattan," she said, "but neither is the rent. Lieutenants don't get paid all that much, and even with per diem and a housing allowance, it's a stretch."

She ate everything on her plate, the way children were once taught to do, giving the impression buying food might be a stretch as well. I said so.

"Nah," Babe said. "I'm just a girl with a healthy appetite."

She was about five seven and, as I say, solid, with straight blonde hair chopped short just above her shoulders. Very square shoulders; I don't know if that was genes or West Point. None of the rest of her seemed at all square or cut off, and even seated, she moved as well as my tennis player or the ballet dancer, the Russian, swiveling and with everything working together. It does me no credit, but it was on the tip of my tongue to ask if she enjoyed being tied up or some other indecent proposal. I chose discretion, noting a very firm chin that a millimeter more might have turned stern and a gloriously straight nose the Irish don't usually have and blue eyes they sometimes do, the fortunate ones, eyes like fresh mornings in the country.

"I went to the library today to look you up," she said. "The main library on Fifth Avenue, the one with the lions."

"And?" I was inordinately pleased, so much so I stopped having lascivious thoughts about her breasts. Women weren't this candid; they fenced and played games. Babe was admitting interest.

"Hey," she said, "the Pulitzer Prize." And she pronounced it right.

"Well, yeah."

"And you wrote a couple of books. A biography of Chanel and a novel."

"The novel was lousy. The bio was okay."

"I'll read it. I just haven't had time yet."

She'd also punched up my file of stories radioed out from Da Xiang, the stories that got me the Pulitzer.

"When I met you last night I recognized the name." I didn't say anything, and then she said, less ebullient, "It's really gross I missed the 'Nam."

"Babe, you didn't miss a thing."

"Easy for you to say, you were there."

"What were you when Vietnam ended, ten, eleven?"

"About."

"You were too young to go. You had to be eighteen. At least."

"We studied it a lot at the Point," she said. "I actually read about Da Xiang. It was one of the firefights we studied in small unit tactics. It all came back to me when I read your stories in the library. I doubt they had all of them, just the ones that ran in the *Times*. But, I mean, there's Charley coming over the wire at you. I could see it just as clearly from what you wrote."

I cleared my throat, remembering fear.

"You overwrote a bit," she said, "all those adjectives."

"The hell I overwrote." I'd been twenty-one years old and an English major and of course I overwrote; I just wasn't going to get pushed around. She smiled. That smile took away critical sting.

"Okay, so I used too many adjectives. I'm having dinner with my first West Pointer, and she turns out to be a literary stylist."

"I did my senior thesis on Emily Brontë."

This wasn't my vision of West Point.

She also, it turned out, swam, captained the field hockey team, tried but failed to get a women's rugby side sanctioned, and was a battalion commander at the Academy.

I was becoming besotted. "You did it all."

She shrugged. "I missed the 'Nam." She was also stubborn.

I told her stories over wine about Elaine's, about how someone once said, "All the men are suntanned and all the girls are five nine," and about the time the London gossip columnist Nigel Dempster hit George Plimpton's ankle and accused Adolph Green, who has large teeth, of having "stolen someone's teeth" and how Elaine threw out Norman Mailer bodily one night when his girl kept unscrewing light bulbs because they shone in her eyes, and Woody Allen was there so often, Elaine gave directions to the men's room by saying "Go to Woody Allen and turn right."

A bit drunkenly, late that evening, I looked into those blue eyes and said, "Is there anything about you that isn't perfect, Babe Flanagan?"

She nodded.

"I'm not five nine."

Yes, she said, she'd like to see me again.

"But not for ten days. I've got final exams and a date with a cram course and black coffee."

"Ten days?"

"Yes."

I suspected it might be a long ten days.

53 ▣ Surreptitiously urinating into the white wine.

I'VE made the point about Bingo's distaste for personal confrontation. But until now I'd never seen him panic.

We strolled jauntily, the two of us, into the Grill Room of the Four Seasons restaurant where Marsh had his favorite banquette, Bingo waving to and being waved at by various people of significance. Now, as we made our way across the great dining space toward his banquette, Marsh literally froze in midstride.

"Oh, my God!" he said, genuinely stricken.

There, on a neighboring banquette, sat Henry Kissinger, publicly flogged in that week's issue of the magazine on the express instructions of Bingo Marsh. The story dealt with Dr. Kissinger's many advisory and consultancy deals since leaving government service and suggested Henry was something of a crass money-grubber. Marsh kept calling for the story to be brought back, strengthened.

"Nastier, juicier, more stats, more details!" Bingo cried, and when a final, decidedly hostile version was presented for his approval, he giggled in delight.

The headline, dictated by Bingo, read:

"Tin-Plated Iron Chancellor."

The story's opening lines conveyed invidious comparisons to Bismarck.

Now Marsh and Kissinger were in the same room, and the prospect of a scene had Bingo shuddering in alarm.

"For God's sake, Bingo," I hissed, "he's not going to slap you with pearl gray gloves."

"He might," Marsh said mournfully. Then, "Don't look at him, I beg you."

"I won't," I said, trying not to snicker.

It may be Kissinger never saw us. Or hadn't read the story. Or didn't think it was worth making a scene. In any event, nothing untoward happened. But for the first time I'd seen a Bingo Marsh taken by sheer terror.

Nor was Bingo's cowardice restricted to the celebrated and powerful, to men like Henry Kissinger. If an employee had to be chastised, it was someone else who provided the chastisement. There was even a man who did the sacking, one of the magazine's least appetizing characters, the office manager, one Cap'n Andy, his title a relic of undistinguished, if lengthy, membership in the National Guard. Le Boot, who despised him, once blackened both Cap'n Andy's eyes in a fistfight, despite being half the Cap'n's size.

Now it was about le Boot that I went to Bingo.

You could see P.J. deteriorating, fast. His pranks had become more destructive, his binges longer and more violent, the hangovers physical and psychic, more painful. Before going to Marsh, I tried to talk to le Boot.

"P.J., you're killing yourself, kid. Killing this job, too."

"Oh, hell."

He was a tiny, skinny, rather ugly man of enormous energy and magnetism, a splendid editor, a dynamic personality, crazed and rather wonderful. And now he might be going to lose it all.

"Look, Shark," he said finally, "this is the best job I ever had, the most money I ever made. I never thought I'd make it to New York. Or be hanging around with fashion geniuses. It's a sort of miracle. I know that."

"That's part of it, using the designers to get you laid. Bingo is going to go crazy when . . ."

He leaned toward me, shaking his head and grinning.

"And I never knew there were girls like this anywhere. Ten years ago I was picking up women in bars, horny women wearing glasses and with runs in their stockings. Last night I was screwing this kid one of the designers sent, the most beautiful damned face you ever saw and really, a nice kid, funny and open and genuine . . ."

I understood the quid pro quo, a good play in the magazine for the designer's next collection. As managing editor le Boot could arrange such things. Marsh didn't catch everything. And P.J. was so damned candid about his graft.

"I'm forty years old and funny looking and spindle-legged and my wife gets the alimony and here I am screwing the most lovely girls you ever saw this side of a wet dream. You think I'll give that up, Shark?"

How could I argue with him, what could I offer in return?

Now he'd committed another outrage, something so unprecedented and imaginative it was bound to be taken public, embarrassing, if not le Boot, who seemed immune, then Marsh and the magazine.

Drunkenly, or just maliciously, during a charity dinner at the Pierre, P.J. surreptitiously urinated into a half-empty bottle of white wine and then deftly replaced it on the table in front of the pompous garment manufacturer who was his host. The manufacturer, unknowing, did his ludicrous part, refilling the glasses.

"I've talked to him, Bingo," I said, "and he listens, but next time out it's the same thing all over again. I guess it's because I'm younger than he is, and I drink some myself. You've got to pull him short or we're going to lose him. P.J. respects you, I know he does. If you really call him on the carpet . . ."

"How can he do that, urinating in wineglasses? It's so disgusting."

"Well, then, tell him so. Tell him you won't put up with it."

Bingo got up and began pacing his office.

"I can't do it. It would just upset me." He skipped a little. "You talk to him again. Threaten him."

"Bingo, I'm not the boss. You are."

"No, no," he said, shaking his head, "and I don't want to hear any more stories like that business of urine in the wine." He paused, thoughtful. "What was it, a Sancerre?"

I didn't answer him.

54 ▣ Olivier of Hollywood . . . had a nervous breakdown.

BABE called.

"Remember me?"

We'd started off honestly, so I wasn't coy. "The last ten days I've been remembering."

"Good," she said, matter-of-fact as ever.

Then I recalled why it had been ten days. "How'd the exams go? Straight A's?"

"The army expects every officer to do her duty."

We had dinner that night at Le Perigord, over near the river in the fifties. It was the first time I'd ever seen her in uniform.

"I had to attend a meeting on Governor's Island," she said. "Hope uniforms don't make you nervous."

"Me? The hero of Da Xiang?"

"Ha! Some hero. You told me yourself you were scared shitless."

"Told the truth. I wouldn't know which end of a gun to point."

"Weapon," she corrected me primly. "A 'gun' is an artillery piece. Or a smooth-bore weapon like a shotgun. The correct term is . . ."

"Have a drink."

We went back to my apartment after dinner. I was hoping we would, but with Babe you couldn't really predict. Under the uniform, for example, her underwear was decidedly not government issue, black and lacy, even a garter belt.

"I don't usually wear a bra," she said when we were in bed, "but on duty you're supposed to."

She didn't need a bra.

"You're beautiful," I said. "Your hair, your eyes, that mouth, your face, your . . ."

"Tits," she said, "which is what you're staring at."

"Never end a sentence with a preposition."

Two could play English major. But I had been staring.

She was, in ways, the most admirable, and most exasperating, woman I knew. And I got to know her very well that year.

"Shark," she said, "you never exercise. Never do a damned thing, do you?"

"No. I walk a lot." I suspected I was sounding defensive with that.

"And drink too much and chain-smoke cigars. Shark, you'll never live to see fifty. Maybe not even forty."

From the very first I was "Shark." Jack was a perfectly good name but she wouldn't use it. I was "Shark." As in Bingo's magazine, though without the exclamation point.

"I read somewhere," she was saying, "that every flight of stairs you climb adds five seconds to your life. You ever think about that, Shark? You ever think about doing laps? A few reps?"

After our third date she sent me a plant. Practically a tree, growing out of a green plastic pot that must have weighed forty pounds with the topsoil.

"Your apartment is morbid," she said. "No wonder you worry about pigeon lice and pick up soldiers in bars."

She thought the tree might help.

"Famous man like you, big war hero, Pulitzer laureate, celebrity journalist, we lived better in dormitories at the Point."

"Stop carping. Besides, we established I'm not a war hero. I just happened to be there when the shooting started."

She was very intense about that. "Hey, being there when the shooting starts is what makes a career in the military."

I even told her about passing ammo at Da Xiang, about contravening "the Geneever Conventions." She liked that but found it unfair a man, even a civilian, could somehow sleaze his way into a firefight.

She really believed one day they'd change the law that kept women out of combat.

"It's sexist as hell. Like unequal pay for equal work."

She liked some of my friends but not others. She liked Olivier of Hollywood. He'd had another nervous breakdown and lost this New York job and Yves Saint Laurent hired him in Paris just to keep him going. And maybe to borrow a few ideas. Olivier was back in New York to sell his apartment and tidy up loose ends. Babe and I took him to lunch.

"Let me order the wine," Olivier said, "you don't know shit about wine."

"And let you put me into Chapter 11 ordering Pétrus?"

"Let him order, Shark," Babe said. "Always go with the expert."

Olivier, who didn't like women, bathed her in a grin.

"Finally, Sharkey, you find a good girl, hein?"

He ordered the Pétrus '61 and it cost me a hundred and twenty-five.

"God, this is great wine," Babe said.

"A year ago you were drinking Thunderbird," I groused.

When Olivier learned she was in the army, he got excited.

"I always loved soldiers. There was this guy I met in Paris. He . . ."

"Olivier, she's a professional. An officer. A graduate of West Point. Don't start with your love life . . ."

"West Point? West Point?" He pronounced it "West Pwant."

"My God, I am in love with West Pwant. Since I was a little boy. Those uniforms. Those buttons. Those little gray jackets. Those tight pants and the hats. I'm mad for those hats."

"Shakos," she said.

"He's sweet," Babe said, "a little screwed up. But sweet."

Most of my other friends, she thought, were phony.

Not Woody Allen, of course. She thought he was great. Trouble was, Woody and I were not precisely intimate. We sat two tables away at Elaine's, I knew a couple of his pals, Mia Farrow used to say hello, but when Woody came in, the bottles of wine under his arm (Elaine's wine cellar was lousy), he would pass my table head down, terrified of making eye contact. It was okay, I could live with it. But Babe kept trying to meet him.

"I could just go over and sit down and start to talk, very brightly, nothing trite, about his body of work, and, you know, maybe one button too many unbuttoned, and I'd postulate a new approach to the auteur theory, and . . ."

". . . and Elaine would throw us both the hell out, and rightly so."

"Sharrrkkk!"

One night she got away from me. It was early, and for some reason Woody was there alone, staring at the table, counting the weave in the tablecloth fabric, analyzing the fiber content.

"I'll be back, Shark."

I thought she was going to the ladies' room, but when she got to Woody, she didn't turn right. She sat down.

It was a hot evening and she was wearing one of those big, loose, lovely cotton skirts and a tank top, and even Woody, myopia and all, couldn't miss any of it. But he tried to keep looking at the table and she kept talking and I sat there being embarrassed and hoping Elaine wouldn't pick this moment to arrive. Finally, it was over, and Babe sauntered back to the table looking very pleased with herself.

"Well?"

"He was very nice," she said. "I told him who I was and how I liked his work. And I gave him a little advice."

"About movies, you're giving Woody Allen a little advice about movies."

"Yeah."

"Like what?"

"Oh, you know, nothing about camera angles or lap dissolves or any of that technical stuff. I concentrated on his self-confidence, telling him to come out of his shell and stop staring at the tablecloth, think better of himself, that sort of thing . . ."

"Uh-huh."

"Sure, as if I were his commanding officer, more genial than authoritative. You know, an enlisted man with a problem called in for a private little . . ."

The army sent her to Arkansas for a month to help train summer

reservists. They didn't want young officers just hanging around Manhattan being idle and getting into trouble.

I was at Elaine's alone one night, waiting for Peter Maas, and Woody
came in. He started to pass the table, head down as he always did. But
he stopped.

"The soldier," he said, looking at his shoes, "is she here tonight?"

"No, she's away."

He shook his head. "Crazy, that girl. Just crazy. And in the army."

"I know," I said.

55 ▣ *Yale men trust each other.*

WOODY ALLEN happened along maybe once or twice a year. It was
with Bingo I had to deal on a daily basis. Oh, but he was complicated,
Bingo Marsh, as tortured and angst-ridden and contradictory as any
Woody Allen character ever. Until I met Babe Flanagan my horizons
had for years been pretty much defined by Bingo and his magazine and
my work. I thought I knew him. Now I began to think about Bingo
with a certain objectivity, as from a distance. Like the artichoke, you
peeled away leaves to discover what Bingo really was, only to
find . . . more leaves.

Peter Quinn, the protégé before me, the one I was supposed to resemble, had sold a novel which one of his sycophants confidentially
informed Marsh had a character based on him, a nasty piece of work in
the publishing trade. The book was not very good and only slimly re-
viewed and didn't sell, but Bingo went out of his way to chill whatever chance it had. Simon Simone, one of the fashion designers, agreed
to host a book party for Quinn, generating a little ink. Marsh had le
Boot phone the fashion designer to say how hurt Bingo was, how great
was this betrayal, that it was obvious Simone thought more of Peter
Quinn than he valued Bingo, or Bingo's magazine. The threat was implicit.

Simon, reduced to weeping, sent a handwritten note of regret to
Quinn.

People who'd known Quinn took it up with Marsh, one of them saying, "You used to be fond of Peter. You don't use a nuclear device to squash a bug."

"He betrayed me," Bingo said grimly. "I can't forgive betrayal."

I'd never met Quinn, but I, too, thought Marsh was playing the bully. And said so.

"So you turn against me, too," he said lugubriously.

"No, I . . ."

"There's no loyalty anymore. After all I've done for Simon. And Elegant Hopkins. And you. It's Benedict Arnold all over again for thirty pieces of silver. And Judas."

He had an absolute gift for feeling sorry for himself, even when things went well, a strange mix of generosity and spiteful malice. I owed much to Bingo professionally. But my affection derived from the little private pleasures shared: those furtive movie afternoons, the barefoot scamper along Valentino's balcony, our lunches with Olivier of Hollywood, Bingo's hilariously mixed metaphors and mangled syntax, his inability to tell you which was the man, Hero or Leander, his little skip and giggle.

I knew he was wrong in this business of Peter Quinn's little book, and yet I felt, if not precisely Judas Iscariot, vaguely uneasy about criticizing Bingo. He could be nasty, even vindictive, as with Quinn, and then he would do or say something so innocent and unthinking that you wanted to hug him and shelter him from a world all too real and cold for a man so vulnerable.

"Get Ambrose down here," he barked into the phone during one of those moments when you suspended judgment, wondering what he could be up to now, why he was so excited, just why the company lawyer and I had been summoned to the presence. When Ambrose came in and he and I were seated, Bingo started to skip around.

"This is confidential," he said, glancing toward the curtained windows to assure himself no enemy was peering in.

"Not to go outside this room."

I braced myself. What perfidy had some fashion designer committed now?

"Vice President Bush wants me to join his cabinet. Or to represent him in Paris."

Even the usually imperturbable lawyer raised an eyebrow. "He what?"

"Yes," Marsh said, "we had dinner last evening. And Ames. At

Brooke Astor's apartment. And the Vice President took me aside after dinner, just the two of us. He's so bright. Very well informed."

That was just too much for Ambrose.

"Just the other day you were telling me how stilted he is, awkward and gauche."

"The Presidency inspires men," Marsh said primly, "they grow in office."

I thought it time to point out Reagan was going to be President for another few years.

Bingo looked pained. "I know that. We're talking about 1988, when Mr. Bush is elected."

"A long shot, Bingo," Ambrose said.

"He's sure to win," Marsh insisted, "and we both went to Yale and we had such a good chat."

"What exactly did he promise?"

"Well, there were no promises as such. But he seemed very interested in my point of view on any number of matters. And he was impressed that I spent time in Paris."

"Just stroking you, Bingo," the lawyer said matter-of-factly, "setting you up for a rich contribution the next election."

"Things were left unsaid," Marsh said smugly. "But he's so nice. And Barbara."

Ambrose was behaving now like a lawyer, probing. "You get anything in writing, Bingo?"

Marsh looked pained.

"Yale men share a bond, something sacred. They trust each other, I'll have you know. It's not like . . ."

"The Big Ten?" I put in.

"Yes, or NYU or Notre Dame or someplace . . ."

He was such a snob. Ambrose, who'd gone to Notre Dame, couldn't resist:

"Wasn't Bush tapped for Skull and Bones?"

For an instant, Bingo looked genuinely stricken.

"Who knows?" he said airily, having pulled himself together, "and one never says. I'm sure that Barbara doesn't . . ."

Ambrose, now very much the lawyer, said, "Which must mean you were Skull and Bones, too, because if you weren't, you *could* talk about it, right?"

Then Marsh did, for him, a rather clever thing, rolling his eyes and starting to whistle, off-key, and beginning to skip about and clap his hands, much the way stockbrokers on the Paris Bourse are supposed to behave, singing and telling coarse jokes and spitting into the sandboxes, if a woman somehow wanders onto the trading floor, so that she won't suspect anything serious is going on, but simply grown-up boys having sport.

When Ambrose and I got out of there and wandered off toward our respective offices, leaving Marsh still whistling tunelessly, the lawyer said:

"He shouldn't be let out alone, you know. He really shouldn't."

"I know."

I was still hearing his jolly, silly whistle. At such moments I could forgive Bingo almost anything.

56 ▣ *Don't you turn first to the obituary pages of the* Times? *I know I do.*

I didn't tell him of Babe. Not yet. As inured as I was to his snobbery, I didn't think I'd be amused to hear Bingo say she wasn't my sort, "not your sort at all, John," lips pursed and unapproving.

So, in a way, as happens to a man and his parents, no matter how loving, when he finds a wife, Babe was already coming between Bingo and me.

He learned of her soon enough, of course. He had his spies. This time it was Princess Tiny Meat, once more out of Chapter 11 and doing splendidly and with yet another terribly social new wife. Babe and I had a table next to theirs at La Reserve over near Rockefeller Center one evening and we chatted, and, as you might expect, Bingo knew all about her before nine the next morning.

"It's all over town, John. One can't keep such matters confidential. New York talks of nothing else, according to Tiny Meat. And Ames."

While Bingo enjoyed a little romantic gossip, his true specialty was disaster.

173

If a designer had gone mad or a fashion editor was dying or a store president about to be arrested for peculation, Bingo knew about it. When the AIDS crisis began its slaughter of fashion figures, Marsh became a one-man center for disease control and always knew, often even before the victim, just who was carrying the infection and the roster of those who'd lately been to bed with him.

His information was not invariably correct.

"So-and-So's dying," he would inform me, having called me to the office and showily closed the door, "won't last out the year."

Sometimes it turned out So-and-So had a heavy cold.

While announcing impending doom, he attempted, without success, to look distressed and never quite could, skipping about the office and waving his hands.

"It's terrible. He's one of my best friends."

When someone was dying he almost automatically became one of Bingo's "best friends." He collected victims. But when the dying man or woman really was a friend, you could assume any mention of illness would be kept out of the magazine. Which didn't mean Bingo's excitement was cooled, just that he wasn't sharing it.

Mainbocher died, one of the old-school designers, and no favorite of Marsh, who always referred to him in the magazine as "Remember the Main-Bocher." He wrote that obit himself, all piety and venom.

Other designers died, most of AIDS, some of other things. Chester Weinberg, short, squat, and balding, an American of whom it was said Balenciaga was in admiration. Phillippe Guibourge, Bohan's longtime assistant at Dior and later the Chanel designer. Perry Ellis, young, handsome, preppy, who in summer flew to Manhattan by seaplane from Fire Island.

Before Ellis died we had a tremendous debate at the magazine.

"Perry's dying," Bingo announced. "His lover died of AIDS and he's got it."

"We can't say that."

"We can issue broad hints."

Bingo took AIDS seriously, because it killed people he knew. Yet it was also, in his ethic, an item of gossip, who had it and who might, information to be collected and passed on for the enlightenment of others, much as the story of Delavan and the geese. And, in his murky view of Bible history, AIDS represented something of a visitation upon the wicked.

"I don't agree at all with William F. Buckley, wanting AIDS patients to be branded . . ."

"Tattooed, Bingo."

"Or that, either. But you know quite a number of clergymen, eminent divines, consider the disease to be a punishment for sin. Mind you, I'm broadminded, exceedingly so, but there just might be something to that. You know, rather like what happened in the Bible to people."

"Oh?" I said, not being a great Bible scholar myself and unsure just where this was leading. And that was all Bingo needed, someone else's ignorance, to set him off.

"Yes, there was all variety of wickedness in several cities in the Holy Land, Sodom and Gomorrah principally, and God turned everyone into salt right there on the spot except for a few who escaped with Noah in his boat and Job or Lot or somebody who migrated into Africa and turned black from the sun and that was where Elegant Hopkins and all of them came from, many years later, of course, and some people had what was called 'the mark of Cain,' or perhaps 'of Abel,' the fellow who killed his brother over his 'coat of many colors,' I think, and they also suffered a number of plagues, like the plague of fleas . . ."

"Flies."

"Yes, and many ministers and bishops and such believe that's what's happening now to the designers."

Some people in the office agreed with Marsh about whether the magazine should hint that Perry Ellis was dying, others didn't. Everyone in the fashion business knew Perry was in bad shape, one of those open secrets. The ethical question was whether to print the story, even in veiled form, knowing it would bring pain to Ellis's friends and to the designer himself and could damage his business. Bingo called me in.

"I know you don't cover collections, but you ought to attend the Ellis show. It could be a great column."

"Because he's dying."

"Well, his novel use of smocking is said to be very interesting as well and . . ."

"Bingo . . ." By now I was savvy to his bullshit.

175

"Well, yes, because he's dying."

"And we're keeping the deathwatch. A bit ghoulish, isn't it?"

Marsh stared at me. Whenever he suspected he might be wrong he became aggressive.

"I won't be accused of such things, John. This magazine has a responsibility to millions of readers to tell them what's happening, to reveal truth."

In the end I went. Curiosity. I was getting as bad as he was.

When the collection was ended, Perry stepped through the parted curtains, supported by two assistants, gave a little bow, and disappeared. People were cheering and people were crying. Everyone in that room knew this was the last time he would see Perry.

I wrote the scene, not saying he was dying, just how he looked. That was sufficiently brutal. Ten days later he died.

"I told you the Ellis show would make a great column," Bingo said.

I looked at him. "Bingo, are you always this enthusiastic about death?"

"It's not enthusiasm so much as . . . I dunno, curiosity? Don't you turn first to the obituary pages of the *Times?* I know I do."

57 ▣ Madama Butterfly! *Bingo announced authoritatively. It was* Bohème.

I mentioned that I didn't own anything, neither apartment nor house nor car. Marsh owned lots of things. And was forever changing country places. You wondered if Ames, Mrs. Marsh, ever got to unpack the crystal and plate.

In the brief time I knew him the Marshes had places in Barbados, the west country of Ireland, outside Ketchum overlooking Sun Valley, a villa at Lago di Como, and a house on Maui which unfortunately vanished under the lava when a nearby volcano came unexpectedly to life. Of each of these homes he assured you, "It's the last civilized place, really, the very last."

I do not believe he said this about Maui, where his house was eaten, but that was an exception.

Now there was a Greek island. "Surely the last civilized spot on earth."

But he was to spend the weekend in an even more exotic clime.

"Princess Tiny Meat is giving a party. We've got to go. Bring along suitable clothes Friday morning. They're flying us out in a seaplane."

"Fire Island?"

"It's where the fairies go weekends," Bingo said, not precisely letting me in on secrets.

I had no desire to weekend on Fire Island. But it was difficult to deny Bingo. Despite his airy assurance he understood and even tolerated certain behavior, he arranged prudently that we stay at the home of friends in the WASP enclave of Point o' Woods, miles along the beach from Tiny Meat's place at Fire Island Pines. On Saturday, by motorboat, we ventured into the Pines for a lunch billed as a charitable fund-raiser for research into some variety of sexually transmitted infection.

"There's some new genius," Bingo explained Friday evening, "they never run out of geniuses."

That season's genius, a protégé of Princess Tiny Meat, was a young painter, Mel something, who'd discarded his name as bourgeois and now called himself "Jason."

"Jason was something in mythology, wasn't he?" Marsh inquired.

"Yes," said our host, "he sailed in search of the Golden Fleece."

"Now I remember," Bingo said. "There was a course they made us take at New Haven in freshman year. Jason and the Astronauts." He paused, confronted by a sort of stunned but well-bred disbelief. "Yes, that's what it was called. And the Astronauts were his crew."

Jason claimed to have met Marsh. "I don't recall. They all claim to know me. Even Elegant Hopkins says he once worked at the magazine."

"But he did. I met him there." I couldn't let that one go by.

"Who can tell them apart?" Marsh said airily.

Tiny Meat, beaming over his protégé, met us at the dock. His wife was elsewhere, it appeared. Jason, a polite young man with an implausibly perfect profile, welcomed us.

"His face was made in shop," Marsh whispered, "even the cheekbones were broken and reset. Regard the nose! And that plastic stuff they use to plump up lips? It's a scandal."

"Mr. Marsh, so good of you . . . " Jason gushed.

"I wouldn't have missed it. And Mr. Sharkey."

We were ushered up to the house, an enormous affair approached on elevated wooden catwalks erected over ecologically fragile dunes.

"The first course will be at my house," Tiny Meat explained, "prawns, lobster with a stiff mayonnaise I whipped myself, salmon with sauce verte . . ."

Lunch, he said, was to be "a movable feast," the first course here, the entrée somewhere else, the desserts and ices at a third location.

"Isn't that jolly, John?" Marsh enthused, no sarcasm in his voice.

"We all try to share the burden of philanthropy," Jason intoned piously. "I've put up a picture as door prize."

The two-hundred-fifty-dollar-per-head fee had already been paid for us, he said. Bingo made noises about our wanting to pay our way, not meaning it, of course, and Tiny Meat and Jason were sufficiently astute to pay him no heed.

Over preprandial cocktails men drifted in to be greeted by our host, young men and old, some of the latter plump and bald or gray; the young men remarkably fit, lean and muscular.

"Olivier of Hollywood would be in heaven," Bingo said.

Jason and Tiny Meat lounged on one of several broad decks in the midday sun, and people were brought to them, much in the manner of presentations at the Court of St. James's.

"They do everything but curtsy," Marsh said, reading my thoughts.

There were men in swimsuits that resembled G-strings, men with smoothly oiled bodies, men in safari jackets, in tights, in pearl chokers and tiaras, men with glitter on their eyelids and blue lipstick, men with teased hair and silk minidresses, men in formal mess jackets and crisp white ducks, all fluttering about Jason. There was much laughter.

"Darling" . . . "bitch!" . . . "lover" . . . "Bruce" . . . "dear one!" they called to each other, exchanging kisses. The more significant men were taken by hand to Marsh and introduced.

"Oh, my God, Bingo Marsh!" one boy exhaled, flailing at the hot summer air to restore himself.

The second course was several hundred yards east along the beach, rack of lamb, grilled tuna, vast salads, and freshly baked baguettes hot from someone's oven. The wine was extraordinary.

"I work for Marsh," I kept telling people who asked. Those who recognized my name fluttered.

"The Shark!"

At a third, even more magnificent, beachfront house there was English trifle, a cleansing sherbet, and banana split. Here there was also a swimming pool and young men, nude, swam and disported themselves. After lunch, rather drunk, I dozed. There was a disco that opened at midnight but neither Marsh nor I had the gizzard for it. We dined again with his Point o' Woods friends, who listened, agog, as Bingo described the day's events.

"You can't judge fashion designers by the usual criteria," he said ponderously, "they molt so easily."

In the morning I walked down to the local store to get the Sunday *Times*. It was hot and sunny with the Catholics going to church and the Protestants and Jews going for the newspapers and the young men staggering home from the discos, half naked and being supported in their drunkenness, staggering and lustful, by other, older, men. There was some problem with the seaplane that had fetched us to the Island and a momentary panic on Bingo's part ("We're not going to be marooned, are we?") so that we ended up taking the four o'clock ferry to Bayshore.

Jason would not be going back to the city until Tuesday, but, graciously, he came with us to the pier.

"I can't tell you, Bingo (Marsh was now, familiarly, so addressed), how much your visit means to me. My career, everything I am or have . . ."

"Yes, yes," Marsh said impatiently, "I've always thought you were so nice. And Ames."

As the boat eased toward the pier, the crowd of weekenders pressed forward, surging toward the gangplank, fearful of being left behind. Even Marsh seemed caught up in paranoid frenzy.

"It's okay, Bingo," I said, not all that confident, "there's room."

And there was, just. When we were all on board the ferry captain, identified to me as Peppy Zee, sounded a loud whistle, and as ropes slacked off, we moved slowly away from the pier. It was then the sobbing began, both those on board and departing and those still on the dock, the seduced and abandoned.

One young man, hanging from a pile, began to sing a Puccini aria.

"*Madama Butterfly,*" Bingo announced authoritatively.

It was *Bohème*. Another gentleman on the dock was stripping off his designer overalls as a third dove into the ferry's wake.

"A nine point nine!" someone shouted.

More men were singing now.

"It's just like the Gay Men's Chorus," a boy standing near me said admiringly.

"Yes, they're quite good," I said, trying to be congenial.

Now more people were diving into the bay, while on the dock a white-haired man seemed to be masturbating.

Bingo alternated between rolling his eyes and averting his gaze. I had the distinct impression we would not soon again be visiting Fire Island.

58 ▣ *My mother, who as you know, was shot down by Nazis.*

BINGO continued to fly to Paris twice a year to cover the collections. Sometimes he had me go along, more for the company, I suspect, than anything, since I seldom wrote about clothes. He had Regina Stealth and Count Vava for that. I was there to write about people.

Rarely did he attend the Seventh Avenue openings, snubbing the most slavering invitations, humiliating the senders. On occasion a major designer would get Bingo to a privately staged preview late at night a day or two before *Vogue* and the *Times* would see the clothes. These little shows for an audience of one cost thousands to arrange, overtime for the building to be kept open and the elevators run and for the runway models to perform. Marsh shrugged it all off, and often, despite the private showing, *Fashion* ignored the collection.

And he remained exasperating, erratic.

One moment Bill Blass was "my best friend"; the next Blass was threatened for having lunched with somebody of whom Marsh disapproved. Princess Tiny Meat was alternately lionized and ridiculed. Giorgio Armani's name vanished from the magazine for eighteen months when he cooperated with *Newsweek* for a cover story Bingo felt belonged to *Fashion*. Jimmy Galanos was banned. The House of Dior threatened a lawsuit in both France and the U.S. A feud with Pauline Trigere had gone on so long not even she could recall how it began, much as no one remembered what inspired Jarndyce *v.* Jarndyce in *Bleak House.*

As these guerrilla wars raged, I was accused by strangers of being Marsh's lackey. *Time* magazine said I "rode shotgun."

"Doesn't that bother you?" Babe asked.

"I fight with him all the time about stories. I tell him when I think he's wrong."

"Do you?" she said.

"Of course," I said, not quite truthfully. Babe and I were still becoming comfortable with each other, and I was not above giving myself the benefit of the doubt, impressing her. The fact was, my arguments with him were pretty rare, the occasions on which I won even more rare. Not that I agonized over it. Bingo was Bingo, this was his magazine.

Nor was I, in a spasm of newly discovered virtue, about to question him on the fashion. On fashion and its trends, he was uncanny.

When we got back from Europe he was invigorated, enthused, like an addict in the marvelous surge that follows a mainlined injection, summoning the entire editorial staff — artists, writers, editors — to hear his comments on the new clothes. Cables had been sent back, sketches and photos radioed home, but now the staff of *Fashion* was to have the benefit of Bingo's firsthand, eyewitness account of splendors. So many of us packed into his office, spilling over onto windowsills and standing room, there wasn't space for Bingo to skip.

I'd been there with him, had seen for myself the wonders of these latest Paris prêt-à-porter collections, yet no one could bring to the account quite Marsh's enthusiasm. As people looked up bright-eyed, expectant, and poised to take notes, he was almost raving with excitement.

"Consider the scene. A fashion revolution like nothing you've ever witnessed . . .'"

"Call up the tumbrils," Count Vava murmured near me.

". . . incredible stuff," Marsh went on, the words tumbling out. "Dark hints of bondage . . . Tyrolean hats with little feathers, quite authentic, I would think . . . rosary bead necklaces . . . a revival of the

Frye boot . . . big, washerwoman skirts over what looks like attic-insulating material, all pink as in the commercials . . . spandex bicycle shorts worn with leafy codpieces . . . women fainting . . . fistfights among the paparazzi . . ."

"The shapes, Bingo," Madame Stealth cried, serious about her craft, "what are the important shapes?"

Marsh fixed her with a glare which, since she was nearly blind, was lost on her.

"Shapes? Shapes? How often must I preach that fashion is the *spirit* of the clothes!"

There was a cowed silence, and he went on, more under control.

"Imagine the scene. The Margiela collection. Not in a salon but in a large khaki tent pitched in a rubble-strewn dirt lot, with half-naked urchins cavorting at the very feet of the models. The clothes? Seams and stitches showing, as if they'd been turned inside out . . . fabrics like plastic garbage bags. At another show a naked couple parades down the runway wearing appliqués of snakes and four-letter words and Communist slogans. At another house, fabrics made not of cloth but of eucalyptus leaves, medicinal as well as chic, and ecologically respectable. As were the recycled cardboard dresses from Jean-Charles de Castelbajac and Marina Spadafora. Then there was Gaultier, hardly my taste, you know, a fashion brat. But this time, even I had to applaud. He opens the collection with a nun swinging a pot of incense . . ."

He looked out across the office.

"What's that called, the incense pot?"

"A censer," someone called out.

"Good, a nun with a censer, incense rising, and then, suddenly, more nuns, in everything from taffeta hotpants to Day-Glo bodysuits. Bastille was also on something of a religious kick, evidently inspired by the Miracle at Lourdes, with velvet jeans and the cutest little leather backpacks bearing icons of the Virgin."

He paused.

"Was it at Lourdes that Saint Francis spoke to animals or where they changed water into wine?"

There was murmured disagreement over that, and Bingo went on, all about another designer "gone cannibal," embellishing clothes with morsels of flesh and bits of bone, necklaces of vertebrae; about a "Save the Rhinoceros" T-shirt collection; about a London collection billed as

"Britain Must Go Pagan," featuring gold appliqué penises on the fronts of all the dresses.

"And then there was Galliano, not a wop at all, surprisingly, but English, with the most telling stroke of all, men's pinstriped jackets with a third sleeve, worn ever so cleverly as a scarf, or, in the case of some unfortunate accident, an arm sling."

I gave Babe a reasonable summary that night, thinking it would amuse her.

"He's grotesque," she said.

"He doesn't design the stuff; he just tells people about it."

"He loves it. If the designers didn't create it, he'd make up stories. He's as weird as they are."

"Don't be stuffy," I said. "Who says fashion has to make sense?"

But she'd planted doubt, and I asked Bingo about the collections, how he could take it all seriously.

"Look," he said, somewhat sensibly for a change. "Fashion is a language, too. It tells you what people are thinking. Even this new craziness." He thought for a moment. "I read somewhere that in 1939, just before the war broke out, when the French knew the Germans were about to attack Finland . . ."

"Poland, I believe."

". . . whatever. Just before the Germans attacked, a Paris couturier showed a dress in the August collection with the inscription, 'Let's get it over with . . . let's get it over with . . .' Over and over, a little fashion designer, some pansy, calling for war against Hitler."

"Yes," I said, unsure just what the anecdote meant. Bingo looked at me, hurt, as you might be disappointed in a favorite child who fails to execute a somersault while the neighbors watch.

"Well, I just think it's significant that no one knew war was coming and we had to fight Hitler, but this little fairy did."

Then he paused, thinking back.

"And maybe my mother, who, as you know, was shot down by Nazis, some claiming it was Goering himself. Wasn't he a famous flying ace in World War One? Or was that the other fellow, Goebbels? Anyway, one of them may have been personally implicated in her death. Because she and a few fairies knew the war was coming . . ."

It was only a silly conversation, typical Marsh, but that last bit stayed with me. As ignorant and mistaken as he could be, Bingo used to be candid, as when he long ago admitted that his mother was careless and probably just ran out of gas.

Now he was like most people, merchandising legends.

59 ▣ *A sperm whale, perhaps sixty feet long, hung from the ceiling.*

AS Delavan and Mainbocher and Norell died and Donald Brooks drifted into other things and people like Jimmy Galanos aged, a younger generation of designers came along, men and women closer to my age, Calvin Klein and Ralph Lauren and Elegant Hopkins and Donna Karan and Halston. For a time it seemed as if Halston might be the big star.

Some designers are reclusive, suspecting their own inadequacies. Not Halston, a tall, handsome, troubled boy who'd been a milliner and lived grandly, with one of several places high above Fifth Avenue overlooking the Cathedral. I was up there one night to a black-tie party when Halston put down a wooden dance floor, hired a band, and had everyone there, from John Belushi to Scorsese and Isabella Rossellini to de Niro and Pacino and Liza Minnelli. Halston made sport of his own guest list:

"A Cosa Nostra reunion. Everything but Chianti bottles sheathed in straw."

What we drank was champagne. I found myself with Belushi and his wife. Nice people, he slimmer than he looked on television or in films, wearing well-cut evening clothes, pleasant, soft-spoken, intelligent people. A few months later in Hollywood, he was dead. Halston had problems of his own, a drug habit, rumors of insolvency. Then, in a startling coup that would make everything right, a big bucks contract to design clothes for J. C. Penney, the snob Halston label in fourteen hundred Penney stores across the country.

He launched the Penney collection with a gala at the Museum of Natural History, in the Great Hall of the Whales, where a sperm whale, perhaps sixty feet long, hung from the ceiling above us as the models pranced. An incongruous place to show a fashion collection. The deal with Penney turned out just as incongruous. Bergdorf dropped him, of course; so did the other high-fashion stores, and after a few years Penney cut the cord and poor Halston lapsed back into drugs and his financial woes.

The "brilliant" deal with J. C. Penney, the dramatic stroke that was to spark a Halston renaissance, was a ghastly death rattle.

"Omens and portents," Count Vava reminded anyone who would listen of that curious evening in the Hall of Whales, "omens and portents."

When Halston died Marsh claimed to have expected it.

"Fashion designers used to be laughable," he said, "like hairdressers. And I suppose *that's* changing as well. Now they're movie stars, and people prance and caper about them, as people used to play up to Gable and Hepburn and Tracy."

I must have looked bored.

"Did I ever tell you about Delavan and the geese?" Bingo asked, brightening.

"Several times."

I got to know Larry Leeds, whose company owned Perry Ellis. Leeds said that even before Perry got sick he himself started seeing a shrink, "so I'd understand the craziness."

"They're children," Bingo insisted, "whatever their age, designers are children."

Even so and despite WASP snobbery and a titled wife and Yale and all that, Bingo, a relatively rich man himself, had to be impressed by the sheer volume of money. The *Wall Street Journal* reported Calvin Klein and his partner, Barry Schwartz, each made sixteen million dollars a year. Cardin made more; so, too, perhaps, Valentino and Saint Laurent; Lauren was now worth a hundred million. You could almost see Bingo licking his lips. But he was still Marsh:

"Don't waste space writing about money. It's so common."

As I was increasingly doing, I ignored him on this, doing columns about their wealth. How Calvin bought a million-dollar house on the beach at Fire Island, next door to his, and then demolished it to provide room for a new pool shortly before decamping for yet another beachfront place in the Hamptons; how Ralph purchased a small forest and transported it tree by tree on flatbed trucks to his new estate in Westchester to create an avenue of Norway spruce leading to the front door.

"They're children, children with expensive toys," Marsh sneered.

He disliked Lauren. "An editor, not a creator. Good taste and no real imagination."

"*Fashion* magazine is important to me," Ralph told me. "I wish they were friendly. But what can I do? I can't beg. It would debase my work and diminish me."

A touching, quaintly dignified appeal, but when I told him, Marsh was unmoved.

"How can a man his size possibly be diminished?"

He was more favorably inclined to Calvin, perhaps because he saw in him some of his own ruthlessness.

"Calvin's cosmetic line back in '78, '79 was a bomb. So he and Barry just closed down the line and fired the entire staff and even canceled the return airline tickets of salesmen on the road."

Brooke Shields's father, Frank, was head of sales, and when he left on a Christmas holiday, Calvin fired him, too.

Klein started out with a pretty wife and a big talent and then his marriage broke up and he discovered discos and there were stories of facelifts and silicone injections to treat acne scars and he fell in with Liza and Bianca Jagger and Cher and seemed intent on doing a Halston. By '81 he was earning eight million a year; by '86 he was into the vodka, into pills; there were rumors he had AIDS, that he was dying in Mass. General. He and a young woman who worked for him flew to Rome to marry. The following spring he was in a drying-out clinic.

"Children, they're just children."

Ralph Lauren soldiered on, without Bingo's benediction, stubbornly successful despite him, while Calvin, a more subtle man, flattered Marsh with luncheons and small, elegant dinners, earning for a brief season a sympathetic hearing from *Fashion* magazine.

Some of the children, it turned out, were as clever as the grown-ups.

60 ▣ *Pillage and rape . . . spoils of war.*

BABE had her heroes. Her heroines. Serious people, none of them children or designers.

"Boadicea, the warrior queen. Joan of Arc. The Amazons."

"They cut off one breast, you know. So they could shoot arrows more effectively."

"Shark, that's why we had to invent gunpowder."

Short of sacrificing a tit, there seemed to be nothing Babe wouldn't do to further her military career. She read Clausewitz and Admiral Mahan and watched old war movies on television, critiquing the tactics, sparing no one, not even John Wayne.

"The Duke wouldn't have lasted fifteen minutes in a real fight," she said. We were watching *Sands of Iwo Jima,* which looked pretty good to me, but Babe had a lot to say about small unit tactics and fire support. "And John Agar; the Nips would have dropped that sucker before he got out of the landing craft."

She also thought Napoleon would've had a shot at winning Waterloo if he'd moved on the farmhouse an hour earlier.

"Wellington lucked out," she said. "Boney was suffering from piles and lacked concentration."

"They really teach you all this stuff at West Point?"

"The basic material. If you're ever going to make general officer you've got to go way beyond what you get at the Point."

That's what she wanted to be, eventually, a general. I wondered aloud what it would be like to be married to a general.

"*You'll* never know. I can't afford to get married. Being married cuts down on the range of duty options, those plum overseas commands you've got to have to get promoted."

"I wasn't proposing," I said testily.

"I know, Shark, and you're sweet. If I ever did get married you'd certainly be on the short list."

You couldn't really get sore at her, though she could be awfully pushy.

I came home one evening to find her straightening out my kitchen cabinets and stocking the refrigerator.

"I can't believe you. A grown-up who makes good bucks, and your refrigerator has a six-pack of Coors, two bottles of wine, a half bottle of Stolichnaya, mayonnaise, butter, a box of Total . . ."

"Wait a minute. Total provides all my daily requirements of vitamins and minerals and I . . ."

". . . six ice trays and three jars of hot mustard."

She'd bought eggs and oranges and milk and apples and some tomatoes and a head of lettuce and some other stuff.

"And I cleaned out some of that junk under the sink. What did you do, buy out the entire stock of Roach Motels?"

"Well . . ."

Other days she organized my sock drawer, matching up socks and rolling them into balls and folding my handkerchiefs. I had a half dozen sweaters, and I kept them on a director's chair in the corner of the bedroom. Now they were neatly folded and stacked on a shelf in one of the closets.

"I'll never find anything!" I protested.

No matter how late we went to sleep she was always up by six, doing exercises on an old beach towel spread out on the floor of the living room while she watched "Sunrise Semester" on television. And she ironed. She bought an ironing board and a GE iron and she pressed everything, mine and hers. Only woman I know who ironed blue jeans. And I began to find my shirts with tiny initials, mine, embroidered into the shirttails so that only I, and the Chinese laundryman, knew they were there. That first Christmas she bought me a very good leather wallet, which I badly needed.

She was always broke, and only later did she confess to having sold a pint of blood to pay for it.

"The normal, healthy body regenerates a pint in a week. And you really need a new wallet."

How could you not love her?

She was reading American poets now, especially Emily Dickinson; and when I started calling Babe the "poet warrior," she purred:

"You're sweet, Shark," she said. "You know George Patton wrote poetry?"

She had her favorites among the generals. Patton, except for his lack of discipline, Lee, Grant in certain campaigns, Longstreet, George C. Marshall. On Eisenhower she had reservations. "Very good on logistics and how he handled that prima donna Montgomery." She also admired some of the Germans and one or two of the Japanese.

"Yamashita, with that three-week campaign to take Malaya, jungle all the way, five hundred miles of it, and he had twenty thousand troops on bicycles and they took Singapore from the rear, from the land side, while the Brits had all their artillery pointed out to sea."

She was very critical of MacArthur.

"I know up at the Point he's our patron saint and all that, but God, how did they ever let him get away with splitting the Eighth Army into two columns separated by a mountain chain with winter coming on in Korea in 1950? He was damned lucky the Chinks didn't put them all in a bag."

She also admired Tamerlane and Alexander and Attila and the Vikings. "They invented amphibious warfare. The Marines are always patting themselves on the back about amphibious warfare, and it was a bunch of crazy Danes and Norwegians with horns on their hard hats about a thousand years ago."

"Pillage and rape," I said.

"Sure," she said, shrugging, "spoils of war."

The funny thing, for all her intensity and ambition, she enjoyed reading what I wrote and hearing me talk about it. Not that she liked everything; she loved playing critic. And while she didn't nag me about it — she was a pest but never a nag — she thought I ought to try another book. Nonfiction.

"Maybe you're not really Shoeless Joe Jackson when it comes to novels, Shark."

Shoeless Joe was, of course, perhaps the best natural hitter ever in baseball. I understood the allusion.

61 ▣ Madonna's our Grace Kelly.

EVEN as he aged, Bingo manifested a gloriously fresh enthusiasm for new directions in fashion.

When Madonna began to emerge as a major star, wearing her underwear on the outside, Bingo was like a boy, skipping about and calling on Rambush the art director for new prodigies of illustration on the magazine's cover.

"Tyson, she's so nice, Madonna, and those bustiers. But would your wife wear them? I keep asking myself that. And Ames."

Tyson Rambush, who as you know lived with another middle-aged gentleman, said he would work up some sketches.

"Yes," Marsh said, "along the lines of 'lingerie is sweeping the country . . .' Wasn't that a Cole Porter song? Or something?"

Bingo also liked Madonna's pointy, stainless-steel bra cups, the famous "bullet bra."

"They're rather fierce and threatening. But I'm sure that appeals to certain masculine tastes, you know, like being dominated, as with all those Valkyries flying about singing Wagner and scaring Siegfried and the dragons and such. I'm not sure if bullet bras are for everyone, though. Madame Stealth would never wear them, I'm quite certain. And just how comfortable they'll turn out to be is something else again. Mrs. K. . . ." He called his secretary.

"Yes, Mr. Marsh."

"Mrs. K., tell Madame Stealth to get several of her girls, you know, ones with busts, to try on some steel bras and report how they feel. Comfortwise, I mean. If they chafe and so on."

"Yes, Mr. Marsh."

"The Maidenform people and Lily of France will probably know how to handle chafing. They worked that out years ago with the underwire bra. Ask Mr. le Boot to assign a reporter to delve into the brassiere market a bit and find out. Madonna doesn't look to me the sort of woman who'd happily put up with much pain and suffering. She probably wouldn't like *Spanky* magazine at all."

"No, Mr. Marsh."

Sometimes I was called in during such spasms of creativity, often in midthought, so that I was totally unaware of just what the hell Bingo was talking about.

"It occurred to me perhaps it would be a better 'Shark!' column than a straight market report, John."

"What would?"

"The chafing problem Madonna has. Ask whether the lingerie industry can do anything about it. I mean the way they did with underwiring at that point in time. Madame Stealth's girls are trying on some of the new stainless-steel models even as we speak, and you might want to ask them as well how they feel about it." He paused. "You know, it just occurred to me, that metal must be terribly chilly to wear, especially in the morning, don't you think? I mean, unless there was some way to warm them up, you know, like those handwarmers L. L. Bean puts in the catalogue for deer hunters and skiing?"

"Bingo, you'd better start over and just . . ."

"Oh, the designers will all have a point of view, I'm sure, you know how they hate to be left out of any new trend. They'll explain it to you, and at tedious length. I wouldn't see Blass or Trigere or people that age. They'll be totally out of it. But the young ones, Isaac whatever-his-name-is, and Todd Oldham. And Donna, because she's a woman and has to wear bras, which the male designers don't, though I'm sure some of them do in private life and around the house and so on."

In the end I didn't do a column, but *Fashion* ran a cover story about Madonna's stainless-steel bras that included reactions and quotes, one of them especially dear to Bingo's heart. One of the kickier, young, androgynous downtown designers, rhapsodizing about Madonna's influence and inspiration, and wanting to put her into historic context, told the magazine:

"You don't understand. Madonna's *our* Grace Kelly."

62 ▣ *Pardon me, Pinsky. . . . I was in a bad chamber.*

MARSH kept getting reports about Babe, through Princess Tiny Meat and Regina Stealth's operatives and Count Vava and the émigré circles, but whenever he pressed me on her, I became evasive. All these years I'd known him and never been to his home or met his wife. Two could play the privacy game. I invented dodges.

"Just look at this Reuters dispatch," I insisted one morning as he started again to pry. "Do you think there could possibly be anything to it?"

I handed him a teletype just off the office machine.

" 'Lagos, Nigeria,' " he read. " 'People shouting that their sexual organs have been stolen set off riots in Nigeria in which several people have been killed. Bizarre claims about people being able to steal penises and women's breasts by means of a handshake or other casual contact have spread rapidly across the country. Some Nigerians believe the stolen organs are put to magical use in charms and potions.' "

Marsh laughed nervously. But I noticed he folded the dispatch carefully and inserted it into an inside pocket, possibly to be studied later with greater care, his curiosity about my love life forgotten.

He and Nunc were feuding, worse than ever. Perhaps the Nigerians were onto something here he might use against the old man. Nunc took me to lunch at his club, ducking several times into the bar for "phone calls," and complaining throughout about his nephew.

"The magazine's making a lot of money, Mr. Marsh. Circulation at an all-time high." I knew Bingo's worth and wasn't going to hear him trashed.

Facts frightened both Marshes, so Nunc grunted and changed the subject.

"I ever tell you about the time I skied the Headwall at Tuckerman's Ravine?"

"No, but I'd like very much to hear about it."

"Good," Nunc beamed, "why don't you have a drink."

Although he wasn't "our sort," I lunched occasionally with Pinsky, the adman, a decent man and funny.

"They are not an entirely sane family," Pinsky said one day over a cocktail. "You never knew Bingo's father."

"No, he died before I got here."

"A gent. Nothing like Nunc. But also, not like his son. Yet, in his own way, strange. That woman who writes best-sellers about vampires . . ."

"Anne Rice?"

"She could have made a career off the Marsh family. Even the father."

"Oh?" I had the impression Bingham Marsh II was the clan's one balance wheel. Occasionally an old-timer smirked when I made the suggestion but refused to elaborate. Now Pinsky fleshed out the portrait.

"I was their Chicago man for a couple of years, a young salesman with a shine on my shoes and greed in my heart, covering the Midwest, and old man Marsh would come out once a year and make some calls with me, Iowa, Wisconsin, Michigan, whatever. I knew every motel and gas station in the territory. And Mr. Marsh would sit there, amiable, asking intelligent questions about the accounts, about the competition, you know. Not like Elmer at all. Nice man."

This was all leading somewhere, I knew. Pinsky was a salesman, and salesmen don't talk unless they've got a sale to close.

"But every once in a while on these long drives, right in the middle of a conversation, whether it was about an account or last night's Cubs game, old man Marsh would go silent. Just stop talking. Thirty miles, forty miles, nothing. I'd ask him something, or say, 'Are you all right?' No answer. Nothing. Just staring straight ahead through the windshield at the ribbon of road."

"Not saying anything, just staring?" I said.

"Pinsky would not ask that you suspend disbelief."

I nodded, not knowing quite what to say.

"So, there I am, a salesman in a rental car, and my boss, the chief executive officer of this company, is sitting there beside me, stricken mute. I should make a clever remark, I should ask after the health of the children? No?"

I didn't say anything.

"The fact is," Pinsky went on, "I am terrified Mr. Marsh has flipped out, that at any moment he will expose himself, he will seize my throat in his jaws and begin to suck my blood, that he may dash himself to the macadam from a speeding car and the authorities accuse Pinsky of manslaughter."

"So?"

"So," Pinsky said, picking up on my clever line, "so suddenly Mr. Marsh turns around and resumes talking about the Cubs. Or about Carson, Pirie, Scott. Or whatever we were discussing, perfectly cogent, as if nothing had happened, and then he says, by way of explanation, 'Pardon me, Pinsky, but you see, I was in a bad chamber.'

" 'Oh,' say I, befuddled and intrigued, 'a bad chamber. You were in a bad chamber.' "

" 'Yes,' says old man Marsh, 'a bad chamber.' "

Pinsky sampled his martini with a great smacking of lips.

When he put down the glass, he fixed me with a look. "So do not be surprised, Sharkey, by anything that happens in this family. I love them as I love my wife, as I love my girlfriend, but do not expect from these people sanity."

Pinsky was right. Nunc was conniving to sell the company. Or that was the rumor.

When Bingo heard of his villainy he called the lawyer, Ambrose, and me to his office.

"Close the door." This was clearly significant stuff.

"This isn't about geese, is it?" Ambrose asked.

"Mr. Delavan is dead, as you know. This is a crisis." He regarded us sternly and told us what he'd heard. When he finished Ambrose said, sensibly, "He's your uncle, Bingo, why not just ask him what the hell is up?"

Marsh giggled nervously, the prospect of confrontation, even with Nunc, unsettling.

"We mustn't do anything for the moment to alert him," he said murkily. Then, brightening, "He and Miss Fuchs are probably in the shower, anyway."

Ambrose called me at home that evening. "You know, with all the Wall Street mergers and acquisitions these days, if this were a grown-up company, I'd worry."

Well, I said, then there was no reason for concern, was there, none at all.

I didn't really feel that cocky. When you have worked for a family company for a while, you get to appreciate the feeling. Paternalistic it might be, erratic, even flawed, but there was a zone of comfort I occupied at the magazine under Bingo. If *Fashion* were suddenly to belong to the Japanese, to some huge American conglomerate, would it be anything like as much fun, would I be able to write with the same freedom?

More to the point: who could ever replace Bingo, the Krazy Glue that held our house of cards together?

63 ▣ *Nude photos floating about. Right along with the Ivory soap.*

WHATEVER the tensions within our little magazine, fashion designers, like the sea, rose and fell with predictable regularity. Olivier of Hollywood had disappeared, victim of mediocre collections. Princess Tiny

Meat wed for the third time. Calvin and Ralph prospered. Along with, oddly, a woman, Donna Karan. As well as a black.

Elegant Hopkins won that year's Coty Award for fashion design. It exasperated Marsh.

"Bad enough letting women design clothes. But the African Queen?"

Hopkins, who'd begun so humbly at Bingo's magazine, establishing relationships along the bush telegraph of fashion, studying fabric, absorbing lessons of line and perspective from Rambush, was now a famous name, generously financed.

"The most exciting young designer in America," *Vogue* gushed.

"Did God really mean for there to be black designers?" Bingo asked.

I took Bingo to the movies that afternoon, to cheer him up. "It's supposed to be terrifying, a sort of slime monster that . . ."

When we came out, Bingo decided it was too late to go back to the office. I walked with him a few blocks.

"You know, you can take credit for Hopkins. Pride of authorship. You saw something in him when he was very young that eluded other people."

Bingo continued to brood.

"You mean I'm to blame for unleashing him on the world."

"No," I said, being stubborn too, "you created this genius, and people ought to acknowledge it."

Marsh shook his head sadly. "God creates geniuses. I just help out."

He was often like that, wallowing in self-pity. A good horror movie used to be sufficient to bring him out of the funk. Now, he was less easily jollied.

It wasn't just Elegant Hopkins. Or the absence of Olivier of Hollywood. Or Princess Tiny Meat's latest descent into bankruptcy. Or the rise of Donna Karan.

I wasn't alone in noticing his brooding. Ambrose saw it, too. "It's Nunc, finally getting to Bingo with this takeover business."

"I think it's George Bush," I said. As the 1988 election campaign approached, no emissaries arrived from the Vice President to seek the counsel and support of a fellow Old Blue.

"He's odd," people said who didn't really know Bingo, who didn't love him as Ambrose and I did in our various ways. Enemies whispered of curious fixations, of cabalistic rituals, suggesting that Marsh and I, or unnamed others, dabbled in erotica and performed unspeakable acts.

We didn't. And I knew Bingo went home every night to Ames. So while I was able to shrug off base calumny, as fond as I was of him, even I had to admit Bingo these days was, well . . . strange.

One night at a dinner party hosted by cinema people he knew in London, he exceeded himself, stunning even me.

The name of Maria Ouspenskaya had somehow come up, an ancient crone of an actress who'd been a major talent on the European stage, reduced in her waning years to playing Gypsy seers and the mother of werewolves in B movies. Marsh listened for a while to a minor anecdote about Madame Ouspenskaya, nervously fidgeting lest someone steal his glory. When the previous narrator drew breath, Bingo nipped in swiftly.

"Well, you know, she was very old and she had a sexual fixation on this beautiful young actress, not Vera Hruba Ralston but someone like that, I forget the name, and Maria Ouspenskaya liked to take a long hot bath, and one evening she was in the tub . . ."

He paused, and I could sense the table's tensing.

". . . and she had some nude pictures of this young actress she was fixated about, and she was becoming terribly excited, Maria Ouspenskaya, not the young actress, as in those scenes by the Gypsy campfire when the moon filled and the werewolf's hair began to grow, and, voilà!"

He stopped entirely now, looking pleased with his tale.

"Voilà *what?*" a woman demanded from my left. "What does that mean?"

Marsh pursed his lips. He liked an audience. "Well, one can't say in mixed company just what she was doing, but it so thrilled her she slipped beneath the water!" Another pause. "They found poor Maria Ouspenskaya submerged the next morning with the nude photos floating about. Right along with the Ivory soap."

Yet another pause.

"That's the brand that floats, isn't it, Ivory?"

As we got into our coats, a man said next to me, "What an extraordinary chap."

Marsh kept thinking of himself as clever Waldo Lydecker, brittle, spontaneous, spleenful. But he lacked Waldo's killer instinct. What in Clifton Webb caught at your breath with its arrogance would have been faintly ridiculous in Bingo, whose vision was so often clouded, seeing not the reality but a potted version of the world about him.

A world hemmed in by his own myopia and curious obsessions.

When Marsh had to fill a table for ten (twenty-five hundred dollars a person) at a New York Public Library fund-raising dinner in the wood-paneled trustees' room overlooking Fifth Avenue and the library lions and presided over by Vartan Gregorian, I was conscripted.

"Brooke Astor called and told me we had to buy a table. She thinks twenty-five hundred dollars grows like weeds."

". . . grows on trees, I believe."

"Yes, well, you just try to say no to Brooke Astor."

So we were there, Bingo glum and uninterested. Until someone at our table, passing up the meat dish, mentioned he'd been feeling bilious.

"Oh, it's easy to talk about cures for constipation," Bingo began, as he often did in full, conversational flight, frequently in non sequitur. "Bran muffins, citrate of magnesia, even that old standby castor oil."

"Who *was* Castor anyway, Mr. Marsh, or was he even a person?"

This was the sort of dialogue in which Bingo shone. Figuratively rubbing hands briskly together, he launched into his thesis:

"I've wondered that myself. But the fact is nothing taken orally for constipation is even vaguely in the same league as a simple hot saltwater enema."

When his three- or four-minute peroration was complete, a dignified old gent inquired, I thought sarcastically, "Do you often discuss such matters at Brooke Astor's dinners for the Library?"

"Oh yes," he said airily, "and with Brooke herself. She's fascinated, like most of us, with bowel regularity."

64 ▣ *I'll explain I'm a cross-dresser.*

OF course I had acquaintances and a few friends, a life beyond Bingo and the magazine, even before finding Babe. They were journalists and cops and admen, and we hung about in pubs, drinking too much, and talked sports and politics and ogled women. The advertising guys complained how the agency business sucked and spoke vaguely of getting into real estate or operating bowling alleys. One of them bought a sail-boat and was going to live on board during the summer, beating the high price of Hamptons rentals. Can you sail? he was asked.

"I can't even swim."

LaRuffa the contractor worried about his friend Stanley, who was now seventy, a famous submariner during World War II, and living in a small apartment next door to two guys who gave loud parties.

"Stanley hammers on the wall and he's scared they're coming in one night after him, so he bought a .22. He keeps it by the bed, and he figures he can get to it in four seconds if they come through the door and that if you shoot guys in your own bedroom, it's not against the law."

O'Brien the federal agent, a man trained to carry out investigations, wasn't so sure. One chill night O'Brien and I passed a bag lady huddled in a Second Avenue doorway with a bottle of red wine on her head. O'Brien went over, solicitous.

"She's okay," he reported. "It's a Robert Mondavi."

It was a shallow business, male bonding and bad jokes and drunken capering that passed for companionship, for a social life. I recognized that, most of us did. We weren't stupid, just silly, not destructive the way le Boot had become. Then Babe came along, and an empty apart-ment was no longer empty, my pub crawls ever shallower. Surprisingly, and she was forever surprising me, she liked my friends. Most of them.

"Except for the guy in the beanie with the propeller on top of it, it's a lot healthier hanging out with them than Calvin Klein and your pre-cious Mr. Marsh."

"I drink too much when I'm with them. You're always saying that, and I know it."

"You do. But I like the guys you drink with."

They liked her, too. Even in uniform. As one of the admen put it, "I never thought I could be sexually aroused by a first lieutenant."

One of our first pub crawls together she got into a fierce debate with an editor at *Forbes* on Marshal Ney's rearguard actions during the retreat from Moscow.

"That girl's great!" he enthused. "Even if she is full of shit about Ney."

A couple of nights a week she went home from law school to Forest Hills to study and wash her hair and do laundry with her roommate.

The other nights she came home to me, taking over one of my closets and installing a hair dryer and toothbrush and some disposable razors and cosmetics in the bathroom and big bottles of Evian water in the fridge.

"I hope the army doesn't find out," she said. "They don't expect us to be virgins, but they're kind of against career officers living in sin."

"Tell them you just drop by occasionally to drink my Evian water."

"With your bureau half full of bras and panties and pantyhose?"

"I'll explain I'm a cross-dresser."

"But just who is she?" Bingo demanded. "Do you know anything about her family?" His network of spies was at work, but I stayed pretty vague about her. Babe, after all, was my affair, not the magazine's. To Bingo, I realized, such things smacked of betrayal.

"I doubt very much she's your sort."

She threatened to find a maid for me. "Just once a week, once every two weeks." I didn't want a maid, I insisted stubbornly. "I'll find you one," she said, just as mulish. One evening I came home to find her on her hands and knees scrubbing the kitchen floor. Even the refrigerator had been pulled from the wall.

"Shark, I found dead bugs back there that were fossilized. This place is the petrified forest."

"You remind me of a man called Norman Delavan."

"Oh?"

"Yes, he liked to scrub floors. And he had affairs with geese."

She made me tell her that story. And others. Like all of us she enjoyed a little dish. She also knew when to stop, when to be serious, when to pose objections and explore motives.

"You've got this discipline," I said. "You try to do everything right and you're not shy about saying so."

"West Point."

"No," I said, "it's just . . . you."

She smiled, very pleased.

"I know it is," she said. "And I can't tell you how nice it is you recognize that."

That Christmas she bought me a VCR. I don't know how she saved the money, but she did. That, too, was discipline.

"I watch too much junk already," I protested.

"Now you can watch better quality junk."

"I won't be able to work it. I'll be electrocuted."

"I'll teach you. We'll go over the schematics and the instructions together. You can learn, I promise you," she said firmly.

I'd never had a girl like this, none of the cover girls, none of the jet set, no one back in Ohio. I was half ashamed to think it, but my mother never had Babe's set of values.

You had to love Babe Flanagan. Even if she weren't so much fun in bed, where she shed discipline along with her clothes.

65 ▣ *What a dirty old man Wyeth is!*

IN the spring Andrew Wyeth first showed his "Helga" pictures, making in the same week the covers of both *Time* and *Newsweek*.

Marsh was frenzied. He'd actually entertained Jamie Wyeth in his home and felt betrayed. "We should have been on top of this," he lamented. "Every designer in the world is poring over those pictures right now. The braided hair, the ripe flesh, the bovine, almost sluttish poses. And the voluptuousness! Right now Eileen Ford's phone is ringing off the wall with *Vogue* looking for slightly blowzy blondes."

Our art director, Rambush, was summoned for counsel.

"Reubens," Tyson said quickly. "It's decidedly Reubenesque."

"What a dirty old man Wyeth is!" Bingo raged. "Think of what his dear, loving wife is having to put up with. How humiliating! How disgusting!"

Bingo could be pious. Especially when competing magazines published Helga first.

I rather liked the pictures, empathized with Mr. Wyeth. If I could paint, that's how I would do Babe, ripe, nude, sexy, alive!

I told her so.

"Shark," she said, practical as ever, "you're sweet to say so, but you can't draw a line with a straightedge."

She'd found me a maid, a Guatemalan Indian, who left me a note the first day she was there.

"You need a new faction cleenar," the note said.

"You do, you know," Babe said. "That damned thing doesn't pick up anything."

"My faction cleenar is just fine," I insisted. "Neither of you changes the bag often enough."

The maid screwed up my television, not understanding about cable and changing channels and the focus. She also found a Spanish-language station on the bedroom radio and instead of its always being set to news, or to one of Babe's rock stations, we had FM in Spanish.

"She bent one of my venetian blind slats," I complained. Babe defended her.

"Oh, Shark, she's a sweet illegal trying to stay off welfare. Give her a break."

I could hear Marsh. "She's not your sort; not your sort at all."

In ways, he was right, of course. I was cataloguing the rich and beautiful, and Babe was refighting Gallipoli.

"Churchill had the right idea, you know. The soft underbelly of Europe and all that. Anything but beating yourself to a pulp on the Somme. But my God, the officers they sent out to do the job. Was there ever such an incompetent pack of . . ."

"Babe, give it a rest. It happened eighty years ago."

"Seventy."

It was a schizoid relationship. I wondered what Chanel would have made of her. When I said something like that, Babe smiled sweetly.

"She probably would have tried to get me into bed. Wasn't that what your old girlfriend said she always did?"

"Gillian. Gillian was a model. They think everyone is trying to get them into bed."

Babe looked at me solemnly.

"Shark, do you miss those skinny girls?"

I thought of Helga. "Not one bit," I said.

"Good," she said, very matter-of-fact, pleased but not precisely knocked off her feet by it.

Ralph Lauren and his wife, Ricky, had us to dinner one night.

"Don't go," Bingo advised. "He's incredibly boring."

I went. If you conducted your affairs by the revealed truth according to Bingo Marsh, you'd never go anywhere.

I'd seen Lauren's work and liked it. The few times we'd met, I found

James Brady

him inarticulate, a neat, compact man with close-cropped graying hair and a discernible speech impediment. His real name was Lifshitz. His father, a house painter, had changed it when Ralph and his brothers were boys. Bingo didn't accept that.

"It's like Scaasi, 'Isaacs,' spelled backwards."

"Well, so what?"

"John," said Bingo in some exasperation, "would you spell your name backwards?"

"Stop being such a snob. If the guy . . ."

"I am not a snob. I simply have certain standards."

"Then it's your anti-Semitism talking."

He was indignant.

"I am *not* anti-Semitic. I won't have you accusing me of such things. My father always employed Jews. So do I. And Nunc, even. Wasn't my mother killed by Hitler? I'd think Scaasi was ridiculous even if his name weren't Isaacs. It has nothing to do with anti-Semitism. He's a pretentious little Jew, and there's nothing anti-Semitic about it! Catholics and Protestants don't change their names, do they?"

"If you and I had an argument, would you get sore and call me 'a pretentious little Catholic'?"

"Of course not. You're rarely pretentious and you're not at all little. Not like that Scaasi."

How could you win such arguments? On matters like this he was simply opaque. I consoled myself I might be the only person at the magazine permitted to argue.

And, as I say, we argued about Ralph Lauren, who was also small and Jewish and had changed his name. Why such things mattered so to Marsh would have taken a shrink to explain. I'd heard a dishy story about Lauren Bingo would have delighted in, dining out on it, tittering and skipping about. I decided against giving him the satisfaction, keeping the story to myself.

When Ralph did the clothes for The Great Gatsby he'd gotten to know Robert Redford. They were a pair: the super WASP blond and little Lifshitz from the Bronx. But Redford sparked a surprising new ambition in Ralph Lauren. He decided to become a movie star! He was sufficiently well connected that William Morris agreed to explore the notion. The agent described the scene.

"I was assigned to talk to him. He came into the office and I said, 'Well, Mr. Lauren, and what can William Morris do for you?'

"He looked at me for a moment and then, very somber, and looking straight at me with those rather beautiful eyes, he said softly, 'I want to be a thtar.'

"When I heard 'thtar,' I knew we had a small problem."

Over his own dinner table in the Laurens's spare and elegant Fifth Avenue apartment, he was more impressive. You forgot the lisp and his size and even the halting turn of phrase. He talked, intelligently and occasionally with grace, about his role not as designer but as editor, of how he blended an element here, a texture there, a mix of rough Western leather and denim and the hacking jackets and flannels and wool sweaters of an English country house. Fred Astaire, Cary Grant, Gary Cooper, and Kate Hepburn, these were his heroes, his inspiration, he said, admitting with a delightful candor to having spent too many Saturday afternoons in the local movie theater watching double features and in the cool darkness of make-believe, shutting out reality and the Bronx.

He and Mrs. Lauren, a slender, pretty woman, were gracious, friendly. After, Babe said, "I liked them. Mostly I don't like the people you know, but they were good."

I told Marsh I was writing a "Shark!" column about the evening. "Oh, he's a bore. It's unworthy of you."

I went ahead anyway, but Bingo was right. Ralph was nice, Ralph was dull. So, too, the column. It needed an edge, it needed something, and in the end I tossed in the William Morris anecdote as a coda.

Bingo exulted, forgetting entirely he'd told me not to write anything. "I knew you'd get something juicy on him!"

Babe hated the column. "It's contemptible, putting that in about his lisp. You're contemptible. How can you go to dinner at a man's home and trash him? You're just like Marsh!"

The column about Ralph Lauren was the talk of New York for at least a day and a half, which was all Bingo ever demanded. He knew to the millisecond the shelf life of good dish. I shrugged off guilt, made easier by the fact Lauren didn't call to raise hell, too shy, too vulnerable. That was part of my calculation. People told me I'd been cruel, unfair. I shrugged that off, too.

Only Babe couldn't be shrugged off.

"Yes," I agreed, "you're right, it was a calculating thing to do."

"But you did it."

"Yes."

"Shark, you're better than that. Or should be. This Marsh . . ."

"You don't understand the job, the work I do, and what sells magazines . . ."

"I know about fair play and decency and honor."

It was the first real anger ever between us. I kept trying to justify myself, if not to her, then to me. Babe didn't relent, but then neither did she go on endlessly about it.

"I told you what I think," she said. "I made my point and you know how I feel. It's up to you to live your life."

I was glad the fight was over. But uneasy. I felt a little bit like Huck Finn, early in the story, pulled this way and that by the Dark Angel and the Good, as if Marsh and Babe Flanagan were wrestling for my soul.

66 ▣ Cruise the steam room and check out the priests.

WE fought about other things. But not often.

"I like the way you cut your nails."

"Squared off and short? Yeah, it makes more sense. Lots of guys like those long, exotic nails, jungle red and lethal. But I figure if you're reduced to defending yourself with fingernails you're already in considerable difficulty."

"There are sexual overtones to long nails. Those not associated with self-defense."

"Oh, I'm aware of that, Shark. And you ever want me to rake your back out of sheer ecstasy, just give me a little notice."

She traced gentle circles on my chest. I decided I preferred this to being raked. Sabra, the Israeli cover girl who liked to be stretched, would have found us disappointing.

When we did fight, it wasn't sexual. If she liked being tied up with neckties, I certainly would have made the effort. And if I'd wanted my back raked, I'm sure Babe would have let her nails grow. No, our difficulties were more intellectual. But there were frictions. You couldn't be as different as Babe and I and not collide.

I found myself defending causes in which I had little faith.

"Listen to this, an interview with a designer, and it's in your magazine. I'll read this. I want to get it right."

"Go ahead," I said, long-suffering.

"Here's the designer talking: 'I'm thinking nudity for this season. But a nudity that transcends transparency. A nudity that conceals as much as it celebrates.' "

She slammed down the magazine.

"Does that make any sense whatsoever?"

"The language of fashion is hyperbole. You don't take it literally. Besides, it's only Guy Laroche."

"I suppose if Chanel said it, you'd think it was fine."

"Chanel was a great designer. Laroche is barely marginal . . ."

The truth was, I, too, found much of the magazine ridiculous. But to admit that would demean the writing I did, which had validity. So I counterattacked.

"For God's sake, Shark, being in the army, being a career officer, doesn't make me Attila the Hun."

"You and Guderian," I snarled. "German panzers versus Polish lances. Mussolini and the Condor Legion . . ."

"The Condor Legion was German . . ."

"See, you defend the militarists!"

"And you're writing columns about Leona Helmsley."

"Well, yes, but critically. You'll admit I was quite severe in my . . ."

"Your magazine has got to be the most shallow, superficial . . ."

"That's redundant."

". . . pandering, phony, star-fucking, meaningless exercise in journalism since Hearst invented the yellow press."

"It was Pulitzer, I think. With the *New York World*. Or someone in England years ago with a magazine called *The Yellow Book* . . ."

"Spare me Journalism 101."

She blamed me for headlines in the *New York Post* and for Robin

Leach on television, and I suggested she and her "sort" were responsible for everything from the Rape of Nanking to the Beirut hostages.

"He who lives by the sword shall die by the sword," I declared.

And she was hell on Bingo.

"Look," she pressed, "I realize he's a devoted husband who loves his kids and he pays you royally, but, Shark, his obsessions, his Freudian lapses! Those wacky things you keep telling me about as if they're amusing . . ."

"Such as?"

"Well, masturbation. Enemas. Whipping Gypsies. Peeping Tom stuff . . ."

"It was Castillo whipped the Gypsies. And as for the Peeping Tom . . ."

". . . diaper changing . . . bowel movements . . ."

"We refer to those," I said prissily, "as doing number two . . ."

That shut her up, turning diatribe into laughter. Mostly, we got along pretty well.

Olivier of Hollywood briefly resurfaced. One bankruptcy too many had driven him again to Paris, where he worked free-lance. "They throw me a bone," he acknowledged with a candid shrug. Out of nostalgia we took him out to dinner one evening at Grenouille. Reduced in circumstances though he was, there was a certain gallantry to his insistence on choosing the wine, a decided pricey Pomerol.

"It's worth every dollar you'll pay," he informed me.

"Where are you staying?" Babe inquired.

"The A.C."

"The New York A.C.?" she said. It didn't sound Olivier's kind of place.

"Yeah, I cruise the steam room and check out the priests . . ."

Toward the end I asked if he'd seen Bingo.

"Nah, I call a couple times, but he don't answer. For me he's never in."

"But you and he used to . . ."

"Sharkey, you don't know Bingo Marsh as good as I thought. In fact, about Bingo, you don't know shit . . ."

We dropped him at the Athletic Club and went home. "I can't believe Bingo would just shut him off like that. Olivier used to be . . ."

"I love you, Shark," Babe interrupted, "but you have your blind spots."

"I love you, too," I said. And I did, even if she'd have been happier if I were Drew Middleton or Hanson Baldwin or, better still, Shelby Foote, and wrote about wars and generals and strategic planning instead of about Cindy Crawford and Princess Tiny Meat.

"The Peninsula Campaign, now, there's something you would have been able to get your teeth into. Or the Four Hundred at Thermopylae. Or how Gallieni realized the Germans had given him their flank and Joffre could fight on the Marne. When you've got material like that, who gives a damn about the pouff dress?"

Deep down, I knew she was right.

And then, for her birthday, I bought her a pouff dress.

"It's delicious, Shark. I'll wear it everywhere. I do so love you."

She didn't wear it everywhere, not quite, but she wore it. And was wearing it the night she first met Bingo.

I mentioned that for all our professional intimacy, and the very real, if odd, friendship that had grown between us, Marsh and I never socialized. He had his family, his Fifth Avenue apartment, his country places; he had Yale and breeding and the Protestant church; he had money; and for all his tics, a very sure sense of just who he was and why.

That last, in my mid-thirties and nudged on by Babe, I was just starting to figure out.

Bingo also had Ames, a cousin to Sir Edmund Hillary, and herself an "honourable," and until now I'd felt that gave Bingo an advantage, a good woman providing ballast, something we all needed. I knew about Ames; I'd just never met her, Bingo believing firmly in the compartmentalization of life, some people destined to travel first-class, but most of us in steerage.

Then, suddenly, stunningly, we met Ames.

67 ▣ *"Ah yes," said Henry Kissinger, "we all serve in our own way."*

ALICE MASON sold Manhattan apartments to rich people. She seldom advertised; she gave dinner parties that were black-tie and brilliantly choreographed. People came at eight for an hour of drinking and rubbing shoulders and were then parceled out to tables of eight, place cards and all, husbands and wives (or lovers) strictly separated. Alice was very firm about that, and her dinners became so celebrated *New York* magazine did a cover story about them.

Only rarely was there a gaffe. Such as the evening when Bingo Marsh and John Sharkey, employer and employee, were both invited.

Babe liked how everything was so organized. "Very crisply set up," she said approvingly, as if inspecting a military honor guard. Over drinks, when she was introduced to someone and asked where she was from, she said, "Long Island."

"Oh, then you must know C. Z. Guest."

"No, my father was a cop."

"Oh!"

Babe didn't always play the kiss-kiss social game as well as some did. For one thing, it didn't really matter to her that much; for another, there was no doubting her sturdy self-coherence. I might not always be sure of who I was; but, like Bingo, Babe was always quite certain.

The pouff dress didn't hurt, but Babe had a lot going for her that had nothing to do with fashion, and as we lolled in Alice Mason's library, I knocked back the vodka and enjoyed seeing famous and wealthy men, and a few women, make their way at flank speed to where we stood.

"Babe, this is Henry Kissinger. Dr. K., this is Babe Flanagan." *Fashion* magazine's treatment of him had been forgiven if not forgotten.

Henry greeted her with enormous élan.

"I know Mr. Sharkey," he said, "and am not quite sure of him. Of you, Miss Flanagan, I am sure."

"It's 'Lieutenant Flanagan,' Dr. Kissinger," Babe said. "I'm in the army."

"Ah yes," he said, "we all serve, don't we, in our own way."

Within seconds Kissinger and Babe were deeply into a discussion of Soviet hegemony and NATO throw weights. I took a refill on the vodka and then, to my astonishment, saw across the room Bingo and a very pretty, slender blonde woman. Ames, of course.

For a long time I hadn't really believed in her, suspecting she was just a name he bandied about to certify masculinity. Or that in some inexplicably Gothic way she existed, as batty as he, a pale nun gliding through corridors and wringing her hands in a wing of the house shut off to the servants. Bingo seemed just as shocked to see me.

"Sharkey, what are *you* doing here?" It was usually "John"; I knew he was upset.

It was as if I'd just delivered the pizza or come to repair the faucet, an enlisted man by accident in the officers' mess.

"Well, I guess because I was invited, Bingo." Across the room Alice Mason was balancing David Rockefeller and Norman Mailer and looking uneasily our way. Also across the room, drawn from me by the magnetic fields of force of a cocktail hour, Babe chatted, alternating between solemn intensity and laughter, with Jimmy Carter and Misha Baryshnikov. But Bingo was talking to me. And Ames.

". . . and this is John Sharkey, Ames. He writes things for the magazine." He could be patronizing.

She gave him a tolerant look.

". . . and this is my wife, the Honourable Ames Hillary Marsh," Bingo went on, very proud of her.

My annoyance at his snub vanished on the instant, swept away by his obvious love.

Mrs. Marsh bestowed a beneficent smile. An honest smile. "Most people call me Amy, Mr. Sharkey. Bingo is so stuffy about given names and such."

I like you very much, Mrs. Marsh, I thought, and I wanted to hug them both, pleased that I worked for such an odd but occasionally wonderful man, and secure in the knowledge from that moment on, his little verbal "and Ames," would never again be a dangled phrase, but a declaration of love.

Bingo, unaware of my thoughts, looked nervous. He liked to stage-manage social intercourse, and once Ames and I had said our howdy-dos, he was adrift, lacking a script.

David and Helen Gurley Brown came by, offering distraction. Bingo attempted to introduce them, and so shaken was he still by my presence, he got names confused and introduced Brown as "David Gurley Brown."

"Alone, Jack?" Mrs. Brown inquired. "Tonight's extra man?"

"No, I've got a date. She's over there, with President Carter and Baryshnikov."

Ames Marsh turned to look, squinting slightly, which made her even more appealing, less Bingo-ish. "She's lovely. My congratulations, Mr. Sharkey."

Bingo never knew when to leave well enough alone, especially when he was flustered.

"Oh, Sharkey's got lots of girls. Ballerinas and tailored women and everything. Dozens."

His wife looked at him. "Well, let's not share that information with his lady, shall we?"

Peter Jennings and Mary Tyler Moore and the admiral who used to run the CIA were at my table, along with Mrs. Mason, and I don't know who sat with Babe except that Bingo was one of the eight. Dinner was fine and the CIA man said something about how the hostage rescue went wrong in Iran and Jennings, who had actually been to Tehran, corrected him on the location of a key street.

While we queued for our coats, a man named Maurice peered at me through glasses. "That girl of yours is extraordinary," he said. "Did you know she's in the army?"

And Bingo grabbed my elbow long enough to hiss, "She's not your sort at all."

So I knew Babe had done very well, and when we were in the cab heading home, I asked her if she'd enjoyed the evening.

"Oh, it was okay, I guess. But that Marsh, I don't think he's the man you ought to be working for, Shark." She shrugged her shoulders, lovely and bare against the satin of her pouff.

"No?" I said lazily, feeling too good to argue.

"No, he's not your sort. Not your sort at all."

68 ▣ *He killed a man, you know, Claus von Bülow remarked.*

ONE morning I mentioned having seen Olivier of Hollywood, had taken him to dinner. I still didn't quite believe that Bingo would simply drop him.

"Oh?" said Bingo. Then, swiftly, "Have you heard about this new Mickey Rooney film? It's called *Nine and a Half Weeks* or something. All about S and M. And whips. Maybe we should go this afternoon, though I find Mickey Rooney rather old for that sort of role."

If Marsh increasingly seemed less easily defended, I was firm about the journalist's trade.

Babe was increasingly critical of both.

"You know in *La Dolce Vita* how Mastroianni is this gossip columnist for a cheap Rome scandal sheet, and he's a basically nice guy who keeps getting involved with the people he's writing about? How he's sympathetic to them, or repelled by them, or falling in love with them? Or with their glamour and their palaces?"

"Yes?"

"Well, that's what I think is happening to you."

Sometimes I thought she might be right. Other times I thought I was a professional and knew what I was doing and she was an amateur who didn't.

I'd met John de Lorean, before his difficulty, at a Christmas party at Ed Downe's house. De Lorean's wife was beautiful, his new sports car would soon be coming off the assembly line in Ireland, he was an assured and successful figure. Only when I turned from the bar, I found myself right behind de Lorean and looked down at his hands, clenched behind his back like Prince Philip's. Then I noticed how his hands were kneading each other, a man under tension. Reporters tuck such moments away, as I did, and then pull them out to be used on suitable occasions. When de Lorean was arrested, I wrote a column that began with a description of his hands at a Christmas party.

It was easy to be secure about that; the column didn't need a defense, even from Babe. I was more equivocal about other things.

211

Claus von Bülow and his girlfriend had us to dinner. I'd met Claus early in his troubles. A mutual friend had set up a lunch at a West Side restaurant called Jean Lafitte, but it was my impression the choice of place was von Bülow's.

"Is it significant," I asked, "that Lafitte was one of our more famous buccaneers?"

Claus laughed. "You're right, you know, but it never occurred to me."

He was all charm, but I don't know how much you could believe.

There were twenty for dinner, Dershowitz the Harvard lawyer among them. We sat in the drawing room of the lovely Fifth Avenue apartment. It had been Sunny von Bülow's, of course, and now Claus and Andrea Reynolds lived there, along with his daughter, Cosima, who was headed for Brown and who floated through the room as we had cocktails, long, young, and blonde, and I wondered, "What does *she* think about all this?"

Claus made a fuss over Babe.

"He's a shit," she'd said when I told her we'd been asked for dinner. "How can you go to dinner with this guy?"

I said I was curious to see him up close, to see the apartment, a lot of reasons, none of them especially doing me credit.

"He tried to bump off his wife, didn't he, and steal the money?"

"Well, that's what they said. Not proved."

"Ugh."

"Okay, Babe, I'll go alone. I won't impose Claus on you."

"Oh, I'll go," she said. "Is it formal?"

Over drinks Claus told stories. He didn't have much credibility, but he could tell a story. He was talking, in that clipped English aristo way of his, product of a public school and the occasional caning, about men he'd known at school who'd become celebrated, and someone said, "Did you know Jimmy Ewald?"

This was Sir James Ewald, a very successful and apparently quite odious international financier.

"Oh yes, we were never intimate, but I knew him quite well. We were at school together."

People leaned forward, sensing there was more to come. I was taking notes without ever touching pen to paper.

"He killed a man, you know," Claus von Bülow remarked. There were a few gasps and someone said "No!" and Claus went on.

"Yes, one of our masters, a perfectly dreadful old man we all feared and despised, especially Jimmy. The man made Jimmy's life sheer hell. So one day Jimmy tripped him on the steps. The man hit his head and died. It was murder pure and simple, even if there was no prosecution. Murder."

He paused, his timing perfect.

"Though I'm hardly one to talk, am I?"

During dinner I had Claus's lady, Andrea, next to me, and Babe was between Claus and Dershowitz, whom she swiftly engaged in discussion of some arcane point of courtroom pleading. I looked over to her table every so often to see how she was bearing up under the hammer of Claus's charm, but you couldn't tell; she had a good trial lawyer's poker face.

"Your girlfriend is a beauty," Andrea said, "but what a strange profession for a woman."

We had a talk about that and agreed we knew very few career army officers who looked like Babe, and then coffee was served in the library and Claus led us in, all bonhomie and good cheer. Babe took one of the armchairs, and Claus made a great fuss over her, fetching the brandy himself. She seemed to have thawed a bit. But when we were home she said:

"I'm glad I went. You were right, of course, it was something to see that apartment. And the daughter is lovely."

"But . . . ?"

"Well, you know. He's a wonderful host, and a charmer. I was repelled and attracted at the same time. I kept wondering about that poor woman in a coma in a hospital somewhere hooked up to all those tubes, and I kept wondering why I had such a good time and laughed so much . . . at *her* table."

I knew why I'd had a good time at Claus's table; it was my job, it would make a good column. A year ago I wouldn't have understood Babe's reservations. Perhaps common sense was becoming contagious.

69 ▣ *God belongs to everyone . . . even Episcopalians.*

YET there were giggles, small, quirky delights.

Another magazine — regrettably not *Fashion* — discovered that the new editor of *The New Yorker*, Robert Gottlieb, was something of a collector and had in fact, with a collaborator, written the definitive work (profusely illustrated) on his particular collectible. Marsh, reading about Gottlieb's hobby, became frenzied.

"I'd have paid a free-lance writer fifty thousand for that story. A hundred fifty!"

What Mr. Gottlieb collected were plastic handbags, women's purses in plastic, the sort of thing women carried in the forties and fifties, many of them transparent. This was his hobby, and he posed happily lounging on a chaise surrounded by dozens and dozens of plastic hand-bags, looking inordinately pleased.

"I'd have made it the cover story!" Bingo swore, "and given it eight pages inside, in color."

No sooner had editor Gottlieb's odd hobby faded from consciousness than Elegant Hopkins surfaced. In an interview in the Sunday magazine of *The New York Times*, Elegant had unburdened himself of any number of provocative remarks, several of which rather pointedly criticized Bingo Marsh. But they, for once, weren't what drew Bingo's ire. In discussing his recent rejection of Christianity (born a Baptist, Elegant had now embraced Islam), he referred to his growing conviction that any number of significant Christian figures, including the Apostle Paul, had been "self-loathing, repressed gays."

"I mean, John," Bingo exploded, "St. Paul gay?"

"News to me," I said.

"Well, I suppose anything's possible, and that's as may be. Next Elegant will be telling us he didn't drive the snakes out of England."

"Ireland. And it was Saint Patrick."

"Well, they were all very holy, I'm sure."

"Fine men, both," I said respectfully.

"Nothing self-loathing about Elegant. He loves himself and hates everyone else. Including me."

"I daresay."

Marsh became thoughtful. "That stuff about the snakes, wasn't there a plague of frogs . . . ?"

"Yes."

"And which Catholic saint took care of that?"

"It was God and Moses, working together," I said.

Marsh nodded, absorbing fresh information, ever eager to expand knowledge.

"And do Catholics believe God is a Catholic? Or does He belong to all of us?"

"God belongs to everyone, Bingo. Even Episcopalians."

Marsh seemed comforted.

The fashion magazine business was becoming more competitive, even tougher. Hachette, the French publishers, and Rupert Murdoch cut a deal to launch a monthly American version of the very successful French weekly *Elle*; *Vogue* was rumored to be bringing in a smart new editor to stir things up; Norman Lear's ex-wife Frances took the alimony and announced she was starting up a monthly named . . . well, *Lear's.* Even *Harper's Bazaar* bestirred itself, speaking of a redesign and an ad campaign.

Such things concerned Marsh. But it was another sort of magazine entirely that fascinated him. He was still reading *Spanky,* the corporal punishment monthly about which he'd gone on enthusiastically on Capri that summer night so long ago.

"It's good to see a magazine with staying power. So many of them start up with enormous promise and then wither away. *Spanky* seems able to maintain its editorial freshness month after month, though it's beyond me where they come up with all these variations on what is, after all, quite a simple act."

There was another new one now, only in its second or third issue, but showing possibilities. He unlocked a drawer in his desk and slid the magazine across the polished surface. It was the size and heft of that week's *Time* magazine, but its title warned you were in for something different: *Enema Quarterly.*

"Isn't it amazing," Bingo said, "the ingenuity of publishers. I know

I should be envious, but I've got to acknowledge creative enterprise when I see it."

I paged through the magazine, too slowly for Bingo, as it turned out.

"Let me have it back again. I barely skimmed the issue before calling you in. I wonder if Blass subscribes. I'd think he would, what with his interest in firemen and hoses and such."

"It could be," I said, choosing discretion.

We may have spent an hour looking over *Enema Quarterly*. Finally, I said, "Bingo, I've got to go. I'm supposed to . . ."

"Oh, all right," he said testily, shoving the magazine back in the drawer and turning the key.

I think he didn't want to be suspected of reading such magazines alone, that going through them with someone else gave the reading legitimacy, as if we were simply a couple of publishing professionals, fellow magazine men, coolly assessing competitive books, judging the typeface, counting the ad pages, calculating a newsstand sale.

70 ▣ *Certainly no one has better manners than Princess Tiny Meat.*

IT was the time of corporate takeovers and hostile mergers, and Elmer Marsh had apparently found a buyer.

Companies with blood relations feuding were raw meat for the Wall Street raiders. Stupid as he was, Nunc had in some primitive way understood this. Bingo, with his reporter's instinct, had been sniffing out trouble for months, and now he called me and Ambrose to a council of war over lunch at Le Cirque.

"Nunc can't really sell the company, can he, Ambrose?"

Ambrose answered with questions. "How much of the stock does he own, Bingo? *How much do you have?* Who else in the family holds shares?"

Bingo didn't know, not even his own shares. I would have been surprised if he had, but Ambrose was exasperated, sputtering disbelief.

Marsh looked inordinately pleased with himself. "Well, I don't know, so there," he said, delighted to have annoyed Ambrose.

Over the meal and a very good Château la Grave '81, the lawyer tried to tell his employer how these things worked.

"Your Uncle Elmer can sell his shares to anyone he wants, unless there's some sort of caveat in the family's partnership agreement. If Nunc has fifty-one percent, he can sell and the new buyer takes over. You then have the choice of selling your shares for the best price you can negotiate or hanging onto your stock and remaining as a minority partner working for the new owner."

"But it's *my* magazine," he said in what seemed genuine distress. "They can't take *Fashion* away from me, can they?"

"*Fashion*'s part of Marsh Publishing. You could always offer to buy it back from the new owners."

"But I own it already," Bingo said, voice rising and cracking in resentment. "How can someone take something I own when I won't sell my shares?"

"Because Nunc has more shares, *if* he does," Ambrose said.

It was Bingo's toy, and he wouldn't sell; therefore no one had the right to wrest it away. Corporate law and Wall Street were clearly beyond him.

"They're both gaga, you know," Ambrose said later when he and I were alone. He was the company lawyer, but no one, neither Nunc nor Bingo, had introduced him to the mysteries of their stock holdings, paranoid secrecy exacerbated by their own peculiar eccentricities. Finally Bingo was persuaded to go to Nunc, to ask him to see the books. Nunc dithered. In the end Ambrose got a look at Bingo's holdings.

"You've only got thirty-five percent. If Nunc has the rest he could sell tomorrow."

"I won't let him," Marsh said petulantly.

There was one possibility, a white knight, a friendly rival bidder who'd agree to keep hands off *Fashion* and leave Bingo alone. "You don't care about the rest of the company anyway, do you?" Ambrose asked.

"A batch of dull, second-rate papers nobody reads. And Ames."

Nunc dug in. Since he and Bingo weren't talking and communicated only through scrawled, rather insulting notes, I was sent to lunch with Elmer Marsh as emissary.

"I suppose you want a drink," Nunc growled with his accustomed grace.

"Well, yes."

217

Over the club salad he asked if he'd told me how he used to go scuba diving with Captain Cousteau.

"Yes," I lied.

"Oh," he said, disappointed, and then told me how a twisted ankle kept him from Wimbledon the year Don Budge beat von Cramm. Bingo said Nunc could barely get the ball over the net, but I shook my head in admiration. I'd been sent to charm Nunc, not edit his autobiography.

"You know, Elmer, Bingo really thinks the company ought to stay in the family, keeping things as they are now, with you as chairman and not some outsiders giving the orders."

"I'll still be chairman. That's part of the deal."

So he had a firm deal, something we suspected but didn't know. I argued Bingo's case as best I could, his devotion to *Fashion,* how hard he worked, the dedicated staff . . .

"Bunch of hippies," Nunc interrupted.

I wanted to defend our people, but this was no time to quibble. "Who's the buyer?"

"Why don't you have yourself another drink?" Nunc said, grinning maliciously and considering himself one hell of a subtle fellow.

"Find a white knight," Ambrose urged Marsh when I reported back, "someone you can live with."

Bingo looked gloomy. "What do I do, take out an ad or something?"

The lawyer explained about merchant bankers and deal brokers and in the end, defeated, Bingo agreed to let Ambrose go ahead and find someone. A fortnight later the three of us took a cab down to Wall Street to meet at a discreet bankers' club the people Bingo hoped might be his salvation.

"Where's your limo?" Ambrose inquired casually.

"I don't want them to think we just fling money around."

It was never quite clear why I was included. Not a shareholder or even an executive of the company, I was as much a financial illiterate as Marsh.

"Because I *trust* you, John," Bingo said when I asked. I knew he was scared; no one ever trusted me about money. It was too serious a matter.

Our merchant bankers met us there. "Now, don't say anything," we were cautioned, "just an exchange of pleasantries. This is a feeling-out procedure. If there seems a reasonable common ground, we'll closet ourselves with them and haggle. Just smile and discuss the weather."

The "white knights," chief executive and financial officer of one of the major television networks, were amiable enough. Too amiable. A gracious remark about the enormous popularity of *Fashion* magazine got a jittery Bingo talking. Compulsively.

"Nunc doesn't understand designers. He thinks they're all strange. Well, there's Cardin, who went out with Jeanne Moreau. But he makes millions on license deals. And Balenciaga had all those juicy boys around in their smocks. But he's dead. Norman Delavan used to scrub the floor before every show, and it's quite possible he had affairs with geese. Though he claimed it was someone else who told him the story, perhaps Olivier of Hollywood, who couldn't go horseback riding anymore due to excitement. But Calvin's a nice boy, and certainly no one has better manners than Princess Tiny Meat. And Ames. And surely Ralph deserved praise even if he lisps for those white suits Robert Redford wore in *Gatsby*, but someone else got the screen credit. And how could anyone say Chanel was strange? Except perhaps Castillo, who tried to set her on fire and had Gypsy boys whipped in the basement . . ."

When it was mercifully over, everyone shook hands more energetically than was truly called for, and the network boys offered us a lift uptown in their limos.

"Oh no," said Bingo primly, "we *always* take the subway."

The last the merchant bankers saw of us, we were standing forlorn on the corner of John Street while Bingo asked a hot dog vendor where the nearest subway was, and then there was a debate with the token booth clerk when Marsh, not precisely a subway regular, tried to pay our fares with a credit card. Once aboard a Lexington Avenue express headed north, he looked at Ambrose and me with a certain complacency.

"I thought it went rather well, didn't you? They seemed very nice."

Ambrose was still too stupefied to respond, and I studied the advertisements in Spanish for painless treatment of hemorrhoids.

71 ▣ *Wait till you meet "Street Dog."*

PAWING at his great nose in pleasure rather than angst, Elmer Marsh called a press conference to announce the identity of his buyer, a "lad" from Britain who'd cut a deal to buy control of Marsh Publishing, a deal which, unhappily for Bingo, included *Fashion* magazine.

"The lad," a London-based Mittel European named Sir Hugo Grottnex, was in the wallcovering trade, the "Wallpaper King," according to the Fleet Street tabloids, a clever marketing man whose advertising slogans included "Paper without Paste!" and, even more memorably, "Don't Glue! Grottnex Your Walls!"

"Let him glue Nunc," Bingo remarked sourly.

For some years Sir Hugo had been buying up failing newspapers in England and on the Continent and had only recently turned his media ambitions toward America. No matter; his money was good. And, something of a diplomatist who sensed the schism between members of the Marsh clan, he hosted a small dinner on the occasion of the signing of papers. It was to be in a private dining room of the "21" Club.

"But he knows I never go there," Bingo protested.

"How could he know?"

"Everyone does. And Ames."

It would be Bingo's first meeting with Grottnex, his first confrontation with Nunc since the deal was made, and he was very nervous.

"Oh, but I adore the '21' Club," he assured Sir Hugo on being greeted. "Sharkey and I are here all the time. They're so nice. And the Perrier."

"Yes," rumbled Grottnex from somewhere deep inside his great belly, unsure if this endorsement were of the club or the mineral water.

We stood about awkwardly and had drinks, peering, with enormous interest as if they'd never been seen before, at the familiar Frederic Remington paintings. Grottnex, whose accents had been smoothed over by years in London, was slick, dividing time and his charm between the warring Marsh factions, chortling or nodding intently, brow creased, at the most commonplace of remarks from either Marsh. Nunc and Bingo

220

behaved as typecast, the older man snorting and boasting, groping at his nose and relating pointless anecdotes about lads he'd known; while Bingo alternately brooded and skipped about, issuing the odd giggle. One of Grottnex's bankers diverted me, sotto voce, by identifying various of Sir Hugo's aides, Fleet Street newspapermen, most of them Australians.

"The gray-haired fellow, they call him 'Old Blue Rinse.' The lean one with glasses and the Oxbridge stammer is the 'Red Peril.' "

"Do they all have nicknames?"

"Apparently there's a law Down Under," I was assured. "Wait till you meet 'Street Dog' and 'Show Pony.' And the worst isn't here, either, 'Barrier Reef.' "

A large oval table had been set and some wonderful wine poured. People loosened up. Sir Hugo tactfully kept Nunc at his elbow but placed Bingo strategically just opposite, cleverly drawing him again and again into the table chat.

"Never drink weeknights," Nunc announced, "but just this once."

He'd been knocking back the Scotch and now the wine, becoming garrulous, spinning yarns about enormous feats with this "lad" or that. He was off on some tale of skiing at North Conway back in the long-thong era when a Grottnex lawyer, about Nunc's age, asked:

"And was Leslie Spruance one of your gang back then, Elmer?"

"Oh yes," said Nunc, expansive and pawing his nose, "a great lad. He and I shared many an adventure. Why, once . . ."

The lawyer cleared his throat. "Leslie was a girl, Elmer, tall, lanky brunette . . ."

"Oh, *that* Leslie Spruance," Nunc mumbled, diving back into the wine.

Bingo cheered up, always pleased to have Nunc make an ass of himself, and was enthusiastically comparing notes with Sir Hugo on the relative virtues of Savile Row tailors. I didn't drink as much as normally I would, not wanting to let down the side, and nervous about Bingo, wondering if Savile Row would lead him into jolly accounts of life among the fashion designers, tales of Tiny Meat et al. Then someone asked Grottnex about the current value of the dollar and the economic outlook, the sort of comfortable talk rich men enjoy. Sir Hugo had somewhat diffidently launched into a soft-spoken but impressive *tour d'horizon*, when Bingo suddenly interrupted.

"Elmer?"

"Yes?"

"I have a very important question, Elmer."

Grottnex tensed, wondering if the family feud were about to be reignited at the very moment of his triumph.

"Yes?" Nunc repeated vaguely, confused and groping at his nose.

"Elmer, how old do you have to be to stop being a 'lad'?"

When I got home Babe was sitting up in bed, looking lush despite reading glasses, a bar exam cram text on her lap, one spaghetti strap of her nightgown slipped provocatively off a shoulder.

"How went the banquet?"

I told her about Bingo and Nunc. About Old Blue Rinse and Street Dog and the Red Peril. And about the Wallpaper King.

"It sounds heaven. Why don't you ever take me to parties like that?"

"Cheer up," I said, savoring the surprise I'd nursed until I was sure it was on. "I'm taking you to France. Ballooning with Malcolm Forbes. In June."

She dropped the book.

"Shark! A real hot-air untethered balloon, honest?"

"I guess so. That's how it's billed."

"Hey, maybe they'll let me take a parachute up and you can watch me jump."

I was already a bit nervous about a simple balloon flight, and she wanted to jump out of the damned thing.

Babe grabbed my arm and pulled me down next to her in the bed.

"Let me brush my teeth first," I said, remembering the postdinner cigars.

"Shut up, Shark, and let me worry about your teeth."

That's how she was, an easy girl to please. A week in France, a hot-air balloon ride, maybe a parachute jump, and she didn't care about your breath.

"Making love," she murmured as I undressed, "isn't a Crest commercial."

72 ⊡ *It would have been such fun visiting Clive in prison.*

HUGO GROTTNEX had barely been digested when further disaster loomed.

"Close the door. I don't want this out."

I glanced about furtively as I usually did, knowing it unnerved Bingo. He got up from behind the big desk and skipped across the carpet with a newspaper clipping in hand.

"Just look at this. Clive Neville arrested in London. They caught him in the bushes with a young guardsman."

I took the clipping. For once, Bingo was approximately accurate. There had been an arrest, the preliminary charges were sodomy and public lewdness, the place was Hyde Park.

"It says the young man was a greengrocer's apprentice."

"Whatever," Bingo said airily. "In the best literature it's always a young guardsman. Oscar Wilde and so on."

"I'm sure you're right."

"Of course I am. Clive's too much of a snob to tamper with a green-grocer's apprentice." He paused, brow creased in thought. "Though with those tight trousers guardsmen wear, it's a wonder they can do any-thing."

"It says he's out on bail and isn't supposed to leave England."

"He must be awfully pleased. He so loves England."

"But under these circumstances . . . ?"

Marsh was up again. And skipping. "Perhaps a committee should be formed. You know, 'Set Clive Neville free!' as they did with that fellow who was going to blow up Parliament . . ."

"Guy Fawkes?"

"No, the Irishman in World War One, Roger Casement. Wasn't he gay as well? I believe they hanged him or something."

"Yes, it was wartime and . . ."

". . . and a defense fund established. Not that Clive can't very well hire his own lawyers, but there's always something civic-minded about raising money for a noble cause and not just for the Jews or cancer."

"He might prefer the less said the better."

"No, that's out of the question. Brooke Astor should certainly be approached. And Laurance Rockefeller. David's too stuffy. And Pamela Harriman. And the Trump woman, the one married to the brother and not that tacky Hungarian . . ."

"I believe she's Czech."

". . . and editorials. We'll run one in *Fashion* of course, suggesting encroachment . . ."

"Entrapment?"

". . . or a momentary lapse of some sort. A midlife crisis and mention how vital Clive's work is to the nation. And so on. Weren't there all sorts of editorials, and quite effective, too, when that Jewish general was sent to Devil's Island for stealing the war plans?"

"Captain Dreyfus?"

"That's the fellow! I remember seeing a movie about him once, where they tore off his epaulets right there in front of everyone. Givenchy did an entire collection with epaulets one season, a brilliant collection that sold exceedingly well. I'm sure he saw the same movie."

"Well, actually, it was an historic event in France, and as a young French boy in school Givenchy probably . . ."

"They'll steal a good idea from anyone, designers."

Now his eyes filmed over a bit, possibly recalling details of the Givenchy collection that featured epaulets. I nudged him back.

"But you were planning to clear Neville's name and save him from jail."

"Yes. And so we shall. Wasn't there a very important book about Colonel Dreyfus, *I Deny* or some such?"

"*J'Accuse,*" I said. "*I Accuse.*"

"Yes, by Proust."

"Emile Zola. It's quite famous, you . . ."

"Whatever. Perhaps Princess Diana would testify. Clive claims he's been asked to the palace more than once. Hardy Amies and Mary Quant, as well."

"Well . . ."

"Is Nan Kempner in town? She's on more committees than Mario Buatta. And certainly Suzy must do a column about poor Clive . . ."

"And Liz Smith."

Marsh looked at me sternly. "Liz and Suzy do not get on. Either you have Suzy saving Neville from prison or you have Liz do it. You do not have *both*."

The greengrocer's apprentice, or young guardsman, or whatever he was, was paid off and declined to testify, and Clive Neville, somewhat subdued, returned safely to New York, where Bingo immediately gave a small dinner party to celebrate his escape while, at the same time, regretting the thing had blown over so swiftly.

"It would have been such fun visiting Clive in prison and sending him things." He stopped, his face solemn.

"Why do you think the British spell 'gaol' like that instead of 'jail'?"

"I have no idea."

Bingo buzzed his secretary. "Mrs. K., phone Mr. Neville and ask him why they spell prison 'gaol.' "

"Yes, Mr. Marsh," the woman said. I believe she drank at night. I hope so.

73 ▣ *. . . an Australian. The loud kind, a disheveled Errol Flynn.*

BINGO really tried to work with (or more accurately, *for*) Hugo Grottnex. He really did. But he was bleeding inside. For nearly twenty years the magazine had been his baby. Now social workers from the foster home had taken it away. On the first Monday after the takeover he called me into his office and pointedly shut the door. There was no skip in his gait.

"Would it be appropriate to introduce Sir Hugo to a few of the more presentable designers?"

I didn't know. "Just which ones?"

"Well, Blass, he's polite."

"He might start telling Grottnex about firemen, about hoses and phallic symbolism . . ."

"Yes, there's that."

"What about Ralph Lauren?" I suggested.

"Oh, he'd just talk about merrie old England, the moors and the grouse, and how he admires Fred Astaire."

"Beene?"

"Geoffrey's too fat. I don't want Sir Hugo to think that's what designers are like."

"Too bad Norman Delavan is no longer with us," I said. "He could tell Grottnex about the geese."

"Don't be malicious."

In the end Grottnex didn't meet any of the fashion designers, nor did he evince any interest in so doing. His empire, even beyond the pasteless wallpaper that covered half of Europe on both sides of the Iron Curtain, now comprised more than forty publications and a range of television and other properties, and *Fashion*, while a desirable asset with a very good cash flow, was hardly his only concern. But he was a good businessman; he kept in touch:

By imposing Barrier Reef on us. This time both Ambrose and I were summoned urgently to Bingo's side.

"There's this man Sir Hugo is sending down, a legate so to speak, to function as overseer. His name's Nigel Reef. I understand he's Australian."

"Barrier Reef," I said.

"A friend of yours?" Marsh said in surprise.

"Only by reputation."

Ambrose wasn't pleased. While the magazine didn't have a general manager's title, that was pretty much what Ambrose did, look after money and personnel and manage.

"You sound like Nunc," Bingo told him. "Don't be so picky. We've all got to make adjustments. Even I."

Barrier Reef was indeed an Australian. The loud kind, a disheveled Errol Flynn.

"Mates," he informed the staff on their first meeting, "I've worked everywhere from tea boy at the *South China Morning Post* to head reporter in Sydney to general manager on Fleet Street. So if anyone bloody comes the acid with me, I'll know about it." "To come the acid," we learned, meant phonying an alibi.

To Ambrose's undisguised glee, Reef had no intention of devoting himself exclusively to personnel and finance; he would be looking over all our shoulders. Marsh, his titular superior, took to ducking into anterooms and offices when he saw him coming. Barrier was, we soon learned, truculent, loud, and a drunk. He was, however, very good at his trade, watching expenses and cracking down on waste. He could sniff out a phony business lunch receipt the way nuns smell out sin. Even Pinsky, another thoroughgoing professional, gave him grudging respect.

"If Pinsky approves, that's approval," he confided to me after two weeks of Barrier Reef. "Like? Pinsky does not hastily award 'like.' "

I went drinking with Reef one night and thereby earned his confidence. Leaning boozily close, he inquired, "And how do you put up with all the poofters, mate?"

"Poofters? Poofters?" Bingo demanded indignantly next morning. "Does he mean fairies?"

"I think he does."

"Well, then, many of my closest friends are 'poofters.' And Ames."

Cap'n Andy, the office manager, eager to suck up to the new power, pulled Reef aside to say how he admired direct action, how he himself broke in by checking the men's room toilets for shirking copyboys. Barrier gave the Cap'n little encouragement.

"Don't let me bloody well catch you at narrow dealing either, mate."

Once Sir Hugo Grottnex and a small entourage descended for Bingo's weekly editorial luncheon in the rubbed-wood dining room, at which senior editors and writers sat in, Marsh presided, and the previous week's issue was dissected and the next discussed. It was usually, barring Bingo's eccentric judgments and pronouncements, a fairly tweedy, relaxed, clubby affair, everything but the vintage port going 'round the table. Sir Hugo listened to it all, laughed heavily once or twice at intramural joshing, made a sensible comment or two, thanked us and left.

Only Marsh, all the Marsh family paranoia in full flight, was unsettled. He'd noticed that one of Grottnex's aides de camp, the Red Peril, had taken notes throughout.

"I could see him," he told me. "Shorthand. He was taking everything down, every word said."

"Fleet Street trains journalists that way," I said. "Probably just a reflex action, taking a few notes."

"They're checking on us. They're checking up. I know it."

I left Bingo to fret. Babe and I were leaving in early June for France, and I gave the Red Peril's shorthand no further thought.

74 ▣ *French workmen and idlers called to her.*

THERE was no wind at all, not even a breeze.

That surprised me. In Normandy there was always wind, but now, nothing. And when the propane burner was switched off, no sound, just the huge balloon floating silent above green fields and hedgerows and darker green stands of wood, at precisely the speed of the air itself. There was no resistance. Bombard, the professional balloonist, lighted a match.

"See, it doesn't even flicker."

I stood braced against the side of the wicker basket of the hot-air balloon as it sailed across northern France toward the Channel over small farms and the occasional château and old battlefields. With me were Bombard and a rather pretty English girl with a title I hadn't caught and a brigadier of the Pakistani army. To my surprise, I was enjoying myself.

Perhaps that was simply a function of temporary release from Bingo's asylum.

"Look!"

The brigadier grabbed my arm, pointing down. A hundred feet below, a big boar, all tusk and snout, crashed through the forest, dodging the bigger trees and snapping off saplings and branches, running fast and looking competent and mean.

"I say!" said the Englishwoman, leaning out to see.

I nodded happily. The brigadier was lean and brown and terribly Sandhurst, but he was excited.

"You know, I've never before seen one, full grown. Not even in the Kashmir."

A grin split his narrow, mahogany face, not at all "Sandhurst" now. I suspected I, too, was grinning.

"Don't lean out too far," Bombard cautioned, laughing, "you don't want to meet that fellow at close range."

How far from New York and the world of Bingo Marsh.

Babe and I flew Air France to Paris and then took the train down to

Caen. We were stabled at the Château de Balleroy, Malcolm's place, in a bedroom without a bath under the eaves four or five creaky flights up. Babe examined the place before nodding in satisfaction.

"Not bad, Shark. When do we get to meet Elizabeth Taylor?"

"After we get some sleep." We'd been traveling for fifteen or sixteen hours. The platformed bed, narrow but comfortable, was sufficient.

"I've slept worse," Babe admitted.

That first evening was informal, with half Forbes's guests not yet arrived. Miss Taylor would not come down from Paris until next morning when Malcolm's jet, "The Capitalist Tool," would fly her in to Caen airport along with a personal assistant, a hairdresser, a hairdresser's assistant, and several tame photographers. Henry Grunwald of *Time*, like us an early arrival, told Forbes in considerable delight, "Malcolm, do you know that in Bayeux there is a supermarket called 'le Conquérant'?"

William the Conqueror had sailed from Bayeux to conquer England, and the locals had never forgotten.

The Comtesse de Breteuil came from Marrakesh, where she had a house. Someone else mentioned having been there once, staying with Yves Saint Laurent. "Yves now has *two* pools," said the comtesse, wickedly, "one for him; one for everyone else. He insists on swimming alone."

By some miracle the Normandy sun continued to shine, and I went up in one of the first flights, and saw the wild boar.

That night there was a welcoming dinner under a striped marquee, with Norman horns and dancers. People drifted in late, muddied balloonists whose flights had outdistanced their chase cars and trucks. Some had landed in cultivated fields, heavy with manure, where they placated irate farmers with bottles of chilled champagne flown along for the purpose. Most people were up at dawn the next day. Dawn and late afternoon were the best time to fly, when the updrafts were strongest. Babe flew with one of the teams, Dutchmen, all three of whom promptly declared their undying devotion to her.

"We had a few beers up there, Shark," she admitted.

The revels continued for three days, and on Monday morning we took the train up to Paris and stayed in one of the attic rooms of the Hotel San Regis, where they had beds that were not at all narrow and Babe was better able to exhibit her agility, properly to thank me for having taken her along. She'd never been to Paris and liked to stand in the French doors looking out over the roofs and the chimneys and the little *balcons* under the spring sky, but since she liked to do this wearing very little, or occasionally nothing, French workmen and idlers called to her from distant rooftops and balconies. She waved back enthusiastically.

"I like the French," she said, "really friendly. Not anti-American or hostile to strangers the way you always read."

I took her to places I liked, restaurants and bars and parks and bookstores and bridges I remembered and loved. She was pleased that I wanted her to see these places, too.

"I like it you know all these things and all those famous people we met at Balleroy," she said, "but it doesn't change you, make you phony or impressed. You just say 'Hi' and shake hands and that's it."

"Well, I guess so."

"I like that, Shark."

Babe was also enthusiastic about Chez Lipp, on the Left Bank, where we ate choucroute and the cold beer came in glasses classified by size as "*sérieux*" and "*distinguée*" and so on.

"I like the '*sérieux*' best," she said. "The '*distinguée*' tends to intimidate."

"It looks as if you like the choucroute pretty well, too."

Choucroute was sausage and ham and potatoes and 'kraut, boiled in the style of the Alsace, eaten with globs of hot mustard and washed down with beer.

"I do, you know. I could eat here every day. Are they open for breakfast?"

"Breakfast? Choucroute for breakfast?" It was difficult to visualize.

"Sure," she said, "it has all the basic requirements of vitamins and minerals. Just like Total."

"Have another '*sérieux*,' " I said.

I saved Chanel for near the end, taking her to the boutique of the Maison Chanel on the rue Cambon, where I bought her one of those trademark quilted leather handbags. While it was being wrapped, I showed Babe the mirrored stairs at the top of which on lazy, drunken afternoons the old lady fed me Scotch and ran fingers through my hair and whispered, "Mon Indien, mon petit Indien . . ."

"She really loved you, didn't she, Shark?"

"In a way, I guess, she must have."

We crossed the street to the small bar of the Ritz, another shrine revisited, and had a martini.

"To your Coco," Babe said, lifting the glass.

I drank.

"And to us . . . ," she said, leaving doors ajar.

I should have said something meaningful then but didn't. This was the best girl I'd ever had, the best friend as well as lover. And still I backed away. Her career, my careless ways, these were the excuses. I knew the real reason, that empty place into which I retreated, unready for commitment, wary of taking risks.

75 ▣ A *Paul Profonde* collection is a powerful mystical experience.

DESPITE his own awkward, sometimes goofy, behavior, George Bush was clearly leading a Dukakis proving earnest but inept, so much so Marsh was already preparing himself for his role in the new Administration, almost ready to forgive Mr. Bush for Dan Quayle. Though not quite.

"When they have cabinet meetings, does the Vice President attend? I certainly hope not. Snubbing him privately is one thing; doing it in front of everyone wouldn't be polite."

But as November neared, no summons arrived from the Bush crusade.

There were other pressures on Bingo, changing him, and not for the better. Perhaps nothing more brutally illuminated how he was changing than the absurd, yet cruel, business of the French designer Paul Profonde.

Nunc and Barrier Reef had been seen carousing of an evening ("plotting, I suppose," Bingo concluded). Sir Hugo, though rarely seen, was now very much owner of his beloved magazine (graffiti scrawled in the elevator, "Don't Glue! Grottnex!" sent Marsh home ill at three one afternoon). Perhaps it was simply midlife crisis, one symptom a dinner Bingo hosted for the Trumps.

"You can't stand Ivana. And you're having them for dinner?"

"John, I'm certainly free to entertain friends. And Ames."

A new set of values. And now, *"l'affaire Profonde,"* as the snippier Paris dailies labeled it. No one was quite sure which was cause, which effect, or just why Marsh went suddenly so sour on the designer.

Around the magazine it had long been said, behind his back, of course: "Paul Profonde cuts a skirt on the bias and Bingo has an orgasm." Profonde, known to the fashion intellectuals as Pipi, had for a dozen years been one of the top men in Paris, up there with Saint Laurent and Ungaro and Cardin and Givenchy. I once asked Marsh why Paul was so good, why *Fashion* and the other leading magazines had so canonized him.

Bingo gave me a long-winded lecture which culminated in something that at least sounded genuine: "Seeing a Paul Profonde collection is a powerful mystical experience."

I had visions of Saul of Tarsus being struck from his horse on the Damascus road and said so, earning me from Marsh an exceedingly bleak look.

Even in seasons when Profonde's work was somewhat off, *Fashion* raved. There were theories, of course: the two men were lovers; through Pipi's manager Gerant they'd invested great sums jointly in financial enterprises; or, less subtly, a numbered Swiss account to which Marsh had the second key. To anyone who really knew Bingo, such murky explanations were rubbish. Pipi was a wonderful fashion designer, and Marsh recognized this and liked and admired the Frenchman and had for a long time. What came between them was never satisfactorily explained. Some said Pipi's snub of a ceremony enrolling Bingo into the Légion d'Honneur for services rendered to French exports; others held Profonde objected to an adjective in a recent *Fashion* line review.

Marsh announced the outbreak of hostilities at his weekly editorial meeting.

"Pipi is finished," he said, getting up from his chair and doing a mirthful skip, "and there's a new man to be crowned. His name is Christian Lacroix."

Barrier Reef, lounging in a corner of the room, hung over and bored by talk of matters alien, came to life. Accustomed to the rough-and-tumble of the Fleet Street tabloids, he understood regicide and king-making.

"And what's this deity's name again, mate?"

"La-croix," Bingo said slowly and in some irritation, "a brilliant young man of whom you will shortly hear more. Much more."

He didn't lie. In the next issue there was a Lacroix cover and six pages inside, ten days before his new collection was to be shown in Paris. The cover photo was of a Lacroix invention of two seasons back, now updated, the pouff dress.

"But how do you sit in the bloody thing, mate?" Reef demanded.

A week later, four more pages of Lacroix with comments from top buyers and elegant women everywhere, all of them frantic in their praise of the new star. No mention of Paul Profonde, none. The following issue had Lacroix himself on the cover, smiling broadly, arms entwined around the slender waists of two models in pouff dresses. Inside, an editorial signed by Bingo declaring Lacroix a genius in the tradition of Dior, Balenciaga, Chanel.

There was no coverage whatever of Pipi's new line, which the *Times* called brilliant and everyone else quite good.

Asked how the magazine could afford to ignore Profonde totally, Bingo remarked piously, "It's only decent, the man's gone down so. It would be cruel to chronicle his decline."

John Fairchild's *Women's Wear Daily* ridiculed Bingo for trying to play God. Another rival editor assailed him for "making a fashion king out of an obscure male seamstress named Christian Lacroix." *USA Today* did a lip-smacking, gossipy account:

"Why is Bingo Marsh so cross?" meowed the headline.

Monsieur Gerant, Pipi's manager, announced *Fashion* magazine was now banned from the house. "One does not invite criminals into one's home." Faye Dunaway, a faithful client of Profonde, was photographed wearing a Lacroix. "I adore Lacroix," she said diplomatically, "but Pipi is king." The First Lady confided in Zizi Orlando, "I'd love to wear a pouff. It would be marvelous with my legs. But give Bingo Marsh the satisfaction?" Jackie Onassis went right ahead and bought a Lacroix. Bingo wrote the front-page headline himself: "Her Elegance Goes Pouff!"

In Paris Paul Profonde went underground, shunning his usual table at Lipp, his other haunts.

"He's dying of something," Bingo said darkly. Other papers picked up rumors about Pipi's health. I smelled Marsh's influence and challenged him.

"I don't just make these things up," he told me in an injured tone.

"But you do, Bingo. You're forever making things up. Most times it's all good fun. But planting rumors a man's dying isn't fun anymore. Think of his friends, of his business."

"Well, I didn't make this up. Maybe I do, sometimes, but not about Pipi. And my instincts are often very good, even when there's no proof."

Now, almost miraculously, firsthand proof there was something seriously wrong with the designer. A French eyewitness was found, not someone cooked up by Bingo but real, a petit bourgeois, middle-aged functionary who lived in the rue des Acacias near Paul Profonde's apartment, who claimed to have had a frightening encounter with the designer the preceding weekend, babbling about "a great, hairy rascal that leaped out at one!"

Marsh spent hours on the transatlantic phone to get the neighbor to recount his adventures to a lawyer in front of a notary, a transcript received by telex at the office:

"My wife and I had just emerged toward midnight from the cinema, a rather entertaining trifle by Besson, no plot to speak of but an amusing film, when suddenly, coming out of the shadows, and you know how the trees are along there, I saw this hunched, distended figure, long-haired, grotesquely bloated, snuffling and grunting, lurching toward us. I recoiled, not knowing if we were to be attacked. My wife cowered behind me, as a woman does, *tu sais*, whimpering and telling her beads, but the thing shambled past without doing harm, perhaps seeking more vulnerable victims, hurrying into the night, and it was only then as it passed that in the light of a street lamp I saw it in full profile. It was, *messieurs/dames*, our most celebrated neighbor, a man well known ('*bien connu*') in the *quartier*. The monster was monsieur Paul Profonde!"

Bingo was desperate to run the neighbor's account on a full page in large type facing another full-page sketch of the scene by our art department.

"Just read this, Tyson," he told Rambush, the art director. When Tyson had read the report, he handed it back, eyes rolling toward the back of his head. Marsh, at his most winning, inquired, "Tyson, what do you think Pipi would look like at midnight if he came at you and your wife in this way outside the movies and was all swollen up and hairy and galloping at you, frothing and such?"

Rambush, who had no wife, said he would work up a few sketches.

"Tyson's wonderful," Marsh enthused, "he always knows precisely what to do."

Neither story nor sketch ever ran. The lawyers protested. Always before, Bingo had his way. But these were Sir Hugo's lawyers.

"No bloody way, mate," Barrier Reef informed Marsh. "That's bloody actionable on the face of it. And malice besides."

Disconsolate, Bingo continued to hammer Profonde and to puff Lacroix in the magazine until, out of patience, Pipi canceled his advertising contract. Substantial money but Marsh shrugged it off. "Church and state, church and state," he told people.

Grottnex's money man, Old Blue Rinse, wasn't as cavalier, but, unable to confront an evasive Marsh, he took it out on the rest of us.

"That's nearly a million dollars American, mate, a million out the bloody door with the trash."

"It's how he's always run the magazine," I said. "You lose a few ads from time to time but controversy causes talk and builds readership and the increased circulation brings in more ads. Lots of them."

Old Blue Rinse looked bleak. "I'm all for bringing in more ads but not losing what you've bloody got."

Profonde chose this moment to shut down production of a marginal perfume.

"Pipi's perfume stinks up bottom line," *Fashion* gleefully headlined the event.

When I grumbled, I got little consolation from Babe.

"Find a grown-up job. It isn't healthy. *Marsh* isn't healthy."

I was growing tired of defending Bingo. A few years earlier the battle with Paul Profonde would have been fought with imagination and irony; not with this heavy-handed adulation of a nearly unknown rival and virtual censorship of Pipi. I remembered another Bingo, giddy and giggling, skipping about the room and reminding me we got paid for having fun while so many others were employed at joyless work.

"I miss that Bingo," I told her, but she hadn't known him then.

Now I was to suffer another loss.

76 ▣ *Lunatics like Marsh and girls like me . . .*

I came home one evening to find Babe sitting on the kitchen floor with the "faction cleenar" taken apart in what seemed hundreds of oily pieces.

"It's very simple, as easy as field-stripping a weapon. Your average small electric appliance is as basic a device as the fulcrum and lever. Pure mechanical advantage. Even you ought to be able to handle something like this, Shark."

It was a warm night, and she was sweaty and smudged with oil.

"Shark?"

Her voice had changed.

"Yeah?"

"I got my posting. My overseas assignment."

Something fell heavily inside me.

"Oh?"

She continued to look down, studying the vacuum cleaner with extraordinary concentration.

"Yeah, Manila. The twentieth of next month. Legal officer handling civilian claims against American military forces."

"Babe," I said.

"Yeah," she said, "great, isn't it?"

Tears were coming down her cheeks, and I started to cry, too.

"Look," I said, "you can always . . ."

"No," she said, shaking her head. "I've been after this two years, Shark. I gotta take it. I gotta go . . ."

Had it been two years? Had we been together that long? And never seriously considered the future . . . ?

First, Bingo. Now Babe.

Her face glistened with tears, but she was smiling. Or trying to.

We both knew the day would come; it was something she was forever rattling on about; but when it happened I never thought it would be like this. Babe was caught up in the frenzy, the rush, the excitement. She had that. I had only a yawning emptiness.

If ever I were going to commit myself . . .

Instead, I fell back on shopworn, superficial concerns.

"It's the worst time for it to happen. Bingo going nuts and Australians crawling all over the place and now you're leaving . . ."

I despised myself for not saying more, for not being honest, the old fear of hurt, abandonment, too powerful.

She'd stopped crying, I guess reckoning this was all she was going to get from me, maybe that I wasn't worth tears.

"Shark," she said, all cheer now, "get yourself a life. Lunatics like Marsh and girls like me . . ."

She was right. She and Marsh, some pair. And I loved them both.

Babe didn't believe in wasting time. She had four weeks to wrap up her affairs in New York and travel ten thousand miles to a new job, a new life, and there she was at Berlitz on Fifty-seventh Street taking a crash course in Tagalog.

"I can skim by in Spanish. But I've got very little Tagalog."

Bingo, as he usually did, had somehow learned she was leaving.

"I know you'll miss her, John, but she wasn't really ever your sort."

Babe gave me instructions about the maid.

"Now don't yell at her. Try to be nice, huh? She's a good ol' gal trying to make her way with the 'faction cleenar,' and she doesn't need grief."

I didn't know what to do to celebrate our last days together. "Celebrate" was hardly the word to use anyway; "memorialize" was more like it, but that sounded morbid.

As the time approached, she got more cheerful, and I didn't.

"This legal stuff can't possibly occupy all my time," she said.

"No, there's probably a pretty active social life," I said gloomily, reeking with self-pity.

"Oh, hell, Shark, that isn't what I mean. I'm talking about getting upcountry, bandit territory, seeing the rebels on their own ground, that sort of thing."

"You be damned careful of those rebels."

"Sure, sure, come on, I'm the career military officer, you know, not some feather merchant like you. Besides, it could be Manila's the place to hang around. They say Cory is out of it, there could be a coup anytime. That'd be something," she said, a dreamy look coming over her face, "a real live coup d'état with jets screaming in over the palace

and tanks whamming away at one another on the main drag and the
paras coming in from the hills shooting up the town and the American
Embassy under siege and Marines running around and roadblocks being
set up and people on balconies tossing Molotov cocktails and . . ."

"Babe," I said.

"Yes, Shark?"

"Babe, this is Manila you're going to. Not West Beirut."

She looked thoughtful.

"I could get lucky," she said.

77 □ *The decline of decency and civility*
in America . . .

IF the Paul Profonde affair opened the eyes of Sir Hugo Grottnex, Marsh
was also learning about Sir Hugo.

"He thinks we should have television stars on the cover. People I
never even heard of. Some black woman, even. 'Opera' something . . ."

"Oh, dear, a black person on *Fashion?*

"It's not funny, John. I have nothing against blacks. Ames and I
always watch Bill Cosby, and didn't I give the African Queen his start?
And we're always doing stories on Patrick Kelly and other talented colored people . . ."

Marsh said he told Grottnex the magazine quite frequently ran celebrity covers.

"Oh, quite right," Sir Hugo had responded, "but this Donna Karan
person no one ever heard of . . . ?"

Bingo was apoplectic. "Can you imagine, not knowing who Donna
is?"

"Did you tell him?" I said.

"Of course not. I'm not getting into unseemly debates over cover
stories."

That was Bingo, carping and whining to people who worked for him,
but refusing to stand up to Grottnex. It was his way, how he'd always
been. When Old Blue Rinse came around, sniffing over the books,

Bingo ordered all of us to deny we kept records. "He's prying and snooping. And he'll just tell Nunc everything."

Then came the officers' meeting on Paradise Island, a three-day event in the Bahamas at which Grottnex and his senior aides talked business and planned the year ahead.

"He wants me to go," Bingo announced in a panic.

"Of course he does. You run one of his finest properties, and he wants to show you off to the other top people in his company."

"No one goes to Paradise Island except gangsters and cheap hookers. A dreadful, vulgar place. Now if it were Lyford Cay . . ."

But greater atrocities were planned. "Hugo wants me to come to dinner. And Ames."

Dinner was but the opening wedge. There were evenings at the theater and weekends at his country place and black-tie events at which Grottnex had purchased a table. I suspected such invitations might come as something of a divertissement for Mrs. Marsh. Bingo, the snob, agonized.

"Well, just tell him you can't go. Or won't."

He was contemptuous of Sir Hugo but too timid to say so.

Nigel Reef, more commonly "Barrier," became the cross we all bore, taking it on himself to counsel me solicitously in affairs of the heart, appalling poor Bingo with his cheerful vulgarity.

Somehow he'd learned of Babe's flight, of my solitary nights.

"Ought to get yourself someone, y'know. Man was not meant to abide alone. Nothing wrong with a good wank once in a while, but not every night."

A "wank" was masturbation, or as Barrier delicately put it, "a date with merry fist."

I asked Marsh if he knew about "wanking" and got an extremely pained "Oh, dear" in response." Then, brightening, "At times like this don't you miss Olivier? It's a word he'd surely like."

Reef certainly did not "abide alone." He was out drinking most nights and had found a woman. We were told there was a wife in Sydney. Or in London. Perhaps both. Now he had a girl, tall and pale and gaunt, with deep, smudged eyes. Her name around the office, a name Reef himself had bestowed, was Deadly Nightshade. We met one morning with Reef and Old Blue Rinse, the money man. Reef looked terrible most mornings, but on this occasion especially so. When he left the room briefly Marsh inquired, solicitously, "Is he well? He looks drained."

"Well," said Old Blue Rinse, "if you closed the pubs every night and then for a couple of hours the Deadly Nightshade sat on your face, you'd bloody well look bad, too."

Bingo adjourned the meeting shortly after and left the building.

Beset by Australians, afraid of Grottnex, his magazine slipping away, Marsh lapsed into depression. Ambrose and I, perhaps other friends, attempted to divert him, even at this late date to broaden horizons. Occasionally he came out of his funk, shaking off despair, to be again for a brief, shining moment the old, silly Bingo we loved.

We'd lunched, and Bingo and I were standing at adjoining urinals in the Racquet Club, "doing number one."

"Ugh," said Bingo, "there's a cockroach."

"Yes," I said. It was undeniably so, a small, brown cockroach scuttling across the tile.

"You ought to do a column about it. 'The decline of decency and civility in America . . .' Something along those lines."

"Bingo," I said, zipping my fly, "it's your club. Do you really want to trash it?"

"But it's so tacky having cockroaches in the little boys' room. And what's the purpose of having a magazine if you don't use it constructively, to improve the quality of life?"

I shrugged, not intending to do a column about cockroaches, just wanting to torment him.

"Members will blame you, you know. They'll see the column and make connections. Could be unpleasant for you . . ."

"I don't care," he said, stubborn as a child being told not to get his feet wet.

Then, as we exited the men's room, Marsh stopped. He'd gone pale.

"Wait a minute. Is Sir Hugo a member here? He'd be upset if you wrote anything . . ."

A year ago Bingo wouldn't have been prey to such doubt. He'd have been confident of his ability to slip out from under by lying, by saying someone planted the cockroach story, that he'd been out of town, or stricken with tumors.

Now the hand of Grottnex, the Wallpaper King, lay heavy on his soul.

78 ⊡ *Is Cristina Ford still around?*

MY soul, too, was leaden. Babe flown west, the apartment had never been as empty, nor had I. I signed up for piano lessons. Lonely, I purchased a dog. It bit me. I began accepting weekend invitations. At a barbecue in the Hamptons, hot dogs and burgers and jolly good fun, I asked the wife of a friend to dance.

"Oh no," she said. "Those baked beans. I'm afraid I'll fart."

Out of desperation I did what Babe, I thought, cured me of: I dated a cover girl.

She was six feet tall and her name was Niki and the fashion magazines described her as having Christie Brinkley's hair, Christy Turlington's cat-eyes and cheekbones, and Elle Macpherson's body. I met her after a Todd Oldham fashion show and asked if she'd like to meet me that evening for a drink and go uptown to Elaine's.

"Well, I don't drink much, Mr. Sharkey," she said. "My mom doesn't let me."

It turned out she was sixteen years old. We didn't go uptown to Elaine's. I wasn't quite yet ready to turn into P.J. le Boot.

To get away, as much as to salvage Marsh, I volunteered, along with Ambrose, to travel with him. Ambrose's turn came first, dinners in the South with executives from Stevens and Milliken and West Point Pepperell, seeking their business.

"At one place the waitress chilled a red Bordeaux and Bingo went mental. 'No problem, mister,' she said, and started warming it over a candle."

On one trip Marsh wanted to attend services on Sunday morning but couldn't find an Episcopal church. I suggested he drop into the Catholic church across from our hotel, the ritual being quite similar.

Bingo regarded me tolerantly. "Don't try to lull me, John. I've seen *The Exorcist,* and I know all about those ushers standing just inside the door sprinkling holy water on people. They'll sniff out a non-Catholic in an instant."

"Oh?"

"Yes, when the steam starts rising from the holy water, turning instantly to vapor on Protestants or Jews."

Bingo didn't like Japan, where Grottnex was considering a foreign edition of *Fashion*.

"All that bowing and taking baths with perfect strangers and eating live fish. It's disgusting. I resent having to take my shoes off so often. My shoes are perfectly acceptable in this country; why not there? Lobb makes them."

But it was the bowing that irritated him most. "Have you ever seen three or four Japanese businessmen sharing a limousine? They keep bowing one another toward the door while the driver stands there. Even if it's pouring rain. They bow and they bow and nobody gets in. That's my definition of the slowest thing on earth: four Japs trying to get into one limo."

I wondered whether, while in Japan, he called them "Japs." It wouldn't have been Bingo, otherwise. Still, I did ask.

"Why shouldn't I? We won the war, didn't we?"

He also got the Chinese and the "Japs" mixed up, and declined to visit China on an official junket of American journalists and business leaders.

"Maybe the Chinks didn't attack Pearl Harbor. But they were certainly capable of it."

On his return Ambrose and I gave it yet another old college try.

We talked Bingo into going to a World Series game with us. I wangled an invitation for both of us to the Gridiron Dinner in Washington. Ambrose introduced him to a justice of the Supreme Court, and I recommended books he might read.

His ignorance remained invincible.

"Clive Neville says Elizabeth Taylor has regular electrolysis treatments or else she'd have a clearly discernible mustache. It all comes of taking hormone treatments for her back problems."

For all his Yale education, he really did share the mentality of people who bought magazines at supermarket checkouts.

"I draw the line at UFO's or that Hitler is really still alive in Argentina," he told me once, "but I believe firmly in dowsing rods and ghosts."

He'd seen a ghost himself, once. "And Ames. We were staying with friends in a manor house in Kent and playing with a Ouija board and there were the usual rappings and creaking noises and mysterious moans you always get in an old house and then our hostess said, 'Hark!' and clear as you are to me now, a nun walked through the wall and across the room and out the other side, rattling her beads and sobbing. Most amazing thing."

"They were serving brandy at the time?"

"No, actually," Bingo said, oblivious to sarcasm, "it was a very decent old port."

He was trying to get the Big Three automakers to spend more advertising money in the magazine and we flew to Detroit for a lunch at some prestigious club where auto executives gathered and they'd arranged a very pleasant private room and an audience of the senior people at Ford. The Ford executives were smooth, making the introductions, appending charming little grace notes of background for each man. Then Bingo introduced our party. When he got to me he said brightly:

"Like Henry Ford himself, Mr. Sharkey is also from the Midwest. From Iowa, the Cornhusker State."

"But isn't Nebraska the Cornhusker . . . ,"one began.

"I'm actually from Ohio," I said, trying to move the conversation along to more constructive lines.

"Whatever," Bingo agreed cheerfully.

Drinks were served around by liveried waiters, and the talk became more general, including a brisk discussion of just which network news people preferred to watch these evenings.

"I always watch CBS," Bingo said, as proud as if he owned the network.

"You like Dan Rather?" a Ford man asked, swirling the ice in his glass.

"No, Mr. Paley."

"Friend of yours?"

"I see him around Manhattan," Bingo said, "and he's always very nicely dressed. Well-tailored suits, and his shoes look English."

"Oh?"

"Most television people wear blazers and such. Mr. Paley maintains a certain standard."

"So that's why you watch . . ."

"It's things like that by which we're all judged, don't you think?"

Now the conversation moved on to current headlines, turning at one point to General Noriega and the Panamanian situation. Bingo listened for a few minutes.

"I never understood how canals work," he said, "you know, how water flows uphill just because they have locks."

"Hydraulics, Mr. Marsh, simple hydraulics. But that isn't the root of our problem with Noriega. You see, he's a drug dealer whose government in a few years will take control of the canal under terms of . . ."

"But just *how* does it flow uphill?" Bingo insisted.

A patronizing explanation ensued which seemed to satisfy Marsh. Then, shifting gears, he said, "You know, I think Princess Tiny Meat was originally from Panama. He's some variety of spic, certainly, whatever his name."

"Princess Tiny Meat?" someone asked, wondering what this might have to do with the Canal Zone and Noriega.

"Yes, you know, that's what Fire Island calls him."

Before we left, Bingo distinguished himself with one final, nearly awesome, gaffe.

"Cristina Ford, is she still around? We used to put her in the magazine a lot, so much more fun than Mr. Ford's other wives."

He had these blind spots, totally opaque. Trouble was, he kept sharing his ignorance with others.

"Did you know Paul Newman was Jewish? It certainly stunned me. I realize anyone can have a nose job but those blue eyes . . ."

When Eastern Europe began to stir and tyrants fall, Bingo wondered aloud, "Which Germany is the Commie part?" He thought "Becket" was about the man who wrote *Waiting for Godot*, something else he'd never seen or read. "I believe two men sit in garbage cans and converse. It's an allegory about something but I forget what."

He was quite convinced he had the solution to the AIDS crisis.

"They ought to all stop putting their things in one another's bottoms," he said. "Before I had the fight with Profonde, I told him so. I said, 'Pipi, do something else with your friend if you must, but please stop doing that.' And, you know, I really think if he took my advice he wouldn't be so swollen up today."

Such memorable moments now became all too infrequent as Bingo slid deeper into a personal slough of despond, and even the competition seemed to be ganging up.

Years before he'd talked of *Fashion* as the "new" *Vanity Fair*. And when Condé Nast relaunched a real *Vanity Fair* in the early eighties, he was delighted at how feeble it was.

"Some Alex Liberman sleight of hand on the art direction and a marvelous Hollywood column by Nick Dunne, and that's about it. It was paranoid of me to think it meant trouble."

When the first editor and publisher were dismissed, Bingo rubbed his hands in genuine glee. When old Leo Lerman was seconded from *Vogue*'s "People are talking about . . ." feature to act as interim editor at *Vanity Fair*, Marsh clucked sympathetically. If patronizingly.

"I hope it doesn't tire him unnecessarily. Such a good and faithful servant."

When Newhouse hired Tina Brown, a young Brit then in London editing (at the age of twenty-six) *Tatler*, Bingo welcomed her snidely to New York, calling her "the latest boy wonder." That was 1984. By now, Marsh was no longer rubbing his hands, no longer sympathetic, had ceased being snide. *Vanity Fair* was by now a "hot" book; it was, in fact, what *Fashion* had been ten years before. Tina Brown, virtually alone, had turned a flop into what even Marsh called "un succès fou."

"The most depressing thing that's happened to me since Babe Paley died," he informed friends.

"But, Bingo, it's not as if it's *Vogue*. *Vanity Fair* isn't your competition."

"Of course they are," he insisted.

"But *Vanity Fair* doesn't even cover fashion."

"Of course they do," Marsh shouted. "Fashion isn't clothes. It's . . . it's . . . life!"

Then, one unhappy afternoon and quite innocently, trying to be sociable, Barrier Reef delivered the coup de grace.

He'd dropped by Marsh's office unasked, something that always upset Bingo, and when admitted reluctantly to the presence, perched himself on a corner of Bingo's Louis Quinze table.

"We don't get much chance to talk, mate," said Barrier, "and I thought it might be matey one of these evenings if you and I stopped by a pub, so to speak, and went on the piss together."

I really think that was what did it for Bingo.

79 ▣ *Sows' purses out of silk.*

"I'M quitting," said Bingo Marsh.

I'd been summoned to his place at Arcachon, in southwest France, sixteen hours, two planes, and a rented car from New York. He stood on the doorstep as I drove up the long gravel along the avenue of cedars, unable, or unwilling, to skip the final dozen paces to greet me.

"Emotion is exhausting. And Ames," he said, extending a languorous hand.

In fairness, he looked exhausted. His hair had once been blond and then salt-and-pepper and finally gray, and it was now pure snow. Only a month had passed since last I saw him and his hair had gone suddenly white, dead white, a great shock of it. I was stunned to see how he looked.

Now, voice piping, words spilling out, he catalogued unhappiness, how Grottnex and Nunc and Barrier, with his unwanted intimacy, and even the AIDS crisis and the "pansies" were to blame.

"I'm sending Sir Hugo a short note, courteous but definite. And I'll assuredly wish him and the magazine well."

I was shocked into silence. And we still stood on the doorstep. In ten years it was the first of any of Bingo's houses I'd actually been invited to, and now, after traveling thirty-five hundred miles to get here, it appeared as if I were not to be asked inside.

"Bingo," I said loudly, "I've been driving for a while, and I'd like very much to go inside and to wash up."

"Oh, you mean do number one?"

Ames wasn't with him nor were any of the children, and after being permitted to "do number one" or any of his euphemisms, I was led out onto a splendid verandah overlooking the sea. Our vervain tea came in cups from Moustiers. I didn't know this but was so informed by Marsh. Then a cassis, in special stemware whose name I have already forgotten. The sun fell over the *bassin* toward the still, mirroring water and we sat there under the great pines of the Landes, staring out toward the oyster beds. Jet-lagged, I fear I nodded.

"Yes," said Marsh, "I'm putting all this in writing to Hugo."

I came out of my funk.

"Bingo, you can't quit. This magazine is your baby, your life. But if you go, you've got to tell Grottnex personally. You simply don't do things like this in the mail."

"Oh," he said airily, "I'll send it by hand, by private courier, as Olivier of Hollywood used to send his dirty socks." He looked very pleased with himself.

I bit my tongue, cutting off a taunt, knowing he was afraid of Grottnex and would never go through the trauma of quitting in person. Instead, I resumed trying to change his mind.

"Bingo, the man paid you and Nunc nearly half a billion dollars. Don't you owe him something? You promised to stay on for five years, to run the magazine that makes all the dough. You're the editor and the heart of . . ."

"They'll do very well without me," he said primly.

"Bingo," I said, almost pleading.

He got up now and skipped across the verandah, quite cheery, as if tremendous weights had been shucked off.

". . . and I'll buy that ski resort I've told you about so often. And Ames."

It angered me, this emphasis on *him*, on *his* future, what I saw as dereliction of duty. For ten years I'd worked for this man and his magazine and couldn't imagine either the magazine or my work without him. Glumly, not really expecting an answer, I said, "And just who becomes editor? Barrier Reef? Cap'n Andy?"

"No," Bingo said brightly, "you will."

Now I was the one pacing the polished tile, mine the voice cracking with emotion.

"Bingo . . . ," I stormed in protestation, "I'm a writer. I've never edited . . ."

"There's no one else. Count Vava's got his conspiracies. Madame Stealth is blind. Le Boot, a drunk. The women are hopeless, once a month they stay home and you're not permitted to ask why. No, it's got to be you. You're the only one."

We railed at each other, hashing out arguments. He ended the debate in typical Marsh fashion:

"You can too make sows' purses out of silk."

Eventually he permitted me to surrender to exhaustion and tumble into an upstairs bed, having pointed out the quilt the maid had just turned down had been sewn up by hand by peasant women in the Camargue.

As we breakfasted next morning in the gazebo ("of local manufacture by artisans; hand-wrought and doweled, not a nail to be found in it anywhere") on oranges "flown in daily from Tangier" and wicked black coffee in Giverny cups, Bingo returned to his theme, insisting I had no choice.

"I entreat you to do this for me, John. I realize you're not a trained editor. But you've got taste and brains and instinct. More important, I trust you. I'm leaving the magazine's fate in your hands. Who knows what atrocities might be committed otherwise? Not Grottnex, of course, he's a decent man even if another sort entirely."

This was a new category: not *our* sort but "another sort entirely." But this was no time to prick Marsh's snobbery or indulge myself. His face reflected genuine concern.

"You really do care about the magazine, don't you?"

"Care? *Care?* It's all I care about in the world. And Ames."

"Suppose Grottnex has his own ideas? Suppose he wants Reef as editor?"

"Oh, he values my output," Marsh said, loftily and imprecisely. "He'll name you."

There was more of this, and then I got back in the car to drive to Bordeaux for the plane to Paris. Bingo ordered a servant out into the road to alert me to oncoming traffic, and as I backed the car slowly along the graveled drive, Marsh walked on the grassy verge beside me. I noticed again how white his hair had turned and, subconsciously, raised a hand to run fingers through my own hair. He noticed and smiled, rather shyly, and unlike him.

"Yes," he said, "old. We're getting older."

"Well," I said, looking for words. Bingo saved me from emotion.

"You remember what Hillary said as he started up Everest?"

" 'Because it's there'?" I said, falling in with his jest. But he shook his head, lips pursed.

"No." Then, after a brief pause, and with a joyous shout:

"Tippicanoe and Taylor too!"

He got even that wrong, but my mouth fell gaping, inspiring him to skip happily along the drive.

"See, you didn't think I knew things like that. About history and such . . ."

He'd tried to make a joke, and he loved me for recognizing it. Or so I thought, watching him for a few minutes in the rearview mirror until, small and indistinct, he skipped from sight.

80 ▣ *They'll cheat you, these lads, if they're dead.*

GROTTNEX went along with Marsh, and I was named editor the following week.

My salary was nearly doubled, I was offered Bingo's office (and declined it; you don't dance on graves). I called the staff together to say the obvious, that I wasn't Marsh, nor an editor, but a writer and journalist who believed in them and in this magazine.

"Was Bingo dumped? Did Grottnex fire him?"

Reporters are paid to be skeptics, and I didn't resent the question. "No," I said, "he resigned."

There were sly, knowing looks. At a certain level of celebrity, no one is ever fired; people "resign."

"What's all this stuff about changing the magazine, putting Diane Sawyer on the cover?"

"The magazine will continue to be what Mr. Marsh made it," I said, feeling prissy. I also felt like a liar, knowing what Sir Hugo had tried to talk Bingo into doing.

That first night as editor I went home drained. I wrote a letter telling Babe I was proud to have been named editor but unsure of my professional qualifications.

"It's fine editing my own stuff. Less sure about editing other people's. And without Bingo as a goad, where do the ideas derive week after week? What do I do about Vava and Madame Stealth? Bingo kept them sullen but not mutinous. Can I do that? The art department and Tyson Rambush are a total mystery. Paperwork, administration, personnel, haggling over people's salaries and expense accounts . . . such things appall me. I'm not as smart as Tina Brown or Anna Wintour or John

Fairchild. Murdoch's said to be starting a new magazine, *Mirabella*. There are too many fashion mags already, and we all compete for the same reader, the same advertising. Now I know why editors get paid so much . . ."

Within a week she wrote back, chewing me out.

"You're as smart as any of them. Just work hard and treat people decently and pick their brains for ideas and remember what you always told me, the advantage *Fashion* has in being a weekly over all those monthlies. See, Shark, I did learn something from you. So stop feeling sorry for yourself. All love, Babe."

Nunc, of course, objected to my appointment. Sir Hugo, plump bonhomie and smiles, heard him out, Nunc, after all, holding considerable stock in the Grottnex empire. "Well, let's give the lad a fair trial, eh?" Nunc grunted, which Sir Hugo took as assent, and when I encountered Nunc one morning in the lobby and he pawed at his nose, I assumed this was meant to be congratulatory. Marsh's departure was major news in the papers, front page in the *Times*. My appointment drew somewhat less attention, for which I was grateful. P.J. le Boot resurfaced, took me out for drinks, and got so drunk in his elation he fell down and I had to get him home. Pinsky sent a basket of fruit.

"Pinsky does not do champagne suppers. But consider this a token."

Cap'n Andy sent me an effusive letter pledging fealty. Tyson Rambush rolled his eyes and called me "Mister Sharkey." Ambrose the lawyer commiserated over dinner he paid for with his own cash. "No one replaces Bingo; no one's that odd." Once a week I went uptown to go over the issue with Grottnex. Barrier Reef was around, of course, and I assumed he spied and gave periodic reports.

Occasionally I was summoned upstairs to Nunc's suite of offices.

"That lad Thaxter, did you know him?"

"No. Who is he?"

"Before your time, I imagine, retired years ago. A copy editor. I think the lad is dead and someone's bilking the company, cashing his pension checks."

I suggested Nunc send someone, Cap'n Andy perhaps, to Thaxter's last known address to find out.

"Good idea," Nunc said. Such direct action had never occurred to him.

A week later came another call. "That lad Thaxter . . ."

"Yes?"

"He's alive, eighty-five years old. But it was a good thing we sent someone. They'll cheat you, these lads, if they're dead."

I realized again how much I missed Bingo, who would have clapped such a line to his bosom and treasured it.

81 ▣ *"Didn't Marsh sack you?" I asked Elegant Hopkins.*

BINGO MARSH'S retirement was like the sightings of comets in Shakespeare, omen and portent of an ordered world tumbled into inelegant chaos. Had volcanoes erupted and continents moved and earthquakes set the Richter Scale to mad vibration in the tiny universe of fashion, the shock could not have been any more dramatic.

"That son of a bitch," some muttered, victims of Marsh and his magazine.

"Fashion will never be the same again," a few lamented, who'd not felt his lash.

"A great man, a force for elegance," the president of Saks Fifth Avenue told the *Times*.

"What a prick," remarked a senior executive for Bloomingdale's, another victim.

But these were mere emotional responses, and to be expected.

The world of fashion was forever shuddering under the impact of enormous events, sea changes which had absolutely nothing to do with Bingo's farewell address.

It only seemed that way, cause and effect.

In Paris, after thirty years, the great House of Dior sacked its designer, Marc Bohan, and hired . . . an Italian! Headlines exploded in the French newspapers: "A Shameful Day for France . . . Another Italian Betrayal." The unfortunate Italian, Gianfranco Ferre, muttered, "*Scusa,*" and asserted lamely that "fashion has become international."

251

"*Mangia spaghetti!*" cried the aggrieved of the Paris couture, and re-minded people Mussolini, too, had ended badly.

Around the corner, André Courreges was abandoned by his Japanese financial backers and brought suit. What does one expect of such trai-torous people? it was asked. The Chambre Syndicale, which had booted Courreges out of its union, snickered.

Karl Lagerfeld fired his longtime friend and favorite model, Ines de la Fressange, remarking with something less than gallantry, "She was getting too big for her little brain."

Men with whom Marsh had feuded — Giorgio Armani and Paul Pro-fonde — marked his demise with solemn masses in the more fashionable churches of Milano and Paris. Men whose careers he'd advanced ingra-tiated themselves with his rival, John Fairchild, another who never forgave a slight.

There were new and grotesquely clinical rumors. Yves Saint Laurent was near death. Saint Laurent promptly hosted a costume ball to prove them inaccurate.

The grand old Maison Lanvin was bought up by financiers. Bernard Lanvin, handsomest man in the couture, said modestly he would play a lesser role in management. The new owners, vulgar little people, made it clear Bernard would play no role at all.

In New York the impeccably well-bred society woman Annette Reed divorced her blue-blooded husband to marry the widowed Oscar de la Renta.

Olivier of Hollywood was said to be ill, a recluse in an unfashionable French province. Halston, too, was ailing, amid the usual ghastly ru-mors. Giorgio de Sant'Angelo really did fall ill, and shortly died. Then, as not to disappoint, so did Halston.

Lagerfeld, enjoying a vintage season, engineered the sacking of his own boss, the president of Chanel. In a face-saving maneuver the woman was given a grandiose new title. Lagerfeld ensured no one would be fooled by it. "They say she's the director of special projects. But we have no special projects."

Princess Tiny Meat sought protection in Chapter 11. And Elegant Hopkins, said to be having an affair with a woman, issued a statement of indignant denial.

Rupert Murdoch, having started up a fashion magazine headed by

Vogue's old editor, Grace Mirabella, sold off his half of *Elle*. The Lacroix pouff dress Marsh had championed was on the markdown racks at Filene's Basement. The Canadian real estate man, Campeau, who'd purchased Bloomingdale's with junk bonds, collapsed into bankruptcy. Giorgio's, on Rodeo Drive, sold itself to Avon for $165 million, and the owners, Mr. and Mrs. Hayman, divorced. Emanuel Ungaro, longtime friend of actress Anouk Aimée, married a young Italian noblewoman. And Count Vava was arrested and briefly held on munitions charges.

"I was simply keeping some hand grenades for a friend, Sharkey," he assured me.

None of this mattered. Without Babe, my nights and weekends echoed vacantly. Attempting to compensate by filling my days, I found myself constantly turning to ask an absent Bingo what he thought, only to realize again that he was gone. For the first time in nearly two decades he would not be goading *Fashion* magazine into decreeing just who was In and who Out, not telling a hundred million American women where to wear their hemlines, was not going to determine just who was that season's "greatest fashion designer ever!"

Did anyone else regret he was gone? He had no real friends. People had feared him or lusted after his benediction, cozying up to power. Society women wanted him to publicize their charitable efforts. Designers craved good reviews. Retailers wanted their stores labeled smart, chic. Filmmakers and Broadway impresarios and choreographers and novelists and publishers and columnists and network executives had sought his patronage, knowing that while *Fashion* could neither make nor break them, it could make life easier. Or infinitely more difficult.

Now that his magazine was owned by foreigners and run by commonplace people like me, with Marsh in exile, they turned on him, all the sycophants, pariah dogs worrying a bit of raw meat. I thought of his protégé Quinn, discarded years before, a Kleenex relationship. Maybe we really do sow what we reap.

Such metaphysical musings gave way to reality when, at a very posh dinner party, I again encountered the African Queen, by now the great man of American fashion, threatening even Calvin and Ralph. And not only a great designer, but a significant cultural figure, exemplar of the deconstructionist school of thought which held that, given an open

253

mind, nothing that Shakespeare or Ibsen or Dante had accomplished was equal to what certain anonymous Eskimo and Ugandan artists offered the world.

We were all in black tie, all but Elegant Hopkins, who now affected a dashiki that topped bare legs encased only in the leather, knee-high thongs of the Roman centurion. I remembered the Savile Row suits he wore when first we met and how shabby we all felt next to him.

Over the first course someone brought up Bingo's name.

"Oh, he's so tiresome, really, with his petty feuds," said Elegant. "Every magazine has its time and its season. *Fashion,* clearly, had its."

He knew I was at the table; he intended the insult. I couldn't resist being as phony as he.

"Didn't Marsh sack you?"

Elegant looked hurt. "I passed a brief apprenticeship at his little paper before moving swiftly on to better things."

A lady with a handsome ivory bosom, fawning over the Queen, shot me a vicious, triumphant look. Not being terribly good at bitchy repartee and feeling I was acting the fool, I got into the wine and shut up. A professor fellow from California went on at great length about scorch marks found on antelope hides in a recently unearthed Hopi Indian cave dwelling in Arizona, markings he said predated and were as rich in literary merit as anything Homer had written.

Elegant Hopkins stirred from his languor.

"More so, in all likelihood," he opined. "One finds the Greeks arid and jejune, doesn't one?"

They'd moved on to the tremendous cultural and artistic contributions of Haiti when I muttered something rude, bowed thanks to my hosts, and left. Next morning Barrier Reef, whose spy network was developing nicely, called me aside.

"Careful of the boongs, mate. You know the way they are."

"Boongs?"

"Wogs," Reef said cheerfully. "Dark-complected gentlemen. They resent accusations of voodoo, you know. Sensitive souls."

A few of the designers loyally stuck by Marsh. Blass did, though I don't know why, and Ungaro and Oscar and poor, bankrupted Tiny Meat. Most, like piranhas, swam in to tear off chunks of whatever influence and reputation remained to him.

Unexpectedly, for Bingo despised the man, Barrier empathized.

"People suck up when you're on top and piss in your shoe when you're not. Marsh ought to have understood that, being a bit of a sod himself on occasion."

I didn't have to be told.

But I continued to defend Bingo. After all, had the tables been turned, if I were the wounded stag at bay, torn by my enemies, Marsh would do the same for me.

82 ▣ Remember George C. Scott in Patton?

NOW Marsh returned to the city, his mysterious errands wound up or on hold. There were rumors he would start a competing magazine, would go to work for Newhouse, was writing his memoirs. I sought him out immediately. How amused he'd be by Elegant Hopkins's absurd get-up and pretensions, how helpful professionally would be his counsel to me. He'd taken office space in Rockefeller Center, something called vaguely Marsh Enterprises. I dropped by 30 Rock one afternoon without notice to be greeted in some dismay by his secretary. As Bingo always had, Mrs. K. lied badly.

"He isn't here. He's at lunch. Out of town. He . . ."

I tried to comfort the woman. "Don't worry. It's okay. I realize he's busy. Just tell him I dropped by to say hello. Nothing vital."

It would be typical of Marsh, I realized, to hide away, to avoid people, to go to ground until he was ready with the announcement of some dramatic coup. Or that was my assumption. A week later I actually got through to him on the phone, his secretary being away from the desk. He was distant, more arch than usual, hurried. I put it down to strain, to a sense of loss on his part. Then people we both knew reported, with a certain human glee, that Marsh had been sniping at me, suggesting disloyalty and brash ambition, blaming my columns about the Republicans for his failure to win a cabinet post. I sloughed off such gossip.

"That's just Bingo being bitchy. He's out of the loop and resents it.

He'll find another toy soon enough and snap out of it." I refused to let people drive wedges between us.

Failing again to get through by phone I wrote a long letter, telling him candidly what I'd heard from third parties and how hurt I was, how he knew better than anyone that I'd been loyal, a good and faithful servant, that it was his idea for me to become editor. "I never wanted your job and told you so at Arcachon. And you know that, Bingo."

My letter was returned, unopened.

Shortly before he resigned, I'd lent Marsh an out-of-print book he wanted particularly to read, and now I sent another note, this one stiff, simply asking if he'd finished the book to send it back. A reply came from Mrs. K.

"Mr. Marsh knows nothing of such a book and doesn't understand your request."

Like the long-ago Peter Quinn, I had become a nonperson.

Other mail brought consolation: long, weekly letters from the Philippines. Babe celebrated a birthday, and I sent a ten-speed bike, the sort of thing after which she'd lusted but couldn't afford in law school days. It had never occurred to me to give her a ring; a bicycle more neatly symbolized our relationship. In letters, she talked about her work as legal officer for U.S. Army advisers working out of Clark Air Force Base and the Subic Bay naval station.

"You know, if a tank runs over someone's water buffalo on its way to rescue the Filipino people from genocide and the farmer sues for a hundred bucks, I try to bully him into admitting the buff has a history of aberrant behavior. Failing that, I negotiate the bribe, which is legalese for 'settling out of court.' Most buffalo go for about forty, maybe forty-five on a good day.

"It's a lot of fun here. I ride my bike a lot, and every week there's an attempted coup. Sometimes even a real coup. Mrs. Aquino (whom everyone calls 'Cory') doesn't have a clue. No coups ever happen weekends, however, because the colonels who organize the coups reserve weekends for golf or visiting their mistresses. Everyone has a mistress or several. I've received a number of flattering offers myself, substantially better than the going price for water buffalo. Sometimes the rebels (there are Communist rebels and Moslem rebels, both in addition to the coup-ists, who are all in the army), who do not play golf and therefore have their weekends free, try to blow up an American vehicle or an adviser. Occasionally you hear gunfire just beyond the perimeter, which I theorize is mostly GI's who are jumpy. I've informed the base commander of my theory on this, but he resents West Pointers and in so many words told me to stick to my torts and leave the fighting to him. Some fighting. I keep hoping we'll have a real firefight with guys coming over the wire as per your famous adventures at Da Xiang. But so far, no luck.

"You'd love Manila," she wrote, "a combination of 'Miami Vice' and the Gaza Strip. Everyone drives a hundred miles an hour and drinks too much, and you can buy a little girl or little boy (Olivier of Hollywood would have loved this joint!) for about ten dollars. And everyone carries a gun. The nightclubs have a checkroom just for guns, and all the doormen at office skyscrapers and posh apartment buildings keep loaded 12-gauge shotguns just inside the front door. What with the boozing and the mistresses and everyone having guns, someone gets shot every fifteen minutes and the Manila newspapers make the *New York Post* seem reticent.

"It's a terrific place and the people are swell and you ought to come out for a visit. And you know how I nag you about drinking too much? All that 'wine of the country'? Well, you'd be dried out pretty soon here because the 'wine of the country' stinks. All else is pretty good, hot and steamy and beautiful with palm trees and three-inch cockroaches and except for the coup-ists and the rebels, people are hospitable and on a Yank salary everything's cheap. With your money you could rent the best one-bedroom apartment in town, with a pool out back.

"Did I mention I ride my bike a lot?"

I wasn't sure the redundancy was intended. But I liked that she was riding it.

Over the next few months I made several more attempts to reach Bingo and finally gave up. I wrote about it to Babe.

"What a pompous, pretentious twit he is. You were right about him. After all these years he refuses to have lunch or even acknowledge my existence. You'd think it was my idea to sell the damned company and not Nunc's. Not a day goes by I don't hear from someone that he's trashing me as an ingrate and a traitor. The bastard."

Babe wrote back a week later.

"Remember George C. Scott in *Patton*? '*L'audace, toujours l'audace*?' You ought to try a little '*audace*' on Bingo Marsh."

I'd seen him once or twice in restaurants and had cut him dead, too sore to acknowledge his existence. But Babe was right. That wasn't how to handle Marsh, with his neurotic fear of confrontation, not at all the way.

"*L'audace, toujours l'audace.*"

Inspired by Babe (and by George C. Scott), I conceived of a simple and yet horrific plan of vengeance. Since Marsh was avoiding me, concealing himself behind secretaries and money and lies, denying my existence, sending me to what his father would have termed a bad chamber, I would simply refuse to be ignored.

An opportunity soon manifested itself. Dior was celebrating an anniversary, and Bloomingdale's was giving a black-tie party. I was invited, of course. It was inconceivable Bingo would not have been asked.

I arrived early, paid my respects to Monsieur Rouet of Dior, paid similar obeisance to Marvin Traub of Bloomie's, and sheltering behind a vodka on the rocks, waited my prey. It was not a long wait. Not fifteen minutes after I got there, Bingo arrived, heading toward the receiving line (and me) from the Lexington Avenue end of the store, bouncing along with a little skip thrown in every few steps, his dinner jacket superbly cut, his pouty face wreathed in smiles as he spied Rouet. Polite greetings were exchanged, a few words, then on to Traub, the ritual repeated. I bided my time behind the vodka and ice. Then, with Marsh totally relaxed, a champagne flute in his hand, I sprang at him, crying his name loudly.

"Bingo, my dear fellow, Bingo Marsh!"

Heads turned toward us. Bingo's mouth fell and eyebrows rose simultaneously as I threw myself upon him, seizing his right hand in mine, pumping it energetically and with vast enthusiasm, repeating his name several times and with emotion, calling out how good it was to see him again, "after all this time!" and then, quite abruptly, breaking off with a final shouted cry of "We must have lunch!"

Marsh was reduced to a stammering repetition of my name in a cracking voice as he retrieved a hand-rolled Irish linen handkerchief with which to mop a suddenly slick brow and flushed cheeks. Marvin Traub, who knew there was bad blood between us, stood there marveling while Monsieur Rouet, mystified, tugged at Traub's sleeve for explanation. Tony the paparazzo shook his head in admiration.

"He's gone, Shark, I saw him heading for the cloakroom." He paused, then went on, impressed. "You chased him, you know."

"Yes," I said, "I believe I did."

After that, whenever we met, I sprinted toward Bingo, calling his name, seizing one or both hands: on Fifth Avenue, in the Grill Room of the Four Seasons, queuing up for his coat at Le Cirque. So upset would he become, he sometimes left the place without having made his purchase or eaten or, in one instance, without returning to his aisle seat at the theater.

Then, almost overnight, Marsh disappeared from the city. People said he was ill, had retired to the islands, was living with various Hillary relatives on a great estate in England. I knew better, and was taken in by none of this.

I had driven Bingo from New York by sheer amiability.

83 ▣ The designer's own wife wept openly throughout . . .

THINGS went less well at the magazine. Not that I didn't try. I had some splendid story ideas. Writers always think they know better than the editors, and now that I was the boss I'd have an opportunity to shape and inspire the entire magazine and not simply craft my own column. It just didn't work out that way. Ten years earlier I'd realized I wasn't much of a novelist; I now began to suspect I wasn't going to be such a terrific editor. Having failed to become Willie Maugham, I was not going to be Henry Luce, either. Reef, with his gift for the pungent phrase, may have put it best:

"You see mate, the way we run our newspapers and magazines, the editor is paid most handsomely to anticipate the shit before anyone else even smells it."

Bingo Marsh had that instinctive gift; it was swiftly evident that I didn't.

Still, the editor's job held its perquisites and small pleasures. I assigned myself to attend the French ready-to-wear collections, sitting alongside Count Vava in the huge, billowing tents set up outside the Louvre and at the Marais and wherever in Paris there was open ground, watching the models pass the collections while, just opposite, Madame Stealth sat with our sketch artists and her current Seeing Eye dog. I left the actual fashion coverage to them, of course, and focused instead on the sideshow, at times as ripely entertaining as a carnival with its dwarfs and fakirs and tattooed lady.

At one show in midcollection a summons was served to the designer by a former partner. At another fights broke out among the paparazzi, cheerfully swinging Nikons at each other for camera angles. Sylvester Stallone attended several of the shows, perched, preening, in a front-row seat while his latest girlfriend undulated past, modeling the clothes. At one collection the disco music was so loud and persistent the designer's own wife wept openly throughout and editors cried "*Assez!* . . . enough!"

"In the sacred name of Christ and his mother," a woman shouted, "turn it down!"

Count Vava, who had seen at least one revolution and was intermittently plotting another, was delighted, nudging me at each new offense and muttering about the decline of the West.

There was a wonderful incident at Karl Lagerfeld's show featuring Bingo's own nemesis, John Fairchild, where the competition for front-row seats spun out of control, with people actually exchanging blows. I scribbled furiously, trying to get the entire scene down in words. Unfortunately, just alongside, a *New York Times* man named Hochswender, who had a nice touch for such moments, witnessed the same outrage and got it into print first:

"At one point John Fairchild of *Women's Wear Daily* gripped his program and began batting nicely dressed Frenchwomen who, as is their manner, stepped all over everybody while chirping, 'Pardonnez-moi.' "

Having had my own insteps dented by their spike heels, I empathized with the irate Mr. Fairchild while recognizing how nice it was to be back in Paris, where no emotion is ever concealed. Still, it was a shame not to have had Bingo there with us to savor the marvelously wacky spectacle of his great rival assaulting the elegant.

That evening, seeking to calm my staff, to thank them for their efforts, to soothe opposing factions, I hosted a little dinner at the Grand Comptoir in les Halles. With a deceptive geniality we chatted about the affairs of the day, the clothes themselves as well as the shouting and the tumult.

"Ah," said Madame Stealth portentously over the claret, "but isn't the fashion show simply a metaphor for life?"

"Rubbish!" Vava exploded, bounding to his feet and knocking over glassware. "First, blind; now sodden with drink!"

The faithful Seeing Eye dog began to sob uncontrollably, and the maître d'hotel rushed to our assistance in some alarm as I tugged at the Count's arm and urged peace.

But if Vava and Regina Stealth continued hostilities, and if many of my schemes didn't work out, Sir Hugo was tolerant. And more. For all the vaunted bluster and vulgarity of those about him, Grottnex was turning out to be a gentleman. No backbiting, no lies, no wild exaggeration, no dodging the consequences of an action. When we disagreed it was straightforward, open, nothing of what one came routinely to expect of Bingo. In a letter to Babe I wrote, almost gushing, "Grottnex is a good and decent man."

Competition was tougher now: this sprightly new American version of *Elle,* the fashion monthly created virtually overnight by Murdoch; the ever-growing popularity of *Vanity Fair;* a new and offbeat something called *Details* . . . Bingo would have complained, "They do these things just to annoy me. They know how upset I get."

Grottnex understood such vast competitive enterprises were "just business." With Grottnex there were no tantrums, no pettiness or vindictive malice.

Then, from one of our best writers, came a perfectly wonderful story out of Los Angeles, about how a cabal of local millionaires, early backers of Ronald Reagan, planned to buy a modest little Bel Air mansion and present it to the President and First Lady, free, once they'd left the White House and retired to private life. No rent would be charged; the Reagans would apparently have an option to buy, but what they were really getting was free, subsidized housing. The Chief Executive who railed against subsidized housing for the poor was feathering his own nest.

"It's bound to get out, Shark," the writer told me by phone. "These Kitchen Cabinet types may be able to keep their mouths shut. But not their wives. This'll be the talk of Rodeo Drive in a couple of days."

I scheduled the story to lead the magazine the following Monday. It was too late to change the cover art but we could get a good, big cover line on there:

"Free housing for the homeless Reagans."

That was to be the cover line. It never appeared. Sir Hugo called me in, alerted by Reef that a politically dangerous story was about to be published in a Grottnex weekly, a story that would, quite understandably, annoy a President of the United States.

"You see, Sharkey, don't you, this isn't really a propitious time for our organization to irritate the Republicans."

"Sir Hugo, this is a great story."

"Well, you know, a retiring President, rather a nice gesture, don't you think?"

"It's a goddamned hustle."

"Now that's a bit brisk, don't you think?"

"Sir Hugo, you weren't here when we did that piece on Nancy Reagan getting free clothes and the loan of Harry Winston jewels. That was a great story. Sold a lot of magazines. And this thing is bigger than that . . ."

Hugo was polite but wouldn't be budged. Later I learned he had a major filing before the Securities and Exchange Commission. It wasn't time to tweak the man who gave George Bush his chance.

Reef commiserated over drinks.

"The Chief thinks the world of you, mate. He wouldn't put up with your shit from just anyone."

Such words were enormous consolation.

I went again to Grottnex with the proposal for a new and important series on AIDS. He listened, thoughtful, none of Bingo's childish skipping about.

"Not really our line of country, is it, Sharkey? Important, I grant, excellent *New York Times* stuff. But for a slick fashion magazine?"

"Yes, I think it is. We've got an enormous readership in an industry riddled with AIDS. On Seventh Avenue alone . . ."

I lost again.

"Bad for advertising, mate," Barrier told me. "Soft goods business is off as it is, all these mergers and such. Doesn't help to have women out there thinking their pantyhose and bras are being sewn up by poofs with running sores, does it?"

I lost other battles, one a well-researched piece on anti-Semitism in Palm Beach, where John Weitz and the fabulously wealthy Estée Lauder were turned away from the better clubs, even as luncheon guests, bias in its rawest form. Reef again took me aside.

"Sir Hugo's new to this country. Doesn't want you Yanks thinking he's the sort of bloke comes in and throws his weight around and tells Americans how to live and so forth."

I don't mean to imply all the stories I assigned were noble. There was still outrage and fun and the odd bitchery. But gradually it came to me that Marsh, a coward who never stood up bravely to anyone, hadn't killed a single story on grounds it discomfited the powerful. While Sir Hugo, a "good and decent man," clamped down on us an iron censorship.

In a confused and frustrated funk, I thought I could hear Bingo now, hear the echoes of his silly, piping voice:

"Vex them! Vex them anew!"

84 ▣ *A slap in the face of Bingo.*

THEN, a loss of another sort, during a fashion show presented by, of all people, Elegant Hopkins.

One of the more salutary consequences of Bingo's departure was that the magazine was no longer honor bound to carry on his feuds. We were now permitted to make our own enemies and to sign peace treaties with the past. In the case of the archtraitor Hopkins, after a hiatus of some years, *Fashion* magazine would cover his line.

"A slap in the face of Bingo," Count Vava said gloomily. "I realize he's gone but this is not something we should do casually."

I agreed. In the end it was decided that Vava and I would continue to absent ourselves ("Elegant will draw the proper conclusions," Vava felt) in tribute to Marsh's memory. Madame Stealth would represent the magazine, accompanied by flunkies, and so, on the appointed day, off she went to 550 Seventh Avenue. Hopkins, triumphant, broke precedent by coming out early to conduct the old woman to her place in the front row, actually pulling out a little gold chair and gallantly seating her before disappearing backstage to prepare to present the collection.

"Oh, the clucking," I was later informed by those on the scene, "Elegant Hopkins sucking up to white people. What a sensation!"

When it was over, tremendous ovations, cries of "Bravo! Bravissimo!" Elegant Hopkins prancing in delight along the runway, throwing kisses, being embraced, weeping the requisite tears of emotion, pontificating into microphones, giving his better profile to the television minicams, the usual postcollection scene. As the salon emptied, the crowd of departing journalists milling their way toward another show about to begin six floors below, Madame Stealth's Seeing Eye dog made her way to the coat check to reclaim Madame's wrap.

By now the showroom had nearly emptied, rolled-up programs strewn about, the routine litter of a fashion show, a workman kneeling on the pearl gray carpet of the runway with a staple gun, coping with an errant corner of carpet, the last of the TV news crews making their way noisily from the room. Madame Stealth continued to perch there on her little gold chair, staring, as she always did, in the wrong direction.

"Madame," said the Seeing Eye dog, "I have your wrap."

No reply. It was when she placed it around the old lady's shoulders that Madame Stealth began to topple, very slowly, to one side.

"Madame!" the girl screamed.

It was too late. Regina Stealth had slipped through her grasp and fell to the pearl gray floor, dead.

Elegant Hopkins told the *Times* he read enormous significance into her passing.

"You know, in an odd way it was the closing of a circle. A childhood spent learning at her knee and then, the unfortunate and quite clearly racist enmity of her employer, shutting me and my work from the pages of their magazine. Finally, now that Marsh has been driven from the business under a cloud, for Regina, dear, faithful Regina, to return to pay homage to her one-time protégé, it almost seems poetic, quite appropriate, that at this extraordinary moment, her life would come gently to its end."

A *Post* reporter asked the great man:

"Yeah, Elegant, but didja actually see the old dame croak?"

By now Hopkins could handle the tabloids as deftly as he might *Vanity Fair*.

"That's the curious thing. I actually believe I did. I caught a glimpse of her face, terribly ashen, looking not at the runway but entirely in the other direction, toward the door, and then her eyes seemed slowly to close, as if blessedly in sleep, her happiness fulfilled. I noticed because I was peering through the curtain to see the reaction to number twenty-nine on the runway, and it was then I *knew* she was dead, because it was hardly the time to doze off, not with number twenty-nine out there, that sportive apricot blazer over the pleated flannel slacks, the one that's just going to walk out of stores if you can believe Saks. . . ."

Bingo didn't attend the funeral. It was said he was out of town.

Count Vava, who insisted, wrote the obituary for *Fashion*, and people for weeks after spoke of his tribute, its sensitivity and grace.

"I'll say this," Vava confided in me, "before her eyes went, she accurately predicted a revival of the peplum."

His voice fell.

"And such a thing," he went on, "is not lightly to be dismissed in fashion journalism . . ."

"No," I hurriedly agreed.

". . . the old bitch!"

85 ▣ *A decent, God-fearing place with the finest modern plumbing.*

THAT winter, President Bush took office (without naming Marsh our ambassador to France) and Bingo found the pubic hair in his bath at the Hotel Gallia.

It turned out he wasn't in Milano attending the collections as a critic, but as a buyer, shopping for fabrics for the interiors and clothes for the staff of his latest passion.

After all and despite the odds, Bingo had purchased that famous ski resort he mentioned when first we met and about which he occasionally went on. Next door to Aspen, an entire mountainside of his own, magnificent country eight thousand feet up, a main lodge and outbuildings and a score of dollhouse cottages where they might have filmed *Heidi*. The place was instantly a success, *People* magazine doing a spread on the celebrity of its clientele, *Architectural Digest* on the gemütlichkeit of its public rooms, the steamy comfort of its hot tubs, the elegance of its Sister Parish–appointed suites, *Gourmet* magazine on the quality of service, the subtlety of its wine cellar, the qualifications of its chef. There appeared, in these magazines and others, photos of Bingo and Ames and their handsome children, suntanned and smiling against the snow. Bingo seemed to have touched up his hair, looking a decade younger. Sir Edmund Hillary, the famous alpinist and Ames's distant cousin, was reportedly intent on spending a holiday with the Marshes, translating his perpendicular talents to skis.

I permitted myself a small resentment. Having abandoned me to struggle with the magazine he'd created and pretended to love, Marsh had now moved on smoothly, almost seamlessly, to another enormous success, a rich man growing richer. Then, early in March, in what the Associated Press termed, with considerable restraint, "an untoward incident," Bingo Marsh was arrested.

The news came in newspapers and on television. The man who loved gossip was now gossip himself; the man who despised Brokaw and Dan Rather and Jennings found himself, and unhappily, on the evening news.

Bingo didn't like Arabs; that was how it began as well as anyone could reconstruct the story. Of course Bingo didn't like a lot of people. But Arabs ranked fairly high on the list, slightly above Jews and below Japanese and people with false teeth. Just how Marsh permitted himself to accept these particular Arabs at his ski resort was never satisfactorily explained. The chief Arab, Sheikh Mohammad, a Harvard man whom American pals called "Mo," was a friend of a friend, and somehow the thing was arranged, twenty-five rooms in the main lodge and a dozen more in various cottages reserved. It was then, even before their arrival, that Marsh began to get nervous. Troublemakers, playing on his ignorance and prejudice, filled him with terrifying misinformation as well as facts, even more frightening. With his accustomed gullibility Bingo lapped up the stories that tended to reinforce beliefs, most of them erroneous, he'd held since childhood.

I remember his telling me long ago a story he'd heard from a neighbor who fought in North Africa during the war.

"These Arab gentlemen looked spotless, walking toward you in those flowing white robes. But once they passed, if you looked after them, you could see they were all brown and smelly in back, with flies droning about. Because they don't have toilet tissue, as we do, so they use their robes to wipe themselves."

Now, having accepted the Sheikh's money, the nightmares returned. Suppose it was true there were religious taboos about using Western toilets? Suppose Mo and his entourage just squatted whenever the spirit moved them? Would their ski trousers be smelly and flyblown?

"Stop worrying," Ames Marsh told her husband, "remember Farah Diba and the Shah at St. Moritz? The most fashionable people on the slopes."

Bingo was briefly relieved until a helpful source explained, "The Iranians, while Moslem, are not Arabs."

Marsh lapsed again into funk.

The entourage flew into Colorado by private jet, and a convoy of limos fetched them to Bingo's mountain. The Sheikh himself, several aides, and a French blonde, a cover girl who may or may not have converted to Islam, arrived by chopper, landing on the sun-brilliant snow in front of the lodge. Bingo, atwitter with nerves, skipped out to meet them.

"Ah, Mr. Marsh," said the Sheikh, hand outstretched and smiling, "what a magnificent panorama, this island in the sky of yours . . ."

It was a gracious opening. Anyone but Bingo would have responded with equivalent charm, conveying welcome. Instead, red-faced and pouty, voice cracking and infinitives split, Marsh blurted out with his accustomed subtlety:

"See here, Sheikh, this is a decent, God-fearing place with the finest modern plumbing. I won't have people doing things in corners and hallways and the like."

Mohammad, stunned and uncomprehending, took a step backward as if fearing he was about to be attacked.

"Mr. Marsh, I haven't the foggiest notion of what you're talking about. We've reserved suites and rooms, not 'corners and . . .' "

"Don't give me that. I know you fellows. And North Africa in the war. Flowing white robes all right, sure, that was up front. But be-hind . . . ah, I know all about behind . . . brown and smelly and flies buzzing . . ."

The Sheikh was glacial.

"I'd like to know precisely what you're trying to say."

Marsh smirked. He had the man now!

"As if you didn't know, going into dark corners, lifting your robes and doing number two . . ."

Mohammad, disbelieving, attempted to maintain dignity. "Mr. Marsh, not only as a member of the Saudi Royal Family, but as an honors graduate of Harvard, I must protest this irrational . . ."

"Don't you tell me about Harvard. I'm a Yale man and . . ."

No one is quite sure who struck the first blow (an open-handed slap, I was quite confident), but within seconds the two men were rolling about in the snow, flailing at each other, while Arab retainers from the Sheikh's entourage and faithful employees of Bingo's hotel (in their livery by Gianfranco Ferre) tried to pry the combatants apart, beating at them with ski poles and Louis Vuitton handbags, the Yale man and the Harvard locked in ineffectual combat, small boys battling over honor and possession of the sandbox.

86 ▣ *No more sucking up to Grottnex?*

UNLIKE Marsh, who thought himself many things, expert on enemas and Mount Everest, on Arab customs and the ozone layer, and was none of those things but just a great fashion editor, now I knew precisely what I was and who: a pretty good nonfiction writer whose small gifts fled when I approached the novel. And I knew something else.

I was never meant to be an editor.

The realization had been growing almost from the moment Sir Hugo anointed me in Bingo's stead. He and I had clashed, and I had lost, on any number of editorial matters. The final break involved advertising. Barrier Reef delivered the bad news.

"We seem to be the only magazine in the category that doesn't smell, mate."

"You mean fragrance inserts?"

"Just so. Research tells me there's millions in it. *Vogue* gets the money, *Elle* gets it, so do *Mademoiselle* and *Glam* . . ."

"I know," I said, "Marsh was adamant. Said he wouldn't have his magazine tarted up with cheap scents. One of the few things he ever really felt strongly about, keeping the magazine pure."

Reef tossed an issue of the new *Vanity Fair* on my desk, opened to a glossy and rather foul-smelling fragrance insert on which the copy read:

"A cologne of raw sensuality!"

He rocked back and forth on his feet like a cop on the cover, a half-smile on his face.

"The Chief says we'll be accepting this kind of advertising in future, mate. Soliciting it, in fact."

"Raw sensuality." How Bingo would have shuddered. And I knew that on this question of principle, I owed it to Marsh to make a last stand. I lost again.

I asked for a meeting, and Grottnex, as he always had, listened graciously to my little speech of resignation.

"The world moves on," he said philosophically. "When I first got into wallpaper they all told me, 'You can't keep it up without glue, y'know,' all the great men of the trade, wiser men than I. But I pushed on. Proved them wrong. Same thing with fragrance inserts. New technology, new opportunities. What makes a country great, what ennobles a people . . ."

Grottnex said he understood my reasons, that he respected me, and so on. I think he was relieved to be rid of me. I took my severance pay plus a generous additional sum Sir Hugo threw in and left, pausing to tell Barrier Reef good-bye and that he'd been right about stinking up the paper and I'd been wrong. There was talk of installing him as editor pro tem, and I wanted to wish him well. He thanked me warmly, mentioning "a bloody marvelous cover story in the works," a profile of Zizi Orlando, an intimate it turned out not only of the Reagans but of George and Barbara Bush.

The headline would read: "The White House's favorite guest."

For nearly ten years I'd been writing for the magazine, and when I went, two men, Pinsky and another, took me out for drinks. One of the senior women promised to call about lunch. She never did. Count Vava, out on bail on the munitions charge, avoided me, confiding to people, "I never believed in Sharkey. He lacks the style." Cap'n Andy hurried in locksmiths to change the tumblers lest I plunder the building. I trekked up to the twelfth floor to tell Elmer Marsh good-bye.

"No more sucking up to Grottnex, eh?" he said with his customary grace.

"I guess not."

Nunc, looking for an argument and not getting one, poured himself a glass of water from the thermos on his desk and drank it off, a pinky finger elegantly extended. In ten years I'd seen him do this perhaps a hundred times. Never once had it occurred to him to offer his guest a glass.

"Well . . . ," I said.

He put down the glass to paw at his nose, ripely seeded and more than ever resembling a vast raspberry. Then, leaning conspiratorially toward me, resentful and sour, he said:

"You ever learn how Sir Hugo does it?"

"Does what?"

"Get the damned wallpaper to stay up there without glue?"

I had money for a year, perhaps two, plenty of time to try yet again to write a book. Not Vietnam this time.

Ever since Bingo finally stood up to fight on a matter of principle out there in Colorado (being Bingo, a principle founded on ignorance, and fallacious), I'd been thinking of another breed of book entirely. A book about Bingo and me.

One that would set the record straight on just what happened between us and how it wasn't Babe's fault or Sir Hugo's or Barrier's or even to be blamed on Nunc. A book about Olivier of Hollywood on the Blue Train and how Nunc never took a drink at lunch and about le Boot pissing in the wine and about that precious phony Elegant Hopkins and the night on Capri when Bingo and I capered drunkenly outside the bedrooms and when we climbed Tyson Rambush's tree and how Princess Tiny Meat went bankrupt and about interviewing Streisand and the bad pizza at Valentino's and the Gypsy boys being whipped and how sore we got Nancy Reagan and getting drunk with Coco Chanel and most of all, the fun we had, Bingo Marsh and I.

Maybe no one will believe it or care, maybe such a book won't sell. The hell with that; maybe I just want to tell the story so as to have it clear in my own mind. And isn't that the yarn most worth telling? The one you write for yourself?

270

87 ▣ Western values . . . and the ingenuity of American plumbing.

HAVING made that decision, I considered doing the writing somewhere other than New York, where I knew too many people and spent too many evenings in bars. The money would last longer overseas, in Ireland, perhaps, where they practically subsidized writers, or the South of France, where I could speak French and go occasionally to Paris on the Blue Train, as Olivier of Hollywood once did. Maybe I should go someplace I'd never been, where a complete change might help the prose. I dropped Babe a line, all very cool and noncommittal, asking if good apartments were really all that available, and did they sell decent bikes in Manila or would I have to bring my own, and did she think I should try piano lessons again.

I'd never told Babe about my dad, what happened back there in Ohio when I was nine that made me so wary, and she deserved to know about it. But not in a letter. That was something you talked about in person, the two of us sitting late over brandy or during a long walk on an empty beach. Or maybe in bed, where I wasn't all that cool and noncommittal.

I thought, too, of writing Bingo.

That would have to be quite a long letter, and not as cool, thanking him for all he'd done for me over the years and saying I was sorry it ended badly, something like that, maybe slipping in there that it was his fault and not mine, subtly of course. But I couldn't seem to get it right. Maybe because I wasn't sure of my real feelings. Did I resent him, did I still love him? What could you say to a man who was at once the patron of your talent, such as it was, and permitted you to toss it idly away on silly, superficial work? No, that was unfair; if there was a wastrel of my gifts it wasn't Bingo. How could I penetrate the morass of his cluttered mind and those smug biases and tell him, without being sappy, how much he'd meant to me over a long time and in a variety of ways?

In the end, the long letter, both hail *and* farewell, was too long, too self-conscious. Better to put it all into the book, between hard covers, to say what I felt about him with whatever eloquence I could muster. Though, knowing Bingo, it was quite likely he wouldn't recognize him-

271

self in any of it, and would go about wagging his head and telling friends Sharkey was writing fiction again and doing it badly.

Still, I owed him a salute, a reminder of happier times, of movie matinees and Clifton Webb typing in the tub and Rodan eating the Japs and chamber pots and Olivier's horseback rides and Bingo's contraband bike at Yale. But most of all I owed him something for his silly, gallant, despairing gesture in the snows when he defied the Sheikh and all his works and pomps.

I could still see Bingo on the courthouse steps in falling snow after the hearing, Ames at his side, as television reporters shoved microphones into his face and camera lenses closed in. How Bingo hated such display, how inwardly he must have cringed. And I could yet hear his voice, quavering a bit but defiant, as if in an odd way he found joy in the battle, the first he'd ever really fought on his own and not through the magazine or surrogates.

"I'm terribly sorry about all this. And Ames," he said. "But long ago President Bush and I were taught at New Haven the time might come when someone, somewhere, would have to stand up for decency. And Western values, as my mother once did fighting Hitler. And in this case, surely, on behalf of American plumbing and not going off in corners and such . . ."

When he was finished Bingo had given a sappy little grin, and I could almost imagine the beginnings of a skip, but then the camera cut back to Dan Rather and Marsh faded, perhaps forever.

I balled up the failed letter and chose instead that terse, and in ways most eloquent form of contemporary communication, the fax machine, tapping out the number of Marsh's place in Colorado, reading the single sentence once more, and signing it in my own hand: "John."

It was okay, it was fine, saying just what I wished to say. Satisfied and at peace, I sent it crackling west, a brief note in a small bottle:

"God bless you, Bingo Marsh."